THE EXODUS QUEST

Will Adams has tried his hand at a multitude of careers over the years. Most recently, he worked for a London-based firm of communications consultants before giving it up to pursue his lifelong dream of writing fiction. His first novel, *The Alexander Cipher*, is about a modern-day quest to find the lost tomb of Alexander the Great. A top-twenty UK bestseller, it has been translated into thirteen languages. *The Exodus Quest* is his second novel.

Visit www.AuthorTracker.co.uk for exclusive updates on Will Adams.

Also by Will Adams

The Alexander Cipher

WILL ADAMS

The Exodus Quest

HARPER

Harper
An imprint of HarperCollins*Publishers*
77–85 Fulham Palace Road,
Hammersmith, London W6 8JB

www.harpercollins.co.uk

A Paperback Original 2008
1

A catalogue record for this book
is available from the British Library

ISBN: 978-0-00-725088-2

Set in Sabon by Palimpsest Book Production Ltd,
Grangemouth, Stirlingshire

Printed and bound in Great Britain by
Clays Ltd, St Ives plc

*In fond memory
of my friend and cousin
Mark Petre*

ACKNOWLEDGEMENTS

The theory that Moses and the Exodus might somehow be connected to the reign of the heretic pharaoh Akhenaten has been around for decades, most famously advocated by Sigmund Freud in his work *Moses and Monotheism*. But the possible link between Akhenaten's capital city at Amarna and the Essene settlement of Qumran is a more recent development, stirringly advocated by the British metallurgist Robert Feather in his book '*The Copper Scroll Decoded*', a fascinating read for all fans of Egyptian history.

Many people helped me with this book, both in Egypt and in England, and I'm very grateful to them all. But I would particularly like to thank my agent Luigi Bonomi and my editor Wayne Brookes for their unfailing support, insight, enthusiasm and advice, without which writing would be a much harder job than it already is.

PROLOGUE

The southern shore of Lake Mariut, AD 415

The plaster had dried at last. Marcus scooped up handfuls of dirt and sand from the floor, smeared them across the fresh white surface until it was dulled and dark and virtually indistinguishable from the rest of the wall. He held his oil lamp close to examine it, added more dirt where needed until satisfied, though in truth it needed the eyes of a younger man. A last walk through the old, familiar passages and chambers, bidding farewell to his comrades and ancestors in the catacombs, to a lifetime of memories, then up the steps and out.

Late afternoon already. No time to waste.

He closed the wooden hatch, shovelled sand and stone down on it. The crash and scatter as it landed, the swish of robes, the crunch of his iron-shod spade. He began to hear in these noises the distant chanting of a mob. It grew so strong, so convincing, he paused to listen. But now there

1

was only silence, save for his heavy breathing, the hammer of his heart, the trickle of settling sand.

Nothing but the fears of a solitary old man.

The sun was low in the west, tinting orange. They usually came by night, as evildoers will, though they were growing bolder all the time. He'd seen strange faces in the harbour that morning. One-time friends muttering amongst themselves. People whose diseases he'd treated without thought for his own safety looking at him like contagion.

He began to shovel again, faster and faster, to quell the panic before it could overwhelm him.

He'd thought they'd be able to ride it out. Their community had survived many previous pogroms and wars, after all. He'd imagined, foolishly, that their ideas would prevail in the end because they were so much stronger and more rational than the pious cruel nonsense of the so-called right-thinking. But he'd been wrong. It was human nature, when fears were stirred, that reason lost all power.

Poor Hypatia! That beautiful, wise and gentle woman. They said her lynching had been ordered by Pope Cyril himself. Epiphanes had witnessed the whole thing. A mere boy; too young for such a sight. The mob led by that sanctimonious monster Peter the Reader. No surprise there. They'd torn her from her chariot, stripped her naked, dragged her to their church, cut her flesh from her bones with oyster-shells, then burned her remains.

Men of God they called themselves. How was it possible they couldn't see what they truly were?

The sun had set. The night began to cool. His pace slowed. He was far from the prime of youth. But he didn't stop altogether. The quicker he finished, the quicker he could set off, catch up his family and fellows in their quest for sanctuary near Hermopolis or perhaps even Chenoboskion, depending on how far this madness had spread. He'd sent them on ahead with all the scrolls and other treasured possessions they'd been able to carry, the accumulated wisdom of centuries. But he himself had stayed behind. They'd grown lax these past few years. It was no secret they had an underground complex here, he knew; not least because absurd rumours about their wealth and hidden treasures had found their way back to him. If these villains looked hard and long enough, they'd every chance of finding these steps, however well he buried them. That was why he'd plastered up the entrance to the baptism chamber, so that some small fraction of their knowledge might survive even if the underground complex itself was discovered. And maybe one day sanity would return, and they could too. If not himself, then his children or grandchildren. And if not them, then perhaps the people of a future age. A more rational, enlightened age. Maybe they'd appreciate the wisdom of the walls, not hate and vilify it.

He finished filling in the shaft, trod it down until it was hard to see. Time to go. The prospect dismayed him. He was too old for such adventures, too old to start again. All he'd ever sought in life was the peace in which to study his texts, learn the nature of the world. But that was now denied him by these swaggering cruel bullies who'd made it a sin even to think. You could see it in their eyes, the pleasure they took in the wanton exercise of their power. They wallowed in their villainy. They raised their hands up high as though the blood on them shone like virtue.

He was travelling light, just his robes, a small sack of provisions, a few coins in his purse. But he hadn't walked ten minutes before he saw a glow over the ridge ahead. It meant nothing to him at first, too lost in private thoughts. But then he realized. Torches. Approaching from the harbour. The direction of the breeze changed and then he heard them. Men and women shouting, singing, jubilant in the anticipation of another lynching.

He hurried back the way he'd come, his heart pounding. Their settlement was on a gentle hill overlooking the lake. He reached the crown and saw the glow on every side, like a pyre just lit, flames licking up the tinder. A cry to his right. A rooftop began to blaze. A second and then a third.

Their homes! Their lives! The clamour grew louder, closer. That hateful baying! How these people loved their work. He turned this way and that, seeking a path out, but everywhere he went, torches forced him back, penning him into an ever-smaller space.

The cry went up at last. He'd been seen. He turned and fled, but his old legs weren't up to it, even though he knew the penalty of capture. And then they were all around him, their faces enflamed with bloodlust, and there was nothing more he could do save go with dignity and courage, try to shame them into compassion. Or, failing that, perhaps when they woke in the morning, they'd look back on their work this night with such horror and revulsion that others might be spared.

That would be something.

He fell to his knees on the rocky ground, his whole body trembling uncontrollably. Tears streamed down his cheeks. He began to pray.

ONE

I

Bab Sedra Street, Alexandria

Daniel Knox was walking north along Sharia Bab Sedra when he saw the earthenware bowl on the street-trader's flapped-out tablecloth. It was filled with matchbooks and packets of white napkins, and it was propping up one end of a line of battered Arabic schoolbooks. His heart gave a little flutter; he suffered a moment's *déjà vu*. He'd seen one like it before, he was sure of it. Somewhere interesting, too. For a few seconds he almost had the answer, but then it eluded him, and the feeling slowly faded, leaving him merely uneasy, unsure whether his mind was playing tricks.

He paused, crouched, picked up a garish plastic vase with wilting artificial yellow flowers, then a ragged geography textbook with all its pages falling out, so that out-of-date maps of Egypt's topography and demographics fanned out over the tablecloth like a deck of cards swept by a magician's hand.

'*Salaam alekum*,' nodded the trader. He couldn't have been more than fifteen years old, made to look even younger by hand-me-down clothes at least two sizes too big.

'*Wa alekum es salaam*,' replied Knox.

'You like this book, mister? You want to buy?'

Knox shrugged and put it back, then glanced around as though uninterested in anything he saw. But the young hawker only gave a crooked-toothed smile. He wasn't a fool. Knox grinned self-deprecatingly and touched the earthenware bowl with his finger. 'What's this?' he asked.

'Sir has a fine eye,' he said. 'A wonderful antique from Alexandria's rich history. The fruit bowl of Alexander the Great himself! Yes! Alexander the Great! No word of a lie.'

'Alexander the Great?' said Knox. 'Surely not?'

'No word of a lie,' insisted the young man. 'They find his body, you know. They find this in his tomb! Yes! The man who find Alexander, he is a man called Daniel Knox, he is my very good friend, he give this to me himself!'

Knox laughed. Since that particular adventure, he'd been everyone's very good friend. 'And you're selling it out here on the street?' he teased. 'Surely if it belonged to Alexander, it's worthy of the Cairo Museum itself!' He picked it up, again felt that reprise of *déjà vu*, a curious tingling in his chest, a dryness at the back of his mouth, a slight pressure at the base of his cranium.

He turned the bowl around in his hands, enjoying the sensation of touch. He was no expert on ceramics, but all field archaeologists had a certain knowledge, not least because about nine out of every ten artefacts on any given site were some kind of pottery, a fragment from a plate, cup or jar, a shard from an oil lamp or perfume flask, perhaps even an ostracon, if it was your lucky day.

But this wasn't broken. It was some seven inches in diameter and three inches deep, with a flat base and curved sides and no rim to speak of, so that you could hold it in both hands and drink directly from it. From the smooth texture, the clay had evidently been well sieved for grit and pebbles before it had been hard-fired. It was pinkish-grey, though coated with a paler wash that gave it a swirling texture, like cream just stirred into coffee. Maybe local provenance; maybe not. He'd need an expert to determine that. He had little more success with the dating. Fine-ware like oil lamps and expensive crockery had changed constantly with prevailing fashions, if only to show off the wealth of their owners; but coarse-ware like this had tended to keep its form, sometimes for centuries. Circa AD 50 at a guess, plus or minus a couple of hundred years. Or a couple of thousand. He put it back down, intending to walk away, but it just wouldn't let him go. He squatted there, staring at it, rubbing his jaw, trying to read its message, work out how it had put its hook in him.

Knox knew how rare it was to find valuable artefacts in a street market. The hawkers were too shrewd to sell high-quality pieces that way, the antiquities police too observant. And there were artisans in the back streets of Alexandria and Cairo who could knock out convincing replicas in a heartbeat, if they thought they could fool a gullible tourist into parting with their cash. But this particular bowl seemed too dowdy to be worth the effort. 'How much?' he asked finally.

'One thousand US,' replied the young man without blinking.

Knox laughed again. Egyptians were expert at pricing the buyer, not the piece. Clearly he was looking unusually wealthy today. Wealthy and stupid. Again he made to walk away; again something stopped him. He touched it with his fingertip, reluctant to be drawn into a haggle. Once you started, it was rude not to finish, and Knox wasn't at all sure he wanted this piece, even if he could get it cheap. If it was a genuine antiquity, after all, then buying it was illegal. If it was fake, then he'd feel annoyed with himself for days at being taken in, especially if his friends and colleagues ever got to hear about it. He shook his head decisively, and this time he did stand up.

'Five hundred,' said the young hawker hurriedly, sensing his fat fish slipping through his fingers. 'I see you before. You a good man. I make you special price. Very special price.'

Knox shook his head. 'Where did you get it?' he asked.

'It is from the tomb of Alexander the Great, I assure you! My friend give it to me because he is a very good—'

'The truth,' said Knox. 'Or I walk away now.'

The boy's eyes narrowed shrewdly. 'Why I tell you this?' he asked. 'So you call the police?'

Knox fished in his back pocket for some cash, letting him see the banknotes. 'How can I be confident it's genuine unless you tell me where you got it?' he asked.

The trader pulled a face, looked around to make sure he couldn't be overheard. 'A friend of my cousin works on an excavation,' he murmured.

'Which excavation?' frowned Knox. 'Who runs it?'

'Foreigners.'

'What kind of foreigners?'

He shrugged indifferently. 'Foreigners.'

'Where?'

'South,' he waved vaguely. 'South of Mariut.'

Knox nodded. It made sense. Lake Mariut had been hemmed around by farms and settlements in ancient times, before the inflows from the Nile had silted up and the lake had started to shrink. He counted his money slowly. If this bowl had indeed come from an archaeological site, he had a duty to return it, or at least to let someone there know that they had a security problem. Thirty-five Egyptian pounds. He folded them between his thumb and forefinger. 'South of the lake, you say?' he frowned. 'Where, exactly? I'll need to know precisely if I'm to buy.'

The young man's eyes refocused reluctantly from the money to Knox. A bitter expression soured his face, as though he realized he'd said too much already. He muttered an obscenity, gathered the four corners of his tablecloth, hoisted it up so that all his wares clattered together, hurried away. Knox made to follow, but a colossus of a man appeared from nowhere, stepped across his path. Knox tried to go around him, but the man simply moved sideways to block him, arms folded across his chest, a dry smile on his lips, inviting Knox to try something. And then it was too late anyway, the youngster swallowed up by crowds, taking his earthenware bowl with him.

Knox shrugged and let it go. It was almost certainly nothing.

Yes. Almost certainly.

II

The Eastern Desert, Middle Egypt

Police Inspector Naguib Hussein watched the hospital pathologist pull back a flap of the blue tarpaulin to reveal the desiccated body of the girl within. At least, Naguib assumed it was a girl, judging by her diminutive size, long hair, cheap jewellery and clothes, but in truth he couldn't be sure. She'd been dead too long, buried out here in the baking hot sands of the Eastern Desert, mummified as she'd putrefied, the back of her head broken open and stuck fast by congealed gore to the tarpaulin.

'Who found her?' asked the pathologist.

'One of the guides,' said Naguib. 'Apparently some tourists wanted a taste of the real desert.' He gave an amused grunt. They'd got that, all right.

'And she was just lying here?'

'They saw the tarpaulin first. Then her foot. The rest of her was still hidden.'

'Last night's windstorm must have uncovered her.'

'And covered any tracks, too,' agreed Naguib. He watched with folded arms as the pathologist continued his preliminary assessment, examining her scalp, her eyes, her cheeks and her ears, manipulating her lower jaw back and forth to open her

13

mouth, probing a spatula deep inside, scraping froth and grit and sand from the dried-out membrane of her tongue, cheeks and throat. He closed her mouth again, studied her neck, her collarbones, the bulging, dislocated right shoulder and her arms, folded awkwardly, almost coyly, down by her sides.

'How old is she?' asked Naguib.

'Wait for my report.'

'Please. I need something to work on.'

The pathologist sighed. 'Thirteen, fourteen. Something like that. And her right shoulder shows signs of post-mortem dislocation.'

'Yes,' agreed Naguib. Out of professional vanity, he wanted the pathologist to know he'd spotted this himself, so he said: 'I thought perhaps that rigor set in before she could be buried. Perhaps it set in with her arm thrown up above her head. Perhaps whoever buried her dislocated it when they were trying to wrap her up in the tarpaulin.'

'Perhaps,' agreed the pathologist. Evidently not a man for uninformed speculation.

'What time would that give us after death?'

'That depends,' said the pathologist. 'The hotter it is, the quicker rigor sets in, but the quicker it passes, too. And if she'd been running, say, or fighting, then it would be quicker.'

Naguib breathed in deep to quell any hint of impatience. 'Approximately.'

'Shoulders are typically the last muscle groups to develop rigor. Onset takes at least three hours, often six or seven. After that . . .' He shook his head. 'It can last for anything from another six hours to two days.'

'But a minimum of three hours, yes?'

'Usually. Though there are cases.'

'There are always cases,' said Naguib.

'Yes.' With his finger, the pathologist tickled out the fragile links of a chain around her neck, a silver charm hanging from it. A Coptic cross. He glanced around at Naguib, the two men no doubt sharing a single thought. Another dead Copt girl. That was all this region needed right now.

'It's a nice enough piece,' muttered the pathologist.

'Yes,' agreed Naguib. Which argued against robbery. The pathologist lifted the girl's skirts, but her underclothes, while ragged, were intact. No sign of sexual assault. No sign of *any* assault, indeed; except, of course, that the back of her skull had been smashed in. 'Any indication how long she's been here?' he asked.

The pathologist shrugged. 'I'd be guessing. I'll need to get her back to base.'

Naguib nodded. That was fair enough. Desert corpses were notoriously tough. A month, a year, a decade; out here they all looked the same. 'And the cause of death? The blow to her head, yes?'

'Too early to say.'

Naguib pulled a face. 'Come on. I won't hold you to it.'

'Everyone tells me that. And then they hold me to it.'

'Okay. If not the blow to her head, maybe her neck was broken?'

The pathologist tapped his thumb against his knee, debating with himself whether to say anything or keep quiet. 'You really want my best guess?' he asked finally.

'Yes.'

'You won't like it.'

'Try me.'

The pathologist stood up. Hands on his hips, he looked around at the arid yellow sands of the Eastern Desert stretching away as far as the eye could see, shimmering with heat, broken only by the rugged Amarna cliffs. 'Very well, then,' he smiled, as though aware opportunities like this wouldn't come his way too often. 'I rather suspect she drowned.'

III

Knox found Omar Tawfiq kneeling on his office floor, the casing and innards of a computer spread out in front of him, a screwdriver in his hand, a smudge of grease on his cheek. 'Don't you already have enough to do?' he asked.

'Our computer people won't come out until tomorrow.'

'So hire new ones.'

'New ones will charge more.'

'Yes. Because they'll come out when you need them.'

Omar shrugged, as if to accept the truth of this, though Knox doubted he'd act upon it. A young man who looked even younger, he'd recently been promoted interim head of the Supreme Council for Antiquities in Alexandria; but everyone knew that he'd got the job because Yusuf Abbas, the Cairo-based secretary general, wanted someone pliable and disposable he could bully while he manoeuvred one of his own trusted lieutenants into the permanent role. Even Omar knew this, but he was too diffident to resent it. Instead, he spent his time hiding from his bemused staff in his old office, filling his time with comfort-zone tasks like these. He stood, wiped his hands. 'So what can I do for you, my friend?'

Knox hesitated. 'I saw an old bowl in the market. Hard-fired. Well-levigated. Pinkish-grey with a white slip. Maybe seven inches in diameter.'

'That could be anything.'

'Yes. But it gave me that feeling, you know?'

Omar nodded seriously, as though he had

respect for Knox's feelings. 'You're here to check our database?'

'If that's possible.'

'Of course.' Omar was proud of his database. Building it had been his main responsibility before his unexpected promotion. 'Use Maha's office. She's away today.'

They walked through together. Omar sat at her desk. 'Give me a minute,' he said.

Knox nodded and walked to the window, looked down at his Jeep. It had cost him a fortune to have it repaired after the Alexander business, but it had been good to him over the years, and he was glad of his decision.

'Any word from Gaille?' asked Omar.

'No.'

'Do you know when's she coming back?'

'When she's finished, I imagine.'

Omar's cheeks reddened. 'All set,' he said.

'I'm sorry,' sighed Knox. 'I didn't mean to snap.'

'It's okay.'

'It's just, everyone keeps asking, you know?'

'That's because we like her so much. Because we like you both.'

'Thanks,' said Knox. He began working his way through the database, colour and black-and-white photos of cups, plates, figurines, funerary lamps. Mostly, he flipped past them without a second glance, the old computer groaning and sighing as it strained to keep up. But every so often an image would catch his eye. Yet nothing quite matched. Ancient artefacts were like this. The closer you looked, the more potential points of difference you found.

Omar came back in with a jug of water and two glasses on a tray. 'Any luck?'

'Not yet.' He finished the database. 'Is that it?'

'Of local provenance, yes.'

'And non local?'

Omar sighed. 'I wrote to a number of museums and universities when I was setting this up. I didn't get much of a response at the time. Since my recent appointment, however . . .'

Knox laughed. 'What a surprise.'

'But we haven't entered the data yet. All we have are CDs and paperwork.'

'May I see?'

Omar opened the bottom drawer of the filing cabinet, pulled out a cardboard box of CDs. 'They're not in any order,' he warned.

'That's okay,' said Knox. He slid one into the computer. The chuntering grew louder. A page of thumbnails appeared. Fragments of papyrus and linen cloth. He clicked to the next page, and then the third. The ceramics, when he found them, were colourful and patterned, nothing like what he was looking for.

'I'll leave you to it, then,' said Omar.

'Thanks.' The second CD was of Roman-era statuary, the third of jewellery, the fourth corrupt. Knox's mind began to wander, triggered perhaps by Omar's earlier question. A sudden memory of Gaille, taking breakfast one morning on the Nile Corniche in Minya: the way she licked her upper lip free of the slight glaze from her pastry, her dark hair spilled forwards, her smile as she caught him watching.

The eighth CD was an anatomy lecture demonstrating how to distinguish manual labourers from the idle rich by bone thickness and spine curvature.

Gaille's mobile had rung that morning in Minya. She'd checked the number, shifted in her seat, turning herself away from him to hold a stilted conversation that she'd quickly ended by promising to call back later.

'Who was that?' he'd asked.

'No one.'

'You want to get on to your service provider, if you keep getting calls from people who don't exist.'

A reluctant sigh. 'Fatima.'

'Fatima?' An unexpected stab of jealousy. Fatima was *his* friend. He'd introduced the two of them barely a week before. 'What did she want?'

'I guess she'd heard about Siwa being postponed.'

'You guess?'

'Fine. She'd heard about it.'

'And she rang to commiserate, did she?'

'You remember how interested she was in my image software?'

The eleventh CD was of Islamic artefacts. The twelfth was of silver and golden coins.

'She wants you to go and work for her?'

'Siwa's not exactly about to happen, is it?' Gaille had said. 'And I hate doing nothing, especially on a salary. I hate being a drain.'

'You're not a drain,' he'd said bleakly. 'How could you think yourself a drain?'

'It's how I feel.'

The thirteenth CD was of pre-dynastic tomb paintings. He started checking the fourteenth on autopilot. He'd got halfway through when he sensed he'd missed something. He paged back to the previous screen, then the one before. And there it was, top right, the twin of the bowl he'd seen, only upside down, resting on its rim. Same shape, same colour, same texture, same patterning. But there was no description of it, only reference numbers.

He fetched Omar, who pulled a ring binder from the filing cabinet. Knox read out the reference numbers while he flipped through the pages, ran his finger down the entries, came to the right one, frowned in puzzlement. 'But that can't be right,' he said. 'It's not even a bowl.'

21

s it, then?'

A storage jar lid.'

grunted. Obvious, now that Omar pointed it out. Not that it helped much. Egypt had been the breadbasket of the ancient world. Huge quantities of produce had passed through Alexandria's multiple harbours. Making jars to store and transport it had been a vast industry. 'My mistake,' he agreed.

His admission did little to mollify Omar. 'But it's not from anywhere near here,' he said. 'It's not even from Egypt.'

'Where, then?'

He squinted at Knox, as though he suspected himself the victim of a bad joke. 'Qumran,' he said flatly. 'It's what the Dead Sea Scrolls were found in.'

TWO

I

Assiut Railway Station, Middle Egypt

Gaille Bonnard was beginning to regret coming inside the station to meet Charles Stafford and his party. She usually enjoyed crowds, the clamour and camaraderie, especially here in Middle Egypt, with its effusively friendly people, not yet soured by overexposure to tourists. But tensions had grown palpably over recent weeks. A protest march was even taking place that afternoon elsewhere in the city, which presumably explained why she could see only three men from the Central Security Forces on the platform, as opposed to the usual flood of uniforms. To make matters worse, an earlier train had broken down, so twice the usual number of passengers were waiting to board, all girding themselves for the inevitable squabbles over seats.

The tracks started to rattle. Vermin scurried. People manoeuvred for position. The ancient train rolled in, windows already being lowered, doors crashing open, passengers spilling out, laden with belongings, fighting through the scrum. Hawkers walked along the line of windows offering translucent bags of *baladi* bread, paper cones packed with seeds, sesame bars, sweets and drinks.

Away down the platform, a strikingly good-looking thirty-something man emerged from the first-class carriage. Charles Stafford. Despite his two-day stubble, she recognized him at once from the jacket photographs on the books Fatima had lent her the night before. She'd skimmed through them out of courtesy, though they were the kind of populist history she deplored – wild speculation backed by outrageously selective use of the evidence. Conspiracies everywhere, secret societies, lost treasures waiting beneath every mound; and never a dissenting voice to be heard, unless it could be ridiculed and dismissed.

Stafford paused to put on a pair of mirror shades, then hoisted a black leather laptop case to his shoulder and descended onto the platform. A stumpy young woman in a navy-blue suit came after him, tucking wilful strands of bright-red hair back beneath her floral headscarf. And an Egyptian porter followed behind, struggling beneath mounds of matching brown-leather luggage.

An elderly woman stumbled against Stafford as he pushed his way through the crowd. His laptop swung and clipped a young boy around the ear. The boy saw instantly how wealthy Stafford looked and promptly started bawling. A man in dirty-brown robes said something curt to Stafford, who waved him arrogantly away. The boy bawled even more loudly. Stafford sighed heavily and glanced around at the redhead, evidently expecting her to sort it out. She stooped, examined the boy's ear, clucked sympathetically, slipped him a banknote. He couldn't suppress his grin as he danced off. But the man in the brown robes was still feeling stung from Stafford's dismissal, and the transaction only irritated him further. He declared loudly that foreigners evidently now thought they could batter Egyptian children at will, then pay their way out of it.

The redhead gave an uncertain smile and tried to back away, but the man's words struck a chord with the crowd, and a cordon formed, trapping them inside, the atmosphere turning ugly. Stafford tried to barge his way out, but someone jolted him hard enough that his shades came off. He grabbed for them but they fell to the ground. A moment later Gaille heard the crunch of glass as they went underfoot. A scornful laugh rang out.

Gaille glanced anxiously over at the three CSF men, but they were walking away into the ticket hall, heads ducked, wanting nothing to do with this. Fear flared hot in her chest as she debated what to do. This wasn't her problem. No one even knew she was here. Her 4x4 was parked directly outside. She hesitated just a moment longer, then turned and hurried out.

II

'But it's just a lid,' protested Omar, as he hurried down the SCA's front steps after Knox. 'There must have been thousands like it. How can you be so certain it came from Qumran?'

Knox unlocked his Jeep, climbed in. 'Because it's the only place Dead Sea Scroll jars have ever been found,' he told Omar. 'At least, there was one other found in Jericho, just a few miles north, and maybe another at Masada, also close by. Other than that . . .'

'But it looked perfectly ordinary.'

'It may have looked it,' replied Knox, waiting for a van to pass before pulling out. 'But you have to understand something. Two thousand years ago, jars were used either for transporting goods or for storing them. Transportation jars were typically amphorae, with big handles to make them easier to heft about, and robust, because they had to withstand a lot of knocks, and cylindrical, because that made them more efficient to stack.' He turned right at the end of the street, then sharp left. 'But once the goods reached their final destination, they were decanted into storage jars with rounded bottoms that bedded into sandy floors and were easy to tip whenever people needed to pour out their contents. They also had long necks and narrow mouths so that they could be corked and their contents kept fresh. But the Dead Sea Scroll jars weren't like that. They had flat bottoms and stubby necks and fat mouths, and there was a very good reason for that.'

'Which was?'

His brakes sang as he slowed for a tram clanking across the junction ahead. 'How much do you know about Qumran?' he asked.

'It was occupied by the Essenes, wasn't it?' said Omar. 'That Jewish sect. Though haven't I heard people claim that it was a villa or a fort or something?'

'They've suggested it,' agreed Knox, who'd been fascinated by the place since a family holiday there as a child. 'I think they're wrong, though. I mean, Pliny said that the Essenes lived on the northwest of the Dead Sea. If not Qumran itself, then very close to it, and no one has found a convincing alternative. One expert put it very succinctly: Either Qumran and the scrolls were both Essene, or we have a quite astonishing coincidence: Two major religious communities living almost on top of each other, sharing similar views and rituals, one of which was described by ancient authors yet left no physical traces; while the other was somehow ignored by all our sources but left extensive ruins and documents.'

'So Qumran was occupied by the Essenes,' agreed Omar. 'That doesn't explain why their jars are unique.'

'The Essenes were fanatical about ritual purity,' said Knox. 'The slightest thing could render a pure receptacle impure. A drop of rain, a tumbling insect, an inappropriate spillage. And if it did, it was a major headache. I mean, if a receptacle became tainted, then obviously anything in it was immediately tainted too, and had to be chucked. But that wasn't the worst of it. Liquids and grain are poured in a stream, you see, so the real issue was whether the impurity climbed back up that stream and infected the storage jar too. The Pharisees and other Jewish sects took a relaxed view, but the Essenes believed that everything would be contaminated, so they couldn't risk pouring out contents in a stream. Instead, they'd lift the lid a little, dip in a measuring cup and transfer it that way. And because they no longer had to tip their storage jars, they could have flat bottoms, which made them much more stable; and short necks and fat mouths, too, to make them easier to dip into.'

'And jars with fat mouths need bowls for lids,' grinned Omar.

'Exactly,' nodded Knox. They were nearing the Desert Road Junction. He hunkered down in his seat to scan the road-signs. A quick review of the records in Omar's office had shown just four foreign-run sites in the vicinity of Lake Mariut, but there was nothing currently happening at Philoxinite, Taposiris Magna or Abu Mina; which left only one worthwhile candidate: a group called the Texas Society of Biblical Archaeology excavating out near Borg el-Arab.

'So what would the lid be doing here?' asked Omar, once Knox had navigated them onto the right road.

'It may well have come centuries ago,' shrugged Knox. 'The Dead Sea Scrolls were known about in antiquity. We have reports from the second, third and fourth centuries of texts being found in Qumran caves. Origen even used them to write his *Hexapla*.'

'His what?'

'The Bible written out six times in parallel columns. The first in Hebrew, the second in Greek, and then a series of edited versions. It helped other scholars compare and contrast the various versions. But the point is, he relied heavily on Dead Sea Scrolls.'

'And you think they might have been brought here in this jar of yours?'

'It's got to be a possibility.'

Omar swallowed audibly. 'You don't think we might actually find . . . *scrolls*, do you?'

Knox laughed. 'Don't get your hopes up. One of the scrolls was inscribed on copper – a treasure map, would you believe? But all the rest were on parchment or papyrus. Alexandria's climate would have chewed those up centuries ago. Besides, there's another explanation. A more intriguing one. To me, at least.'

'Go on.'

'We're pretty sure the Essenes didn't live only in Qumran,' said Knox. 'Josephus mentions an Essene Gate in Jerusalem, for example, and several scrolls laid down rules for how Essenes should live outside Qumran. Besides, we know there were several thousand Essenes, whereas Qumran could only hold a few hundred. So obviously there were other communities.'

'You mean here? In Alexandria?'

Knox grinned. 'Have you ever heard of the Therapeutae?' he asked.

III

The Reverend Ernest Peterson surreptitiously dabbed his brow. He didn't like being seen to sweat. He didn't like showing any sign of weakness. Fifty-two years old, ramrod straight, grizzled hair, fierce eyes, a hawk's nose. Never without his copy of the King James Version. Never without his preacher's livery. A man proud to show through his own unyielding purpose a faint glimmer of the irresistible strength of God. Yet the sweat kept coming. It wasn't just the humidity in this cramped, dark underground labyrinth. It was the vertiginous sense of what he was on the verge of achieving.

Thirty-odd years before, Peterson had been a punk – a petty thief, always in trouble with the law. Under arrest one night, dozing on a police bench, glancing up at a Heinrich Hofmann print of Christ hanging high up on the wall, his heart suddenly starting to race crazily, like the most violent panic attack, but which suddenly dissolved into the most intense and serene vision of his life, a blinding white light, an epiphany. He'd stumbled from the bench after it was done, searching for a reflective surface in which to see what imprint it had left upon him: bleached hair, charred skin, albino irises. To his astonishment, there'd been no physical change whatsoever. Yet it had changed him, all right. It had *transformed* him from within. For no man could look upon the face of Christ and remain untouched.

He dabbed his forehead once more, turned to Griffin. 'Ready?' he asked.

'Yes.'

31

'Then do it.'

He stood back as Griffin and Michael heaved a first block of stone from the false wall to reveal the open space behind that had been indicated by their probes. Griffin reached in his torch, twisted it this way and that, illuminating a large chamber that flickered with shadow and colour, provoking murmurs and gasps from his young students. But Peterson only nodded at Nathan and Michael to continue dismantling the wall.

It said in the Good Book: *The Lord seeth not as man seeth; for man looketh upon outward appearance, but the Lord looketh on the heart.* The Lord had looked upon *his* heart that night in custody. The Lord had seen something in him that even he hadn't realized was there.

A sufficient gap had been created for Griffin to step through, but Peterson put a hand on his shoulder. 'No,' he said. 'I'm going first.'

'It should be an archaeologist.'

'I'm going first,' repeated Peterson. He rested his palm on the rough crumbled mortar, stepped through into the new chamber.

He'd not merely been transformed that night; he'd been given purpose. Of all God's gifts, perhaps the greatest. It hadn't been easy. He'd wasted years on the medieval make-believe of the Turin Shroud and the Veil of Veronica. Yet he'd never once doubted or contemplated giving in. The Lord didn't hand out such missions on a whim. And finally he'd found the right lead, had followed it relentlessly, was now within touching distance. He felt it. He *knew* it. The time of the light was coming, certain as sunrise.

He shone his torch around the chamber. Thirty paces long, ten wide. Everything covered in dust. A deep bath embedded in the floor, a wide flight of steps leading down into it, divided by a low stone wall, so that community members could descend unclean down one side and emerge purified from the other. Walls plastered and painted in antiquity; pigments dulled by neglect, cobwebs, dirt and wormcasts. He brushed an area with his hand, shone his torch obliquely at the revealed scene. A woman in blue with a child on her lap. He had to blink away tears.

'Reverend! Look!'

He glanced around to see Marcia shining her torch up at the domed ceiling, painted to represent the sky, a glowing orange sun near its apex, constellations of yellow stars, a creamy full moon, red coals of planets. Day and night together. Joy effervesced in his heart as Peterson stared up. He fell to his knees in gratitude and adoration. 'Let us give thanks,' he said. He gazed around until all his young students had fallen to their knees. And then even Griffin had to follow, compelled by the power of the group.

'I know that my redeemer liveth,' cried Peterson, his voice reverberating loudly around the chamber. 'And that He shall stand at the latter day upon the earth: And though worms destroy this body, yet in my flesh shall I see God.'

Yes, he exulted. *In my flesh shall I see God.*

IV

Naguib Hussein was on his way back to the Mallawi police station to make his report when he decided it might be as well to make a detour to Amarna, ask the people there if they'd heard anything about a missing young girl, if only to take the opportunity of introducing himself.

A tourist policeman was fooling around on his motorbike, gunning his engine, braking sharply, spraying huge arcs of dust and sand with his back wheel: entertainment for his officer and two comrades drinking *chai* on wooden benches beneath a makeshift sunshade. Naguib braced himself. Relations between the services were strained around here, each looking down on the other. He waited for the officer to acknowledge his arrival, but he continued to ignore him until Naguib's cheeks grew warm. He scowled and walked across the officer's line of sight, giving him no choice but to notice him, though he still didn't get up. 'Yes?' he asked.

Naguib nodded at the eastern crescent of hills. 'I've just come from the desert,' he said.

'If they'll pay you for it.'

'One of the guides took some tourists out last night. They found a girl.'

'A girl?' frowned the officer. 'How do you mean?'

'I mean they found her body. Wrapped in tarpaulin.'

The officer set down his glass, stood up. A tall man, beautifully presented, razor-cut hair, manicured nails, a silken moustache, making the most of his uniform. 'I hadn't heard,' he said, suddenly earnest, offering his hand. 'Captain Khaled Osman, at your service.'

'Inspector Naguib Hussein.'

'Are you new here, Inspector? I don't recall seeing you before.'

'Six weeks,' admitted Naguib. 'I was in Minya before.'

'You must have done something pretty bad to get posted here.'

Naguib gave a wry grunt. He'd been investigating military equipment on the black market, hadn't dropped it even when the trail had led him to the top, not even after he'd been warned off. He hated Egypt's culture of corruption. 'They told me it was a promotion,' he said.

'Yes,' agreed Khaled. 'They told me that, too.' He glanced around. 'You'll join us for some *chai*?'

Naguib shook his head. 'I need to get back to the station. I just thought I'd ask if you'd heard anything.'

Khaled shook his head. 'I'm sorry. I'll ask around, if you like. Keep an ear to the ground.'

'Thank you,' said Naguib. 'I'd be most grateful.' He returned to his Lada feeling cheered. His wife always said that a drop of courtesy could solve a world of ills. She knew what she was talking about, his wife.

THREE

I

Gaille unlocked the Discovery and climbed inside. She sat there for a moment, breathing hard, studying herself in the rear-view. Her tan, head-scarf and local clothes gave her anonymity if she wanted it. She could drive away and no one would ever know. Only that wasn't quite true. *She'd* know.

She grabbed her camera from the glove compartment, hurried out and back through the ticket hall where the police were still hiding, her heart pounding, chills fluttering across her skin. Stafford and his companions were still hemmed in on the platform, wrestling for their luggage with two youths. She stepped up onto a bench, wielded her camera like a weapon. 'CNN!' she cried out. 'Al Jazeera!' Attention shifted instantly to her, a wave of hostility, quickly replaced by fear, people instinctively ducking their faces, not wanting to be captured on film. She panned around to the men from the Central Security Forces. The officer scowled and snapped out orders. His men hurried out, opened a precarious corridor with their batons that Stafford, the redhead and Gaille all hurried down, out to the Discovery.

'What are you waiting for?' yelled Stafford, slamming the passenger door behind him. 'Get us out of here.'

'What about your porter?'

'Fuck him,' snapped Stafford. 'Just get us out of here, will you?'

'But—'

'He's one of them, isn't he? He can look after himself.'

The CSF men were waving them away, as though they couldn't guarantee them protection much longer. Gaille thrust the Discovery into gear, surged away. Traffic was gridlocked the way she wanted to go; she turned left instead. The streets quickly narrowed, aged, turned into a bazaar, forcing her to slow right down, wend her way between irritated shoppers. With all the twists and turns, she quickly became disoriented. She leaned forwards in her seat, scanning the skyline for a familiar landmark by which to navigate.

II

Captain Khaled Osman kept his smile fixed to his lips as he waved off the police inspector. But it vanished when he turned to his men. 'Time for a patrol, I think,' he said. 'Faisal. Nasser. Abdullah. Come with me, please.'

Khaled sat stiffly in the passenger seat as Nasser drove and Abdullah and Faisal cowered in the back. There was silence apart from the blast of the engine. The silence of anger. The silence of fear. They reached the Northern Tombs. Khaled climbed out; his men followed, forming a desultory line, sagging like sacks of rice. He'd done his best to instil some pride of uniform in these men since being forcibly transferred into the tourist police out of the army, but it was futile, they were worthless, all they cared about was gouging *baksheesh* from the tourists. He walked back and forth in front of them, their heads bowed in shame like the miserable pups they were. 'One job I give you!' he spat. 'One damned job! And you can't even do that!'

'But we did exactly what you—'

Khaled slapped Faisal across the cheek, the crack echoing off the cliff walls behind. 'How could you have done?' he yelled, saliva spraying over Faisal's face. 'They found her, didn't they?'

A smile tweaked Abdullah's lips, evidently

relieved that Faisal was taking the brunt. Khaled grabbed his collar and clutched it so tightly that his face turned red and he started struggling for breath. 'If this goes wrong . . .' vowed Khaled. 'If this goes wrong . . .'

'We never wanted any part of this, sir,' protested Faisal. 'It was all your idea. Now look!'

'Shut up!' snarled Khaled, letting go of Abdullah, who gasped for breath, massaged his raw throat. 'You want to spend your whole life poor? Is that what you want? This is our chance to be rich.'

'Rich!' scoffed Faisal.

'Yes, rich.'

'There's nothing there, sir! Haven't you realized that yet?'

'You're wrong,' insisted Khaled. 'It's in there. I can smell it. One more week and it'll be ours.' He wagged a finger at them. 'But no more mistakes. Understand? No more mistakes.'

III

Knox drove west out along the new Desert Road into a palette of extraordinary colours, the ice-packs of the salt farms dazzling white to his right, the chemical sheen of Lake Mariut glowing almost purple to his left, and, up above, the wisps of late-afternoon cloud making for a Jackson Pollock sky.

'The Therapeutae?' frowned Omar. 'Weren't they early Christians?'

Knox shook his head. 'They had Christian attitudes and practices, and they were claimed as Christians by certain early church fathers, and it's even possible they *became* Christians. But they can't have *started* out as Christians, not least because they were living in and around Alexandria before Christ started preaching. No, they were Jews, all right. Philo admired them so much he almost joined them, after all, and he was certainly Jewish. What's more, he implied a very strong connection between them and the Essenes. The Therapeutae were his ideal of the contemplative life, the Essenes of the active life. But their beliefs and practices were otherwise virtually indistinguishable.'

'In what ways?'

'Both were extremely ascetic,' said Knox, scratching the resinous scab of a mosquito bite on his forearm. 'It's commonplace now, but no one used to think there was much virtue in poverty before the Essenes. Their initiates had to hand over most of their worldly belongings when they joined, as did new Therapeutae. Both rejected slavery and considered it an honour to serve others. Both held their elders in great esteem. Both were vegetarian and disapproved of animal sacrifice, perhaps because both believed in reincarnation. Both dressed in white linen. Both were renowned for their medical skill. Some argue that the words Essene and Therapeutae actually derived from Aramaic and Greek for healers, though it's more probable they both meant "servants of God".' He turned south onto the low causeway across Lake Mariut, where a few fishermen were idling away their day on the rocky verges. 'Purification rituals mattered hugely to both. Both were largely or completely celibate, sustaining their numbers through recruitment rather than procreation. Both sang antiphonal chants. In fact, some Passover hymns found at Qumran might well have been composed by the Therapeutae. Both used a solar calendar, as opposed to the usual Jewish lunar calendar. And both had a ritual three hundred and sixty four days to their year, even though they knew the real figure.'

They arrived south of the lake, a barren landscape of Bedouin farms, vast industrial complexes, expensive verdant villas and large stretches of rocky waste-ground that no one had yet found a use for. Knox pulled into the side to consult their map. A grey heron looked quizzically at him from a reed-bed. He winked at it and it flapped leisurely away.

'The Essenes and the Therapeutae,' prompted Omar.

'Yes,' nodded Knox, pulling away again, turning west, the map open on his lap, keeping as close to the lake as the roads allowed. 'Both were keenly interested in the hidden meanings of the scriptures. Both knew secrets they couldn't divulge to outsiders, such as the names of angels. Geometry, numerology, anagrams and word-plays held special meaning to both, as did jubilees. The Therapeutae held a feast every seven days, a more important one every fifty days. Fifty was a very special number, you see, because it was the sum of three squared plus four squared plus five squared; and any triangle with the lengths of its sides in the ratio of three, four, five is a right-angled triangle, which they held to be the building-block of the universe.'

'Right-angled triangles? Isn't that more Greek than Jewish?'

'Absolutely,' agreed Knox, turning left down a narrow lane, flat tilled fields to their right, bare limestone bedrock to their left. 'They had an amazing amount in common with the Pythagoreans. Diet, calendar, rituals, beliefs. All the things I just mentioned. And clear traces of sun-worship too. Ancient Alexandrians actually claimed that Pythagoras derived all his knowledge from Moses, that his religion was essentially Egyptian. He did spend twenty years here, after all. So maybe he got it all from the same place as the Therapeutae.'

An irrigation canal ran along the left-hand side of the road, its banks grazed by goats. This whole area was a lattice of channels distributing fresh water from the Nile. By his reckoning, the excavation should be somewhere the other side. He kept going until he saw an earthen bridge ahead, guarded by two men in uniform playing backgammon on a wooden trestle table. He turned left over the bridge, pulled to a stop beside them. 'Is this the Texas Society dig?' he asked.

'What do you want?' asked the elder of the guards.

'To talk to the chief archaeologist.'

'You mean Mister Griffin?'

'If that's his name.'

'You have an appointment?'

'This is Mr Tawfiq,' said Knox, nodding at Omar. 'He's head of the Supreme Council in Alexandria, and he wants to speak to the chief archaeologist. I suggest you let him know we're here.'

The guard held Knox's eye, but when Knox didn't look away, he stood, turned his back, held a muttered conversation on his walkie-talkie. 'Very well,' he said gruffly, once he was done. 'Follow this track to the end. Wait by the cabin. Mister Griffin will meet you there.'

'So?' asked Omar. 'Do we know where these Therapeutae of yours lived?'

'Not exactly,' admitted Knox. 'Philo did give us some clues, though. For example, he said that their settlement was on a slightly raised plain within reach of the sea breezes. And that they were close enough together to defend each other from attack, yet far enough apart to be alone with their thoughts. Oh, yes, and he told us one other thing.'

'Which was?'

The two men topped a small rise. A wooden cabin with a canvas extension came into view, two battered white pick-ups and a 4x4 parked outside. And, in the distance, the flat blue sheen of Alexandria's great lake. Knox turned to Omar with a slight smile. 'That their settlement was on the southern bank of Lake Mariut,' he said.

FOUR

I

Lily Auster stared bleakly out the window of the Discovery as Gaille drove them slowly through the narrow wending alleys of the Assiut bazaar. Two days into her first proper overseas assignment, already a train wreck. She clenched her fist until her nails dug pale crescents in her palm. *Get a grip, girl*, she told herself. *A setback, that's all*. It was her job to deal with setbacks and then move on. If she couldn't deal with such things, she should find a new career. She forced a smile first onto her lips and then up into her eyes and leaned forwards between the front seats. 'So you're Gaille Bonnard, yes?' she asked with all the brightness she could muster.

'Yes,' agreed Gaille.

'I rang Fatima while we were on the train,'

nodded Lily. 'She said you'd be meeting us. Thanks so much for helping out back there. I thought we were toast.'

'Forget it,' said Gaille.

'I'm Lily, by the way. Lily Auster. And of course you recognize our star, Charles Stafford.'

'Of course,' agreed Gaille. 'Pleased to meet you both.'

'Bloody maniacs!' muttered Stafford. 'What was wrong with those people?'

'Things are very tense around here at the moment. Two young girls have been raped and murdered. And they were both Copts. Egyptian Christians, that is.'

'I know what a Copt is, thank you,' said Stafford.

'Those poor girls,' said Lily, checking herself in the rear-view mirror, her eyes flicking instinctively to her cheek. The laser treatments had done exactly what the brochure had promised, reducing her vivid port-wine birthmark to a reddish-brown glow that people barely even noticed any more. But she'd discovered an unwelcome truth about disfigurement: suffer it long enough, and it became a part of who you were, your personality. She still felt ugly, no matter what the mirror tried to tell her. 'But why is it significant they were Copts?'

'The last time anything like this happened – a

murder – the police simply rounded up hundreds of other Copts. It caused an awful lot of friction with the West. People assumed it was religious discrimination, you see – Muslim on Christian; though it wasn't, really. It's just how the police investigate around here. They grab all the nearest people and beat them until one of them talks. But this time, instead of rounding up Copts, they've used it as an excuse to grab all the local Islamic firebrands and beat them instead. And their friends and families blame people like us. There's a big march on through the city this afternoon.'

'Charming,' nodded Stafford, his interest fading fast. He turned to Lily. 'What luggage did we lose?'

'Just clothes, I think,' said Lily. 'I saved our equipment.'

'*My* clothes, I suppose.'

'Both our clothes.'

'What the hell am I supposed to wear on camera?'

'We'll find you something. Don't worry.' Her smile had become strained these past few days. Working for Stafford would do that to you, particularly if your colleagues had jumped ship, as hers had. Last night over dinner he'd gone on about his recent trip to Delphi. *Gnothi Seauton*, the Oracle had advised. *Know thyself.* Stafford had sat back in his chair and claimed it as his prescription for a fulfilled life. Her unintentional snort had sprayed atomized droplets of white wine across the tablecloth. She'd never met a man with such little self-awareness, yet he'd done absurdly well, was both successful and happy. Oh, to be a narcissist, with unshakeable faith in your own beauty and wonderfulness. And to have people admire you for it too! Because they did: people were such fools, they took others at their own estimate. She turned back to Gaille. 'Fatima said you'd come with us tomorrow. That's so kind of you.'

'Tomorrow?' frowned Gaille. 'How do you mean?'

'Didn't she mention it?'

'No,' said Gaille. 'She didn't. Why? What's happening?'

'We're filming in Amarna. Our guide went AWOL.'

'Good riddance to him,' muttered Stafford. 'Man had an attitude.'

'That's why we had to take the train,' said Lily. 'Your professor said she'd come with us. But now apparently something's come up. So we're really stuck. It's not just that we need an expert to talk to camera, though that would be great. It's that neither of us speak Arabic. I mean, our documentation's in order and everything, but I don't know how things *work* around here. Every country has its own ways, you know?'

'I'll have a word with Fatima when we get back,'

sighed Gaille. 'I'm sure we'll be able to sort something out.'

'Thanks,' said Lily, squeezing Gaille's shoulder. 'That's brilliant of you.' A pang of shame, quickly suppressed. It was one of the hidden penalties of ugliness that no one ever volunteered their help; you had to find other ways to get what you needed: flattery, bargaining, bribery, throwing yourself on their mercy.

They drifted to a halt. Lily glanced through the windscreen. The way ahead was blocked by metal barricades, ranks of riot police in black uniforms and helmets, the protest march passing the other side, fervent young men in robes, the perfect oval faces of the women in their hijab, others completely veiled by their niqab. A sweet stab of longing low in Lily's stomach. As a girl, how envious she'd been of Muslim women, able to hide behind the sanctuary of burkha. 'I hate to ask,' she murmured, 'but are you sure this is the right way?'

II

Knox and Omar leaned against the Jeep as they waited for Griffin. 'Maha said these were bullet-holes from that Alexander business,' said Omar, fingering the patched-up bodywork. 'They're not really, are they?'

'Afraid so.'

Omar laughed. 'You do live, Daniel.'

'Only just.' He stooped to check the ground. The site was on a gentle hummock of limestone, almost completely bare of soil, useless for farming and untouched by industrialization or property development. If people had lived here in ancient times, there was a fair chance traces of them would have survived. He looked up at the scuff of footsteps. Two middle-aged men emerged from behind the cabin, their clothes and hair grey with dust and cobwebs. 'Mister Tawfiq,' said the first, thrusting out his right hand, revealing a dark crescent of sweat beneath his armpit. 'I understand you're the new head of the SCA in Alexandria. Congratulations.'

'Oh,' said Omar. 'I'm only interim head, you know.'

'I met your predecessor, of course. A terrible tragedy to lose such a good man so young.'

'Yes,' agreed Omar. He turned to Knox. 'And this is my friend, Mister Daniel Knox.'

'Daniel Knox?' asked the man. 'Of Alexander's tomb fame?'

'Yes,' acknowledged Knox.

'We are honoured,' he said, shaking his hand. 'I'm Mortimer Griffin. Chief archaeologist of this excavation.' He turned to his companion. 'And this is the Reverend Ernest Peterson.'

'An excavation with its own chaplain?' asked Knox.

'We're really a training dig,' explained Griffin. 'Most of our crew are very young, you know. Away from home for the first time, a lot of them. Their parents feel better knowing they have moral guidance.'

'Of course,' said Knox. He offered to shake Peterson's hand, but Peterson just stood there, his arms folded, staring back with a granite smile.

'So what can we do for you gentlemen?' asked Griffin, pretending nothing had just happened. 'All this way without an appointment. It must be important.'

'Yes,' agreed Knox. 'I'm beginning to think it might be.'

III

Stafford sighed loudly as Gaille pulled to a stop by the barriers. 'Don't tell me we're lost!'

'I had to get us away from the station,' said Gaille defensively. She leaned forwards. Late afternoon sun blurred like a headache on her dusty windscreen. There was no indication of when the march might end and the barricades be removed. Nothing for it: she pulled an awkward five-point turn in the narrow street, headed back through the bazaar and emerged onto the square outside the crowded train station, the traffic and emerging passengers forcing her to slow almost to walking pace as she worked her way through the crowd.

Two men were laughing good-naturedly as they tussled over a straw hat. 'That's mine!' scowled Stafford. He lowered his window, grabbed for his hat. The two men danced off yelling cheerful insults, bringing the Discovery to general attention. People walked in front, forcing Gaille to a stop. 'What are you doing?' protested Stafford, raising his window back up.

'I thought you wanted your hat.'

'Get us out of here.'

Gaille pressed her palm on her horn, revved her engine until the throng reluctantly parted, allowing her to squirt through a gap and away. But the traffic lights ahead turned red, a three-wheel van blocking their escape. Gaille glanced back. A tall youth was swaggering after them, swinging his shoulders, probably only wanting to impress his friends; but the seconds passed and the lights didn't change, and he drew closer and closer, so that Gaille knew he'd have to do something or look ridiculous. She checked to make sure the doors were all locked, looked around again. The man stooped, picked up a stone the size of an egg from the edge of the kerb, threw it hard. It clanged on their roof, skittered off down the street. Others began to near. A clod of earth exploded on their back window, leaving an ugly brown smear. The lights finally turned. The three-wheeler struggled to get away. Suddenly they were surrounded, people banging on their windows. A man reached beneath his robes just as an explosion, like a fire-cracker, made Gaille's hands jump on the steering wheel. A wisp of smoke leaked apologetically from the three-wheeler's exhaust as it finally picked up speed. She stamped her foot down indignantly and accelerated away.

FIVE

I

'Well?' said Griffin. 'Won't you tell us why you're here?'

'I was offered an artefact in Alexandria this morning,' replied Knox. 'The seller said it was from an excavation south of Mariut.'

'You shouldn't believe what those people tell you. Anything for a sale.'

'Yes,' agreed Knox.

Griffin's eyes narrowed. 'What kind of artefact exactly?'

'A storage-jar lid.'

'A storage-jar lid? You came all this way for a storage-jar lid?'

'We came all this way because we think antiquities theft is a serious matter,' said Omar.

'Yes, of course,' nodded Griffin, suitably chastened.

'But you must realize there used to be a substantial pottery industry out here. They made jars to transport grain and wine all around the Mediterranean, you know. Good wine, too. Strabo commended it highly. So did Horace and Virgil. They even found some amphorae of it off Marseilles, would you believe? Walk along the old lake-front here, you'll find great heaps of ancient pottery fragments. Anyone could have picked up your lid from one of them. It didn't have to come from an excavation.'

'This lid wasn't broken,' said Knox. 'Besides, it was . . . *unusual*.'

'Unusual?' said Griffin, shading his eyes from the sun. 'In what way?'

'What exactly *is* this site?' asked Omar.

'An old farm. Of no great interest, believe me.'

'Really?' frowned Knox. 'Then why excavate here?'

'This is primarily a training excavation. It gives our students the chance to experience life on a real dig.'

'What did they farm here?'

'All kinds of things. Grain. Vines. Beans. Madder. Papyrus. You know.'

'On limestone bedrock?'

'This is where they lived. Their fields were on all sides.'

'And the people?'

Griffin scratched beneath his collar, beginning to feel the pressure. 'Like I say. This was an old farm. They were old farmers.'

'What era?'

Griffin glanced at Peterson, but found no help. 'We've found artefacts from the Nineteenth Dynasty on. But mostly Graeco-Roman. Nothing later than the early fifth century AD. A couple of coins from 413 or 414, something like that. There seems to have been a fire around that time. Luckily for us.'

Knox nodded. A good blaze would put a carbonized shell over a site, protecting it from the worst ravages of time and weather. 'The Christian riots?' he suggested.

'Why would Christians burn down a farm?'

'Why indeed?' agreed Knox.

'Perhaps you could give us the tour,' suggested Omar into the ensuing silence. 'Show us what you've been finding.'

'Of course. Of course. Any time. Just make an appointment with Claire.'

'Claire?'

'Our administrator. She speaks Arabic, you know.'

'That's good,' said Omar. 'Because I can barely speak a word of English myself.'

Griffin had the grace to blush. 'I'm sorry. I didn't mean it that way. It was just if you had one of your people make the appointment for you.'

'Can't we speak to her now?'

'I'm afraid she's not on site. And this season may not be easy. Rush of work. So much to do. So little time.' He waved vaguely at the desert behind him, as though they could see for themselves. But of course they could see nothing.

'We wouldn't get in your way,' said Knox.

'I think I'm the best judge of that, don't you?'

'No,' said Omar tersely. 'I think *I'm* the best judge.'

'We report to Cairo, not you,' said Peterson, speaking for the first time. 'I'm not quite clear what your jurisdiction here is.'

'Do you have an SCA representative here?' asked Omar.

'Of course,' nodded Griffin. 'Abdel Lateef.'

'May I speak with him?'

'Ah. He's in Cairo today.'

'Tomorrow, then?'

'I'm not sure when he'll be back.'

Knox and Omar shared a glance. The SCA representative was supposed to be on site full time. 'You have an Egyptian crew, I assume. May I speak with your *reis*?'

'By all means,' said Peterson. 'Just show us your authorization.' He waited a moment for Omar to produce it, then shook his head in theatrical disappointment. 'No? Well do come back when you have it.'

'But I'm head of the Supreme Council in Alexandria,' protested Omar.

'Interim head,' retorted Peterson. 'Drive safely, now.' And he turned his back on them and strode away, leaving Griffin to hurry after him.

II

Gaille was waved to a stop at a checkpoint a couple of kilometres north of Assiut, assigned two police cars for the return journey north. It was like that round here. In her headscarf, driving alone, Gaille was effectively invisible; but once she had such obvious Westerners as Stafford and Lily for passengers, there was little chance of avoiding an escort. Gaille hated driving in convoy like this; the police here drove at breakneck pace, wending wildly through traffic, forcing her to drive frighteningly fast just to keep up. But they reached the end of the police jurisdiction without incident and the two cars vanished as quickly as they'd appeared.

'So what's your programme about, then?' asked Gaille, slowing with relief to a more comfortable speed.

'I've a copy of the synopsis for this segment, if you'd like,' said Lily from the back, unzipping her bag.

'That's confidential,' snapped Stafford.

'We're asking Gaille to help,' observed Lily. 'How can she if she doesn't know what we're working on?'

'Very well,' sighed Stafford. He took the synopsis from Lily, glanced through it to make sure it contained no state secrets, then rested it on his knee and cleared his throat. 'In 1714,' he began sonorously, as if for a voice-over, 'Claude Sicard, a French Jesuit scholar, came across an inscription cut into the cliffs at a desolate site near the Nile in the heart of Egypt. It turned out to be a boundary marker for one of the most remarkable cities of the ancient world, the capital city of a previously unknown pharaoh, a pharaoh who'd inspired the birth of a new philosophy, a new style of art, and – most of all – of bold new ideas about the nature of God that had shattered the status quo and irreversibly altered the history of the world.'

As opposed to reversibly altering it, you mean? thought Gaille, struggling not to smile.

Stafford squinted at her. 'Did you say something?'

'No.'

He pursed his lips, but then let it go, picked up where he'd left off. 'The new ways had proved too much for the Egyptian establishment, however. Extraordinarily, it would transpire, this city hadn't just been abandoned, it had been deliberately *dismantled*, brick by brick, to remove any evidence of its existence. And all across Egypt, every mention of this man and his reign had been meticulously erased so that the seas of time closed over his head without a trace. Who was he, this heretic pharaoh? What crime had he committed that was so monstrous, it had had to be expunged from history? In his latest groundbreaking book and companion documentary, iconoclastic historian Charles Stafford explores the astonishing multiple mysteries of the Amarna era, and puts forward a revolutionary new theory that not only shatters the way we think about Akhenaten, but will also rewrite our notions of the history of the ancient Near East.' He folded the sheet back up, tucked it away in his inside jacket pocket, looking rather pleased with himself.

A donkey was standing in the middle of the road ahead, its front legs hobbled so that it could move only in feeble bunny-hops. Gaille put her foot on the brakes, slowing right down, trying to give it time to reach the verge, but it didn't move, it just stood there, terrified and bewildered, so that she had to cut into the other lane to drive around it, provoking angry bursts of horn from other traffic. 'Your programme's really going to do all that?' she asked, checking anxiously in her rear-view until the donkey had vanished from sight.

'And more. Much more.'

'How?'

'He's suggesting Akhenaten had a disease,' volunteered Lily from the back.

'Oh,' said Gaille, disappointed, as she turned left off the main Nile road onto a narrow country lane. The grotesque images of Akhenaten and his family were one of the most fiercely debated aspects of the Amarna era. He himself had often been portrayed with a swollen skull, protruding jaw, slanted eyes, fleshy lips, narrow shoulders, wide hips, pronounced breasts, a potbelly, fat thighs and spindly calves. Hardly the heroic picture of manhood that most pharaohs had aspired to. His daughters, too, were typically shown with almond skulls, elongated limbs, spidery fingers and toes. Some believed that this had simply been the prevailing artistic style. But others, like Stafford it seemed, argued that it portrayed the ravages of some vicious disease. 'Which are you going with?' she asked. 'Marfan's Syndrome? Frohlich's?'

'Scarcely Frohlich's,' sniffed Stafford. 'It causes sterility. And Akhenaten had six daughters, you know.'

'Yes,' said Gaille, who'd worked on her father's excavation in Amarna for two seasons while still a teenager, and who'd studied the Eighteenth Dynasty for three years at the Sorbonne. 'I did.' Even so, there was only so much of the relentless *'child of his loins, his alone, no one else's, just his'* inscriptions that you could read before wondering whether someone wasn't protesting a mite too much.

'We spoke to a specialist before coming out,' said Lily. 'He reckoned Marfan's Syndrome was the most likely candidate. But he did suggest others too. Ehler's-Danlos. Klinefelter's.'

'It was Marfan's,' asserted Stafford. 'It's autosomal dominant, you see. That's to say, if a child inherits the relevant gene from *either* parent, they'll inherit the syndrome, too. Look at the daughters; *all* portrayed with classic Marfan's symptoms. The odds against that happening unless the condition was autosomal dominant are enormous.'

'What do you think, Gaille?' asked Lily.

She slowed to bump her way across a thick carpet of sugar-cane husks laid out to dry in the sun, fuel for the furnaces of the black-honey factories, their thick black smoke still visible despite the growing late-afternoon gloom. 'It's certainly plausible,' she agreed. 'But it's not exactly new.'

'Yes,' smiled Stafford. 'But then you haven't heard the groundbreaking bit yet.'

III

'This is bad,' muttered Griffin, whey-faced, hurrying after Peterson. 'This is a disaster.'

'Cleave ye unto the Lord thy God, Brother

Griffin,' said Peterson. 'No man will be able to resist you.' The visit of Knox and Tawfiq had, in truth, exhilarated him. For was not Daniel Knox a one-time protégé of that shameless abominator Richard Mitchell? Which made him an abominator himself, a servant of the Devil. And if the Devil was sending his emissaries on such missions, it could only mean he was worried. Which in turn was proof that Peterson was close to fulfilling his purpose.

'What if they come back?' protested Griffin. 'What if they bring the police?'

'That's what we pay your friends in Cairo for, isn't it?'

'We'll need to hide the shaft,' said Griffin, holding his belly as if he had a stomach ache. 'And the magazine! Good grief. If they find those artefacts . . .'

'Stop panicking, will you?'

'How can you be so calm?'

'Because we have the Lord on our side, Brother Griffin. That's how.'

'But don't you realize—?'

'Listen,' said Peterson. 'Do as I tell you and everything will be fine. First, go and talk to our Egyptian crew. One of them stole that lid. Demand his colleagues give him up.'

'They never will.'

'Of course not. But use it as an excuse to send

them all home until your investigation is complete. We need them off the site.'

'Oh. Good thinking.'

'Then call Cairo. Let your friends know our situation, that we need their support. Remind them that if there's any kind of enquiry, we might not be able to prevent their names from coming up. Then move anything that could cause us a problem out of the magazine and back underground. Store it in the catacombs for the moment.'

'And you? What are you going to do?'

'The Lord's work, Brother Griffin. The Lord's work.'

Griffin paled. 'You're not seriously planning to go on with this?'

'Have you forgotten why we're here, Brother Griffin?'

'No, Reverend.'

'Then what are you waiting for?' Peterson watched disdainfully as Griffin slouched away. A man of terrible weak faith; but you had to use the tools to hand when you did the Lord's work. He strode up a hummock of rock, relishing the tightness in his hams and calves, the burnish of the setting sun upon his nape, the long sharp shadow he cut in the sand. He'd never for one moment imagined he'd feel such affinity for Egypt, away from his church and flock and home. Yet there was a quality to the light here, as though it too had suffered in the flames and been purified.

He breathed in deeply, filling his lungs. The earliest Christian monks had chosen this place to answer God's call. Peterson had always imagined that an accident of history and geography; but he'd soon realized that there was more to it than that. This was a profoundly spiritual place, all the more so the further you ventured into the desert. You felt it in the blazing sun, in the sweat and ache of labour, in the way water splashed gloriously over your parched skin and lips. You glimpsed it in the voluptuous golden lines of the dunes and the shimmering blue skies. You heard it in the silence.

He paused, looked around to make sure no one could see him, then went down into the slight dip in which they'd found the mouth of the shaft two years before. That first season, and the next, he'd allowed himself to be constrained by Griffin's anxieties, excavating the cemetery and old buildings during the day, only going about their true business once their Egyptian crew had left for the night. But his patience had finally run out. He was an Old Testament preacher by temperament, scornful of the divine social worker championed by so many modern religious leaders. His God was a jealous God, a stern and demanding God: a God of love and forgiveness to those who submitted utterly to him; but a God of furious wrath and vengeance to His enemies and to those who let Him down.

Peterson had no intention of letting his God down. He had one night to complete his sacred mission. He intended to make the most of it.

SIX

I

'The groundbreaking bit?' asked Gaille.

Stafford hesitated, but he was clearly proud of his ideas and wanted to impress her: the maverick historian showing up the establishment academic. 'I'll not tell you everything,' he said. 'But I'll say this much. Yes, nearly every modern work on Akhenaten mentions the possibility of some disease or other. But as an adjunct, you know. A *sidebar*. They get it out of the way and then move on. But I don't think you can get it out the way and move on. If it's true, after all, it would have had the most profound impact. Think about it. A young man suddenly developing a bewildering, disfiguring and incurable disease. And no ordinary young man, but one of almost unlimited power, viewed as a living God by his sycophantic court. Can't you see how that would be a catalyst for all kinds of new thinking? Priests devising new theologies to explain his ravages as blessings not curses; artists striving to represent disfigurement as beauty. Akhenaten was constantly pledging never to leave Amarna because it was the spiritual home of his new God, the Aten. But actually his vows sound much more like the wheedling of a frightened young man finding excuses to stay home. Amarna was sanctuary. People here knew better than to make him feel a freak.'

'Maybe,' said Gaille.

'There's no maybe about it,' said Stafford. 'Disease explains so much. His children all died young, you know.'

They'd reached the last of the cultivated fields, and now passed between a thin line of trees out shockingly into the raw desert, nothing but dunes between them and the high ridge of sandstone cliffs ahead. 'Christ!' muttered Lily from the back.

'Quite a sight, isn't it,' agreed Gaille. It felt like true border territory this, the tall grey water towers every kilometre or two resembling nothing quite so much as guard-posts struggling to keep the hostile desert at bay. She pointed through her windscreen. 'See that walled compound with the trees in front? That's where we're going. It used to be the local power station, but they abandoned it for a new one further south, so Fatima took it over.

It's almost exactly halfway between Hermopolis and Tuna el-Gabel, which puts us right in the—'

'I'm sorry you find my theories so boring,' said Stafford.

'I don't at all,' protested Gaille. 'You were telling us about how all Akhenaten's children died young.'

'Yes,' said Stafford, a little mollified. 'His six daughters certainly, and Smenkhkare and the famous Tutankhamun too, if they were his sons, as some scholars suggest. Marfan's Syndrome drastically reduces life expectancy. Aortic dissection mostly. Pregnancy is a particularly dangerous time because of the additional pressures on the heart. At least two of Akhenaten's daughters died in childbirth.'

'So did a lot of women back then,' pointed out Gaille. Life expectancy for women had been less than thirty years, significantly less than for men, largely because of the dangers of pregnancy.

'And Akhenaten is often criticized for letting his empire fall apart while he lazed around worshipping the Aten. Marfan's causes extreme fatigue. Maybe that's why he's never portrayed doing anything energetic, except riding his chariot. And it would explain his love of the sun too. Marfan's sufferers really feel the cold, you know. And their eyesight is afflicted, so that they need good light to see anything.'

'Quite a risk, isn't it? Basing your whole thesis on such a speculation.'

'You academics!' snorted Stafford. 'Always so frightened of being proved wrong. You've lost your nerve; you hedge everything. But I'm *not* wrong. My theory explains Akhenaten perfectly. Can you offer another theory that even comes close?'

'How about the opium-den theory?'

Stafford slid her a glance. 'I beg your pardon?'

Gaille nodded. 'You know they've got the mummy of Akhenaten's father, Amenhotep III, in the vaults of the Cairo Museum?'

'So?'

'It's been examined by palaeopathologists. His teeth were in a wretched state, apparently.' She glanced around at Lily. 'They used to grind up their grain with stone,' she said. 'Little bits of grit were always getting in the mix. Like eating sandpaper. All Egyptians of a certain age had worn-down teeth, but Amenhotep particularly so. He must have been constantly plagued by abscesses. Have you ever had a tooth abscess?'

Lily winced sympathetically, touched a hand to her cheek. 'Once,' she said.

'Then you'll know just how much pain he'd have been in. No antibiotics, of course. You just had to wait it out. He'd almost certainly have drunk to numb the pain. Wine, mostly, though the Egyptians loved their beer. But there's another possibility. According to something called the Ebers Papyrus, opium was well known to Eighteenth

Dynasty medics. They imported it from Cyprus, made it into a paste and spread it as an analgesic over the sore area: the gums in Amenhotep's case. Is it really too much of a stretch to imagine doctors prescribing opium for Akhenaten too, particularly if he was suffering from some disease, as you claim?'

They reached the outside of Fatima's compound. The gates were closed, so Gaille gave a short squirt of horn. 'Maybe he got the taste for it. Opium was certainly used at Amarna. We've found poppy-shaped juglets there, with traces of opiates inside. The Minoans used opium to induce religious ecstasy and inspire their art. Isn't it possible that Akhenaten and his courtiers did the same? I mean, there's something rather hallucinogenic about the whole Amarna period, isn't there? The art, the court, the religion, the hapless foreign policy?'

Lily laughed. 'You're saying Akhenaten was a junkie?'

'I'm saying it's a theory that explains the Amarna era. One of several. As to whether it's right or not . . .'

'I've never heard it before,' said Stafford. 'Has anyone published on it?'

'A couple of articles in the journals,' said Gaille, as the front gates finally swung open. 'But nothing major.'

'Interesting,' murmured Stafford. 'Most interesting.'

II

'They've found something,' said Knox, as he drove away from the Texas Society site. 'They're hiding it from us.'

'What makes you think that?' frowned Omar.

'Didn't you notice how their hair was matted with cobwebs and dust? You only get that when you've found something underground.'

'Oh,' said Omar gloomily. 'But they're archaeologists. They wouldn't have been awarded the concession if they couldn't be trusted.'

Knox gave an eloquent snort. 'Sure! Because no one ever took *baksheesh* in this country. Besides, didn't you see the way that preacher glared at me?'

'It was like he knew you from somewhere,' nodded Omar. 'Have you met him before?'

'Not that I can remember. But I recognize that look. You remember Richard Mitchell, my old mentor?'

'Gaille's father?' asked Omar. 'Of course. I never got to meet him, but I heard plenty of stories.'

'I'll bet,' laughed Knox. 'You heard he was homosexual?'

Omar coloured. 'I assumed that was just malicious gossip. I mean, he was Gaille's father, after all.'

'The two aren't incompatible, you know. And just because gossip is malicious, doesn't make it wrong.'

'Oh.'

'The thing is, because I worked with him so closely, lots of people assumed I was his boy, you know. I never bothered to put them right. Let them think what they want, right? Anyway, most people in our business don't much care. But a few do. You soon get to recognize a certain look in their eye.'

'You think Peterson's like that?'

'The Bible's pretty intolerant of homosexuality,' nodded Knox. 'People try to gloss it over, but it's there all right. And some Christians exult in the opportunity to be spiteful in the name of God. That's fine, up to a point. They're entitled to their opinion. It's just, if I've learned one thing in archaeology, it's never to entrust a sensitive site to anyone who's convinced of the truth before they start. It's too easy for them to fit the evidence to their theories, rather than the other way around.'

'I'll call Cairo first thing in the morning. We'll come straight back out.'

'That will still leave them all night.'

'Then what do you suggest?'

'We go back now. We look around.'

'Are you crazy?' protested Omar. 'I'm head of the SCA in Alexandria! I can't go sneaking around archaeological sites at night. How would it look if we were caught?'

'Like you were doing your job.'

Omar's cheeks flamed, but then he sighed and bowed his head. 'I *hate* this kind of thing! I'm no damned good at it. Why on earth did Yusuf Abbas appoint me?'

'Maybe because he knew you wouldn't cause him any trouble,' said Knox ruthlessly.

A dark scowl flickered like a passing cloud across Omar's face. 'Very well,' he said. 'Let's do it.'

III

Gaille showed Stafford and Lily to their rooms, then went in search of Fatima. No surprise, she was at her desk, swaddled in blankets, looking cadaverous with exhaustion beneath her shawl. It was sometimes hard for Gaille to believe that so frail and shrunken a frame could house so formidable an intellect. Born just east of here, she'd discovered her passion for Ancient Egypt young, had won a scholarship to Leiden University in Holland before becoming a lecturer there, returning to Egypt each year to excavate at Berenike. But her illness had drawn her back here, close to her family, her roots. 'I saw you were back,' she smiled. 'Thank you.'

Gaille put her hand upon her shoulder. 'I was glad to help.'

'What did you make of our friend Mister Stafford?'

'Oh. I really didn't have much of a chance to get to know him.'

Fatima allowed herself a rare laugh. 'That bad?'

'He's not my kind of historian.'

'Mine, neither.'

'Then why invite him?'

'Because we need funds, my dear,' said Fatima. 'And, for that, we first need publicity.' She clenched her eyes and produced a blood-red handkerchief, the inevitable prelude to one of her violent coughing fits.

Gaille waited patiently until she was recovered. 'There must be other ways,' she said, as the handkerchief vanished once more beneath Fatima's robes.

'I wish there were.' But they both knew the reality. Most of the SCA's constrained budget went to Giza, Saqqara, Luxor and the other landmark sites. So few people ever visited this stretch of Middle Egypt, it wasn't considered an attractive investment, despite its beauty, friendliness and historical significance.

'I don't see how having Stafford here will help,' said Gaille mulishly.

'People read his books,' replied Fatima.

'His books are nonsense.'

'I know they are. But people still read them. And they watch his programmes too. And some of them will no doubt be prompted to learn more, maybe even come here to find the truth for themselves. All we need is enough traffic to support a tourist infrastructure.'

'They said something about me going with them to Amarna tomorrow.'

Fatima nodded. 'I'm sorry to land that on you,' she said. 'But my doctor came today. He's not happy with my . . . *prognosis*.'

'Oh, no,' said Gaille wretchedly. 'Oh, Fatima.'

'I'm not looking for sympathy,' she said sharply. 'I'm explaining the situation. He's ordered me to hospital tomorrow for tests. So I won't be able to accompany Stafford as I'd promised. Someone must take my place. I've already banked my fee and I assure you I'm not paying it back.'

'Why not one of the others?' asked Gaille. 'They know more than I do.'

'No they don't. You spent two seasons excavating Amarna with your father, didn't you?'

'I was only a teenager. It was over a decade ago.'

'So? None of my people have spent anything

like that much time there. And you studied the Eighteenth Dynasty at the Sorbonne, didn't you? And haven't you just been back there with Knox? Besides, we both know that Western audiences will respond more positively to a Western face, a Western voice.'

'He'll make it seem like I'm endorsing his ideas.'

'You won't be.'

'I know I won't be. But that's how he'll make it look. He'll take what he needs and ignore everything else. He'll make me a laughing stock.'

'Please.' Fatima touched her wrist. 'You don't know how tight our budget is. Once I'm gone—'

Gaille winced. 'Don't talk like that.'

'It's the truth, my dear. I need to leave this project in good financial health. It's my legacy. And that means raising the profile of this region. I'm asking you to help. If you feel you can't, I suppose I could always postpone my tests.'

Gaille blinked and clenched her jaw. 'That's unfair, Fatima.'

'Yes,' she agreed.

The wall-clock ticked away the seconds. Gaille finally let out her breath. 'Fine,' she sighed. 'You win. What exactly do you want me to do?'

'Just be helpful. That's all. Help them make a good programme. And I want you to show them the *talatat* too.'

'No!' cried Gaille. 'You can't be serious.'

'Can you think of a better way to generate publicity?'

'It's too early. We can't be anything like sure. If it turns out we're wrong—'

Fatima nodded. 'Just show them the place, then. Explain how your image software works, how you recreate those old scenes after all these centuries. Leave everything else to me. My doctor insists I eat, after all. I'll join you for dinner tonight. That way, if anyone's made a laughing stock over this, it'll be me.'

SEVEN

I

Night fell as Knox and Omar headed back towards the excavation site, avoiding the route they'd taken before, wary of being spotted. They took farm tracks instead, crossing a wooden bridge over another irrigation channel into a field, then navigating by moonlight until their further progress was balked by a high stone wall. By his reckoning, the Texas Society site lay across a lane just the other side. He trundled on a short distance until he spotted a padlocked steel gate, rolled to a stop.

His white shirt glowed treacherously in the moonlight when he got out of the Jeep, so he rummaged in the back for a dark polo-neck jersey for himself, found a jacket for Omar too. Then he patted his pockets to make sure he had his camera-phone, and set off. A bird hooted and flapped lazily away as they climbed the gate. They crossed the lane, reached the irrigation channel. Knox grinned at Omar, enjoying himself, but Omar only grimaced in response, his discomfort clear.

Knox clambered down the near bank, taking a cascade of earth and stone with him, stepped across the dank ribbon of water at its foot, scrambled up the far bank on his palms and knees, peered cautiously over the top. The landscape was flat and featureless, making it hard to get a fix. He waited for Omar to arrive then crouched low and headed on in. He'd barely gone fifty metres before he trod on a fat stone and turned his ankle, stumbling to the ground. There were many such stones, he now saw, pale-grey and rounded, some even arranged in rough cairns, all aligned in the same direction. He came across a tent of translucent plastic sheeting, pulled it back to expose a pit beneath, a crumbled wall of ancient bricks at its foot, filtered moonlight glowing on a domed skull, thin curved ribs and long bones. 'Neat rows of white stones,' he murmured, taking a photograph, though without his flash attachment he wasn't sure quite what would show up. 'Just like the cemetery at Qumran. Skeletons pointing south, their faces turned to the rising sun. And see how the bones are tinted slightly purple?'

'So?'

'The Essenes used to drink a juice made from

madder root. It stains bones red, if you drink enough of it. And didn't Griffin say they used to grow madder around here?'

'You think your lid came from one of these graves?'

'It's possible.'

'Then can we leave now?'

'Not yet. We still need to see—'

A snarl behind them. Knox whirled around to see a mangy dog, ribs showing through its flanks, moonlight reflecting brightly from its black eyes and silvery slobber. Ancient Egyptian cemeteries had typically been sited on desert fringes; good quality farmland had been too valuable to waste. They'd consequently become the haunts of scavengers, one reason why the jackal-god Anubis had been so closely associated with death. Knox hissed and waved. But it only growled louder, bared its fangs, its territory infringed.

'Make it go away,' said Omar.

'I'm trying,' said Knox.

Torchlight flared away to their left, vanished then came back, stronger and nearer. A security guard on his rounds, swinging his torch back and forth, painting yellow ellipses on the ground that came perilously close. They ducked down behind the plastic tent, allowing the dog to approach to within a few feet, snarling and sniffing. Omar jabbed a finger back the way they'd come, but it was too late, the security guard was almost upon them. Knox gestured for Omar to crouch low, hold his nerve.

The guard heard the dog, picked it out with his torch, then stooped for a stone that he hurled hard. It missed its target but provoked a furious barking. The guard came closer. Knox could see dots of moonlight gleaming on his polished black boots. His second shot caught the dog a glancing blow on its hind leg. It yelped and bounded away. The guard laughed heartily then turned and walked off.

'Let's get out of here,' pleaded Omar, once he'd vanished from sight.

'Just a little further,' said Knox, dusting himself down. He hated playing the bully, but this place needed checking out. They soon came to a sandy embankment, a yellow glow on the other side. Knox crawled up on his elbows and knees, that familiar metallic tang at the back of his mouth as he peered over the top. Griffin and a young man with buzz-cut blond hair were standing by the rear of a pick-up backed against the open door of a squat brick building, its interior light on. Two more young men emerged with a crate that they lugged onto the flatbed. Their hair was cropped short too, and they were wearing identical cornflower blue shirts and khaki trousers.

'That'll do for now,' said Griffin. 'We'll have to

come back anyhow.' He locked up the building, got into the pick-up, the three young men climbing up onto the back.

'What are they doing?' whispered Omar as the truck drove off.

'Clearing out their magazine. So that we won't find anything incriminating tomorrow.'

'Let's go to the police. We'll tell them everything.'

'They'll have hidden it all by the time we get back.'

'Please, Daniel. I hate this kind of business.'

Knox took out the keys to his Jeep, closed Omar's hand around them. 'Go wait for me,' he said. 'If I'm not back in an hour, go get the police.'

Omar pulled a face. 'Please come with me.'

'We need to find out where they're putting this stuff, Omar. You must see that.' And before Omar could protest, Knox got to his feet and jogged across the broken ground after the pick-up, its rear lights shining like a demon's eyes in the darkness.

II

Lily felt a little sheepish as she emerged from Stafford's room. 'He has some urgent phone calls to make,' she told Gaille, waiting outside. 'Is it essential that he comes with us?'

'It's your documentary,' shrugged Gaille. 'Fatima just thought you might be interested, that's all.'

'And we are. Don't think we don't appreciate it. It's just . . .'

'He has phone calls to make,' suggested Gaille.

'Yes,' said Lily, dropping her eyes. Stafford had discovered the Internet connection in his room, was now happily catching up with his email, checking out his latest sales figures and running searches of his own name to see if anyone had written anything nice about him recently.

She followed Gaille out of the compound's back gate straight into the desert. Her feet sank into the soft dry sand, making her camera equipment feel twice as heavy.

'You want help with that?' asked Gaille.

'If you wouldn't mind.'

'So you're Stafford's camera-woman, are you?' said Gaille, taking a bag.

'And producer,' nodded Lily ruefully. 'As well as sound engineer, gofer, runner – everything else you can think of.' Stafford had apparently been all for luxury and large crews while he'd been working on someone else's dime. But he'd grown increasingly affronted at the thought of anyone else making money from his work, so he'd set up his own production company, intending to hawk the finished product to broadcasters. He'd duly cut costs to the bone, hiring inexperienced staff like herself and bullying them so mercilessly that her three colleagues had walked out just a week before, landing this whole nightmare of a trip on her shoulders. She'd hoped to be able to rely on local help, but Stafford's high-handed manner had driven even those away. 'Not that I get to do as much camerawork as I'd like. Charles does his own whenever he can.' She allowed herself a small smile. 'I think he has this image of himself as an intrepid solo desert adventurer. He likes to keep adjusting the settings while talking to camera, so that viewers will think him out here on his own. I just film when he's interviewing people, or if we need a pan or zoom.' They reached the entrance to the site. Gaille unlocked the wooden door, turned on the generator, gave it a few moments to warm up before flipping switches and leading Lily down eerie corridors of crumbling sandstone to a cavernous new space. 'Wow!' murmured Lily. 'What is this place?'

'The inside of a pylon of a Nineteenth Dynasty Temple of Amun.' She pointed to a mound of bricks in the far corner. 'And these are what I brought you to see. They're Ancient Egyptian bricks called *talatat*. They were used by—'

'Whoa, whoa,' interjected Lily. 'I can film this, yes?'

'If it's light enough in here, sure.'

Lily patted the side of her Sony VX2000. 'This

thing's a marvel, believe me. It'll look wonderfully atmospheric.' She'd grown to love cameras. It hadn't always been that way. When she'd first encountered them, at children's parties and at school, she'd feared and hated them. It was bad enough having other children stare at her birthmark in her presence, but at least she'd been there to make sure they didn't say anything too cruel. Cameras had allowed them to take her ugliness away with them, to look at it whenever they chose, to poke fun at her and laugh and insult her to their heart's content, with no way for her to defend herself against it.

She'd been cursed with a runaway imagination, Lily. At times the thought of what the other children were saying about her had tormented her so severely that her only way of soothing it had been to imagine the moment of her own death, the sweetness of release. She'd started deliberately hurting herself, slapping herself across her cheek, jabbing scissors into her arm. But then one day her uncle had almost negligently given her his cast-off camcorder. She still shivered at the memory. Just holding the viewfinder to her eye concealed her birthmark, which had been wonderful in itself. But it was the power that it had given her that had been transforming. The power to make others look good or bad as she chose. The power to make them look gracious or sullen, ugly or beautiful.

And she'd used that power too. She'd discovered a real talent in herself. It had given her identity and self-esteem. Most of all, it had given her a path.

She unpacked and set up the equipment, plugged in and put on her headphones, checked sound and light levels, hoisted the camera to her shoulder, turned it on Gaille. 'You were saying?' she asked.

'Oh,' said Gaille, taken aback. 'I thought you'd be filming the *talatat*, not me.'

'I want both,' said Lily, well accustomed to soothing stage fright. 'But don't worry. Charles already has his script. He's highly unlikely to make changes this late, believe me. And you'd need to sign a release anyway, so if you don't like it . . .'

'Okay.'

'Thanks. Now crouch down. That's it. Straighten your back and look up at me. No, not like that. Lift your chin. A little more. That's it. Perfect. Now rest your right hand on the bricks.'

'Are you sure? It feels very odd.'

'But it looks great,' smiled Lily. 'Trust me. I'm good at this. Now start at the beginning. Assume I know nothing. Which is, I'm afraid, shamefully close to the truth. So, then. What is this place? And what exactly are *talatat*?'

III

The pick-up's brake lights flared red and then vanished over a ridge. Knox kept his eyes fixed upon the spot and slowed to a gentler jog to gather his breath. He reached the ridge, crouched down to peer over it, but there was nothing the other side. He wandered the darkness for a while, was beginning to give up hope, when he heard a clang away to his right. He climbed another ridge to find the pick-up parked in a slight hollow on the other side, its engine off, lights out, no sign of life except for a gentle yellow glow emanating from a pit next to it.

With any kind of GPS, he'd simply have logged the coordinates and headed off to fetch the police. But without GPS, getting a fix was virtually impossible. The skyline was featureless except for the distant orange flame of natural gas burn off, the dark outline of twin power-station chimneys. He crept forwards. The pit proved to be a flight of steps leading down through a hatchway to some kind of atrium, a generator muttering away inside. He went over to the pick-up, just three boxes left on the flatbed. There was an earthenware statue inside the first, a young boy with a finger to his lips. Harpocrates, a deity popular among Egyptians, Greeks and Romans. He photographed it, was about to open the second box when he heard footsteps. He dropped instantly to the ground, slithered beneath the pick-up. The three young men emerged, came over, their boots by Knox's face, kicking up dry dust that made his throat tickle. They picked up the last boxes and went back down. But they passed Griffin on the steps, and he emerged a moment later, breathing hard. He came over and sat heavily on the flatbed, making its suspension creak, trapping Knox underneath. A minute passed. Two. The young men reappeared.

'Let's get that last load then,' muttered Griffin. They all climbed aboard and set off, leaving Knox exposed. He tucked his hands beneath his stomach, pressed his face into the hard earth, expecting to be spotted at any moment. But they vanished over the ridge without incident. Knox picked himself up, went back to the mouth of the pit. The light was still on at its foot, the hatchway open. Too good a chance to miss, even though Omar would doubtless be going frantic by now. He tiptoed down to the atrium, his heart in his mouth. No one inside, only a generator chuntering away in the corner. It suddenly started stuttering and coughing, sending vibrations through the floor, the lights dimming for a moment before they picked up again. He waited for his heart to resettle, checked his watch. Griffin would surely be at least fifteen minutes. He could allow himself ten.

Arched passages led left and right. He went left. The passage snaked this way and that, following the path of least resistance through the limestone. Lamps were strung out every few paces on orange electrical flex, their light coaxing nightmarish shadows from the rough-cut bedrock. The passage opened abruptly into a large catacomb, its walls cut with columns of square-mouthed *loculi*, an island of crates and boxes stacked in the centre. He photographed a skeleton in one of the burial niches, eye-sockets staring blindly upwards. The Essenes had considered death unclean; burial inside a communal area like this would have been unthinkable. It was a big blow to his Therapeutae theory.

A camera and ultraviolet lamps were fixed to a stand on a worktable. There were trays and boxes stacked beneath, a processing sheet taped to each, artefacts to be photographed. Knox opened one, found a clay oil lamp in the form of a leering satyr. The next box contained a silver ring; the third a faïence bowl. But it was the fourth box that gave him the shivers. It was divided into six small compartments, and lying inside each of them was a shrunken, mummified human ear.

EIGHT

I

'We're currently inside the pylon of a Temple of Amun,' began Gaille, her voice echoing in the large chamber. 'It was completed under Ramesses II, but it fell into disrepair before being extensively rebuilt by the Ptolemies.'

'And its connection with Amarna?' prompted Lily.

'Yes,' blushed Gaille. 'Forgive me.'

'No need for forgiveness. You're a natural. The camera loves you.'

'Thanks.' Gaille smiled wryly, her scepticism clear. 'As you know, Egyptians typically built their monuments and temples with massive blocks of quarried stone, as with the pyramids. But cutting and transporting them was expensive and time-consuming, and Akhenaten was in a hurry. He wanted new temples to the Aten in Karnak and Amarna, and he wanted them now. So his engineers came up with a different type of brick, these *talatat*. They weigh about a hundred pounds each, light enough for a single construction worker to heave into place by himself, though it wouldn't have done much good for their backs. And after the walls were completed, they'd be carved and painted into grand scenes, like a huge television wall.'

'So how did they get here?'

Gaille nodded. 'After Akhenaten died, his successors determined to destroy every trace of him and his heresy. Did you know that Tutankhamun's name was originally Tutankh*aten*. He was pressured into changing it after Akhenaten died. Names were incredibly important back then. The Ancient Egyptians believed that even *saying* someone's name helped sustain them in the afterlife, one reason why Akhenaten's name was deliberately excised from temples and monuments across the land. But his *talatat* suffered a different fate. When his buildings were dismantled, the bricks were used as hard-core for building projects all across Egypt. So every time we excavate a post-Amarna site, there's a chance we'll find some.'

'And recreate the original scenes on Akhenaten's walls?'

'That's the idea. But it isn't easy. Imagine buying

a hundred jigsaw puzzles, jumbling all the pieces up together, then throwing away ninety per cent and bashing up the rest with a hammer. But making sense of such things is what I do. It's why Fatima invited me down here. I usually work with ancient texts, but the principle's the same.'

'How do you go about it?'

'It's easiest if I explain with scrolls. Imagine finding thousands of fragments from different documents all muddled up together. Your first task is to photograph them all to scale and at very high resolution, because the original fragments are simply too fragile to work with. You then examine each one more closely. Is the material papyrus or parchment? If papyrus, what weave? If parchment, from what animal? We can test the DNA these days, would you believe, to see if two fragments of parchment come from the same animal. What colour is it? How smooth? How thick? What does the reverse look like? How about the ink? Has it smudged or bled? Can we analyse its chemical signature? Is the nib thick or thin, regular or scratchy? And what about the handwriting? Scribal hands are very distinctive, though you have to be careful with that, because people often worked on more than one document, and some documents were written by more than one scribe. Anyway, all that should help you separate the initial jumble into different original scrolls; rather like separating the jigsaw pieces I mentioned earlier into their different puzzles. Your next task is to reassemble them.'

'How?'

'Often we're already familiar with the texts,' answered Gaille. 'Like with the *Book of the Dead*, for instance. Then it's just a question of translating the fragments and seeing where they fit. But if it's an original document – a letter, say – then we look for other clues. Maybe a line of text that runs from one fragment to the next. If we're *very* lucky, multiple matching lines, putting it beyond doubt. More usually, however, we'll put similar themes together. Two fragments on burial practices, say. Or two episodes about a particular person. Failing that, fragments are, by definition, damaged. Is there a *pattern* of damage? Imagine rolling a sheet of paper into a scroll, burning a hole through all the layers with a cigarette, then ripping it up. The burn-holes won't just help you reassemble the scroll, they'll also tell you how tightly it was rolled in the first place, by the steadily decreasing distances between them. And scribes often scratched guidelines on their parchment to keep their writing level. We can match those scratches from one fragment to the next, by tiny variations in the gaps between them, like checking tree rings.'

'And there are similar indications with *talatat*, are there?'

'Yes,' nodded Gaille. 'Though they tend to be more elusive. For example, *talatat* are made either from limestone or sandstone. Limestone *talatat* typically go with limestone; sandstone with sandstone. And the composition of the stone is useful, too, because walls were often built with stone from a single quarry. But you can't rely too heavily on that. Paint residue can also be helpful, as can weather-damage. Maybe the bricks have been sunbleached. Or maybe there was a leaky pipe nearby, and they've got matching water stains. Anyway, once we've done what we can, we try to reassemble them into scenes. *Talatat* are typically decorated either on their long side, which we call "stretchers", or on their short side, which we call "headers". Egyptians used alternate courses of stretchers and headers. That really helps. After that, it often really is a case of putting heads on torsos. Fortunately, many of the scenes are duplicates of each other, or of scenes that have already been reconstructed from *talatat* found elsewhere, so we know what we're looking for.'

Lily's ears pricked up. 'But not all?' she asked shrewdly.

'No,' acknowledged Gaille. 'Not all.'

'You've found something, haven't you? That's why you brought me down here.'

'Maybe.'

'Well? Aren't you going to tell me?'

'Oh,' said Gaille, dropping her eyes. 'I think Fatima wants that pleasure for herself.'

II

Knox picked up one of the shrivelled ears. The tissue had a slight sheen to it where it had been severed from the body, suggesting the cut was recent. He checked the *loculi*, quickly found a mummy missing its right ear, then another. He frowned, baffled, before belatedly remembering he was on the clock. His self-imposed deadline had already passed. He needed to get out of here.

He hurried back to the atrium, up the steps, was about to rush away when he heard an engine, and suddenly the pick-up reappeared over the rise, its headlights sweeping the shaft's mouth like a lighthouse beam, so that Knox barely had time to duck out of sight and retreat back down to the atrium.

Griffin and his crew were storing everything in the catacombs, so he headed the other way instead, down the right-hand passage. He soon reached another chamber, a huge mosaic on its floor, tesserae bright from a recent clean, though rutted from ancient footfall. A grotesque figure sat naked in the lotus position inside a seven-pointed star surrounded by clusters of Greek letters. He took a photograph, then a second, before hearing a grunt from back along the corridor, someone struggling with a box – and coming his way. He hurried deeper into the site, a confusion of passages and small chambers, the walls decorated with colourful ancient murals: a naked man and woman reaching up in supplication to the sun; Priapus leering from behind a tree; a crocodile, dog and vulture sitting in judgement; Dionysus stretching out on a divan, framed by vines and ivy leaves and pine cones. He was photographing this last one when he heard footsteps and turned to see Griffin approaching down the passage, squinting through the dappled gloom as though he needed glasses.

'Reverend?' he asked. 'Is that you?'

III

Inspector Naguib Hussein was writing out his report at the station when his boss Gamal came over. 'Don't you have a wife and daughter to get home to?' he grunted.

'I thought you wanted our paperwork up to date.'

'I do,' nodded Gamal. He perched on the corner of the desk. 'Word is, you found a body out in the Eastern Desert.'

'Yes,' agreed Naguib.

'Murder?'

'Her head was bashed in. She was wrapped in tarpaulin and buried beneath sand. I'd say murder was a possibility.'

'A Copt, yes?'

'A girl.'

'Investigate, fine,' scowled Gamal. 'But no waves. This isn't the time.'

'How do you mean?'

'You know how I mean.'

'I assure you I—'

'Haven't you learned yet when to speak and when to shut up?' asked Gamal in exasperation. 'Don't you realize how much trouble you caused your colleagues up in Minya?'

'They were selling arms on the black market.'

'I don't care. There are crimes we can solve and crimes we can't. Let's deal with the ones we can, eh?' He gave a companionable sigh, as though he didn't like the way things worked any more than Naguib did, he was just more realistic. 'Haven't you been following what's going on down in Assiut?' he asked. 'People out on the streets. Fights. Anger. Confrontation. Just for a couple of dead Coptic girls. I won't risk that spreading here.'

'She may have been murdered,' observed Naguib.

Gamal's complexion was naturally dark. It grew darker. 'From what I understand, no one has reported her missing. From what I understand, she could have been there years, maybe even decades. You really want to provoke trouble at a time like this over a girl who may have been dead for decades?'

'Since when has investigating murder been a provocative act?'

'Don't play with me,' scowled Gamal. 'You're always complaining about your workload. Concentrate on some of your other cases for the moment: don't go chasing off into the desert after djinn.'

'Is that an order?'

'If it needs to be,' nodded Gamal. 'If it needs to be.'

NINE

I

'Reverend!' said Griffin again. 'A word please.'

Knox turned sharply and hurried away along the corridor, glad that the gloom evidently made his white shirt look sufficiently like a dog collar against his dark polo neck to fool Griffin.

'Reverend!' cried Griffin in exasperation. 'Come back. We need to talk.'

Knox continued walking as fast as he dared. The passage straightened out, hit a dead end some twenty paces ahead. Just before that, there was a high heap of ancient bricks and plaster fragments and a gaping hole in the wall, through which he could hear Peterson reading from the Bible; though, from the accompanying hiss, it sounded more like an old recording than the real thing.

'"*And there came two angels to Sodom; and*

Lot sat in the gate of Sodom: and Lot seeing them rose up to meet them."'

Knox reached the hole, glanced through. There was a large chamber on the other side, young men and women kneeling on dustsheets cleaning the walls with sponges moistened with distilled water and soft-bristled brushes. The men had the standard crew-cuts, the women short-bobbed hair, and they were all wearing the same cornflower-blue and khaki livery. They were too intent on their work to notice him step through into the chamber. Only once inside did he see Peterson to his left, deep in earnest discussion with a young woman, while his voice incongruously continued to declaim scripture on the portable CD-player in the centre of the chamber.

'"*Behold now, I have two daughters which have not known man; let me, I pray you, bring them out unto you, and do ye to them as is good in your eyes.*"'

Griffin was still approaching down the corridor. Knox had only one possible hiding place, the baptismal bath. His foot slipped as he hurried down the wide flight of stone steps so that he had to fight for balance, but he found the shadows even as Griffin poked his head in. 'Reverend!' he said. Peterson gave no sign of having heard him, however, so he said it again, louder this time, until one of the young women turned the volume down on the CD-player. 'Why on earth did you walk away from me?'

Peterson frowned. 'What are you talking about, Brother Griffin?'

Griffin scowled but let it go. 'We've emptied the magazine,' he said. 'It's time to close up.'

'Not yet,' said Peterson.

'It's going to take hours to fill in the shaft,' said Griffin. 'If we don't start now we'll never finish before—'

'I said not yet.'

'But—'

'Have you forgotten why we're here, Brother Griffin?' blazed Peterson. 'Have you forgotten whose work we're doing?'

'No, Reverend.'

'Then go back outside and wait. I'll tell you when to start.'

'Yes, Reverend.'

Footsteps faded as he walked away. The young woman turned the volume back up.

'"*For we will destroy this place, because the cry of them is waxen great before the face of the Lord; and the Lord hath sent us to destroy it.*"'

Knox waited a few moments before risking a glance over the rim of the baptismal bath. Everyone was once more concentrating on cleaning their section of wall, bringing an array of scenes back to life: portraits, landscapes, angels, demons, texts in Greek and Aramaic, mathematical calculations, signs of the Zodiac and other symbols. Like a madman's nightmare. He photographed the ceiling, two sections of wall, then Peterson and the woman examining a mural.

'"*The sun was risen upon the earth when Lot entered into Zoar. Then the Lord rained upon Sodom and upon Gomorrah brimstone and fire from the Lord out of heaven.*"'

'Reverend, sir!' said a young man. 'Look here!'

Knox ducked down, but not quite quickly enough. One of the women saw him as she turned. Her mouth fell open in shock. She pointed at him with a trembling finger and began to scream.

II

Meals with Fatima were notoriously frugal affairs usually, but tonight the table was laden with a colourful and fragrant spread of dishes in honour of Stafford and Lily: *ta'amiyya*, *fu'ul*, hoummos, beans, tahina, a salad of chopped tomatoes and cucumber seasoned with oil and garlic, stuffed aubergines, chicken dressed in vine leaves, all looking succulent in the rippling candlelight. There were even two bottles of red wine, from which Stafford poured himself a liberal glass that he drained and immediately refilled. For all Gaille's dislike of him, she had to admit he was looking rather dashing, wearing a borrowed *galabaya* while his own clothes were being washed in readiness for the morning.

Lily was looking nervously at the food, as though apprehensive both of local etiquette and cuisine. Gaille gave her a reassuring nod and helped herself to some of the safer dishes, allowing Lily to emulate her, which she did with a grateful smile.

'Will you be in Egypt long?' asked Fatima, as Stafford sat next to her.

'Amarna tomorrow, then Assiut the day after for an interview. Then off to the States.'

'You're packing an awful lot in to two days, aren't you?'

'We were supposed to be here for the best part of a week,' he shrugged. 'But then my agent got me on the morning shows. I could hardly turn that down, could I?'

'No. I suppose not.'

'It's the only market, the States. If you're not big there, forget about it. Anyway, we're only filming a short section here. We're coming back later in the year to film in . . .' He caught himself on the verge of his indiscretion, smiled as though she'd almost wheedled great secrets out of him. 'For the other sections of my programme.'

'Your programme, yes. Won't you tell me a little more about it?'

He took another swallow of wine as he considered this. 'Will you give me your word that you won't repeat what I tell you?'

'Of course. I wouldn't dream of telling anyone your theories, believe me.'

'Because it's explosive, I assure you.'

'It always is.'

Stafford's cheeks pinked, as though he'd only just realized she'd been having a little sport with him. He lifted his chin high, giving himself a swan-neck for a moment. 'Very well, then,' he said. He waited for silence to fall around the table, for them all to be still. Then he waited a little longer, building the suspense. An old storyteller's trick, yet effective all the same. When finally he had their complete attention, he leaned forward into the candlelight. 'I intend to prove that Akhenaten wasn't just another Eighteenth Dynasty pharaoh,' he said. 'I intend to prove he was also founder of modern Israel. That's right. I intend to prove beyond doubt or argument that Akhenaten was Moses, the man who led the Jews out of Egypt and into the Promised Land.'

III

Heads swivelled to see what had made the woman cry out. A shocked and frozen silence fell as they saw Knox crouching there in the baptismal bath, camera-phone in his hand. But it was Knox who acted first. He raced up the steps, dived headlong through the hole in the wall, crashed onto the passage floor outside.

'Stop him!' thundered Peterson. 'Bring him back!'

Up to his feet, sprinting through islands of lamplight, yells behind, Knox glanced around as an athletic young man, face contorted with the joy of duty, flung himself into a tackle, taking his legs. He went down hard, grazing his palm and elbow on the rough stone, wind punched from his lungs, but twisting around, throwing the young man off, up and away towards the atrium.

Griffin and one of the young men appeared in the doorway ahead, standing shoulder-to-shoulder to block his escape. No way could he fight past both of them. He reached down and yanked the electrical flex from the generator, plunging the passage into sudden darkness, then shoulder-charged Griffin flat onto his back, fought his way through his flailing arms into the atrium then up the steps. The two other young men were coming across, summoned by the commotion. Knox cut the other way, over a low ridge, running headlong until he crashed into the wire-mesh fence of the neighbouring power station.

He ran alongside it for a couple of hundred

metres, trying to work out where he was, how best
to get back to Omar and the Jeep. But his efforts
were taking their toll, a stitch worsening in his
side, his breath coming short and fast. He glanced
back, silhouettes all around, shouting exhortations
and instructions to each other, the moonlight too
strong and the terrain too bare for him to go to
ground. He gritted his teeth and kicked again. But
his legs were growing heavy and his pursuers were
gaining all the time.

TEN

I

'Ah,' sighed Fatima. 'Akhenaten as Moses. That old chestnut. I can't tell you how many first-year students of mine have come to the same conclusion.'

'Perhaps for a very good reason,' said Stafford tightly. 'Perhaps because it's true.'

'And you have evidence to support such a bold claim, I assume?'

'As it happens.'

'Won't you share it with us?'

Lily bowed her head and looked uncomfortably down at her plate. This wasn't the first time she'd been ringside when Stafford had launched into one of his lectures. She hated it, not least because it always seemed to be down to her to smooth things over once he was done.

'It's not so much that I've discovered anything new,' he acknowledged. 'It's just that no one else has put the pieces together in quite the right way before. After all, even you have to admit some link between Akhenaten and the Jews, if you're honest with yourself.'

'What exactly do you mean by that?'

'Everyone knows that Egyptologists have their heads buried in the sand when it comes to the Exodus. It's too sensitive an issue for a Muslim country in this day and age. I'm not criticizing you for this—'

'It sounds that way to me.'

'I'm only saying I understand why you'd look the other way.'

'Quite a feat, what with my head already buried in the sand.'

'You know what I mean.'

'Yes,' said Fatima. 'You believe I'd distort the archaeological record for personal convenience or professional advancement.'

'Forgive us,' said Lily hurriedly. 'Charles didn't mean that. Did you, Charles?'

'Of course not,' said Stafford. 'I was talking about the establishment in general. So-called Egypt experts who refuse even to consider that the Bible might have light to shed upon Egyptian history.'

'Which people are these?' asked Fatima. 'I've never met any.'

'I don't suggest for a moment that the Bible is strictly factual,' continued Stafford. 'But clearly it's by far our best account of Judaism's origins. Who can doubt, for example, that a slave population later known as the Jews were present in Egypt in large numbers sometime during the second millennium BC? And who can doubt that they came into conflict with their Egyptian masters and fled in a mass exodus, led by a man they called Moses? Or that they stormed and destroyed Jericho and other cities before settling in and around Jerusalem. That's the skeleton of what happened. Our job as historians is to flesh those bones out as best we can.'

'Oh,' said Fatima. 'That's our job, is it?'

'Yes,' said Stafford complacently. 'It is. And if we do, we straightaway encounter a problem. Because there's no obvious Egyptian account of any such exodus. Of course, it wasn't anything like so significant for the Egyptians as for the Jews, just the flight of a group of slaves, so that's understandable enough. And it's not as though we're completely without clues to work with. For example, Genesis credits Joseph with bringing the Hebrews to Egypt. And chariots are mentioned not once, not twice, but *three* times in Joseph's story. But the Egyptians didn't *have* chariots before the Eighteenth Dynasty, so the Jews can't possibly even have *arrived* in Egypt before the mid sixteenth-century BC. And then there's the Merneptah Stele, which records a victory over the tribe of Israel *in Canaan*, so the Exodus must have already taken place by the time it was inscribed, around 1225 BC. So now we have a bracket of dates: 1550–1225 BC. Or, to put it another way, sometime during the Eighteenth Dynasty. Agreed?'

'Your logic appears impeccable,' said Fatima.

'Thank you,' said Stafford. 'Now let's see if we can't narrow it down further. The Ptolemies commissioned a man called Manetho to write a history of Egypt. His King List still forms the basis for our understanding of the ancient dynastic structure.'

'You don't say.'

'Manetho was an Egyptian high priest, and he had access to the records of the Temple of Amun in Heliopolis. He identified a man called Osarseph as the biblical Moses. This Osarseph was high priest to a Pharaoh Amenhotep, and apparently he built up a following among outcasts and lepers. He became so powerful that the gods came to Amenhotep in a dream and ordered him to drive Osarseph from Egypt, but Osarseph drove out Amenhotep instead, establishing a thirteen-year reign before he was finally expelled. So. Not only do we have our independent confirmation of the Exodus, we also have a massive clue in our search for Moses. This man Osarseph. This Pharaoh Amenhotep.'

'There were four Pharaoh Amenhoteps during the Eighteenth Dynasty. Which one do you suppose Manetho was referring to?'

'He said that the pharaoh had a son called Ramesses. Ramesses was a Nineteenth Dynasty name, so Manetho was clearly referring to one of the later, not earlier, Amenhoteps.'

'Ah. I see.'

'Now, Osarseph's thirteen-year reign might appear to be a problem, because we have no other record of a Pharaoh Osarseph, or of any Eighteenth Dynasty pharaoh ruling for thirteen years. But let's take a closer look at our various candidates. Ay or Horemheb, maybe. Neither was of royal birth, one being a vizier before he ascended the throne, the other a general. But Ay reigned just four years; and Horemheb's nineteen years were largely orthodox and prosperous. Smenkhkare lasted just a few months, while Tutankhamun was only a youngster when he died. None of them fit. But we have one possibility left. Akhenaten. He succeeded his father Amenhotep III. And though he ruled for seventeen years in all, something extraordinary evidently happened during his fifth year. Not only did he change his name, he also founded his new capital city of Akhetaten, the place we know as Amarna, from where he ruled until 1332 BC. Thirteen forty-five to 1332. Tell me: how many years is that?'

'Thirteen,' said Fatima.

'Exactly,' nodded Stafford. 'So we have our match, superficially at least. But that raises other questions. For example, why would anyone consider Akhenaten an interloper? He was the legitimate pharaoh, after all. And, apart from Manetho's assertion, is there anything else to connect Akhenaten with Moses?'

Fatima spread her hands. 'Well? Aren't you going to put us out of our suspense?'

II

Knox crossed a low hummock of rock, glanced around. The pursuit was getting closer all the time. His breath was hard and hot, his stitch jabbing sharp. The moon slid behind a rare drift of night-time cloud. He used the greater darkness to cut right, away from the fence, running almost blind. But then the moon reappeared and he saw plastic sheeting ahead. The cemetery. A cry went up behind him. He ran towards the irrigation channel, slith-ered down the bank, splashed wearily through the water at the foot, clambering up the other side, his shoes clotting with water and mud.

A pair of headlamps appeared to his right, one of the pick-ups. It accelerated down the lane towards him, doors flying open, two young men jumping out. Knox vaulted the gate near where he'd parked, but there was no sign of Omar or the Jeep on the other side – other than the tracks it had left in the earth, at least.

He juddered to a halt, hands on his knees, heaving for air, his thighs weighted down with lactic acid. Three young men arrived at the gate behind him, climbing it without great hurry, confident they had their man. The breeze pressed Knox's soaking shirt against his skin. The chill of the night, coupled with apprehension, rippled a shiver right through him.

An old engine roared. Knox turned to see the Jeep bumping towards him, Omar at the wheel, its passenger door already flapping open. Knox ran to meet it, tumbled inside, slammed and locked the door even as his pursuers made a last effort to catch him, surrounding the Jeep, pounding on the windows, faces ugly with frustration as Omar swung the wheel around, crunching up through the gears as they jolted their escape across the field.

III

Peterson gripped his King James Version tight as he stared at the painted section of wall that had been drawn to his attention by Michael just before Knox had been discovered. The distilled water had cleaned off the thick coat of dirt, and revived the underlying pigments too, so that the mural glowed clearly: two men in white robes emerging from a cave, a figure in blue kneeling before them, a single line of text beneath.

Peterson had come late to languages, but his Greek was good enough for this, not least because the phrase had showed up in his nightmares this past decade, ever since he'd first encountered the Carpocratians.

Son of David, have mercy on me.

The blood rushed from his head, leaving him so dizzy that he had to put a hand against the wall to steady himself.

Son of David, have mercy on me.

And Knox had had a camera! Of all people! *Knox!* A heavy dull thumping in his chest, like a distant steel-press. *What had he done?* He looked around. Everyone else had chased off after Knox, leaving him alone. That was something. He picked up a rock hammer and attacked the wall furiously, venting his rage and fear on it, hacking wildly at the plaster until it lay in dust and fragments on the floor. He leaned against the wall, breathing heavily, before sensing he had company. He turned to see Griffin staring horrified at him, at what he'd done.

'Well?' demanded Peterson, turning defence into attack. 'Did you catch him?'

Griffin shook his head. 'Tawfiq was waiting in the fields.'

'You let them get away? Don't you know what damage they can do?'

'They can't get far. The only way out of those fields is by that old bridge. Nathan's gone to wait there.'

He nodded. That was something. But this was now too delicate a situation to leave to anyone else. He needed to take personal command. 'Close this site up,' he ordered Griffin. 'I don't want to see a trace of it when I come back. Understand?'

'Yes.'

Peterson tossed the rock hammer negligently away into the corner, as though it were nothing, what he'd just done to the wall. Then he checked his pockets for his car keys and strode towards the hole in the wall with such purpose that Griffin had to jump back out of his way.

ELEVEN

I

'Monotheism,' declared Stafford.

'I beg your pardon,' frowned Fatima.

'Monotheism. That's the key. Moses was the original champion of the One True God. "*Thou shalt have no other gods but me.*" And what sets Akhenaten apart from any other pharaoh?'

'Monotheism?' suggested Fatima.

'Exactly. Monotheism. Before him, Egypt had always had a multitude of gods. But under Akhenaten, everything changed. For him, there was only *one* God. The sun disc. The Aten. All others were fabrications of the human mind and the craftsman's art. And he did more than pay lip service to this idea. He acted upon it. He closed the temples of rival gods, particularly those of Amun, the Aten's chief rival. In fact, he had Amun's name excised from monuments all over Egypt. You'll acknowledge that much, I trust?'

'Acknowledge it? I wrote a book on the subject.'

'Good. Now, Manetho – he who claimed that Osarseph was Moses – based his history on the records of the Temple of Amun in Heliopolis. And what do you imagine the priests of Amun would have thought of Akhenaten, the man who'd closed down their temples and excised their God's name across the land? Do you not think they'd have considered him an interloper? His supporters lepers?' He took another swallow of wine then wiped his mouth, smearing dark hairs against his wrist. 'Good,' he said, taking silence for assent. 'Now, let's take another look at Moses. A Hebrew child, we are told, set upon the Nile in a basket of rushes, rescued by the pharaoh's daughter who gave him the name Moses because it was Hebrew for "drawn out". But that whole tale has the ring of folklore, doesn't it? Why would a pharaoh's daughter give a foundling a Hebrew name, after all? She wouldn't have *known* he was Hebrew, for one thing. Nor would she have spoken Hebrew, not least because it didn't exist back then. No. The true explanation is simple. Moses means "son" in Egyptian, and it's a common part of pharaonic names, as in Tutmosis, son of Thoth, or Ramesses, son of Ra. The foundling myth was merely a retrospective attempt to claim Moses as a born Jew; but the truth is that he was born an Egyptian prince.'

'The Bible says he murdered an Egyptian soldier, doesn't it?' frowned Fatima. 'And that he fled to the land of Kush. I can't recall Akhenaten doing that.'

'You're never going to get a perfect match,' said Stafford. 'The question is whether the fit's close enough. It clearly is. And that's without even going into the remarkable parallels between the doctrines of Akhenaten and Moses.'

'Which parallels are those exactly?'

'I'll tell you, if you give me a chance.'

'Please,' said Fatima. 'Be my guest.'

'I already am your guest,' observed Stafford, gesturing grandly with his glass, slopping wine like blood onto his borrowed *galabaya*. He brushed the droplets irritably away, then composed himself to complete his thesis.

II

Inspector Naguib Hussein was usually good at forgetting his police work once he'd closed his front door for the night. Normally, his wife and daughter were a tonic to his spirits. But not tonight, not even as he stooped low for Husniyah to throw her arms around his neck so that he could lift her up. He tried not to let her see his anxiety, however, as he carried her through the bead curtain into their kitchen, kissing her surreptitiously on her crown, noting with a warm stab of pain and pride how springy and black her hair was, the thin pale valley of scalp that showed through beneath.

Yasmine looked up from her cooking, eyes tired, complexion shiny with vapours. 'That smells good,' he said. He tried to pinch a morsel from the pot, but she smacked his hand and made him drop it. They shared a smile. Thirteen years of marriage, and still he could be surprised by the freshness of their affection. Husniyah sat cross-legged on the floor, a pad of paper on her lap, drawing pictures of animals and trees and houses. He watched over her shoulder, praising her skill, asking questions. But soon he fell into a reverie, brooding on the evils of the world, and it was only when Yasmine touched his shoulder that he realized she'd been talking to him. He shook his head to clear it, mustered the warmest smile he could. 'Yes?' he asked.

'Something's on your mind,' she said.

'Nothing particular.' But he couldn't prevent his eyes from swivelling to his daughter.

'Husniyah, beloved,' said Yasmine gently. 'Could you please leave us a moment?' Husniyah looked up, puzzled; but she'd been brought up to be obedient, so she gathered her things and left without a word. 'Well?' asked Yasmine.

Naguib sighed. Sometimes he wished his wife didn't know him so well. 'We found a body today,' he admitted.

'A body?'

'A young woman. A girl.'

Yasmine's eyes flashed instinctively to the bead curtain. 'A girl. How old?'

'Thirteen. Maybe fourteen.'

It took Yasmine an effort to get her next question out. 'And she was . . . murdered?'

'It's too early to be sure,' answered Naguib. 'But probably. Yes.'

'That makes three in a month.'

'The other two were down in Assiut.'

'So? Maybe they moved here because things were getting too hot down there.'

'We don't know how long this one has been there. There's no reason to suspect the cases are connected.'

'Yet you do suspect it, don't you?'

'It's possible.'

'What are you doing about it?'

'Not much,' he confessed. 'Gamal has other priorities.'

'Priorities that come before finding the murderer of three young girls?'

'With all this tension and everything, he doesn't

think this is the right time . . .' Naguib drifted lamely to a halt. The other side of the curtain, Husniyah started singing, ostensibly to herself, but actually so that her parents could hear her, be aware of her, protect her.

'Tell me you're going to go after whoever did this,' said Yasmine fiercely. 'Tell me you're going to catch them before they kill again.'

For a moment, that wretched mummified mess reappeared in Naguib's mind, still wrapped in her tarpaulin shroud. Who knew whose face he'd find next time? He met his wife's eyes directly, as he always did on the important matters, when he needed her to know she could trust him. 'Yes,' he promised. 'I am.'

III

'Any good?' asked Omar, leaning over from the driver's seat to check Knox's photographs on the screen of his camera-phone.

'Just watch what you're doing, will you?' said Knox, as Omar crunched the Jeep's gears again.

'Huh!' said Omar. 'They're pretty dark, aren't they?'

'Maybe I should send them to Gaille,' said Knox. 'She'll be able to make something of them, if anyone can.'

'She'd better. We need more than that to show the police.'

'Says the man who didn't think we needed photographs at all.' He started composing a text message, not easy as they bumped across the field, without even a seat belt to hold him in place. *Took the attached at poss Therapeutae site! Light terrible. Can you help? All speed appreciated! Love, Daniel.* He frowned in dissatisfaction, replaced *Love* with *Much love* then *All love* and finally *All my love*. None felt right. Everyone protested their love these days. The word had been cheapened into meaninglessness. He sat there feeling ridiculous. This was scarcely the time to fret over such things, after all. Yet he fretted all the same. He stabbed out some other words with his index finger, stared down at them for several seconds, unnerved by how plaintive they sounded. But he'd already wasted too much time, so he attached the photographs and sent them on their way before he could change his mind.

Omar muttered a curse, slowed, came to a halt. Knox looked up to see headlights crisscrossing a main road a kilometre away. 'What's the matter?' he asked.

'Down there.'

Now Knox saw it, moonlight glowing on a pick-up parked by the wooden bridge. 'Bollocks,' he muttered.

'What now?'

'There has to be another way out. Let's keep looking.'

The engine screeched as Omar tried to force it into gear. 'Mine's an automatic,' he said with a wince.

'You want me to drive?'

'It might be best.'

They switched seats. Knox belted up, thrust the Jeep into gear, headed off in search of another way out. The pick-up lumbered after them, obviously wanting to keep them in sight, but staying a wary distance behind, between them and the bridge.

Knox crossed a rise, swung around. The moment the pick-up reappeared, he floored the pedal, accelerated towards it, jolting violently over the rutted ground. Omar clutched the door-handle, stamped on imaginary brakes. But Knox kept his foot to the floor. The pick-up swung round, aware it was a race for the bridge. He sped past it, but it quickly caught up, its engine newer and more powerful.

'We'll never get away,' cried Omar.

'Hold tight,' said Knox, weaving back and forth to prevent the pick-up from pulling alongside, wheels spitting clods of mud. He swung out wide then turned sharply back towards the bridge. He was almost there when a 4x4 surged out of the darkness on the far side, its headlights springing on full and dazzling, so that Knox had to throw up a hand to shield his eyes, slam on the brakes, but too late, tyres losing grip, slithering sideways, missing the bridge and hurtling instead into the irrigation channel, flinging out his arm in an instinctive effort to pin Omar in his seat, their bonnet smashing into the opposite bank, metal crumpling, windscreen exploding in a great cacophony of glass, hurling him against his seat belt, his head snapping violently back, something crashing into the back of his skull, and everything going black.

TWELVE

I

Lily put her hand surreptitiously on Stafford's arm, an effort to calm him down a little, but he merely shrugged her off, refilled his wineglass, and continued. 'People have Judaism all wrong,' he declared. 'They read about Abraham, Noah, Jacob and all those other patriarchs, and assume that the Jews arrived in Egypt with their beliefs and practices fully formed, that they retained them during their sojourn, then left without being one whit influenced. But it can't have been like that. It *wasn't* like that. Look dispassionately at Judaism and you'll see that its roots lie in Egypt, specifically in the monotheism of Akhenaten.'

'That's quite a claim,' said Fatima.

'Just look at the creation account in Genesis, if you don't believe me. The notion that everything

133

came from the void was an Egyptian conceit, as
was the idea of mankind as God's flock, crafted
in His image, for whom He made heaven and
earth. There are countless passages in the Bible
stolen virtually verbatim from Egypt. Take the
Negative Confessions of the Book of the Dead. "I
have not reviled the God. I have not sinned against
anyone. I have not killed. I have not copulated
illicitly." Replace "I have not" with "Thou shalt
not" and you have the Ten Commandments. Psalm
Thirty-four is based on an Amarna inscription;
Psalm One hundred and four is a rewrite of
Akhenaten's Hymn of the Aten.'

'A rewrite!' frowned Fatima. 'They have a few
images in common, that's all.'

'A few images!' scoffed Stafford. 'It's word for
word in places. But even if you won't allow me
that, you surely can't dispute the similarity of the
Bible's Proverbs to Egypt's Wisdom texts; or that
the so-called "Thirty Sayings" are nothing but a
rehash of Amenemope's "Thirty Chapters".
Granted, on their own, each might conceivably be
coincidence. But they *aren't* on their own. They're
part of a pattern. The very name Hebrew is a
corruption of the Egyptian word *'Ipiru*, people
who've stepped outside the law. Jewish priestly
robes are virtual replicas of the costumes of
Eighteenth Dynasty pharaohs. The Ark of the
Covenant is almost identical to an ark found in

134

Tutankhamun's tomb. And, speaking of the Ark, during the Exodus the Jews housed it in a great tent called the Tabernacle, just like the tent Akhenaten lived in when he first settled in Amarna. Tithes were an Egyptian practice taken up by the Jews. Magic likewise. Did you know that Egyptians wrote down their spells, soaked them in water, and drank the resulting brew, precisely as advocated in the Book of Numbers? Egyptian voodoo dolls are mentioned in the Psalms. And circumcision wasn't originally a Jewish practice, you realize? It was *Egyptian*; they even found a clay model of a circumcised penis in Akhenaten's tomb. "They are in all respects much more pious than other peoples," claimed Herodotus. "They are also distinguished from them by many of their customs, such as circumcision, which for reasons of cleanliness they introduced before others; further, by their horror of swine. In haughty narrowness they looked down on the other peoples who were unclean and not so near to the god as they were." Was he talking about the Jews? No, the Egyptians.'

'The best part of a millennium later.'

'Atenism was sun-worship,' asserted Stafford, barely breaking stride. 'So was early Judaism. Ezekiel, chapter eight, talks bluntly about worshippers in the Temple of the Lord adoring the rising sun. On Mount Sinai, Moses' God describes himself by the Tetragrammaton YHWH: "I am

135

who I am." The Egyptian *Prisse Papyrus* describes an Egyptian God as *"nk pu nk"*. You know what that translates as? Yes. "I am who I am."'

'The *Prisse Papyrus* was—'

'Everywhere you look, there's compelling evidence that Judaism was originally Egyptian, derived from Akhenaten's monotheism. But do you know what the smoking gun is? The absolute, incontrovertible proof?'

'Go on, then.'

'The Hebrews called the Lord their God Adonai. But in ancient Hebrew the "d" was pronounced "t", the suffix "ai" was optional. Yes. That's right. The Hebrews worshipped a God called Aten, which means that Moses' admonition to his people *Shema Yisrael Adonai Elohenu Adonai Echad* translates as "Hear, O Israel, the Aten is the only God." Refute *that*, Professor. Refute *that*.'

II

'Oh Lord,' muttered Nathan feebly, getting out of the pick-up, staring white-faced down at the creaking, lurching wreckage of the Jeep, the motionless body of the passenger, flung through the windscreen and now lying on the far bank. 'Oh heaven.'

'Pull yourself together,' scowled Peterson.

'Good grief. Good grief. What did you do that for? You made them crash.'

'They made themselves crash,' snapped Peterson. 'You understand? Anything that happened here, these people did to themselves.'

Nathan pulled his mobile from his pocket. 'How do I get an ambulance?'

'Are you crazy?' demanded Peterson. He slapped Nathan stingingly across his cheek, turned him to face him. 'Listen,' he said. 'Forget ambulances. It's too late for ambulances.'

'But I—'

'I said listen to me. You're to do exactly what I tell you. No more, no less. Understand?'

'Yes, Reverend, but—'

'Be quiet and listen,' yelled Peterson. 'This is a heathen country. The people here are heathens. Don't you understand? The police here are heathens. The judges. All of them, all heathens. They'll revel in the opportunity to smear the name of Christ, because that's what heathens do. They smear the name of Christ. Do you want to help heathens smear the name of Christ? Is that truly what you want?'

'No, Reverend. Of course not.'

'Good. Now listen. No one needs to know what happened here. It was an accident, that's all. Foolish people driving too fast through fields at night. What else did you expect?'

'Yes, Reverend.'

'Go back to the site. If anyone asks, tell them you drove around for a while but saw nothing. Understand?'

'Yes, Reverend. And you?'

'Don't worry about me. Just get out of here.'

'Yes, Reverend.'

Peterson watched him drive away. That was the trouble with kids. Their clay was too soft, not yet fired by the furnaces of righteous conflict. He'd have to handle this all by himself. He climbed down to the foot of the ditch, keeping clear of the worst of the carnage. He had a camera-phone to recover.

THIRTEEN

I

Fatima allowed a few moments of silence to pass before responding to Stafford, perhaps so that he might see for himself just how ugly and excessive his vehemence had been. Then she said quietly: 'Refute it? Refute what, exactly?'

Stafford looked confused. 'My thesis.'

'But you promised me evidence,' replied Fatima, her voice so low that Gaille had to strain to hear her. 'How can I refute this thesis of yours until I've heard your evidence?'

Stafford looked blankly at her. 'How do you mean? I've just given you my evidence.'

'Really?' frowned Fatima. 'You call *that* evidence. All I've heard so far is speculation. Well-informed speculation, I admit. But speculation nonetheless.'

'How can you say that?'

'My dear Mister Stafford, let me explain something. I do not personally believe in the Bible or its God. But perhaps you do. Perhaps you believe that He created the world in seven days, and that those animals Noah took aboard his ark were the only ones to survive the flood, and that we speak different languages because God took offence at mankind's effort to reach the heavens by building the Tower of Babel? Is that what you believe?'

'I've already said I don't take the Bible literally.'

'Ah. Yet you still believe that we should consider it as somehow *special,* as having validity even when it is contradicted by the historical and archaeological record?'

'I'm not saying that.'

'I'm glad to hear it. For let me tell you what I think of the Bible. I think it is the folk-history of a particular Canaanite people. No more, no less. And I think its historical validity should be assessed as scrupulously as any other folk-history, not accorded special treatment just because many people still consider it sacred. You'd agree with that, wouldn't you? As a fellow historian, I mean?'

'Yes.'

'Good. Now if you want to test folk-history for validity, do you know what you must first do? You must discard it completely from your mind, then interrogate the independent record until you've established the truth as far as possible, and *only then* refer back to your folk-history to see how well it fits. Any other approach is special pleading. And do you know something?'

'What?'

'Do it that way and the Bible falls apart, particularly the early books. There's no evidence *whatsoever* to suggest its stories are true. There's no evidence that the Jews existed as a distinct people in the time of Akhenaten, or that they lived in Egypt in any great numbers, or that they left in some mass exodus.'

A flush in Stafford's cheeks, a cocktail of alcohol and defiance. 'So where did those stories come from, then?'

'Who can say? Many were clearly borrowed from other, older cultures. There are recognizable traces of the Mesopotamian Epic of Gilgamesh, for example. Others seem to be variations on the same story, presumably because the writers of the Bible wanted to drum home their moral message. Man makes covenant with God. Man breaks covenant. God punishes man. Again and again this same motif. Adam and Eve evicted from Eden. Cain exiled for murdering Abel. Lot's wife turned to salt. Abraham fleeing Egypt. Babel. Noah. Isaac. Jacob. The list goes on and on. Because it isn't history. It's *propaganda*. Specifically, it's religious propaganda, put together after the Jews had been defeated by the Babylonians to convince them that they'd brought their destruction and exile upon themselves by failing in their obligations to their God.'

She broke off a moment, sipped water to moisten her mouth and throat, forced a smile to release some tension. 'Do you know something?' she said. 'Whenever historians have been able to test folklore against known history, they've discovered what one might expect: that it proves reasonably accurate for events within living memory, but the further back one goes, the less reliable it becomes, until it bears almost no relation to the truth. With one exception. Founding myths typically have a seed of truth in them.

'So let's apply this to the Jewish people. Their founding myth is clearly the Exodus. The Bible is built around it. So I'm quite prepared to accept some sort of flight from Egypt. The trouble is, the only evidence of such an exodus during the second millennium BC is that of the Hyksos. But the Hyksos were a full two centuries before Amarna. So how is it that this mass flight of yours left no imprint? We're not talking about a few hundred people, remember. Not even thousands. According to the Bible, we're talking about *over half* the population of Egypt. Even allowing for massive exaggeration, don't you think that *someone* would have noticed? Do you know, Mister Stafford, there's a stele recording the flight of two slaves from Egypt to Canaan? *Two!* Yet you'd have us believe that *tens of thousands* of valuable artisans suddenly upped and left, and no one said a word. And don't you think someone would have found *some* trace of their forty years in Sinai? *Any* trace. Archaeologists have found settlements from pre-dynastic times, from dynastic times, from the Graeco-Roman and Islamic eras. But from the Exodus? Nothing. Not a coin, not a potsherd, not a grave, not a campfire. And it's not for lack of looking, believe me.'

'Absence of evidence isn't evidence of absence,' observed Stafford.

'Yes, it is,' countered Fatima. 'That's exactly what it is. Not *proof* of absence, I grant you. But evidence, certainly. If the Hebrews had spent significant time there, they'd have left traces. No traces means no Hebrews. To argue otherwise is simply perverse. And where we do find evidence, it flatly contradicts the biblical account. You mentioned Jericho, the city felled by Joshua's trumpets. If your thesis is correct, it should show evidence of destruction circa 1300 BC. But the archaeological data is conclusive. Jericho wasn't even *occupied* at that time. It was destroyed in the sixteenth century BC and left virtually abandoned through to the tenth.'

'Yes, but—'

'The early Bible is make-believe, Mister Stafford. It wasn't even written until after the Babylonian exile, circa five hundred BC; over *eight hundred years* after the death of Akhenaten.'

'From records that go back much further.'

'According to whom? Do you *have* any of these records? Or are you just assuming their existence? And if they did exist, how would you explain all the anachronisms? Camels in Egypt a thousand years before they were actually introduced. Cities like Ramses and Sais that weren't founded for hundreds of years after Akhenaten. A landscape of kingdoms that didn't exist in the thirteenth century BC, yet which maps almost exactly onto the seventh and sixth.'

'What about the parallels between the religions?' asked Stafford weakly. 'You can't deny those.'

Fatima shook her head dismissively. 'Eighteenth Dynasty Egypt was the great regional power. Its armies occupied Canaan for hundreds of years. Even after their occupation ended, they remained Canaan's key trading partner. Their practices and rituals were admired and emulated just as French and British practices are still visible in former colonies. As for their monotheism, have you considered the possibility that it might just be a coincidence? Monotheism isn't complex. It's "my god's bigger than your god" taken to its logical extreme. Long before Akhenaten proclaimed the

Aten the Sole God, Egyptians had done the same for Atum.'

'Yes, but—'

'And let's compare the gods themselves. The Aten enjoys an exclusive relationship with Akhenaten. The God of Moses makes His covenant with every single Jew. The Aten is notional and pacific, an aesthete's God. The God of Moses is vengeful, jealous and violent. Or take their creation myths. Actually, you can't. The Aten has *no* creation myth; Genesis has two. The God of Moses dwelt in the enclosed Holy of Holies; the Aten was worshipped in wide-open spaces. Read how Moses received the Ten Commandments: it couldn't be clearer that his God is a volcano God. But there *are* no volcanoes in Egypt or in Sinai.' She shook her head angrily. 'Let me tell you something. You claim that I have my head in the sand because I assert there's no connection between Akhenaten and Moses. But you're wrong. All I assert is that there's no evidence for such a connection. I'm an archaeologist, Mister Stafford. Bring me evidence and I'll gladly endorse your views. Until then . . .' And she gave a dismissive little wave of her hand.

Stafford's jaw clenched tight as walnuts in his cheeks. 'Then it seems we'll just have to agree to disagree,' he said.

'Yes,' agreed Fatima. 'It does.'

II

Peterson knelt beside Omar Tawfiq on the far bank, rough diamonds of shattered glass shining pale blue in the moonlight all around. His head was twisted back in a hideous and unnatural position, his lacerated face covered with both fresh and congealing blood. Peterson was so sure he was dead that it gave him a jolt when he opened his mouth suddenly and gasped in air.

The Jeep was lying on its side, screeching and groaning and hissing, as if it too were in great pain. He squatted down to look through the empty frame of the windscreen. Knox was belted into the driver's seat, slumped against the driver's door, his hair slick and glistening, the bubbles of blood at the corner of his mouth expanding and shrinking as he breathed. He opened his eyes, looked at Peterson with a faint flicker of recognition. Then his gaze went distant and his eyes closed once more.

Peterson rested his hand on the buckled bonnet, reached through the vacant windscreen, rummaged around in search of Knox's mobile phone. He patted down his right-side trouser pocket and found only a wallet, which he left. He strained to reach his left trouser pocket, felt something compact and hard inside, though he couldn't quite get hold of it. He tried to release the seat belt instead, pull Knox towards him, reach his phone that way, but the catch had jammed and wouldn't come free. He backed away, frustrated, squatted down, thinking it through.

Severe concussion tended to destroy short-term memory, he knew. As a young man, before finding God, he'd fallen off the roof of a house he'd been breaking into, had come to his senses lying on the asphalt drive, his partner-in-crime laughing his head off. To this day, he had no memory of what had happened in the twelve hours leading up to his fall. So it was quite possible, even probable, that Knox wouldn't recall the crash or the events leading up to it. But what if he did? What if he survived and remembered everything? So the question was, was there a simple way to take care both of the camera-phone and of Knox?

Such questions were beyond the wisdom of mortal man, but that didn't make them unanswerable. Peterson knelt at the foot of the ditch and bowed his head in prayer. The Lord always spoke to those with ears to hear. He didn't even have to wait long. The numbers twenty and thirteen began to blaze like bonfires in his mind's eye. They could surely only refer to Leviticus 20:13.

If a man also lie with mankind, as he lieth with a woman, both of them have committed an abomination: they shall surely be put to death; their blood shall be upon them.

So be it. When the Lord spoke with such clarity, man's only task was to obey. He went around to the exposed undercarriage. A small puddle of diesel had collected on the dried-out mud bank, dripping from a hairline fracture in the tank. His 4x4 had a cigarette lighter in its dash. He pushed it in, went hunting for a rock. He found a goodly chunk of flint, took it back down to the Jeep, hammered at the tank until the drips of diesel turned to a stream and the puddle became a pool. He went back up again, tore a strip of paper from his car-hire documentation, lit it from the orange coils of the cigarette lighter, nursed it back down the slope, dropped it into the pool of diesel, leapt back before it could take his eyebrows.

It went up with a violent whoomp like a great orange balloon launching into the night sky. But after its first furious blaze, it burned itself out, leaving soft flames licking at the Jeep's undercarriage; and though the fabric of the ripped seats was smouldering with a rich black choking smoke, much of it was escaping through the broken windows, sucking the fresh air back in.

Peterson scowled. Even should Knox asphyxiate, he'd still need to retrieve his phone. He knelt once more on the buckled bonnet, poked his head inside, braving the intense heat. The seat belt was still jammed. He worked furiously at the release, tugging, jiggling and pushing until finally it came free. He gave himself a momentary respite from the fierce heat and smoke, then went back in, grabbed Knox's collar, hauled him forwards while reaching for his pocket and—

'Hey!'

Peterson guiltily let go of Knox, jumped backwards. Two men in fluorescent yellow bibs were standing on top of the ditch, spotlighting him with their torches. The taller scrambled down, the name Shareef emblazoned in a Highways Maintenance badge upon his chest. He said something in Arabic.

Peterson shook his head blankly. 'I'm American,' he said.

Shareef switched to English. 'What happened?'

'I found them like this,' said Peterson. He nodded at Knox. 'This one's still alive. I was trying to get him out before the smoke gets to him.'

Shareef nodded. 'I help you, yes?'

'Thank you.' They hauled Knox out through the windscreen, over to the bank, laid him gently down. The second highway maintenance man was carrying on a fraught conversation on his mobile. 'What's going on?' asked Peterson.

'Big crash in Hannoville,' explained Shareef. 'No ambulances. The hospital ask can we bring them in ourselves.' He nodded at his own vehicle, just a cab with a crane on the back, then at Peterson's Toyota, still parked by the bridge. 'We take yours, yes?'

Peterson nodded, trapped. Argue now, he'd only raise suspicions. 'Where's the hospital?' he asked.

'Follow us,' said Shareef, stooping to pick Knox up once more. 'We show you.'

FOURTEEN

I

The evening meal was cleared away, coffee brought in its place. Gaille clasped her hands beneath the table and wondered how quickly she could excuse herself. Perhaps Lily sensed her restlessness, for she leaned forwards into the candlelight. 'I was fascinated by the *talatat* Gaille showed me earlier. She hinted you might have something interesting to share with us.'

'Yes,' agreed Fatima. She turned to Gaille. 'You don't need to be here for this, my dear. Perhaps you should update our Digging Diary.'

Gaille felt a prick of shame. 'I can do it tomorrow,' she said.

'Please,' said Fatima. 'It doesn't pay to fall behind.'

Gaille nodded and stood. 'Goodnight, then,' she

said, touching Fatima's shoulder in gratitude as she passed.

'Are we all set for the morning?' asked Lily. 'Only we really need to film the sun rising over Amarna.'

'You may not find that possible,' said Fatima, answering for Gaille. 'The ferry won't start running until dawn. You should film from the west bank anyway. That's how Akhenaten first saw it.'

'We'll need to leave by a quarter to five,' said Gaille. 'That should give us plenty of time.' She nodded goodnight, trying not to let any resentment show as she closed the door.

It reopened almost immediately, however, and Lily came out. 'I'm really sorry about this, Gaille,' she said.

'Sorry about what?'

'About manoeuvring you into coming with us tomorrow.'

'It's okay.'

'It's not okay. I've used your good nature against you, we all have, don't think we don't know it. And I just wanted to say sorry. I hate doing things like that to good people. If anyone tried it on me . . .'

Gaille laughed. 'It's fine,' she said; and suddenly it was.

Lily gave a rueful yet charming smile. 'This is my first overseas assignment. I don't want it to be my last.'

'You're doing great.'

She threw a glance at the door. 'That's not what *he* thinks.'

'Don't worry about him. I've worked with his kind before. He'll think himself wonderful and everyone else awful no matter what happens. The only thing you can do is not let it get to you.'

'I won't. And thanks again.'

Gaille found herself in an unexpectedly good mood as she reached her room, humming a half-remembered tune as she turned on her laptop and connected to the Internet. Their Digging Diary did need an update, though it wasn't exactly urgent, especially considering the precious little traffic the site got. But Fatima liked keeping it fresh. Anything to spread the word. She posted a summary of recent finds, added a photograph, her mind wandering back to the dinner table, wondering what Fatima was telling Lily and Stafford about the *talatat* they'd found.

Akhenaten had routinely been portrayed with breasts in sculptures and paintings. Some said it was the prevailing artistic style; others attributed it to disease. But one statue showed him completely naked, and not only did he have breasts but he had a perfectly smooth groin too, no hint of genitalia. In some cultures this might have been prudery, but Eighteenth Dynasty artists had been anything but coy. Some had argued that Akhenaten must therefore have been a woman, like Hatshepsut, who'd disguised her sex to ascend the throne. Others had even claimed Akhenaten an hermaphrodite. But then it had been pointed out that the statue had been designed to wear a kilt in antiquity, so that drawing such extravagant conclusions from it was completely unsafe. Yet their cache of *talatat* threatened to revive the controversy, for Gaille had assembled a plausible portrait of Akhenaten, naked, with pronounced breasts, yet without genitalia. And that was what Fatima was telling Stafford and Lily right now.

Her update finished, Gaille yawned, eager for bed. But she checked her hotmail account just in case. Her heart gave a little jolt when she saw she had an email from Knox. She opened it up.

> *Took the attached at poss Therapeutae site! Light terrible. Can you help? All speed appreciated!*
> *I miss you.*
> *Daniel.*

She reached out and touched the screen, fingertips tingling with static. She'd had many reasons for accepting Fatima's invitation to join her team for a month's work, but the strongest had been her growing certainty that having Knox's friendship wasn't going to be enough for her. She'd needed his respect as well.

I miss you.

Suddenly she felt wide-awake again, vibrant. She began downloading his photographs to her hard disk, eager to get to work on them.

II

Peterson never cursed out loud, but there were moments during the drive to the hospital when he came precious close. It was partly because he'd not had an opportunity to retrieve Knox's phone, for Shareef was in the back of the Toyota ministering to him and Tawfiq. But mostly it was from trying to keep up with Shareef's colleague in the Highway Agency cab. The man was crazy, driving recklessly fast, pumping his horn and flashing his lights as he wove through thickening traffic, road signs and markings whistling by like tracer fire.

He roared past an articulated lorry, braked sharply for the off-ramp, up through the gears again, speedometer needle whipping around the dial. They emerged from an underpass, took such a sharp right that Peterson had to wrench the Toyota's steering wheel with his whole body, bumping down a potholed road, a barrier ahead being raised even as they approached, then racing into the hospital grounds, past the cement mixer and two pyramids of sand being used for ongoing building works, screeching to a halt outside the hospital front doors.

The place was already abuzz with emergency staff from the Hannoville crash. A medic and two porters hurried out. The back of the Toyota flew up. The medic clamped masks over Omar's and Knox's mouths; had them put onto trolleys. Peterson got out, running alongside Knox as he was wheeled inside, his hand resting by his left hip, eyes on the bulge in Knox's pocket. He glanced around. Everyone was frantic, calling out orders, no one watching him. He reached for the—

They crashed hard into swing doors, the surprise forcing Peterson to drop back. By the time he caught up again, Knox had been turned onto his side, his shirt off, blackened skin beneath. A nurse took off his shoes, unbuckled and pulled down his jeans. Peterson tried to grab them from her. 'My friend,' he said.

But the nurse yanked them from him and pointed emphatically back at the swing doors. He turned to see Shareef standing there with a policeman, a bull of a man with small piercing eyes and a bitter line to his upper lip. Peterson forced a smile, made his way to join them.

'This is Detective Inspector Farooq,' said Shareef. 'He was here for that other crash.'

'A long night for you,' said Peterson.

'Yes,' agreed Farooq tersely. 'And you are?'

'Peterson. The Reverend Ernest Peterson.'

'And you found these two, yes?'

'Yes.'

'You want to tell me about it?'

'Perhaps I should move my car first,' said Peterson. 'It's blocking the entrance.' He nodded to them both, walked out through the front doors, thinking furiously about what story to give. The policeman had a look about him, the kind who distrusted everyone, who automatically assumed all witnesses were lying to him, until he could establish otherwise. He started up the Toyota, headed into the parking area. Stick to the truth. That was the key in such situations. Or, at least, stick as close to the truth as you could.

III

Gaille smiled as she opened the first of Knox's photographs. He hadn't been kidding about the light. The screen was almost completely black, except for a yellow tint of moonlight top left. But she was good at this, and soon she'd coaxed from it a dark but clear picture of a partially exhumed grave. She saved it and moved on. A few of the pictures proved beyond her skills, but most responded well. In fact, once she'd worked out which adjustments to make, it became almost repetitive. The content of the pictures kept her rapt, however. She couldn't believe what she was seeing. Catacombs, human remains, oil lamps, murals. But the most striking photograph was of a mosaic: a figure sitting inside a seven-pointed star, surrounded by clusters of Greek letters. Gaille frowned. She'd seen other such clusters recently, she was sure of it. But she couldn't think where.

She finished the photograph, saved it and moved on. When she'd completed the last photograph, she composed a reply to Knox, attaching all the images she'd been able to enhance. Then she checked the time with a heartfelt groan. She was supposed to be setting off for Amarna in just a few hours. She hurried to get ready for bed to grab what little sleep she could.

FIFTEEN

I

Farooq watched from the hospital's front doors as Peterson parked his Toyota 4x4 in an empty bay. 'Maybe I was just imagining things,' murmured Shareef. 'Maybe it was nothing.'

'Maybe,' agreed Farooq.

'It was just . . . I kept getting this impression. That we were in his way, you know. That he was looking for something. And I wasn't imagining what I told you about the seat belt.'

'Foreigners,' muttered Farooq, spitting a fleck of tobacco from his lip. He loathed them all, but the English and Americans most. The way they behaved: they thought it was still the old days.

'You need me any longer?' asked Shareef.

Farooq shook his head. 'I'll call if I have any questions.'

'Not before morning, okay? I need my sleep.'

'Don't we all?' He threw down his cigarette as Peterson arrived back at the hospital's front doors, then led him to the makeshift office he'd been given, motioned for him to take a chair, turned over a fresh sheet on his notepad. 'Go on, then,' he grunted. 'What happened?'

Peterson nodded. 'You should know first that I'm an archaeologist,' he said, spreading his hands wide, giving what he no doubt imagined was a sincere and candid smile. 'I'm here on excavation in Borg el-Arab. Earlier today, yesterday now, I suppose, we had a visit from Doctor Omar Tawfiq, he's head of the SCA in Alexandria, you know, and a man called Daniel Knox, a British archaeologist.'

Farooq grunted. 'You're not going to tell me one of those two men you brought in is head of the SCA in Alexandria?'

'I'm afraid so.'

'Hell!'

'We spoke for a while. We informally arranged a full site tour. Then they left. I thought no more of it. But then, after dark, we had an intruder.'

'An intruder?'

'It's not uncommon,' sighed Peterson. 'The local Bedouin farmers are all convinced we're finding great treasures. Why else would we be digging, after all? We're not, of course. But they won't take our word for it.'

'So this intruder . . . ?'

'Yes. We chased him off the site. He got into a car. Someone else was driving.'

'And you went after them?'

'You can't just let people run over your site. They'll contaminate important data. I wanted to give them a piece of my mind. I thought it might deter others. I was way behind them though. Then I saw flames.' He shrugged. 'I got there as quick as I could. It was awful. One of them, the man Knox, was still inside. I was worried he'd asphyxiate. I managed to release his seat belt. That's when the Highway Maintenance men arrived, thank heavens.'

A tired-looking doctor knocked and entered. 'Bad news,' he said. 'The man from Borg. The Egyptian one.'

'Dead?' asked Farooq gloomily.

The doctor nodded. 'I'm sorry.'

'And the other?'

'Grade three or four concussion, smoke inhalation, moderate burns. The smoke and burns should both be manageable. The concussion is more problematic. You can never be sure, not this soon. It depends on impact damage, how the intracranial pressure builds, how the—'

'When will I be able to talk to him?'

'Give it two or three days and he should be—'

'He may be responsible for the other man's death,' said Farooq tightly.

'Ah,' said the doctor, scratching his cheek. 'I'll take him off the morphine. With luck, he'll be awake by morning. Don't expect too much though. He'll probably suffer retrograde and anterograde amnesia.'

'Do I look like a doctor?' scowled Farooq.

'Sorry. He's highly unlikely to remember anything from immediately before or after the crash.'

'All the same,' said Farooq. 'I need to speak to him.'

'As you wish.' He nodded and withdrew.

'What terrible news,' sighed Peterson, when Farooq had translated the gist for him. 'I only wish I could have done something more.'

'You did what you could.'

'Yes. Is there anything else?'

'Your contact details.'

'Of course.' Peterson turned the pad to face him, jotted down a phone number, directions to the site. Then he got to his feet, nodded and left.

Farooq watched him out. Something wasn't right, but his brain was too tired right now, he needed sleep. He yawned heavily, got up. Just one more thing to take care of. If Knox was truly to blame for the death of Alexandria's senior archae-ologist, he needed to be kept under watch: his own room, a man outside his door. Then he'd come back tomorrow and find out just exactly what the hell was going on.

II

Gaille was drifting to sleep when suddenly she jolted awake, sat up, turned on her light. Stafford's two books were on her bedside table. She grabbed the one about Solomon's lost treasures, flipped through the pages to a photograph of the Copper Scroll, most mysterious of the Dead Sea Scrolls: a treasure map written in Hebrew, but containing an anomaly that no one had ever satisfactorily explained: seven clusters of Greek letters.

ΚεΝ ΧΑΓ ΗΝ Θε ΔΙ ΤΡ ΣΚ

She took the book over to her laptop, turned it on, brought up Knox's photograph of the mosaic. A thrill shivered her as she saw that the clusters were identical, though arranged in a different order. But the figure in the mosaic was pointing at the ΚεΝ; and the line that made up the seven-pointed star went past the other six clusters in the exact same sequence as in the Copper Scroll.

She sat back in her chair, astounded, confused, electrified. The Copper Scroll had been an Essene document, and thus linked to Knox's Therapeutae site. But even so . . . .

She grabbed her phone. Knox would want to hear this at once, whatever the time. But he wasn't answering. She left messages instead, telling him to call at once. Then she sat there, reading Stafford's book and studying the photographs, brooding on what it might mean, her mind fizzing with the excitement of the chase.

III

Peterson moved his Toyota to the far shadows of the car park, then sat there watching the hospital's front doors, for he dared not leave without first taking care of Knox's camera-phone.

It felt like an age before Farooq finally came out, lit a cigarette, walked wearily over to his car, drove away. Peterson gave it ten more minutes to be safe, then headed back inside. First things first. His face and hands were smeared with oil and soot. If anyone saw him that way, he was bound to be challenged. He found a men's room, stripped down, washed himself vigorously, wiped himself dry with paper towels. Not perfect, but it would have to do. He checked his watch. He needed to get busy.

A family was squabbling in strained, hushed

voices in reception. An obese woman was stretched out on a bench. Peterson pushed through swing doors into a dimly lit corridor. Signs in Arabic and English. Oncology and Paediatrics. Not what he was looking for. He took the back stairs, emerged into a corridor. A doctor scurried between trauma patients on trolleys, the adrenaline long-since worn off, leaving him merely exhausted. Peterson hurried past, pushed through double doors into a small room crammed with six beds. He walked the aisle, scanned faces. No sign of Knox. Back along the corridor, into the next ward. Six people here, too, none of them Knox. He continued checking rooms without success, out into a stairwell, up another floor, through swing doors into an identical corridor. A policeman was snoozing on a hard wooden chair outside the nearest room, his head tilted back against the wall. *Damn Farooq!* But the man was asleep and there was no one else in sight. Peterson approached stealthily, listening intently for any change in the rhythm of his gentle snoring. God was with him and he reached the door without alarm. He opened it quietly, rested it closed behind him.

It was dark inside. He gave his eyes a few seconds to adjust, walked over to the bed. Peterson was a veteran of hospitals. He noted the saline IV drip, the pungent smell of a colloid application. He looked around for Knox's clothes, found them folded on a chest of drawers, a small pile of belongings on top, including his camera-phone. He pocketed it, turned, then paused for thought.

He'd surely never get a better chance to deal with Knox once and for all. The policeman asleep outside the door would no doubt swear blind he'd been wide awake all night, that no one could possibly have got in or out. In a heathen backward country like this, they'd take it for granted that the effects of the crash had simply caught up with Knox. Shock. Trauma. Concussion. Burns. Smoke inhalation. They'd give him only the most cursory of autopsies. And he was an abominator, after all. He'd brought his fate upon himself.

He took a step closer to the bed.

SIXTEEN

I

Stafford and Lily were already waiting by the Discovery's passenger door when Gaille went out at twelve minutes to five. 'Sorry,' she said, holding up Stafford's book by way of an excuse. 'I got carried away.'

'It *is* good, isn't it?' he nodded.

'The Copper Scroll,' she said as she and Stafford climbed in and Lily went to open the gates. 'That's for real, is it?'

'Do you imagine I'm in the habit of populating my books with make-believe artefacts?' he asked sourly. 'Go and visit Jordan's Archaeological Museum if you don't trust me.'

'I didn't mean for real like that,' said Gaille, gunning the engine a little to warm it up before

167

pulling away. 'I mean, how can you be sure it's not a hoax of some kind?'

'Well, it's certainly not a modern hoax,' he said, as Gaille braked to allow Lily to climb in the back. 'Scientific analysis has proved that beyond question. As for an *ancient* hoax, the Essenes weren't exactly known for their frivolity, were they? Especially as the copper was over ninety-nine per cent pure – effectively *ritually* pure; and the Essenes took ritual purity very seriously.'

'Yes.'

'Besides, it wasn't on just one sheet of copper, surely plenty for a hoax, but on three sheets riveted together. And it wasn't inscribed in the normal fashion, with the letters scratched out with a sharp stylus. Someone actually punched the letters out from behind with a chisel. Extremely painstaking work, believe me. No. Whoever went to all that trouble believed it genuine.'

'Believed?' asked Gaille.

He granted her a slight smile, a teacher rewarding a bright pupil. 'The text seems to have been copied from another, older document, probably by someone unfamiliar with the language. So it's possible, I suppose, that some mischief-maker wrote out a hoax on parchment or papyrus, and that this hoax was somehow mistaken by the Essenes for the real thing, and that it became so venerated by them that when it began to disintegrate, they copied it out, only onto copper this time. But that's quite a stretch, wouldn't you say?'

A donkey cart ahead, laden with long green stalks of sugar cane that bounced and swished like the skirts of an Hawaiian dancer, blocked the full width of the narrow lane, forcing Gaille to fall in behind. It was still dark, but the eastern horizon was just beginning to lighten with the first intimations of dawn. Stafford leaned across and tooted the horn again and again until Gaille swatted away his hand. 'There's nowhere for him to pull into,' she said.

Stafford scowled and folded one leg across the other, crossed his arms. 'Do you realize how important this shot of sunrise is for my programme?' he asked.

'We'll get there.'

'Akhenaten chose Amarna as his capital because the way the sun rose between two cliffs mimicked the Egyptian sign of the Aten. That's going to be my opening shot. If I don't get it—'

'You'll get it,' she assured him. The cart finally found a place to pull in. Gaille waved gratefully as she sped by, the acceleration making Stafford's book slip from the dashboard. He picked it up, flipped the pages with authorial pride, stopped to admire a photograph of himself by the Wailing Wall. Gaille nodded at it. 'How come you're so sure these Copper Scroll treasures came from the Temple of Solomon?' she asked.

'I thought you'd read it.'

'I haven't had a chance to finish it yet.'

'The scroll's in Hebrew,' he told her. 'It was owned by the Essenes. So the treasure was unquestionably Jewish. And the amounts involved are staggering, I mean *over forty tons* of gold. That's worth *billions* of dollars at today's prices. The kind of quantities only a hugely wealthy king or a very powerful institution could possibly own. Yet some of the treasures are described as *tithes*, and tithes are paid exclusively to religious organizations. Others are religious artefacts like chalices and candelabras. A religious institution, then. In ancient Israel, that means either the First Temple, the Temple of Solomon, which was destroyed by the Babylonians in 586 BC; or the Second Temple, which was built on the ruins of the first, and which was destroyed by the Romans in AD 70. Most scholars ascribe these Copper Scroll treasures to the latter. But my book proves that impossible.'

'Proves it?'

'It's all to do with dates,' said Stafford. 'The Copper Scroll was found in the Qumran caves, remember. And Qumran was taken and then occupied by the Romans in AD 68, two years before Jerusalem fell. Advocates of the Second Temple theory would have you believe that Jews took the treasure *out* of Jewish-held territory to bury it in

Roman-occupied territory, then hid the map to it right under the noses of a Roman garrison. How crazy would they have had to be to do that? But even that's beside the point. The Copper Scroll was found buried *beneath* other scrolls that had been left there at least twenty years before the Roman invasion. And, as I just said, it was copied from another, older document. And the script itself is a very peculiar version of archaic square-form Hebrew dating to 200 BC or even earlier. Tell me, is it likely the Second Temple treasures were hidden from the Romans hundreds of years before they came rampaging?'

'It does seem odd.'

'So if the Copper Scroll treasure didn't come from the Second Temple, it must have come from the first. QED.'

They reached the Nile road, headed south. The lime, flamingo and turquoise strip lighting of a minaret lit up the darkness like a fairground ride. Gaille turned right and then left, wending through a small village then out between lush fields of budding grain and down a gentle incline to the Nile, flowing sedately by. The glow of dawn was turning the eastern horizon blue, though the sun wouldn't rise over the Amarna cliffs for a while yet.

'Any good?' she asked.

'Perfect,' grinned Lily from the back.

They climbed out, yawned, stretched. Lily set up the camera and checked the sound while Stafford took out his vanity case and primped himself. Gaille sat upon the bonnet, savouring its radiated heat, her mind buzzing pleasantly. Somewhere, in the far distance, a muezzin began his call to prayer.

The Copper Scroll. Ancient lost treasures. She laughed out loud. Knox was going to love her for this.

II

'That'll have to do,' grunted Griffin, as they stamped down the mix of sand, rock and earth with which they'd filled up the shaft. Even with everyone helping, it had been a long night's work, and he felt drained. The two or three hours of sleep they could still get wasn't much, but it was better than none.

'What about the reverend?' asked Mickey doubtfully. 'Shouldn't we wait for him?'

'He's scarcely going to turn up now, is he?' snapped Griffin irritably. Peterson never had to explain himself. He just barked out orders and these damned munchkins ran to obey. 'We'll come back later.'

'I still think we ought to—'

'Just do as I say, all right?' He wiped his hands on his backside, turned and strode over to the truck with as much authority as he could manage, hoping rather than expecting that his students would follow. But when he turned to look, they were kneeling in a circle, arms around each other's shoulders, giving thanks to the Lord.

A familiar sweet stab of envy in Griffin's groin, disturbingly like lust. How fine to release oneself into the group like that, to surrender one's cynicism and doubt. But his own cast of mind had been set decades ago, and it didn't do submission, it didn't do faith. 'Come on,' he said, hating the wheedle in his voice. 'We need to get moving.'

But they didn't pay him any heed. They took their own good time. His impatience turned to something akin to fear, a sense of impending doom. How the hell had it come to this? Nathan hadn't said what had happened to Tawfiq and Knox, but from the state of shock he'd been in, it clearly wasn't good. He'd sent him away before the others could see him, but now Griffin was worried he might have bumped into Claire at the hotel. Claire wasn't like these others. She made her own judgements on things. If she found out that something really bad had happened . . . Christ! This whole house of cards could easily come crashing down.

Finally, they were done. They walked across, still exuberant with prayer, climbed onto the pick-up's flatbed, not one of them joining him in the cab. There were times he *hated* them, how low he'd sunk in the world. A moment of weakness. That's all it had been. The girl had sat front row during his lectures, staring unblinkingly at him with her guileless blue eyes. He'd been unused to the frank admiration of an attractive young woman. It had set his heart pounding. Lecture after lecture, he'd kept glancing her way. She'd still been staring raptly. Then she'd come to his office one lunchtime, pulled a chair up beside him. When their knees had brushed beneath his desk, his hand had moved almost convulsively, with a life of its own, to the warm top of her inner thigh, fingertips pressing down between her legs.

Her shocked shriek haunted him still, made his cheeks burn whenever he thought of it.

No one had taken his side, of course. His boss had seized the opportunity to cut him loose. She'd never liked him. And she must have put the word out too, the vindictive bitch, because no one had even bothered to answer his application letters. No one except Peterson. *What did they expect him to do?* he thought defiantly. *Did they expect him to starve?*

A strange noise reached him over the rumble of the engine. He took his foot off the gas, glanced over his shoulder. They were singing in the back, moonlit faces shiny with devotion, hands raised in ecstasy, worshipping together. His low spirits sank even further. Maybe there was something in religion after all. Maybe if he believed like that, attractive young women wouldn't shriek in horror just because he put his hand on their leg.

Maybe.

III

Knox woke abruptly, nebulously afraid without being quite sure why. It was almost pitch black in the room, at least until some passing headlights painted yellow slats upon the ceiling. But that only made him all the more anxious, because he didn't recognize his surroundings at all. He tried to lift his head, but he had no strength in his neck. He tried to push himself up, but his arms felt atrophied and useless. He worked his eyes instead, left, right, up, down. A catheter taped to his forearm. He followed the translucent tube up to an IV drip on a stand. Hospital. At least that explained why he felt like shit. But he had no recollection whatsoever of what might have brought him here.

Another car passed by, its headlights silhouetting a man standing by his bed, looking down. He tugged the pillow from beneath Knox's head, held it squarely in his hands, made to place it over his face. Heels started clacking on the tiled floor outside, drawing closer and closer. The man vanished into the shadows. Knox tried to call out, but no sound emerged. The heels passed on by, pushing through swing doors and away, leaving only silence behind.

The man re-emerged from the shadows, pillow still in his hands. He placed it over Knox's face, pressed down. Until that moment, there'd been an almost hallucinogenic aspect to the whole experience, like a waking nightmare. But as the pillow pressed down hard and he couldn't breathe, his heart kicked into overdrive, pumping out adrenaline, belatedly giving him some movement and strength. He scrabbled at the man's hands, kicked with his feet and knees, tried to twist his mouth sideways to gain some air. But he had no leverage; his muscles were already tiring, his mind swimming from lack of oxygen, his system closing down. He flung up an arm in a last effort to claw his assailant's face, tugging the IV tube so hard that the stand teetered and then tumbled with a great clatter. The pillow was instantly whipped from his face, falling to the floor, allowing Knox to heave in great gasps of air, savour the oxygen flooding gloriously through his system.

The door flew open. A policeman came in, flapped on the light, saw the fallen IV stand, Knox gasping, went back out into the corridor, shouting for medical assistance, panic in his voice. Knox lay there, terrified his assailant would finish him off, until a doctor finally appeared at the door, two days of stubble on his chin and cheeks, eyes gluey with tiredness. He picked up the IV stand, checked the tube, reaffixed Knox's catheter. 'Why do you do this to me?' he muttered. 'I only want to sleep.'

Knox tried to speak, but his mouth wouldn't work, he could manage only a plaintive croak. A trickle of spittle ran down his cheek. The nurse wiped it sympathetically away. He checked Knox's pulse, raised an eyebrow. 'Panic, yes?' he said. 'Is normal. You have a bad crash, you know. But you're safe now. This is hospital. Nothing bad can happen here. All you need is rest. That's all any of us need.' He picked the pillow up from the floor, plumped it and replaced it beneath Knox's head. Then he nodded in satisfaction, went back to the door, turned off the lights and left Knox at the mercy of this stranger who wanted to kill him.

SEVENTEEN

I

The Nile car ferry was little more than a motorized metal raft. Gaille leaned against the rail and watched the fishermen paddle their sky-blue boats with their flat slats of oars, the floating mats of vegetable matter passing serenely by. A Coptic monk muttered as he ran his finger across the small print of his Bible. Kids dangled their feet over the side, watching for the sudden pale flash of fish. Four young farmers kept looking at Stafford then howling with laughter. But even that couldn't put him out of the cheerful mood he'd been in since he'd bagged his sunrise footage.

They bumped against the east bank, drove up a short hill through a dusty village. Youngsters stared wide-eyed at them, as though they'd never seen tourists before. A shopkeeper polished with spit and cloth his tired display of lemons and mangoes. They passed a cemetery, drove along an empty road to the Amarna ticket office. The shutters were closed, though two tourist policemen were sitting beneath a sunshade by a cabin, sharing a cigarette. One stood, wandered across. 'You're here early,' he grunted.

'We're filming,' Gaille told him. 'Aren't you expecting us?'

'No.'

Gaille shrugged. It was ever thus in Egypt. You got clearance from the Supreme Council, the army, the security services, the police, a hundred different bodies; but no one ever bothered to alert the people on the ground. She beckoned Lily across with her fat file of documentation, offered it to him. He looked blankly at a page or two, shook his head. 'I call my boss,' he said, heading inside the cabin. 'Wait here.'

Gaille returned to the Discovery, opened her glove compartment. It was second nature now to carry a selection of goodies for such occasions. She took a bar of chocolate over to the second tourist policeman, peeled back the silver foil, offered him a chunk, took one herself. They smiled companionably at the sweet flavour, the way it melted in their mouths. Gaille handed him the rest of the bar, motioned for him to share it with his comrade. He nodded and grinned happily.

'Chocolate-bar diplomacy, huh?' murmured Lily.

'It can be a life-saver, believe me.'

The first policeman finished his phone call, made a gesture to indicate that his boss was on his way. They stood around smiling and eating the chocolate as they waited.

'What's going on?' grumbled Stafford. 'Is there a problem?'

'Just Egypt,' Gaille assured him. At last, a truck trundled into view, trailing a cloud of dust. A man jumped down, looking for all the world like an army officer in his beautifully pressed military-green uniform with polished black leather belt and holster. His complexion was unusually soft and pink for Egypt, his hair razor-cut, his moustache silky. Yet there was a hardness beneath the surface vanity. 'I am Captain Khaled Osman,' he declared. 'What's this I hear about filming?' He held out his hand for Lily's file, leafed through it, his frown growing. 'No one tells me about this,' he complained. 'Why does no one tell me?'

'It's all in order,' said Gaille.

'Wait here.' He marched inside the guardhouse, made a phone call of his own that rapidly became heated. He came back out, beckoned to Gaille. 'Where exactly you want to film?' he asked.

Gaille took back the file, flipped through for the shooting schedule. It listed every major site in Amarna, including the boundary stele, the workmen's village, the Northern Palace, the Southern Tombs and the Royal Tomb. 'You really expect to film all these in one day?' she murmured to Lily.

Lily shook her head. 'We started getting permissions before Charles had finished his script. We applied for everything, just in case. All we actually need is the boundary stele, the Northern Palace and the Royal Tomb.'

'Where in the Royal Tomb?' demanded Captain Khaled.

'Just the mouth and the burial chamber.'

He squinted unhappily, but seemed to accept it. 'You will need an escort,' he declared, thrusting the file back at her. 'Nasser and I will come with you.'

Gaille and Lily shared a glance. The last thing they wanted was this man treading on their heels all day. 'That's very kind,' said Gaille, 'but I'm sure we'll be—'

'We come with you,' said Khaled.

Gaille forced a smile. 'That's very kind,' she said.

II

Knox lay petrified in his hospital bed, waiting for the intruder to reappear, grab his pillow, finish what he'd started. But the seconds ticked by and nothing happened. He must have left already. It was a limited comfort, however. Someone wanted him dead, and they knew where to find him too. He needed to get away.

The adrenaline burst had given him a little strength. He moved his right leg to the edge of his bed, let it drop heavily over the side. He waited till he was stable, moved his left leg to join it. It dragged his thighs with it, his backside, then his whole body went crashing to the floor, ripping his catheter free, the IV stand wobbling but remaining upright. He lay there winded, half-expecting the door to fly open. But no one came in. His clothes were on the chest of drawers. He crawled laboriously over, grabbed them down, torn and stained with soot and oil, yet still less conspicuous than a hospital gown. He pulled on his jeans, his shirt, his black jersey. Using the iron bed-frame, he hauled himself to his feet. A dizzying rush of blood, he had to fight past the urge to faint. He let go of the bed-frame, staggered across the room to the door. A moment to compose himself. A deep breath. He opened the door. Morning sun blurred on the facing window. He used the wall to hold himself up as he went out.

'Hey!'

Knox glanced left. The policeman was smoking by an open window. He flicked the cigarette away, folded his arms, assumed a stern expression, evidently expecting that to be enough to bring Knox to heel. But Knox turned the other way instead, stumbled through swing doors into a stair-well, clutching the banister tight as he staggered down a flight.

'Hey!' cried the policeman, from the swing doors. 'Come back!'

Knox lurched out onto an identical corridor, a porter leaning against the wall, warming his hands around a glass of *chai*. He heard the policeman shouting, set down his glass, began striding towards Knox. A door to Knox's left. Locked. Across the corridor to the windows, opened them, looked out. A cement mixer below, a pyramid of sand. He hauled himself onto the windowsill, tipped himself out, just as the policeman grabbed his ankle. Gravity ripped him free, he turned his shoulder, hitting the side of the sand heap, bouncing out onto the driveway, a car swerving around him, the driver shouting and shaking her fist.

He picked himself up, hobbled out past the deserted guard-post onto the road. A lorry forced him back against the wall. A taxi-driver tooted. Knox waved him over, pulled open the rear door, collapsed inside, just as the policeman ran out onto the road.

'You have money?' asked the driver.

Knox's tongue felt as huge and clumsy as a

balloon in his mouth. He couldn't form the words. He searched his pockets instead, found his wallet, produced two tattered banknotes from it. The driver nodded and pulled away, leaving the policeman shouting vainly in their wake. 'Where?' he asked.

The question took Knox by surprise. His only concern had been getting away. But he had questions that needed urgent answers: about this mysterious crash that had put him in hospital, the stranger who'd tried to kill him. His last clear memory was meeting his French friend Augustin for a coffee. Maybe he'd know something. He mumbled his address to the driver, then collapsed exhausted across the rear seats.

III

'Do you have to stand there?' complained Stafford. 'You're in my eye-line.'

Gaille looked helplessly around. Lily had already taken her footage of the boundary stele itself, and now Stafford was setting up the camera to film himself against the desert backdrop, leaving her a choice of standing in his eye-line or actually in shot.

'Come with me,' said Lily, gesturing at a thin track that led up the slope. 'I've done my bit.'

The steep path was treacherous with loose shale, but they soon emerged onto a hilltop plateau with a magnificent view over the bleak sandstone plain to the thin ribbon of vegetation that shielded the Nile.

'Christ!' muttered Lily. 'Imagine living here.'

'Wait till midday,' agreed Gaille. 'Or come back during summer. You wouldn't build a prison here.'

'So why did Akhenaten choose it? I mean there must have been more to it than this sun rising between the cliffs business.'

'Amarna was virgin soil,' said Gaille. 'Never consecrated to any other god. Maybe that was important. And you must remember that Egypt was originally a fusion of two lands, Upper and Lower Egypt, always vying for the ascendancy. This is effectively the border between the two, so maybe Akhenaten thought it a pragmatic place to rule from. Though there are other theories too.'

'Such as?'

Gaille pointed north, to where the crescent of cliffs rejoined the Nile. 'That's where Akhenaten built his own palace. It's got plenty of natural shade, yet it's also close enough to the Nile to have beautiful gardens and pools. And whenever he had business in the main part of Amarna, he rode in on his chariot with soldiers running alongside to shade him from the sun.'

'All right for some.'

'Quite. There were hundreds and hundreds of offering tables in the main Aten temple. Each one would have been piled high with meat and fruit and vegetables during ceremonies. Yet the human remains in the cemeteries here show clear signs of anaemia and malnutrition. And then there's a famous letter from an Assyrian king called Ashuruballit. "Why do you keep my messengers standing in the open sun? They'll die in the open sun. If the king enjoys standing in the open sun, then let him do so by all means. But, really, why should my people suffer? They will be killed."'

Lily frowned. 'You think he was a sadist?'

'I think it's possible. I mean, imagine your boss is right, that Akhenaten suffered from some dreadful disease. It isn't hard to see him taking pleasure in the suffering of others, is it?'

'No.'

'But the thing is, I don't know, not for sure. No one does. Not me, not Fatima, not your boss. We simply don't have enough evidence. You should try to find some way to make your viewers understand that. Everything in your programme will be best guesses, not fact. *Everything*.'

Lily squinted shrewdly. 'Is this about what Fatima told us last night?'

'What do you mean?'

'Those *talatat* showing Akhenaten without

genitalia. You're not comfortable about them, are you? That's why you went to bed.'

Gaille could feel herself blushing. 'I just think it's too early to be sure one way or the other.'

'Then why did she tell us?'

'This is a wonderful part of Egypt. The people are enchanting, the history is magical, but hardly anyone ever comes here. Fatima wants to change that.'

'And we're the bait?'

'I wouldn't put it quite that bluntly.'

'It's fine,' grinned Lily. 'Actually, I'm glad. I'd like the programme to do something good.'

'Thank you.'

Lily nodded. 'Can I ask you a really stupid question? It's been bugging me ever since we got down here, but I haven't dared ask.'

'Of course.'

'It's about pronunciation. I mean, the Ancient Egyptian alphabet didn't have vowels, right? So how do you know how all these names like Akhenaten and Nefertiti were pronounced?'

'That's anything but stupid,' smiled Gaille. 'The truth is, we don't, not for sure. But we do have some good clues from other languages, particularly Coptic.'

'Coptic?' frowned Lily. 'I thought Coptic was a church?'

'It is,' agreed Gaille. 'It all goes back to Alexander

the Great's conquest of Egypt. He introduced Greek as the language of administration, but all the people still spoke Egyptian, of course, so the scribes gradually developed the habit of writing down Egyptian speech phonetically with the Greek alphabet, which *did* have vowels. That eventually became Coptic, which in turn became the language of early Christianity here, and the name stuck. So whenever we find an Egyptian word written in Coptic, we get a very good idea of its original pronunciation. Not perfect, of course, particularly for the Amarna era, which finished over a thousand years before Alexander. Our best guesses for that actually come from Akkadian cuneiform rather than Coptic; and Akkadian is a bastard, believe me. That's why Akhenaten's name has been transcribed in so many different ways over the years. The Victorians actually knew him as Khu-en-aten or Ken-hu-aten, but recently we've . . .' She broke off, put her palm flat upon her belly, her breath suddenly coming hot and fast.

'What is it?' asked Lily anxiously.

'Nothing. Just a little turn, that's all.'

'This wretched sun.'

'Yes.' She gathered herself, found a smile. 'Would you mind terribly if I went back to the car, sat down for a bit?'

'Of course not. You want me to come with you?'

'Thanks, but I'll be fine.' Her legs were unsteady

as she made her way down the path to where the Discovery was parked. The tourist policemen were dozing in the front of their truck. She took Stafford's book from the dashboard, sat sideways on the driver's seat, the dark synthetic fabric feeling gluey from the sun. She flipped through the pages, found what she was looking for.

Yes. Just as she remembered.

But it couldn't be. It *couldn't* be. Could it?

IV

The moment the IV stand had crashed to the floor, Peterson had known his opportunity was gone: the best he could hope for was to get out unseen. He'd hidden behind the door as the policeman had looked in, had slipped out when he'd gone hunting for a nurse, through the swing doors at the end of the corridor, down two floors and out through a fire exit. Then he'd sat in his Toyota, taking a few moments to gather himself, think things through.

He prided himself on his strength of character, Peterson. On his ability to hold his nerve. But he undeniably felt the pressure right now. Knox was sure to blab about the intruder in his room. Even if he didn't remember yesterday's events, he'd have no trouble describing his assailant, and Farooq would make the link in a heartbeat. Straight-out denial wouldn't save Peterson. He needed an alibi. He needed to get back to the dig.

A window on the first floor opened at that moment. He looked up in time to see Knox hauling himself out, tumbling onto the sand pile beneath, then scrambling to his feet and staggering out onto the road.

A huge shiver ran through Peterson. He felt overwhelmed by a sense of privilege. God had wanted him to see this. It followed that He still had work for Peterson to do. He knew in his heart what it was too, and he accepted his mission without hesitation.

He put the Toyota into gear, followed Knox out onto the road, watched him collapse into a taxi. He followed the taxi east across Alexandria until it pulled up outside a tall grey block of flats. Knox climbed unsteadily out, vanished inside. Peterson found a place to park then went to check the names on the buzzers. An Augustin Pascal lived on the sixth floor. A man of that name was Alexandria's most celebrated underwater archaeologist. Surely it was him Knox had gone to see. The lift doors opened. Two women emerged chattering into the lobby. Peterson couldn't afford to be seen. He ducked his head and hurried back to his Toyota to await the opportunity he was certain his Lord would provide.

EIGHTEEN

I

Lily watched curiously as Gaille walked down to the Discovery. The way she grabbed Stafford's book from the dashboard and flipped avidly through it reminded her that Gaille had also pestered Stafford with questions about the Copper Scroll.

Something was up, she was sure of it.

She made her own way down, approaching quietly from behind, drawing to within a few paces before Gaille heard her, snapping Stafford's book closed, holding it down low as she turned, clumsily trying to hide it. 'Christ!' she said, putting a hand over her heart. 'You gave me a fright.'

'Sorry,' said Lily. 'I didn't mean to.' She put her hand on Gaille's shoulder. 'Are you quite sure you're okay?'

'I'm fine. Please don't worry.'

'How can I not? After all you've done for us.'

'It's nothing. Really.'

Lily allowed herself a mischievous smile. 'It's the Copper Scroll, isn't it?'

Gaille's eyes went wide. 'How did you know?'

'Really, Gaille. We need to play some poker before I leave. Come on. Spill.'

Gaille's eyes flickered anxiously up to Stafford, but the need to confide was evidently too strong. 'You won't tell anyone?' she asked. 'Not until I've had a chance to think through what it means, at least.'

'You have my word,' nodded Lily.

Gaille opened the book, showed her the clusters of Greek letters from the Copper Scroll. 'See these?' she said. 'These first three would have been pronounced something like Ken-Hagh-En.'

'Kenhaghen?' frowned Lily. 'You don't mean . . . as in Akhenaten?'

'Yes. I think I do.'

'But that makes no sense.'

'Tell me about it.' Gaille gave a mirthless laugh. 'But the Copper Scroll is a Jewish document, remember, and you're the ones here doing a programme on Akhenaten as Moses.'

'Jesus!' muttered Lily. She looked up at Stafford. 'I'm sorry, Gaille,' she said. 'You've got to let me tell him.'

She shook her head vigorously. 'He won't thank you.'

'Are you kidding? This is dynamite.'

Gaille held up Stafford's book. 'Haven't you read this? He made his money and his reputation on the back of it, claiming that the Copper Scroll treasures came from the Temple of Solomon. You want to tell him he's got it all wrong, that they really came from here?'

'From *here*?'

'If this really is Akhenaten's name,' nodded Gaille, 'that has to be the implication.'

'But the Copper Scroll was in Hebrew,' protested Lily.

'Yes, but copied from another, older document. Maybe the Essenes translated it when they copied it. After all, if you're right about Akhenaten being Moses, the Essenes would be by far his most likely true heirs.'

'How do you mean?'

'Have you read Akhenaten's poem, the Hymn of the Aten? It outlines his way of thinking. Basically, he divided everything into sunlight and darkness, good and evil. That was exactly how the Essenes viewed the world. They called themselves the Sons of Light and they saw themselves as engaged in a life-or-death struggle against the Sons of Darkness. They practised a form of sun-worship too. They thought of God as the "perfect light" and they prayed to the east every morning, beseeching the sun to rise. They even carried trowels with them to bury their faeces so they wouldn't offend the sun. They used a solar calendar, just like they did here. And Amarna faces twenty degrees south of due east, you know, and Qumran is on *exactly* the same axis.'

'Jesus!' muttered Lily.

'Essene ritual linen was Egyptian, as were their dyes. Their burials were Egyptian. Archaeologists even found an ankh inscribed on a headstone at Qumran, and the ankh was Akhenaten's symbol of life, as you know. They marked up their scrolls with red ink too, a practice only otherwise found in Egypt. Then there's the Copper Scroll itself. Ancient Egyptians sometimes inscribed important documents on copper. No one else did – not as far as I know, at least. And the other Dead Sea Scrolls are absolutely packed with references to the Essenes' spiritual leader, a Messiah-like figure known only as the "Teacher of Righteousness". That's precisely how Akhenaten was known here in Amarna.'

'It's true then. It has to be.'

'Not necessarily. Over a thousand years passed between Amarna and Qumran, remember. And everything I just said is circumstantial. No one's ever found a smoking gun.'

'The Copper Scroll isn't circumstantial,' pointed out Lily.

A few moments' silence. 'No,' admitted Gaille.
'It isn't.'

II

The decorators had been out of Augustin Pascal's
flat for nearly a week now, but they'd left their
distinctive smell behind, that sour cocktail of paint
and solvent. It was most noticeable at this time of
the morning, with the unwelcome intrusion of
another dawn, the way it combined with his low-
wattage acid hangover and the mocking empty
space on the mattress beside him. Two weeks he'd
had this damned bed, and still untested. Something
had gone seriously wrong in his life.

A pounding on his front door. His bastard neighbours were always complaining. He turned onto
his side, muffled his ear with his pillow, waited
for them to fuck off. God, but he felt tired. His
expensive new bed and mattress, his fine linen, his
duck-down pillows. He couldn't remember ever
sleeping so badly or feeling such relentless fatigue.

The pounding continued. With a cry of exasperation, he pushed himself to his feet, pulled on
jeans and a sweatshirt, went to open his door.
'What the fuck . . . ?' he scowled when he saw
Knox. But then he noticed his friend's cuts and
bruises. 'Jesus! What the hell happened?'

'Car crash,' slurred Knox. 'Can't remember.'

Augustin looked at him in horror, turned and strode into his bedroom for his jacket. 'I'm taking you to hospital.'

'No,' said Knox. 'Not safe. A man. He put a pillow over my face.'

'What? Who?'

'Don't know. Too dark.'

'I'm calling the police.'

'No! No police. No doctors. Please. Find out what's going on.'

Augustin shrugged and helped Knox to his sofa, then went to his kitchen, poured them each a glass of water, swallowed his own in one. 'Okay,' he said, wiping his mouth. 'From the beginning. A car crash. Where?'

Knox shook his head. 'Can't remember. Last thing I remember was coffee with you.'

'But that was the day before yesterday!' protested Augustin. 'Do you have any receipts? Any way to work out your movements?'

'No.'

'How about your mobile? See who you've called.'

Knox patted his pockets expressively. 'Lost.'

'Email, then.' He helped Knox to his breakfast table, set up his laptop, dialled up a connection. Knox logged into his account, found incoming from Gaille.

Hi Daniel,
I've attached your Therapeutae photos, the ones
I could make anything of, at least. The others
were too badly lit or blurred for the short time
I had, but I'll keep working. Where did you
take them? Are you up to no good again? I'm
dying to hear. I'm on taxi-duty in Amarna today
but I'll call tonight.
I miss you too.
All my love, Gaille.

Augustin's heart thumped as he read the message; he felt the blood draining from his face. 'Everything okay?' asked Knox, looking curiously at him.

'Therapeutae photos?' said Augustin. 'Where the hell did you take Therapeutae photos?'

'How should I know?' retorted Knox. 'Concussion, remember?'

Augustin nodded. 'Then download these damned photos, will you? This is getting interesting.'

III

The appendices of Stafford's book included full transcriptions and translations of the Copper Scroll. Gaille and Lily read the translation together. 'How much did a talent weigh, exactly?' asked Lily.

'It varied from place to place,' replied Gaille. 'Anywhere from twenty to forty kilos.'

'But here's a cache of nine hundred talents,' protested Lily. 'That would be eighteen thousand kilos of gold. That's not possible, surely.'

Gaille frowned. Lily was right. The quantities were simply unbelievable. She checked the transcription of the original Hebrew. 'Look,' she said. 'The weights are designated by the letter "k". That's been translated as talents, because talents were used by the Jews and in the Bible. But if this was Akhenaten, and the treasure came from Egypt, it would surely have been designated in Eighteenth Dynasty units of weight, and they didn't use talents, not then, not for gold. They used something called a kite, which was denominated by the letter "k". And a kite was just a fraction of a talent, only about ten or twelve grams.'

'So these numbers would make more sense?'

'Much more. I mean, it would still make for a huge amount of gold, but plausible, you know. And look at this numbering system. These slashes, this figure ten. That's classic Eighteenth Dynasty.'

Lily took a step back, shook her head. 'But why would Akhenaten's followers bury their gold? Why not take it with them?'

'Because they couldn't,' said Gaille. 'There was a massive reaction after Akhenaten's death, remember. The traditionalists took back over, and they stamped down hard. Most Atenists recanted and moved to Thebes, but not all of them. If you're right about them being the Jews, Exodus says they did a moonlight flit. And you can't take this much bullion with you on a moonlight flit, it would slow you down too much.'

'So they buried it,' said Lily. 'And wrote down the hiding places on a copper scroll.'

'They wouldn't have been too worried,' nodded Gaille. 'After all, this was the One True God's home on earth, and they were fervent believers. It followed that they'd soon be back, triumphant. But of course it didn't happen that way. They fled Egypt altogether, settled in Canaan, convinced themselves that was their Promised Land. And when their original Copper Scroll was in danger from oxidation, or perhaps when they couldn't read Egyptian any more, they made a copy, only in Hebrew this time. And maybe another copy after that. And somehow it ended up in Qumran.' She frowned at a thought. 'You've heard about the End of Days, right? The great battle at Meggido?'

'Armageddon,' said Lily.

'Exactly. Afterwards, God is supposed to reign from a New Jerusalem, a city described in Ezekiel and the Book of Revelations. They found a different "New Jerusalem" scroll at Qumran. Six copies of it, in fact, which suggests it meant a lot to the Essenes. The city's layout is given in precise detail. Size, orientation, roads, houses, temples, water, everything. And it maps onto one particular ancient city with quite startling accuracy.'

'Which city?' asked Lily, though she must have suspected the answer.

'This one,' replied Gaille, spreading her hands. 'Amarna.'

IV

Knox clicked through Gaille's photographs in stunned silence. A half-excavated grave, a statuette of Harpocrates, catacombs, mummified human remains, a box of severed human ears. 'Good Christ!' he muttered, when he brought up the mosaic.

Augustin tapped the screen. 'You know what this reminds me of?'

'What?'

'Ever heard of Eliphas Lévi? A French occultist, like Aleister Crowley, only earlier. He created a famous image of an obscure Templar deity called Baphomet that became the model for modern iconography of the Devil. It showed him in this same posture, legs crossed, right hand pointing up. And he had the same look too. That long chin, those stretched eyes, those accentuated cheekbones. See what I'm saying?'

'Slow down a bit,' said Knox, gesturing at his banged-up forehead.

'No one's quite sure where Baphomet came from,' nodded Augustin. 'Some claim his name was a corruption of Mahomet. Others that it came from the Greek *Baphe Meti*, baptism of wisdom. But there's another theory, based on the Atbash cipher, a Jewish transliteration code that swaps A for Z, B for Y and so on.'

'I know it,' said Knox. 'The Essenes used it.'

'Exactly. Which makes sense if this place belonged to the Therapeutae. Anyway, if you put Baphomet through the Atbash, you get Sophia, Greek goddess of wisdom, firstborn of God. Sophia was female, of course, but Lévi made Baphomet a hermaphrodite with breasts, rather like the figure in the mosaic.'

Knox peered closer. He hadn't picked it up before, but Augustin was right. The figure in the mosaic looked masculine, yet was clearly depicted with breasts.

'Hermaphrodites were sacred back then,' said Augustin. 'The Greeks considered them *theoeides*, divine of form. The Orphics believed that the universe began when Eros hatched as an hermaphrodite from an egg. After all, it's easier to imagine that *one* thing came out of the void, rather than multiple things. And when everything starts from one thing, that one thing must be both male and female.'

'Like Atum,' said Knox. In Egyptian mythology, Atum had arisen from the primordial soup, created only by himself. Feeling lonely, he'd masturbated into his hand, a representation of the female reproductive organs, giving birth to Shu and Tefnut, beginning the cascade of life.

'Precisely. In fact, that's almost certainly where the Orphics got the idea from, though divine hermaphrodites crop up everywhere. Hebraic angels were hermaphroditic, did you know? And Qabbala souls are just like that famous wheel in Plato, hermaphrodites divided into their male and female aspects before entering the world, fated to search the earth for their other half. Even Adam was an hermaphrodite, according to some traditions. "Male and female He created them, and He called their name Adam." That was what Jesus was talking about when he said: "Therefore now are they not two, but one flesh." And Gnosticism is full of it. It's even in the *Sophia* itself, now that I think of it.'

'How do you know all this stuff?'

'I wrote a piece for one of the papers a couple of years back. They lap up this kind of shit. I got most of it from Kostas.'

Knox nodded. Kostas was an elderly Greek

friend of theirs, a font of knowledge on the Gnostics and Alexandria's church fathers. 'Maybe we should give him a call.'

'Let's see what else we have first.' He took control of the mouse, clicked through the remaining photographs. Heavenly bodies on the ceiling, young men and women kneeling on dust sheets cleaning walls. A mural of a figure in blue kneeling before two men at the mouth of a cave, the Greek subscript just about legible. Augustin zoomed in then squinted at the screen. '"*Son of David, have mercy on me*",' he translated. 'Mean anything to you?'

'No.' Knox sat back. 'Have you seen any of this before?'

'No.'

'And you would have, yes? I mean, if a reputable crew had found anything like this round here, you'd know, right? Even if they'd kept it secret from the *hoi polloi* like me, you'd have heard about it?'

'I'd like to think so,' said Augustin. 'But this is Egypt, remember. Maybe I should give Omar a call.'

'Good idea.'

There was no answer on Omar's mobile. Augustin tried his office instead. Knox watched in puzzlement as he turned pale, his expression increasingly bleak. 'What is it?' he asked.

Augustin ended the call, turned dazed to Knox. 'Omar's dead,' he said.

'*What?*'

'And they're saying that you killed him.'

NINETEEN

I

'Why are you looking at me like that?' asked Knox, horrified. 'You don't think . . . you *can't* think I killed Omar?'

Augustin put his hand on Knox's shoulder. 'Of course not, my friend. But we must face facts. Omar's dead. And you said yourself that you were in a car crash, you can't remember anything about it.' He grabbed his jacket, pocketed his wallet, mobile and keys. 'I'll go to the hospital and the SCA, see what I can find out. You stay here. Get some rest. That's often the best way to get your memory back. And don't worry. We'll sort this out.' And he pulled the door closed behind him, locking it on the latch.

II

Lily looked a little dizzily down at the ground beneath her feet. 'You don't suppose . . . I mean, it's not possible that any of these treasures are still here?'

'I doubt it,' said Gaille. 'This place has been pretty well searched over the years. Nothing much has been found. Some Nefertiti jewellery back in the eighteen hundreds. Some bronze temple vessels. I guess they might have been part of it. And there was something called the Crock of Gold too, a jar half-filled with ingots. They used to make them by digging grooves in the sand with their finger, then pouring molten gold into them to set. I've always thought that was most likely someone's life-savings or a goldsmith's stash of raw material, but I suppose it could be part of this.'

'Nothing else?'

'Not that I know of. But then you wouldn't expect to find much. Remember, this whole city was completely dismantled after Akhenaten died.' Gaille gave a dry laugh. 'In fact, maybe that's *why* it was dismantled, not simply demolished or abandoned. Think about it. If the new authorities realised what the Atenists had done, maybe because they found a cache or two, or because someone talked . . .'

Lily nodded vigorously. 'They'd have taken the place apart brick by brick until they'd found the lot.' She touched Stafford's book. 'Does it say where these things were buried?'

Sunlight glared upon the white paper. They turned their backs until it was in shadow. 'In the fortress in the Vale of Achor,' murmured Gaille. 'Forty cubits under the eastern steps. In the Sepulchral Monument. In the third course of stones. In the Great Cistern in the Court of the Peristyle, concealed in a hole in the floor.'

Lily wrinkled her nose. 'Pretty vague, isn't it?'

'You'd expect it to be,' replied Gaille. 'If we're right, the Atenists would have believed their eviction only a temporary setback. They didn't need precise directions, only an *aide-mémoire*.'

'What about these place names? Secacah, Mount Gezirim, the Vale of Achor?'

'They're all near Jerusalem,' admitted Gaille. 'But maybe that's not so surprising, either. I mean, if our theory's right, this is at least a double translation. Egyptian into Hebrew then Hebrew into English. And these places would only originally have been designated by a series of consonants, because neither Egyptian nor Hebrew had vowels. So when the translators came across place names that didn't quite fit their preconceptions, wouldn't it have been natural for them to tweak them until they did? I mean, take the Royal Wadi here. It used to be known as "Vale of the Horizon", or "Vale of Akhet" in Egyptian. Is it really too great a stretch to imagine that being translated as the Vale of Achor? Or that Secacah might originally have been Saqqara?'

'I thought Saqqara was near Cairo?'

'Yes, but it got its name from Sokar, a god of the dead worshipped throughout Egypt. Burial grounds were often—'

Footsteps crunched the crusted sand behind her. She snapped the book closed, whirled around to see Stafford approaching, camera bags hoisted over his shoulder. 'Can't put it down, eh?' he asked complacently.

'No,' agreed Gaille. 'It's quite extraordinary.'

'That's why I wrote it.' He checked his watch, nodded at the Discovery. 'Whenever you're ready,' he said, heaving the camera onto the back seat. 'We are on a schedule, you know.'

III

Peterson was still on watch outside Augustin Pascal's apartment block when a pair of sixth-floor balcony doors opened abruptly and Knox walked out, looking weary and dismayed, as though he'd just had bad news. The building's front doors banged open a few moments later and a man in jeans and a leather jacket emerged. Pascal. It had to be. Pascal took a deep drag from his cigarette, flicked it away across the concrete, then straddled a black-and-chrome motorbike, raising an arm in acknowledgement to Knox as he pulled away.

Knox leaned far out over the balcony railing to wave him off. Watching him, Peterson experienced a most intense waking dream: Knox overbalancing, trying vainly to claw himself back, plunging to his death. Such visions weren't new to Peterson. He took them with great seriousness. Faithless people and the weak of spirit considered prayer as their way to beseech the Lord to give them things they coveted. But true prayer wasn't like that. True prayer was how the faithful found out what the Lord wanted from them.

A man overwrought by the death of a close friend, a death for which he blamed himself. Yes. People would understand if such a man threw himself to his own destruction.

He waited for Knox to go back inside the apartment, then got out of his Toyota and walked calmly over to the front doors.

He always felt calm when he had the Lord's work to do.

IV

'I thought you people weren't in a rush,' remarked the pathologist, leading Naguib through gloomy hospital corridors to his small office.

'Is that what you heard?'

'Yes. That's what I heard.'

Naguib shrugged. 'My boss thinks this isn't the best moment for an investigation like this.'

'You don't agree with him?'

'I have a daughter.'

The pathologist nodded seriously. 'So do I.'

'Have you . . . begun yet?'

'She's scheduled for this afternoon. I could bring her forward if you wish.'

'I'd be grateful.'

'There is one thing,' said the pathologist. 'Not related to cause of death, but you may find it interesting.'

'Yes?'

'My assistant found it while he was bringing her in. A pouch on a string around her neck.'

'A pouch?' frowned Naguib. 'Anything inside?'

'A small statuette,' nodded the pathologist. 'You can take it with you if you like.'

TWENTY

I

Knox caught a whiff of himself as he came in from the balcony. Not a pleasant experience. He went into the bathroom, stripped off. His bandages were looking tired and grey, much how he felt. He washed around them with soap and a flannel, flinching every few moments, less from pain so much as from the dreadful news about Omar.

He went back out. He'd slept here a hundred times, after late nights putting the world to rights, and had never thought twice about borrowing a clean shirt in the morning. But Augustin's bedroom door was closed. And now that Knox thought about it, he recalled how Augustin had stopped on his way out of the apartment, turned back, vanished into his room for a minute, and how he'd closed his door carefully again after he'd emerged.

So maybe he had someone in there. He often did. And while Augustin wasn't coy about such things, maybe the person in there was.

Knox hesitated, unwilling to intrude. But then he remembered how bad his shirt had smelled. No way was he putting *that* back on. He knocked gently. No answer. He knocked louder, called out. Still nothing. He opened the door a short way, peeked inside, pushed it wide open and stood there in surprise. Augustin's flat had always been a tip, particularly his bedroom. Somewhere to bring women back to, as he put it, not somewhere they'd want to stay. It wasn't like that any more. Morning sunlight poured through dazzling clean windows onto deep-pile maroon carpet and a gleaming new brass, king-sized bed. The walls had been stripped of their ragged wallpaper, beautifully refinished and painted royal blue. Lithographs of Egypt's great monuments on the walls. Cornices, skirting and ceiling glowing white. A fitted wardrobe of gleaming mahogany. A matching dressing table and chair. And now that he'd noticed the bedroom, he belatedly realized the main room had been redecorated and re-carpeted too, though less extravagantly. He'd simply been too disorientated to notice before.

He opened the wardrobe. *Bloody hell!* Jackets and crisply ironed shirts on wooden hangers. Shelves of neatly folded underclothes. He flipped through a stack of T-shirts, spied the corner of a purple folder. His heartbeat instantly began to accelerate. He knew instinctively that this was why Augustin had come in here, to hide this. He knew too that he shouldn't look, yet also that he was going to. He took the folder to the window, opened the flap. There were photographs inside. He pulled them out, leafed through them in gathering disbelief, a knot tugging tight in the pit of his stomach as he wondered what it meant. But it was obvious what it meant, and there was nothing to be done about it, not now at least, except to return the photographs to the folder, replace them as he'd found them.

He still needed a fresh shirt, so he peeled one from its hanger, hurried out, closed the door behind him. Then he sat at the kitchen table, brooding on what he'd just discovered, the uncomfortable realization that perhaps he couldn't entirely trust his closest friend any more.

II

Farooq arrived at his desk to find Salem standing there, bleary-eyed from his night's sentry-duty outside Knox's hospital room. 'Yes?' asked Farooq.

'He escaped, boss,' mumbled Salem.

'Escaped?' said Farooq icily. 'What do you mean, escaped?'

'He left his room. He jumped out a window. He got into a taxi.'

'And you just let him?'

Salem pulled a face, as if he was about to cry. 'How could I know he'd jump out a window?'

Farooq waved his hand angrily to dismiss him. But in truth, he felt excited rather than dismayed. Vindicated. His instincts had proved right. Car-crash victims didn't flee hospitals for no reason, not even Egyptian ones. They certainly didn't leap out of windows. Only a man with blood on his hands would go to such lengths.

He sat back in his chair, joints creaking beneath the strain, considered what he knew. An archae-ological dig. An unannounced visit by the SCA. A return visit under cover of darkness. A Jeep crashed in a ditch. One man dead. An important man too. He bit a knuckle in thought. Was it possible there was something on Peterson's site? Something *valuable*? It would certainly help explain things, including his strong sense that it wasn't just Knox who was up to no good, but Peterson too.

He pushed himself to his feet, grabbed his car keys. He needed to go check out this site for himself. But then he hesitated. He had no idea what to look for, after all. And if Peterson did have anything to hide, he'd no doubt try to bury it beneath mounds of jargon. Farooq loathed jargon. It always made him feel uneducated.

He checked his watch. He should go visit the SCA anyway, notify them of the crash, try to find out more about Tawfiq and Knox, why they'd gone to Borg el-Arab in the first place. And maybe, if he asked nicely, they'd lend him an archaeologist to go out there with him.

III

The high sandstone walls of the Royal Wadi made little impression on Captain Khaled Osman as Nasser drove them out along the new road to Akhenaten's Royal Tomb. He'd escorted dozens of tourists this way these past few months, but he'd never felt anything like this nervous before. Perhaps it was because these were TV people, and he knew to his own cost what damage TV people could do.

They reached the generator building. Half a million Egyptian pounds they'd just spent on the new generator! *Half a million!* He felt slightly queasy at the thought of all that money as Nasser drove the short distance down the side-spur that housed the tomb and parked next to the Discovery. He opened his door, jumped down. The sun was still low enough that the spur was in shade. He gave a little shiver. There were ghosts in this place. He put a hand on the holster of his Walther and felt a little better.

His childhood friends had bitterly resented the prospect of conscription into the army, being ripped away from home and family. Only Khaled had looked forward to it. He'd never envisaged any other life for himself. He liked the discipline, relished the cold authority of a weapon, savoured the way women looked at a handsome man in uniform. He'd breezed through basic training, had volunteered for Special Forces. Officers had murmured of him as the coming man.

He walked over to the tomb entrance, unlocked the door, pushed it open, revealing the sloped shaft of steps leading down to the burial chamber below, floor-lamps glowing either side with their soft insect buzzing. He watched sourly as the TV people made their way inside and then down.

His army career had died one afternoon in Cairo. A street urchin had spat at his driver window as he'd been escorting his commanding officer to a meeting at the Ministry. It was a level of disrespect that simply couldn't be tolerated, not with his CO watching. A passing tourist had filmed what had happened next, then passed on the footage to some do-gooder journalist who'd tracked the kid down, had filmed him lying wrapped up like some mummy in his bed. His CO had stepped in, saved him from the courts. But he'd had to agree to a transfer out of the army. He'd had to agree to join these wretched tourist police, be stationed here in the arse-end of nowhere. Six months, he'd been promised. Just until the dust settled.

That had been eighteen months ago.

The TV people reached the foot of the steps, crossed the wooden walkway over the sump into the burial chamber. Khaled turned his back on them. What they got up to down there meant nothing to him. It was only up here they needed watching.

Six months ago, Amarna had been struck by the fiercest of storms, as if the end of the world had come. He and his men had driven around the site the morning after. It had been Faisal who'd spotted her, lying face-down on the rocks a little way from here, one arm flung out above her head, the other bent grotesquely back, her matted hair glued with congealed blood to a blue tarpaulin.

Khaled had knelt beside her, touched her cheek. Her skin had been waxy and cool, speckled with sand and grit. He'd heard stories about local kids scouring the wadis after storms, hoping that the rains had broken open some undiscovered tomb, or more realistically looking for fragments of pottery in the sand, the characteristic Amarna-blue gleaming brightly after the spray-clean of violent rain. *Poor stupid thing. To risk so much for so little.*

'Captain!' Nasser had said. 'Look!'

He'd glanced up to see Nasser pointing at a narrow black slash in the sandstone wall high above their heads. His heart had clenched tight as a fist as he'd realized that the girl hadn't died in pursuit of mere pottery fragments after all. She'd been after bigger quarry.

Men chose their destiny in such moments. Or perhaps they simply learned who they truly were. Khaled had known his duty, that he should report this at once to his superiors. It might even win him a reprieve, a return to soldiering. But not for a moment had he considered it. No. He'd walked straight over to the cliff-face and begun to climb.

TWENTY-ONE

I

There was a thin gap between Augustin Pascal's front door and its jamb, enough for Peterson to see it was locked only on the latch, a trivial challenge to anyone with a past like his.

A door slammed below. He took a step back, stood with his hands clasped respectfully in front, as though he'd just knocked and was waiting for an answer. Elevator cables cranked. Doors opened and closed. The lift disgorged its occupant. The block fell silent again.

He put his ear against the door. Nothing. He quietly released the latch with a credit card, slipped inside. The bathroom door was half-closed; he could hear the splash of a man relieving himself. A laptop was set up on the kitchen table, a photograph of the mosaic from his site displayed upon it. He stared stunned at it. No wonder the Lord had brought him here.

The loo flushed. Peterson hurried across to the bedroom, leaving the door a fraction open so that he could see. Knox came out a moment later, wiped his hands on his trousers. He went into the kitchen, sat down with his back to Peterson, clicked the laptop's mouse, brought up an Internet browser.

He was a naturally powerful man, Peterson, and he kept himself fit. He despised people who let any of God's gifts go to waste. He'd been an accomplished wrestler as a young man too. He'd enjoyed pitting his strength and technique against others, the mutual respect of close combat, the way you had to wear down your opponent like a constrictor its prey, the tautness and ache of stretched muscle, the slick sheen of pressed flesh, faces just inches apart, how that other man became your entire world for those few intense minutes of the bout. Best of all, he'd loved that delicious moment of succumbing, that almost inaudible exhalation when his opponent had known and then accepted his defeat. So he knew he had the raw attributes for the task that faced him now. Yet still he felt nervous. The Devil was a powerful adversary, not one to be taken lightly, and rarely had he sensed his presence so strongly in anyone as in Knox. Besides, even if everything went perfectly, he'd risk at least one moment of exposure. He needed to make sure that should he be seen, he couldn't be recognized.

On the top shelf of the wardrobe, he found a motorcycle helmet. Perfect. He put it on, tightened its chinstrap. The way it reflected his breath sounded strangely like fear. Knox was still absorbed in his laptop. Peterson pushed the door slowly open and crept up quietly behind him.

II

'Was this burial chamber truly built for the man we know as Moses?' Stafford asked rhetorically, as Lily filmed. 'I believe it was.'

Gaille stood quietly outside the burial chamber as he talked, well out of shot and Stafford's eye-line. He had a low tolerance for distraction, a low tolerance for everything.

'No trace of Akhenaten's body was ever found here,' he continued. 'No trace of any body. Think about that. This wonderful burial chamber, yet no one buried here.'

Gaille pursed her lips. Traces of human remains *had* been found here, according to reports, though none had been preserved for analysis. And fragments of a sarcophagus built for Akhenaten had certainly been found, along with numerous *shabtis*, miniature Akhenaten figurines designed to do the menial work in the afterlife so that Akhenaten's own spirit wouldn't have to. Even should Stafford be right about the Jews coming from Amarna, it was hard to accept Akhenaten as Moses. Egyptian society had been fiercely hierarchical. Pharaohs had been obeyed, even heretic pharaohs. While Akhenaten lived, he'd have remained in charge and he'd have had no reason to leave Amarna. On the other hand, she could easily believe he hadn't been buried in this chamber. It would have been too easy a target for vindictive enemies. So maybe they'd taken his body with them, or moved it to the Valley of the Kings, or maybe even somewhere close by.

'So what *did* happen to Akhenaten?' asked Stafford. 'Where did he go? And what about all his followers, his fellow Atenists? Come with me on a marvellous journey, as I reveal for the first time ever the true story of Moses and the birth of the Jewish nation. Join me on my extraordinary Exodus quest.'

A few seconds' silence as Lily panned around the burial chamber, filming the faded gypsum murals. Then she lowered the camera, passed Stafford the headphones, enabling him to review the footage. 'I preferred the first take,' he grunted.

'I told you it was fine.'

'Then let's go back up. Scout our sunset shot.'

'Sunset shot?' asked Gaille.

'From the hill opposite,' nodded Stafford. 'We'll pan around from the tomb mouth to the Royal Wadi. It'll finish this segment off nicely. We start with the sun rising over Amarna, you see.'

'And end with the sun setting on it?'

'Exactly,' nodded Stafford, leading the way up the steps. 'The symbolism, you see.'

'Quite.'

He smiled sourly at her. 'You academics,' he said. 'You're all the same. You'd sell your soul for what I have.' They emerged back out into daylight. He strode across the road to the far side of the wadi without a backward glance, surveyed it for a place to climb.

'Hey! You! Stop!'

Gaille looked around. Captain Khaled Osman was striding belligerently towards Stafford, anger and something like fear in his expression. Stafford decided to ignore him, began to climb, but Khaled grabbed his leg and violently tugged him back. Stafford fell tumbling onto rock, scraping his palms. He stood up, turned incredulously to Gaille. 'Did you see that?' he demanded. 'He put his hands on me.'

'You finish here,' said Khaled. 'Leave.'

'Leave? I'll leave when I'm good and ready.'

'Leave now.'

'You can't do this. We have permission.' He turned to Lily, emerging from the tomb. 'Show him our paperwork.'

Lily glanced at Gaille for some clue of what was going on, but Gaille only shrugged in bewilderment. Lily opened her folder, pulled out several paper-clipped sheets of paper. 'There!' said Stafford, snatching them from her, thrusting them in Khaled's face. 'See?'

Khaled slapped Stafford's hand away. The pages fluttered to the ground like a wounded bird. 'Leave,' he said.

'I don't believe this,' muttered Stafford. 'I don't fucking believe this.'

Lily picked up the pages, flipped through for the authorization to film at the Royal Tomb, and found a wide and deferential smile as she pulled the single sheet out. 'We really do have permission, you know,' she said, offering it back to him.

Khaled's complexion darkened. He took the page from her, tore it into confetti that he flung disdainfully into the air. 'Leave,' he said, putting his hand meaningfully upon his holster. 'All of you. Now.'

Gaille's heart was thumping wildly. 'Let's do as he says,' she murmured, taking Stafford's arm. He scowled but let himself be led back to the Discovery, his bravado punctured. Gaille belted herself in, drove back down the Royal Wadi road and then across Amarna to the car ferry, Khaled and his truck looming like perdition in her rear-view mirror.

III

Knox felt a mild but distinctly illicit thrill as he typed in the web address of Gaille's Digging Diary. He made the occasional visit, curious to know what she was up to. He found it strangely comforting. And this morning, with everything he'd been through, he hankered for that comfort more than usual.

A new thumbnail photograph had been uploaded. Gaille standing outside her room with two of Fatima's Egyptian staff, smiling happily in the sunshine, their friendship and good spirits obvious. He clicked on it; it began to download. He pulled up a second browser while he was waiting, reopened her email.

I miss you too.

That 'too' intrigued him. He'd clearly said it first. It was true enough, of course. It was just that he was surprised he'd said it. Ever since they'd become partners, he'd been scrupulous about not letting his personal feelings affect their professional relationship. Gaille's father had been his mentor after all. His death had left Knox in a strange position. He felt a certain responsibility to her, almost as though he was *in loco parentis*.

The way her hair tumbled when she turned her head. The brush of her fingertips on his forearm as she steered him across the street. There was nothing *in loco parentis* about that.

The photograph finally came up. He was staring at it when he saw a shadowy reflection in the screen, a man in a motorcycle helmet creeping up behind him. He whirled around, but too late. The man grabbed him like a straitjacket, pinioning his arms down by his side. He lashed out with his heels and elbows and the back of his head, but to no effect. The man was too strong for him. He dragged Knox out through the open glass doors onto the concrete balcony, then lifted him bodily and hurled him over the rail and out screaming into space.

TWENTY-TWO

I

Knox threw out his hand as he was flung from Augustin's balcony, instinctively grabbed his assailant's wrist, clung on for dear life, breaking his outward trajectory, falling downwards instead, swinging like a wrecking-ball on the man's arm, crashing numbingly hard into the concrete base of the balcony. The impact knocked the wind out of him, strength from his muscles. He lost grip and tumbled down a storey to land flush on the metal railing of the balcony beneath, his left knee buckling beneath him as he fell outwards again, scrabbling desperately for something to cling to, grabbing a cast-iron stanchion as he whirled past, skin flaying from his palm on the speckled rust, until his wrist crashed into the concrete base and ripped him free once more, yet now swinging inwards far enough to hit the rail beneath and fall onto the balcony itself, the breath once more punched out of his lungs, his whole body bruised and sore, but somehow still alive.

He hobbled to his feet, leaned against the railing, looked up to see his helmeted attacker with his visor up, a glimpse of a compressed fraction of his face provoking a shudder of memory; but he vanished before Knox could quite grasp it, or fix his features in his mind.

He looked around the balcony. A steel shutter stood between him and the main body of the apartment. He tried to work his fingers beneath it to prise it up, but without success. He rattled it, pounded on it, trying to attract attention. No one came. He leaned over the railing once more. The car park below was deserted. He was about to call for help when he thought again. Even if he could get someone's attention, they'd surely only summon the police; and he didn't fancy explaining himself to them right now, not while they still held him responsible for Omar's death. Which left him marooned out here while a stranger in a motorcycle helmet plotted ways to kill him.

II

No one at the hospital was talking, so Augustin headed over to the SCA instead, arrived to find it buzzing with rumour, disoriented by grief. Omar was evidently one of those people only fully appreciated after they're gone. Mansoor, Omar's deputy, was in his cluttered office. 'Terrible business,' he said, shaking his head, looking grey and harried. 'I can't believe Knox had anything to do with it.'

'He didn't.'

'There's a man from the police here who thinks he did.'

'The police!' mocked Augustin. 'What would they know?'

Mansoor narrowed his eyes shrewdly. 'Have you heard something?'

'No.'

'You can trust me, you know.'

'I know,' agreed Augustin. He removed a stack of reports from a chair, sat down. 'But how could I tell you anything? I don't even know what happened. They wouldn't say a damned thing at the hospital.'

'You should talk to this policeman,' suggested Mansoor. 'He'll still be around here somewhere. I promised to go out to Borg el-Arab with him.'

'Borg el-Arab?' frowned Augustin. 'Is that where they crashed?'

'Yes.'

'What the hell were they doing out there?'

'Visiting some training dig apparently.'

'A dig? In Borg?'

Mansoor nodded. 'No one here knows anything about it either. Being administered out of Cairo, apparently.' He went over to his filing cabinet, shifted a boxed aerial-photography kit out of the way to get at a drawer.

'A remote-controlled aircraft,' grunted Augustin, impressed. 'How the hell did you get the budget for that?'

'Rudi lent it to me,' said Mansoor. 'Easier than him shipping it back and forth to Germany every season.' He handed Augustin a dog-eared sheet of paper, the writing so faint that Augustin had to take it to the window to read. Mortimer Griffin. The Reverend Ernest Peterson. The Texas Society of Biblical Archaeologists. An address in Borg el-Arab. Nothing else. But surely it had to be the source of Knox's photographs. 'I'd like to go and see this place for myself,' he murmured.

'Maybe you can,' said Mansoor. 'You've seen how the guys are. My place today is here with them. What if I were to ask this policeman if you could go out there instead of me?'

'Yes,' nodded Augustin. 'What a good idea.'

III

Peterson hurried in from the balcony, aghast that Knox had once again escaped justice. The Devil was working overtime today. The laptop was still open on the kitchen table, reminding Peterson of the urgent need to destroy all Knox's photographs of his site.

There were two browsers open, one showing a photo of a dark-haired young woman with two Egyptian men in *galabayas*, the other an email from a certain Gaille Bonnard, perhaps the woman in the photo. He scanned it quickly, assimilated the implication that she had a set of Knox's photographs. He sat down, typed out a reply.

Dear Gaille, thanks for these. They're terrific. One more thing. Delete all copies, including the originals. Can't explain now. I'll call later. But please do as I say. Delete everything as soon as possible! Before calling me even. Very, very important. Can't stress it too much.
All love, Daniel.

A makeshift solution, but it would have to do. He sent it on its way then deleted her email from Knox's hotmail account, consigning it and all its attachments into oblivion. He was no computer expert, but he'd heard stories about sodomites and other abominators being trapped by images recovered from their hard disks even after they'd thought them deleted. He couldn't risk anyone recovering these, so he unplugged the laptop from its various connections, tucked it under his arm and hurried out.

TWENTY-THREE

I

Captain Khaled Osman stood on the eastern bank of the Nile to watch the car ferry take the Discovery and its TV crew away.

'I don't like this, sir,' said Nasser. 'People are getting too close. We need to shut the place up. We can always go back again once things quieten down.'

Khaled had already come to the same conclusion. With the girl's body having been found, things were too hot. He turned to Nasser. 'You and Faisal have everything you need, right?'

'Already inside, sir,' confirmed Nasser. 'Just give us two hours, no one will ever know it was there.'

The car ferry reached the far bank. The Discovery was a dot that headed up the hill towards the main road, disappeared behind trees. 'Very well, then,' he said. 'We'll do it tonight.'

II

Knox was still trying to prise open the steel balcony shutters when he heard the apartment block's front door slam closed. He looked down over the rail in time to see his assailant, still wearing Augustin's motorcycle helmet, carrying his laptop over to a blue 4x4 in the parking area, too far away for him to make out its licence plate. The man climbed inside before taking off the helmet, giving Knox no chance to see his face. And then he was gone.

Knox turned his attention back to the steel shutter. But he couldn't get through, no matter what he tried. It seemed he was stuck out here until whoever lived here came home. And who could predict how they'd react? They'd almost certainly call the police. He leaned out over the railings. The shutter of the balcony beneath was raised and its glass doors were wide open. He called out. There was no reply. He called louder. Still nothing. He paused for thought. Climbing down to it wouldn't be easy, but he was confident he could manage it safely enough, and it was better than waiting here.

He straddled the railing, turned to face the

building, placing his feet between the stanchions. The breeze didn't feel quite so gentle any more, with nothing between him and the tarmac below. He crouched, grabbed a stanchion in each hand, took a deep breath, then lowered himself, legs kicking air above the drop. His stomach and then his chest scraped on the rough concrete. His chin bumped against it, biceps feeling the strain. He tried to adjust his position, give himself a respite, but his grip slipped and he dropped sharply, shuddering to a halt, hanging there holding desperately onto the base of the two stanchions.

It was at that moment that an overweight woman with silvered hair came out onto the balcony. She saw Knox dangling there, dropped her basket of laundry and began to shriek.

III

Gaille could see the colour rising in Stafford's throat, his fists clenching tighter and tighter in his lap. She found herself leaning away from him in the driver's seat, as if he was a landmine about to go off. But when the detonation finally came, it began more quietly than she'd expected.

'Congratulations,' he said, turning to Lily.

'I'm sorry?'

'For ruining my programme. Congratulations.'

'I don't thinks it's—'

'What the hell am I supposed to do now? Tell me that.'

Gaille said: 'It can't be as bad as—'

'Did I ask your opinion?'

'No.'

'Then shut the fuck up.' He turned back to Lily. 'Well? Your suggestions, please.'

'We'll go on to Assiut,' said Lily. 'I'll make some calls from the hotel. We'll sort it out. We'll come back tomorrow and—'

'We're filming tomorrow,' yelled Stafford, red-faced with anger. 'And then we're on a fucking plane. I've got obligations, you know. I'm expected in America. You want me to cancel my morning shows because you can't do your job properly?'

'I got the permissions,' said Lily defensively. 'Everything was in order.'

'But you didn't arrange it *on the ground*, did you? First rule of going overseas. Arrange it on the ground.'

'I asked to come out. You wouldn't pay my airfare.'

'So it's my fault now, is it? Jesus! I don't believe this!'

'I didn't mean it like that.'

'You're supposed to find ways to sort these things out. That's your job. That's your entire fucking job. That's all I employ you to do.'

'Why not film the sunset here on the west bank?' asked Gaille. 'You'll still get your sunset.'

'But not Amarna. Not the Royal Wadi. Unless you're suggesting that I should perpetrate a fraud upon my public. Is that what you're suggesting?'

'Don't talk to me like that.'

'Don't talk to me like that?' he mocked. 'Who the hell do you think you are?'

'I'm the person driving this car,' replied Gaille. 'And unless you want to walk . . .'

'This is a disaster,' muttered Stafford. 'A fucking disaster.' He turned on Lily again. 'I can't believe I ever hired you. What was I thinking?'

'That's enough,' said Gaille.

'I'm going to warn everyone about you, you know. I'll see to it you never work in television again.'

'That's it!' Gaille pulled into the side, took the keys from the ignition, got out and walked away. Doors opened behind her, she glanced around to see Lily hurrying after her, wiping her wet eyes with the heel of her hand. 'How do you put up with him?' asked Gaille.

'It's my career.'

'Is it worth it?'

'Yes,' said Lily. 'Isn't yours?'

Gaille sighed. It was true enough. She'd put up with plenty in her time. 'How can I help?' she asked.

'Can't you call someone? How about Fatima?'

'She's in hospital.'

'There must be someone. Please.'

Gaille's gaze slid past Lily to Stafford, leaning against the Discovery, glaring at them both. This was how bullies worked, she knew. They made life unbearable for everyone around them until they got their own way. It galled her to do anything to help him out of the mess he'd brought upon himself. 'You've still got your permissions to film, yes? I mean, he only ripped up the one for the Royal Tomb, right?'

'Yes. Why?'

'There is something we could try, I suppose.'

'What?'

'It's a hell of a risk,' said Gaille, already beginning to regret volunteering anything.

'Please, Gaille. I'm begging you. He can ruin my career. He really can. And he will too, just out of vindictiveness. You've seen how he is.'

Gaille sighed. 'Okay. The thing is, there are car ferries every few kilometres along the Nile. Every town has its own. There's another a little south of here. I've used it before when this one was down for repairs. The police don't watch that one.'

'Another ferry?' Lily turned before Gaille could stop her. 'Apparently there's another ferry just south of here,' she told Stafford.

'And I could care less because . . . ?'

'You have permission to film the Southern Tombs,' sighed Gaille. 'That's where many of Akhenaten's nobles were buried.'

'I know what the Southern Tombs are, thank you. I also know I have no need to film them.'

'The thing is, they're out on their own at the southern end of Amarna.'

'So?'

'So if we cross back over the Nile on this other ferry, we should be able to make it there without being spotted. And even if we are stopped, we'll have your authorization to film.'

'Are you stupid or something? I don't want to film the Southern fucking Tombs. I want to film the Royal fucking Tomb.'

'Yes,' said Gaille. 'But once we're there, it's theoretically possible to hike across the hills to the Royal Tomb. It's not that far.'

'*Theoretically* possible?' sneered Stafford. 'What use is that if none of us knows the way?'

Gaille hesitated again. She knew she shouldn't let animosity for this man provoke her into rashness. And yet it did. 'I know the way,' she said.

TWENTY-FOUR

I

The woman stopped shrieking and ran back inside her apartment. Knox's relief didn't last long, however. She reappeared with a kitchen knife, proceeded to hack viciously at his ankles. He tried to hoist himself back up, but he didn't have the grip. He had no choice but to swing away from her and then back in, letting go and landing on her spilled clothes, stumbling forwards onto his hands. She stabbed at his back, the sharp tip piercing through his shirt. He twisted around, holding up his palms submissively, but it did nothing to placate her. He scrambled to his feet, hobbled through her apartment and out her front door.

His ankle was too sore for the stairs. He summoned the elevator. Behind him, the woman was telephoning the police, shouting hysterically for them to come at once. Cables clanked and creaked. The woman came to her front door to yell at him some more, call on her neighbours to save her. Doors opened above and below, people leaned over banisters. The lift arrived. Knox got in, jabbed the button for the ground floor. He limped out of the building, ankle throbbing, left knee clicking ominously. Out on the main road, he waved down a bus, not caring where it was headed, nor that it was already packed. A woman wearing a floral headscarf and sunglasses looked quizzically at him as a police car swept by, siren blazing. Knox ducked his eyes, feeling ridiculously conspicuous.

He got out at the Shallalat Gardens, struggled to the Latin Cemeteries, pushed open the heavy wooden door. An elderly curator was leaning on his broom. Otherwise, the place was deserted. Many of the tombs here had superstructures like shrunken marble temples. Knox found one out of the way, lay down inside with his back to the wall. Then he closed his eyes and cleared his mind, giving his much-abused body some time to rest and heal.

II

Mallawi's Museum of Antiquities consisted of three shabby long halls with high ceilings and low lighting. The curator raised her eyebrows when

Naguib set the figurine from the dead girl's pouch on the glass top of a display case.

'May I?' she asked.

'That's why I brought it here,' said Naguib. He watched her pick it up, turn it in her hands. 'Well?' he asked.

'What do you want to know?'

'What is it? How much is it worth?'

'It's an Amarna-style statuette of Akhenaten in pink limestone. As to what it's worth . . .' She shook her head regretfully. 'Not very much, I'm afraid.'

'Not very much?'

'It's a fake. One of thousands.'

'But it looks old.'

'It *is* old. Many fakes were made sixty or seventy years ago. There was a big market for Amarna antiquities back then. But they're still fakes.'

'How can you be sure?'

'Because all the genuine ones were found decades ago.'

A party of schoolchildren arrived yelling and playing, gleeful to have escaped their classroom prison. Naguib waited until they'd been ushered past by their embarrassed teachers before asking his next question. 'So there are genuine ones?'

'In museums, yes.'

'And you can always tell the difference, can you? I mean, just by looking?'

'No,' she admitted.

'So it's conceivable that one might have been lost? Buried in the sand, say, or in some undiscovered tomb?'

'You'd struggle to convince a buyer of that.'

'I don't have a buyer,' said Naguib tersely. 'What I have is a dead girl who may have been murdered over this. So tell me: how much would a piece like this be worth, if genuine?'

The curator looked down at the figurine with a touch more respect. 'Hard to say. Genuine Amarna artefacts don't often come up for sale.'

'Please. Just a rough idea. In US dollars. A hundred? A thousand? Ten thousand?'

'Oh, more. Much more.'

'More?' swallowed Naguib.

'This wouldn't just be a figurine,' said the woman. 'It would be history. *Amarna* history. People would pay what they must pay. But you'd have to prove it was genuine first.'

'How would I go about that? Are there tests?'

'Of course. Chromatography, spectography. But nothing is conclusive. For every expert who'll tell you one thing, another will say the opposite. Your only real hope is to establish provenance.'

'Provenance?'

'Find this undiscovered tomb of yours. Then we'll believe you.'

Naguib grunted. 'And where should I look for that?'

'In Amarna, certainly. If it was me, I'd check the wadis leading out to the Eastern Desert. A lot of antiquities have been found in them. The storms, you know. They hammer at the cliffs like a million pickaxes. It can still happen that the hidden mouth of an old tomb will simply shear away and its contents wash down into the wadis and then in a great river out into the desert.'

Naguib went a little numb. 'A flash flood,' he said.

'Exactly,' smiled the curator. 'A flash flood.'

III

Augustin waited in Mansoor's office while his friend went off to persuade the policeman to accept a substitute on his trip out to Borg el-Arab. He killed time running an Internet search on the Texas Society of Biblical Archaeologists. It had its own website, group photographs and brief overviews of excavations in Alexandria and Cephallonia. Its 'About Us' page mentioned its affiliation to the UMC, though there was neither link nor explanation. There was, however, a profile of Griffin, surprisingly impressively qualified for so small an organization.

A new search on the Reverend Ernest Peterson returned a huge number of hits. The man was clearly a divisive figure, deplored and feared for his hardline religious views, yet also admired for the hospice, hospital, homeless shelter and rehabilitation centre founded and financed by his ministry. He also financed a private Christian college, the University of the Mission of Christ, presumably the same UMC mentioned on the TSBA website, with faculties of Theology, Creation Science, Law, Political Administration and Archaeology.

Peterson's ministry had its own site. The screen turned dark blue when Augustin clicked the link. A line of white text emerged. '*Thou shalt not lie with mankind as with womankind: it is abomination.*' It faded away. A new one took its place. '*The show of their countenance doth witness against them; and they declare their sin as Sodom, they hide it not. Woe unto their soul! For they have rewarded evil unto themselves.*' A photo of a church appeared, with columns of links either side. The left-hand column was entitled *What Christ said about . . .* with topics such as homosexuality, feminism, adultery, abortion and idolatry beneath, and lists of verses from Deuteronomy, Leviticus, Numbers and other Old Testament books.

The right-hand column bore titles like *The Cancer of Liberalism* and *The Sin of Sodom*. Augustin clicked on *The Abominators Agenda*. An inset screen appeared, Peterson mouthing silently at the camera. He turned on the volume, had to sit back at the torrent of anger and hate that poured forth. He clicked a different link, all by itself, and entitled '*The Face Of Christ*'. Peterson again, but his tone completely different. Emollient. Transcendent. '*You ask how I came to God,*' he said. '*Let me tell you how I came to God. I was a wretched sinner. A thief, a drinker, a man of dishonesty and violence, well known to our police, though still but a youth. And I came to God because one day, my lowest day, in His infinite mercy He sent His Son to bring me to Him. A vision of His Son. And I tell you this: no man can look upon the face of Christ and not believe. And that is the mission God gave me for my time upon this earth: to bring the face of Christ to the whole world. Make it your mission too and together we will surely—*'

The door opened behind him. He looked around to see a policeman standing there. 'Doctor Augustin, yes?'

'Yes.'

'I'm Detective Inspector Farooq. Your colleague Doctor Mansoor suggested you would be good enough to come to Borg el-Arab with me.'

'Yes.'

'Excellent. Are you ready?'

Augustin nodded. He closed down the browser

with a little shudder, got to his feet. 'Let's do it,' he said.

IV

Peterson drove back to the excavation site as quickly as prudence would allow, stopping only to hurl Knox's laptop and mobile phone into the reed-fringed waters of Lake Mariut, watching with satisfaction as they splashed and sank.

Claire came out of the office to greet him. An awkward young woman, all elbows and knees, yet with a certain steeliness too. He'd have done without her if he could, but her medical know-how and fluent Arabic were too useful. 'Are those men okay?' she asked, her arms folded.

'What men?'

'Nathan told me about them last night. He was in a terrible state.'

'They're fine,' Peterson assured her. 'They're in the Lord's hands.'

'What's that supposed to mean?'

'We're all in the Lord's hands, Sister Claire. Or perhaps you think differently?'

'Of course not, Reverend. But I'd still like to—'

'Later, Sister Claire. Later. Right now, I have urgent business with Brother Griffin. Do you know where he is?'

'In the cemetery. But I—'

'Then if you'll excuse me,' he said, striding off.

Griffin must have heard his car, because he met him halfway to the cemetery. 'What the hell happened last night?' he demanded.

'In good time,' said Peterson. 'First, have you done everything I told you to do?'

Griffin nodded. 'You want to see?'

'Indeed, Brother Griffin.'

They visited the emptied magazine, then the shaft. To Peterson's surprise, he had a hard time spotting where it had been, even standing right beside it. 'I suppose it will do,' he said. His greatest worry now was that someone might shoot their mouth off. Specifically, Griffin or Claire. He glanced back towards the office. 'I don't want Claire here should the police or the SCA turn up. Take her back to the hotel. Keep her out of sight.'

'But what will I tell her?'

'Tell her you need to talk to the hotel people about something, and you need a translator.'

'But they speak English at the hotel.'

'Then think of something else,' snapped Peterson. He watched Griffin traipse away, then headed to the cemetery. The authorities were certain to visit sooner or later. His students needed to know what to tell them.

V

Captain Khaled Osman felt uncharacteristically anxious as Nasser drove him and his men out along the Royal Wadi road. He didn't like visiting the tomb before dark, but Faisal had insisted he needed some natural light to work by. It should be safe enough, he told himself. No tourists ever arrived this late; Amarna was simply too big to see in less than half a day. And he'd made it quite clear to the locals that they were not to come down here any more.

They parked behind the generator building. Abdullah walked back a little way along the road to stand sentry just in case, while he, Faisal and Nasser traded their uniforms for old shirts and trousers. It was dirty work, what lay ahead. He'd have let Faisal and Nasser handle it themselves, but he didn't trust them to do good work if they weren't supervised. Besides, he felt the need for one last look.

He belted his holster back on. He felt naked without his Walther, his pride and joy, an unofficial memento of his army days that he'd taken along with an AK-47 and a box of grenades for fishing with. Decent kit too, not like the Egyptian-made pieces-of-shit his men had to put up with. They crossed the drainage channel, picked their way across boulders and scree.

'These damned boots!' muttered Faisal, who always got agitated near where they'd found the girl.

The easiest way to reach the tomb mouth was to walk beyond it, climb the side of the wadi, then cut back across the top to a thin ledge. Faisal led the way. The man was a mountain goat. He reached the mouth, pulled back the sackcloth curtain, invisible from more than a few paces. Dust and grit sprinkled Khaled's hair as he followed him inside. 'How long do you need?' he asked.

'That depends, sir,' said Faisal.

'On what?'

'On how much help I get.'

Khaled stood there uncertainly. There was something about this place that seemed to incite insubordination. 'One last look,' he said, picking up a torch. 'You never know.'

'Sure,' said Faisal. 'You never know.'

Khaled headed along the passage to the burial chamber, still fuming. Who did Faisal think he was? But he put it from his mind in the greater frustration of his failure in this place. Their first visit here, they'd found three statue fragments in the debris, a scarab and a silver amulet. He'd truly believed it was the start of great things. But the finds had dried up, and they'd only fetched a fraction of what he'd hoped because no one believed they were genuine. He hadn't even got enough for them to share anything with his men. It was a paltry return for so much work. Whole sections of ceiling had caved in over the centuries, so that the whole place had been choked with sand and rubble. They couldn't dump it out the mouth, or someone would soon notice, so they'd shifted it from area to area instead, like cleaning house. And all by night, too, their only free time. They'd grown increasingly weary and irritable, yet had never quite been able to give up. That was the cruelty of hope.

There was a sump in front of the burial chamber, just like in the Royal Tomb. So much sand and rubble had fallen down it over the millennia that at first they hadn't even realized it was there. But it was there all right, the full width of the passage. And deep! Once they'd checked everywhere else, they'd turned their attention to it, removing basket after basket, digging ever deeper, until they'd had to bring in a rope ladder to climb down to the foot, and then tie lengths of rope to their baskets so that one of them could stay at the bottom to fill them while the others hauled them to the top for sieving and disposal.

He climbed down the rope ladder for one last look. But his torch lit nothing save their own detritus: empty water bottles, discarded food wrappings, the stub of a candle, a book of matches. Discipline had been an early casualty of failure.

Six metres deep already, and still they hadn't reached the foot! *Six metres!* He shook his head at the absurdity of the ancients. So much effort! And so pointless too.

After all, who on earth needed a sump six metres deep?

TWENTY-FIVE

I

Knox had drifted off into a restorative sleep in the Latin Cemeteries. He woke to footsteps slapping the paving slabs outside. For a moment he feared he was bound to be discovered, but the footsteps passed by without changing cadence. He waited for silence, pushed himself grimacing to his feet, his body stiff. He hobbled out of the cemetery, bought a Menatel card from a general store, then found a secluded phone-kiosk from which to call Augustin.

'*Cedric, mon cher ami!*' boomed Augustin, the moment he recognized Knox's voice.

Knox picked up his cue at once, switched smoothly to French. 'There are people with you?'

'A fine officer of the law. He speaks some English but I think we're okay in French. Hang on a second.' Knox heard some muttering, Augustin's hand clamped over the mouthpiece. Then he came back on. 'We're fine,' he said. 'I just called his mother a fat sow. Not a flicker.'

Knox laughed. 'What are you doing with the police?'

'On our way to Borg.' He gave a quick rundown of what he'd learned about the Texas Society of Biblical Archaeology, their links to UMC, their excavations in Cephallonia. Then Knox filled Augustin in on his mystery assailant, and how he'd made off with his laptop.

'Shit!' exclaimed Augustin. 'I only just bought the damned thing. But you're okay, yes?'

'I'm fine. But I need somewhere to hide out. I thought maybe Kostas. Pick his brains while I'm there. But I can't remember his address.'

'Sharia Muharram Bey. Number fifty-five. Third floor. And tell him I want my copy of Lucretius back. Bastard's had it for months now.'

'Will do,' said Knox.

II

This was the time to visit the desert, the late afternoon sun coaxing sharp contrasts from the same cliffs that had earlier seemed a flat monochrome, tinting the western sky fruit-bowl colours. Gaille cut out past the southern tip of the Amarna cliffs then circled north to the eastern end of the Royal Wadi. She pointed away across the sands. 'The desert road's about five kilometres that way.'

'And it runs all the way down to Assiut, right?' asked Lily.

'Yes.' The car ferries would stop running after dark; they needed to head south on this side of the Nile. She turned into the wadi. There was no sealed road this end, just a rock-strewn floor. Gaille navigated it cautiously, while Stafford sat beside her, his arms pointedly folded, sighing every few seconds, until they reached an impassable barrier of scree.

'I thought you knew the way,' he said.

'You can walk from here. It's straight ahead. Only a couple of kilometres.'

'Two kilometres!'

'Then we'd better set off now, don't you think?' said Lily. 'Unless you don't want this scene any more?' Stafford threw her a caustic look, but got out and strode off down the wadi. 'That's right,' muttered Lily. 'Don't help carry the equipment.'

'What a prick!' said Gaille. 'How do you put up with him?'

'It's just for a couple more days,' said Lily, getting out. She turned back to Gaille, still sitting there. 'Aren't you coming?'

'I'd better stay with the Discovery. Just in case.'

'Sure. I bet this place is just crawling with car thieves.' She tipped her head onto one side. 'Please. I can't take him alone.'

'Fine,' said Gaille, just about managing a smile. She climbed out of the Discovery and locked it behind her.

III

Augustin was growing bored on the drive out to Borg. Farooq was hardly the world's greatest conversationalist. A few blunt questions about Omar and Knox that Augustin had managed to deflect easily enough, then a slump into almost complete silence. He got out his cigarettes, offered them across.

'Thanks,' grunted Farooq, taking one.

Augustin lit his own, passed his lighter to Farooq, then lowered his window, cupping a hand to catch the passing air. A white pick-up was coming towards them, sunlight reflecting off its dusty windscreen in such a way that it was only when they were passing that he saw the driver and his passenger, a young woman with long fair hair, whose eye Augustin caught for the briefest of moments.

They took a sharp right a kilometre further on, headed down a long lane, then turned left over an earthen bridge across an irrigation channel, pulling up to speak to a security guard. They'd just missed Griffin, apparently. That must have been him with the blonde in the pick-up. But Peterson was on site. The guard sent them in to wait by the office. They'd only been there a minute when Peterson arrived. 'Detective Inspector Farooq,' he said. 'An unexpected pleasure. What can we do for you?'

'Just one or two details to clear up. You know Doctor Augustin Pascal?'

'By reputation,' said Peterson.

'He's offered to help me. Explain archaeological terms, that kind of thing.'

'How good of him.'

Farooq nodded, took out his mobile. 'If you gentlemen will excuse me. I need to check in.'

Augustin and Peterson locked gazes as Farooq walked off, sizing each other up, neither backing down. It was a good minute before Farooq came back to join them, looking rather pleased with himself. 'Well,' he said, rubbing his hands vigorously. 'Perhaps we could get started.'

'On what, exactly?' asked Peterson.

'I'd like to speak to your people. Find out what they saw.'

'Of course,' said Peterson. 'Follow me.'

'Thank you,' nodded Farooq, as they set off across the broken ground. 'You told me last night that Knox and Tawfiq visited you yesterday afternoon. That's right, isn't it?'

'Yes.'

'Did they say why?'

'Perhaps you should ask Knox.'

'We will,' promised Farooq. 'The moment we find him.'

'You've lost him?' frowned Peterson. 'How could you have lost him? The man was half dead.'

'Never you mind,' scowled Farooq. 'And I'd like to hear your version anyway.'

'He'd seen some kind of artefact in Alexandria. A jar lid, as I recall. We told him they made jars all around Lake Mariut, so there was no reason to suspect it came from here.'

'And then they left?'

'Yes. We thought no more about it until we had an intruder. In fact, not even then. We had no idea it was them. We just assumed it was some petty thief.'

'I understood this was a training excavation,' murmured Augustin. 'Are you finding things of value here?'

'Not of intrinsic value, no. But the locals don't know that. So there's always a danger they'll trespass and contaminate our data. Surely you appreciate that, Doctor Pascal?'

'So you chased them off.'

'It was just as I told you last night, Detective

Inspector. Nothing has changed.' They reached the cemetery, dusty young excavators exhuming two graves. 'You want to speak to my team,' he said, spreading his hands. 'Well, here they are.'

TWENTY-SIX

I

Gaille's thighs were burning by the time they'd walked along the wadi and climbed the hillside close to the Royal Tomb. They all fell silent without being told, aware that they'd have a terrible time explaining their presence should they meet anyone. But the door of the Royal Tomb was emphatically closed, and the road deserted. Gaille grinned at Lily in unspoken relief.

'We're only just in time,' said Stafford, nodding at the sun, low on the western horizon.

'Then you'd better get started,' suggested Gaille.

'If you'll get out of my eye-line.'

She turned and walked off, not trusting herself to speak. But it wasn't easy to get away. To her left was a deep cleft in the hilltop, as though one of Egypt's gods had attacked it with an axe. And to her right was the cliff's edge itself, and a vertigin-ous drop down to the wadi floor. But at least that way was out of Stafford's line of sight, so she inched as close to it as she dared, saw to her surprise what looked like a ledge a few feet below, a boot-print clearly visible in the dust.

She went a little further along the edge, found a way down onto it. Lily and Stafford were still setting up. They'd be a few minutes yet. Her toes tingled as she started out, but her curiosity proved stronger than her fear of heights, so she steeled herself and pressed on.

II

Kostas always took his own good time answering his front door, blaming either his failing hearing or his failing legs. He took it as a privilege of age to make people wait. But eventually he arrived, patting down his wreath of tangled, snowy hair, producing a pair of half-moon spectacles from his jacket pocket, then peering over the top of them. 'My dear Knox!' he exclaimed. 'What a *delightful* surprise.' But then he blinked and took half a pace back. 'My! You have been in the wars.'

'That bad, is it?' grimaced Knox. 'I couldn't use your bathroom, could I?'

'Of course. Of course. Come in.' Kostas shuffled along his obstacle course of a hallway, using his cane as a white stick to help him navigate between the dusty high stacks of academic tomes and packing chests of exotic artefacts, making the place feel more like a bric-a-brac store than a home. His walls were just as cluttered, a collage of astral charts, lurid occult posters, his own watercolours of herbs and other medicinal plants, framed frontispieces of arcane works and yellowed press clippings of himself in the news.

Knox examined himself in the washbasin mirror. A sight indeed: dried blood on his scalp and forehead, his face haggard, his hair prematurely aged with dust. He lathered up some soap, cleaned himself as best he could. A line of Greek text across the top of the mirror made him smile: NIΨONANOMHMATAMHMONANOΨIN. One of the earliest known palindromes: *Wash your iniquities not just your face*. He dried himself with a hand-towel, turning it an ugly brown, then went back out.

'Well?' asked Kostas impatiently. 'What brings you here in such a state?'

Knox hesitated. It wasn't that easy to explain. 'I don't suppose you're on the Internet, are you?' he asked.

'Sadly, yes,' said Kostas, leading Knox through to his library, where subdued lighting glowed on the burnished leather of innumerable old books.

He opened his bureau to reveal a slimline laptop within. 'One can't do anything without them these days.'

Knox logged on, went to his hotmail account. But, to his dismay, Gaille's email had vanished. That bloody man in his motorcycle helmet must have deleted the photographs. He closed down the browser. 'Looks like I'll just have to tell you,' he said. 'But please bear with me if everything's not entirely clear. I took a bit of a bang on the head.'

'I noticed.'

'It seems I stumbled across some kind of antiquity out near Borg last night. It's being excavated by some biblical archaeologists, and it seems it might have some connection with the Therapeutae. I took some photographs. There was a statuette of Harpocrates. Six severed mummified ears. A mosaic of a figure inside a seven-pointed star that reminded Augustin of a picture of Baphomet by some French guy whose name I can't remember.'

'Eliphas Lévi,' nodded Kostas. 'I know the one.'

'And there was a mural of Dionysus. Another of Priapus. That's about it.'

'What a *fascinating* list,' gloated Kostas, his eyes watering with pleasure. 'You realize of course that the Therapeutae lived out near Borg?'

'Yes.'

'And Harpocrates. The Romans worshipped him as the god of silence, you know, because the

Egyptians depicted him holding a finger to his lips. But in fact that had nothing to do with hush.'

'No,' agreed Knox. It was one of the ways that the Egyptians had indicated youth, like the curled forelock on a prince's forehead.

'His name is actually a corruption of the Egyptian *Har-pa-khared*. Horus the Child. Horus being the falcon-headed god who fused with the sun god Ra to become Ra-Horakthy, rising each morning in the east.'

'I am an Egyptologist,' observed Knox.

'Of course you are, my dear boy. Of course you are. That's why you'll already be aware of the connection between him and Baphomet.'

'What connection?'

'Aleister Crowley's religion of Thelema, of course. Crowley picked up where Eliphas Lévi left off, as you no doubt know. He identified Baphomet as Harpocrates, though to be fair that was mostly due to his extraordinary ignorance. On the other hand, now that I think of it, Harpocrates *was* associated with a particular – and quite fascinating – group of Alexandrian Gnostics.'

'Which group?'

'A cup of tea first, I think,' said Kostas, licking his lips. 'Yes. Tea and cake.'

III

Khaled climbed back up the rope ladder, then contemplated a final visit to the burial chamber. Crossing the sump wasn't a comfortable experience. The only access was on a makeshift bridge of two planks, each just a few centimetres longer than the shaft was wide, and which bowed uncomfortably when you stepped upon them.

It hadn't mattered when they'd first brought them in, for the sump had still been nearly full of rubble, so the fall would only have been a couple of metres. But now, even with a torch, you could scarcely see the foot. Sometimes he had nightmares about tumbling into that great hungry darkness. Yet he hadn't wanted to be the first to suggest they get longer planks. And none of his men had either.

He negotiated the crossing safely, however, entered the burial chamber, high heaps of rubble obscuring much of the walls, completed and plastered but not yet decorated, presumably because the tomb hadn't been—

He froze suddenly. A voice. A man's voice. Coming from above. He listened intently. But now there was only silence. He relaxed, smiling at his foolishness, his heart slowing back down. These ancient tombs! They'd play tricks on your imagination. They'd make you feel—

The voice again. No question this time. He

recognized it too. That damned TV man. He must have come back! He looked in horror up at the ceiling, unnerved by how close he sounded. Maybe he *was* close. There was a cleft in the hilltop above them. And the first time he'd come here, it had been ankle-deep in storm water. So there had to be a fault in the rock. He hurried back across the planks, up the passage to the entrance. Faisal and Nasser had heard the voices too; they'd turned off their lamps, were squatting there by the mouth, sackcloth curtain glowing russet against the setting sun.

'The TV people,' whispered Faisal.

Khaled nodded. 'They'll film and then they'll go.'

'What if they see our truck?'

The other side of the sackcloth, a shoe slithered on shale. Khaled went cold. Faisal sniggered with nerves, clenched his jaw in both hands to stop himself, his eyes blinking maniacally. Khaled quietly unbuttoned his holster and drew his Walther. He aimed at the mouth of the tomb. A sudden sharp vision of home, childhood, the way his mother had boasted of him, all those photographs of him in uniform on her walls. Another scuff on the ledge. A mutter of surprise and then the sackcloth drawing back and the woman Gaille standing there, silhouetted against the sunset.

How quickly a life can turn, thought Khaled

bleakly, as they stared at one another. How suddenly catastrophe can strike. He felt strangely calm, like the one time he'd seen anything approaching action as a soldier, on checkpoint duty in Sinai, waving down a truck laden with timbers and other carpentry supplies, ready to haggle out a small gift of *baksheesh*, glimpsing a gun barrel beneath the tarpaulin. He'd been aware of his bodily reaction then too, the fizz of adrenaline, yet in a bizarrely detached way, watching the scene unfold on TV as much as living it. He'd relished the way his senses had sharpened, data flooding his mind, sharper than it had ever been; hearing breath catch in a throat, seeing the driver glance in his rear-view; feeling the truck lurch slightly as someone reached for their weapon, having all the time in the world to take command, as though they were moving in honey while he alone was free.

But this time it was Gaille who reacted first. She span on her heel, shouting warnings as she fled.

TWENTY-SEVEN

I

Knox took the tray back through to the library, set it down on the low coffee table. He wasn't exactly in the mood for a tea party, but Kostas evidently was, so he tried to master his aches and jitters. He was at least safe here, after all. He poured them each a cup of aromatic pale tea from the silver pot, cut two thin slices of moist chocolate cake. 'You were telling me about Harpocrates and the Gnostics,' he prompted, passing Kostas his plate.

'Yes,' agreed Kostas. He nibbled the end of his cake, washed it down with a decorous sip of tea. 'You see, there was a group of Gnostics actually *called* the Harpocratians. At least, they *may* have been called that, though it's hard to be categorical. They're only referred to once or twice in the sources, you see. And there was another, much better-known group of Gnostics called the *Carpocratians*, founded by an Alexandrian by the name of Carpocrates. So it seems feasible, perhaps even probable, that these two were one and the same.'

'A spelling mistake?'

'It's possible, of course. But our sources were the kind of people to know the difference. So my suspicion has always been that these Carpocratians might have been reputed to worship Harpocrates as well as Christ. That the names were therefore interchangeable, if you like.'

'Is that plausible?'

'Oh, yes,' nodded Kostas vigorously. 'You have to realize that Gnostics weren't Christian in the modern sense. In fact, even grouping them together as Gnostics is really to miss the point, because it implies they had a single way of thinking, whereas in fact each of the sects had its own distinct views, drawn eclectically from Egyptian, Jewish, Greek and other traditions. But the great pioneers of Gnosticism, people like Valentinus, Basilides and Carpocrates, did have certain things in common. For example, they didn't believe Jesus to be the Son of God. Come to that, they didn't believe that the Jewish God was actually the Supreme Being at all, but merely a demiurge, a vicious second-tier creation who mistook himself for the real thing.

How else, after all, could one explain all the horrors of this world?'

'So who *was* the Supreme Being?'

'Ah! Now there's a question!' His eyes were watering freely, his skin flushing. Like many solitary people, Kostas tended to become over-stimulated in company. 'The Gnostics held that it was incapable of description, incapable of even being contemplated, except perhaps in mathematical terms, and only then by the exceptionally enlightened. A very *Einsteinian* God, if you like. And that's where Christ came in, because Gnostics saw him, along with Plato and Aristotle and others, as gifted but essentially ordinary men who'd nursed their divine sparks sufficiently to have glimpsed this truth. But I'm getting away from the point, which is the similarities between Harpocrates and Christ.'

'Such as?'

'Oh my dear Daniel! Where to start? Luxor Temple, perhaps. The nativity reliefs. A newborn pharaoh depicted as Harpocrates. Nothing surprising about that, of course. Pharaohs were the physical incarnations of Horus, so infant pharaohs were by definition Horus-the-child or Harpocrates. But the details of this particular tableau are curious. A mortal woman impregnated by a holy spirit while still a virgin. An annunciation by Thoth, the Egyptian equivalent of the archangel Gabriel. A star leading three wise men from the east, bearing gifts.'

'You're kidding me.'

'I thought you'd enjoy that,' smiled Kostas. 'In fact, the wise men crop up all the time in divine nativity stories, especially among sun-worshippers. An astronomical allegory, of course, like so many religious conceits. The three stars of Orion's belt point towards Sirius, the key to the ancient Egyptian solar calendar and for predicting the annual inundation. Gold, frankincense and myrrh often crop up too. Man's very first possessions, you know, given by God to console Adam and Eve after their expulsion from Eden. Seventy rods of gold, if my memory serves.'

'Rods?' frowned Knox. A rod was a unit of distance, not of weight.

'According to *The Book of Adam and Eve*,' nodded Kostas. 'Or was it *The Book of the Cave of Treasures*?' He sighed wistfully. 'My memory, you know.'

'I don't think it was *The Cave of Treasures*,' said Knox, who'd wasted countless glorious summer afternoons in a forlorn effort to master Syriac by studying that particular text, about a cave in which Adam, Abraham, Noah, Moses and most of the other leading Jewish patriarchs had supposedly been buried. 'Anything else?'

'There are some startling parallels between

Horus's mother Isis and Mary the mother of Christ, of course. You must be aware of those. And Harpocrates was believed to have been born on a mountain, the hieroglyph for which was the same as that for a manger. Ancient Egyptians used to celebrate his birth by parading a manger through their streets. Easier than carrying a mountain.'

'Ah.'

Kostas nodded. 'The Gospel of Matthew claims that the Holy Family fled to Egypt when Jesus was a child to avoid the Massacre of the Innocents. According to Saint Edward the Martyr, they got as far south as Hermopolis, city of Thoth. Which brings us neatly full circle, for Hermopolis was directly across the Nile from the city founded by this pharaoh I mentioned, the one in those Luxor reliefs.'

'You mean Amarna?' asked Knox. 'The pharaoh was Akhenaten?'

'Indeed,' agreed Kostas, allowing himself a little chuckle. 'Just think of it! The New Testament accounts of Christ's Nativity borrowed from the birth of a heretic Egyptian pharaoh. Not something the Church has sought to publicize, for some reason or other.' He held out his cup. 'You couldn't pour me some more tea, could you?'

II

'Come back!' yelled Khaled, hurrying after Gaille, almost losing his footing in his haste. 'Come back!' he shouted again. But Gaille did nothing of the sort. A flash of movement and colour above, a cascade of grit and pebbles. Khaled glanced up to see Lily bringing her camera to bear. Khaled felt sick. He had to stop them getting away, contacting the outside world. He scrambled recklessly along the path, feet slipping on the limestone, clinging on desperately with one hand, trying to holster his Walther with his other. Faisal came up behind and hauled him back to safety, but valuable seconds had been wasted, allowing Gaille to get further ahead.

He reached the top to see her fleeing helter-skelter after her companions, Stafford way out in front, Lily flailing inelegantly with the camera on her shoulder. Khaled put in a burst, closing the gap a little, but not enough. They ran down the hillside into the wadi, clambered east over the scree towards the desert. Khaled couldn't sustain his pace. He slowed, came to a halt. 'Wait!' he panted, hands on his knees, his leg muscles fibrillating wildly. They slowed and turned, if only to catch their breath. 'Let's talk,' he shouted, holding up his hands and smiling in an effort to convince them he was no threat. 'We can sort this out.' But even he could hear the falseness in his voice.

They began to hurry again. He scowled, drew his Walther, fired a single shot into the air. It made them run all the faster. Nasser and Faisal came up alongside him, wheezing for air. They set off again, legs heavy with exertion. The Discovery came into view ahead. Lily looked around to check on their pursuit and promptly stumbled on a stone. Her camera went flying and hit the rocks hard, shattering into component pieces. Stafford reached the Discovery. He tried the door but it was locked. 'The keys,' he yelled at Gaille, who was hauling Lily back to her feet. 'Throw me the bloody keys.'

Khaled heaved for breath. His shirt had tugged free from his belt, he felt obscurely furious at the indignity. He fired another shot but the women didn't even break their stride. He put in a last burst, giving everything to the chase. Gaille took out her keys, pressed the remote. The corner lights on the Discovery flashed orange. Stafford opened the driver door and climbed in. They were going to get away. Khaled stopped, aimed as best he could, squeezed off three rounds. Metal pinged. The driver-side window disintegrated and fell out. The two women stopped dead, as though they believed Khaled some kind of marksman who could pick them off at will. They raised their arms and turned to face him.

He walked towards them, his hand against his side, heaving for breath, trying not to let it show, wanting to appear in control. Beads of sweat dripped down his forehead and trickled chillily down his flanks. Faisal and Nasser came up behind, but he kept his eyes firmly on the foreigners, the sag of their shoulders, their shiny faces and bedraggled hair, their dread-filled eyes, that poignant dash of hope. He scowled, hardening his heart towards them. These weren't people. They were problems. Problems to be solved. Problems to be eliminated. He drew to within a few paces, wondering which one to take out first.

The one with the car keys. Gaille.

He was raising his gun to kill her when a mobile phone began to ring.

III

Knox poured more tea for Kostas and himself, watched his sugar dissolve in the whirlpool of his stirring. 'What about the Therapeutae?' he asked. 'Did they have any links to these Carpocratians?'

Kostas pulled a face. 'I've heard it claimed that Carpocrates was a devotee of the teachings of a Talmudic figure called Jehoshua Ben Panther. A fascinating character. You may have heard of him, because he's been conflated with Christ by some, but he was most probably an Essene leader.'

'Linking him to the Therapeutae.'

'Quite,' nodded Kostas. 'And their doctrines mesh too, though admittedly with one major discrepancy. The Therapeutae were famously chaste, you see, whereas the Carpocratians were notorious for licentiousness and orgies. But almost everything we know about the Carpocratians was written by their enemies, so it's quite possible that that was nothing but malicious propaganda. And if you discount it, the two groups prove a remarkable fit.'

'In what way?'

'In every way. Long initiations. Water baptisms. The rejection of materialism. Carpocrates is credited with the phrase "Property is Theft", you know. Both abhorred slavery. Both believed in some kind of afterlife or reincarnation. Both accorded unusual respect and power to women. One of Carpocrates' most celebrated followers, Marcellina, even became quite a figure in Rome. They both had very Hellenic elements, and shared a great deal with Pythagoreanism. Both included traces of sun-worship. Both studied angels and demons. Both believed in and practised magic. Both prized numbers and symbols. And both were hideously persecuted too. Maybe that's why they both lived outside Alexandria. And, now that I think about it, the Carpocratians appeared around AD one hundred and twenty, around the same time we lose track of the Therapeutae.'

'You're suggesting the Therapeutae *became* the Carpocratians?'

'It's not inconceivable, I suppose. But all I'm really saying is that it's quite possible they *overlapped* in some way. Bear in mind that this whole region was fervid with philosophical and religious energy back then – everyone borrowing, sharing, arguing. Religions hadn't yet *set* in the way they have today. Places that were sacred to one were holy to others too. Many early churches were built on old pagan temples, you know. Even the Vatican. So perhaps they lived together for a while, or perhaps the Carpocratians took over this antiquity of yours after the Therapeutae moved on.'

Knox nodded. It seemed plausible enough, though plausibility was a very different beast from truth. 'What else do we know about the Carpocratians?'

'Founded in Alexandria, like I say, but they flourished elsewhere too. In Rome, as I mentioned. And I believe they also had a temple in . . .' He pushed himself to his feet, went over to his shelves, plucked down a volume, leafed through it, then put it back, shaking his head.

'Come on, Kostas. Just tell me.'

'Patience, young man. Patience.' He pulled out a weighty church encyclopaedia from his shelves, hefted it over to the corner table, licked his thumb and forefinger to turn the thin leaves until he found the page. 'Yes,' he said. 'They had a temple on one of the Greek islands.'

Knox frowned as he recalled his recent phone call with Augustin. 'Not Cephallonia, I don't suppose?'

Kostas smiled quizzically. 'How on earth did you know that?'

'What else does it say?'

He licked his fingertips, turned the page. 'Ha! How about that!'

'How about what?'

'Oh, yes. Oh, you'll like this.'

'Come on, Kostas. Just tell me, will you?'

'You know how Christian groups identified each other with secret signs and markings like the fish and the cross? Well, the Carpocratians had one of their own.'

'What?'

'It doesn't say,' said Kostas. 'All it says is where on their bodies it was tattooed.'

'And?'

Kostas's eyes twinkled. 'It was on the back of their right earlobes,' he said.

TWENTY-EIGHT

I

The mobile continued to ring. 'Turn that off,' said Khaled. Then louder, a touch of panic in his voice: 'Turn it off.' Stafford reached slowly into his pocket, pulled out his mobile, turned it off. But it was too late. The damage was done. Or, more accurately, the ringing had made Khaled aware of a serious problem. Mobile phones emitted as well as received signals, even when they weren't being used. They just had to be switched on, as Stafford's clearly was.

If he disappeared now, it would be a simple matter for the police to trace their movements. They'd come straight here. He and his men would be their automatic chief suspects. Out would come the canes, the hosepipes, the water-boarding. And one of them would surely crack. Faisal, probably. There was something almost womanish about him.

Abdullah had been summoned from sentry-duty by the sound of gunfire. 'What going on?' he panted.

'What does it look like?' scowled Khaled, glaring at the foreigners. The tomb had seemed a gift from Allah. But now he saw it for what it truly was. A satanic trap. Five years in jail, if they were caught. Five years minimum. More likely ten or even more. And Khaled had seen the inside of Egypt's prisons. They were cramped and dirty places, filled with disease and brutality. He wasn't a weakling, but the prospect unnerved him.

'Why don't we just kill them, sir?' asked Nasser, ever the practical one. 'Dump them in the desert, like we did with the girl.'

'Yes,' scoffed Khaled. 'And that worked well, didn't it?'

'We have more time this time. We have all night.'

'All night?' snarled Khaled. 'Don't you know what's going to happen when these people don't appear wherever they're expected?' He pointed his gun at the woman Lily. 'Where *are* you expected?'

'Assiut,' she said, her face drained of colour. 'The Cleopatra Hotel.'

He turned back to Nasser. 'The moment they don't show up, their hotel will notify the authorities. Nothing terrifies *them* more than bad things happening to foreigners, especially to TV people. It jeopardizes their hotel investments, their precious tourist dollars. Believe me, by morning there'll be a manhunt like you've never seen! And the first place they'll come is here. And the first thing they'll do is follow all the tyre tracks in the sand out to this wonderful hiding place of yours.'

'Then let's dump them in the Nile.' Nasser made waves with his fingers to indicate a car vanishing beneath the surface.

Khaled shook his head. 'Without being spotted? And even if by some miracle we get away with it now, the police are sure to drag the river, or some fisherman will snag his net on the car. Anyway, it doesn't matter, their damned mobile phones are going to lead them straight to us.'

'Oh,' said Nasser gloomily. 'Then what are we going to do?'

'I'm trying to think,' scowled Khaled. 'Give me some quiet, will you?' He squatted, not wanting his men to see how baffled he was. Perhaps he could shift all the blame onto them. Make it look like a shakedown gone wrong. A gunfight erupting, leaving the three foreigners and all his men dead. But it was a desperate solution. Even a half-competent investigator would see straight through it. So maybe they should strike a deal. But while these foreigners were scared enough to agree to anything right now, that would all change the moment they were released.

'We should blame it on terrorists,' muttered Abdullah. 'They're always killing foreigners.'

'Excellent idea,' scoffed Khaled, seizing the opportunity to vent some anger. 'But, tell me, which terrorists, exactly?' He waved an arm around the desolate wadi. 'Show me these terrorists of yours and sure, we'll blame it on them.'

'It was only a suggestion, sir.'

'There aren't any terrorists around Amarna. Don't you know that? They're all down in Assiut and . . .' He broke off, a thought coming to him. Abdullah was absolutely right. In Egypt, only terrorists would dare take out foreigners like this. And it was a story the authorities would instinctively believe. The merest hint of terrorism made intelligent people behave like idiots. As far as anyone knew, these three were on their way to Assiut tonight. There'd been major unrest down there recently. He'd been watching it on TV. Riots. Demonstrations. Firebrand Muslims up in arms against the West because five of their brethren had been arrested for the rape and murder of two young Coptic girls. And, just like that, the idea came to him.

'Yes, sir,' asked Nasser, reading inspiration on his face. 'What is it?'

'One moment,' begged Khaled. He thought it through, its implications, the resources they'd need, the steps they'd have to take. It was crazy, yes, but then the situation was crazy and demanded crazy solutions.

'Please, sir,' pressed Nasser. 'Tell us.'

Khaled nodded twice, breathed deeply. 'Okay,' he said. 'This is what we're going to do.'

II

Knox sat back in his chair, leather creaking voluptuously, giving himself a chance to assimilate his new knowledge. Peterson and his team had cut those six ears from the mummies to check them for tattoos under ultraviolet light. That, along with the link to the TSBA's previous excavations in Cephallonia, surely meant that they were here on the trail of the Carpocratians. The only question left was why.

Kostas brooded for a moment or two when Knox put this to him. 'These Texan archaeologists of yours: they're highly religious, yes?'

'Yes.'

'Then there is *one* possibility, I suppose. You see, the Carpocratians were reputed to—' The doorbell sounded at that moment. Kostas broke off, sighed, pushed himself to his feet. 'Excuse me.'

'Of course.' Knox went over to the table. The encyclopaedia was lying open. He scanned the entry for the Carpocratians, but nothing caught his eye. He wandered the shelves instead, pulled down a slim biography of Philo, flipped through the creamy pages, the crumbling leather binding leaving smears like dried blood on his palms and fingers.

The library door reopened. Knox looked around to see Kostas standing there, pale and shaken. 'What is it?' frowned Knox. But then he saw two policemen come into view behind Kostas and instantly went cold. He'd thought himself safe here; had allowed himself to relax. But somehow they'd found him. For a mad moment, he contemplated trying to run for it, but there was nowhere to go. And then he caught the glimmer of a smile twitch on the shorter of the two policemen's lips, as though that was exactly what he wanted, an excuse to lay in to him. So he forced himself to relax instead, go quietly; see if he couldn't find out what the hell was going on, and how they'd tracked him here.

III

Augustin and Farooq were learning precisely nothing from Peterson's archaeology students, crew-cut clones with morons-for-Jesus smiles who all just happened to have exactly the same story to tell. 'And your name is?' Farooq asked the latest arrival.

'Green, sir. Michael Green.' He glanced around at Peterson, standing over his shoulder, as though he needed to check he'd got his own name right.

'And you saw this intruder too?'

'Yes, sir.'

'Tell me about it.'

'Well, sir. It was kind of dark, you know. I don't know that I can—'

Farooq's mobile began to ring. He sighed and raised an eyebrow at Augustin. 'I need to answer this,' he grunted. 'You want to take his statement?'

'Sure,' said Augustin, stifling a yawn. He nodded at the young man as Farooq wandered off. 'Go on.'

'I was just saying, I don't know that I can add much to what the others told you.'

'Try. What was this intruder doing?'

'I'm sorry, sir?'

'Was he standing, kneeling, crawling? Was he coming towards you? Going away? What was he wearing? How tall was he? What colour hair? Did he realize you'd spotted him?'

'Ah.' A touch of colour flamed Michael's cheeks. He glanced at Peterson once more. 'It's difficult to remember, exactly,' he said. 'It all happened so quickly.'

'You must have some recollection.'

Peterson stepped forward. 'Is it really wise to bully witnesses into telling you things they didn't see?'

'I want to make sure he isn't forgetting anything.'

'Are you forgetting anything, Michael?' asked Peterson.

'No, sir.'

'There you go, Doctor Pascal. He's not forgetting anything.'

'Good news,' announced Farooq, finishing his phone call, coming back to join them. 'My men have found Knox.'

Augustin's heart skipped a beat. 'What?'

'Do you know the thing I hate most in this world, Doctor Pascal?' he asked. 'Being taken for a fool. All those people at the Supreme Council this morning. Do you know what they told me? They told me, if I wanted to find Knox, I should talk to you, Augustin Pascal. Pascal will know, they said. He and Knox are best friends. But when I ask you about Knox, you tell me nothing about this great friendship of yours. Not one word. You think I'm an idiot? Is that what you think?'

'Oh, Christ! You speak French.'

Farooq's right hook knocked Augustin clean onto his backside. 'And that's for calling my mother a fat sow,' he said.

TWENTY-NINE

I

The camera was still lying where Lily had dropped it. Its lens and display were intact, but its battery pack had come away from its housing and wouldn't slot back in, however Khaled twisted and pushed. He handed it to Faisal, who was good with such things. 'Fix it,' he scowled.

But it took Faisal only a moment's examination to shake his head. 'I'll need proper tools,' he grunted. He checked through the pouches of the camera bag, found an electrical lead instead. 'This might work,' he said. 'We could try one of the power-points in the Royal Tomb.'

Khaled nodded. It was a good idea, though they'd need to cover up the wall paintings or they'd give themselves away. 'Nasser,' he said. 'Go fetch the blankets and sheets from the other tomb. Abdullah,

293

you turn on the generator.' He walked back over to the foreigners. 'Your possessions, please. Phones, wallets, watches, car keys, jewellery. Everything. On the rocks.' He gave them a cuff or two to keep them compliant, scooped it all up, put it away in the camera bag. 'On your feet,' he ordered.

'What are you going to do with us?' whined Stafford.

'Just move, will you?'

The generator started up just as they reached the Royal Tomb, so that the floor-lights glowed and then grew bright. They herded the foreigners down into the burial chamber. Faisal plugged in and tested the camera. Its operating light came on. About time something went their way. Abdullah arrived, then Nasser with his arms full of dustsheets. There was a crudely cut niche high up in the wall in the far right corner of the chamber. They hung a sheet like a curtain from it, obscuring the murals behind. They spread another on the floor.

Satisfied, Khaled patted his pocket for something to write with, then sat on the floor to compose his message.

II

The policemen put Knox in a small dank holding cell with two other detainees: a tall thin straggle-bearded youth in a tan *galabaya* who fingered beads and muttered incessantly, and a sallow forty-something man in a mussed white suit who lay restlessly on the bench opposite, sitting up every so often, rubbing his hands and cheeks like a deprived addict.

The stone walls, softened by damp, were everywhere scratched with graffiti. Knox read them while he waited. He brooded too. Only Augustin had known he was with Kostas. And the photographs Augustin kept in that folder gave him a motive. But he was also his closest friend, and Knox had never met a man more loyal to his friends than Augustin. No way would he deliberately betray him. There had to be another explanation.

It was a good hour before the door scraped open again and a policeman beckoned. He was led through a recreation room full with off-duty policemen watching the football on a flickering TV screen high up on the wall, then along a narrow corridor to an interview room, where he took a seat at a bare pine table. An overweight policeman arrived a minute later, a notepad in one hand, a carton of juice in the other.

'What's going on?' demanded Knox.

The man sat as if he hadn't heard a word, jotted down Knox's name, checked his watch for the time. He had surprisingly elegant handwriting. 'My name is Farooq,' he said. Knox gave the faintest of snorts, for the name Farooq meant one who could tell truth from falsehood. Farooq looked up sharply. 'You speak Arabic, then?' he said.

'I get by.' It was only then that he realized how he'd been tracked down. 'And you speak French, yes?'

Farooq grinned wickedly. 'I get by,' he acknowledged. 'You've lived in Egypt long?'

'Ten years.'

'May I see your papers?'

'Not on me.'

'If you've lived here ten years, you should have learned to carry your papers at all times.'

'I'll go get them if you like.'

Farooq tapped his pen on his pad, thinking how best to approach this. 'Tell me something, Mister Knox,' he said. 'You were in a serious car crash last night. You were knocked unconscious. You were taken to hospital, seemingly a sensible place for a man who's been in a serious accident. Yet this morning you ran away. Why?'

'I don't have insurance. Those places cost a fortune.'

'A man died last night, Mister Knox. Do you think this is funny?'

'No.'

'Then I ask again: why run away?'

Knox hesitated. The truth would sound implausible, but maybe it was worth trying. 'A man came into my room,' he said. 'He tried to kill me.'

'With one of my officers stationed outside?'

'He put a pillow over my face.'

'You expect me to believe that? You think I'm a fool?'

'Why else would I have run away?'

Farooq tapped his pen some more. 'Describe this man to me.'

'It was dark. I had concussion.'

'Why not call for help?'

'I tried to. I had no voice. But I did pull my IV stand over. It was all I could manage. Your officer came running in. He fetched a nurse. The nurse righted the stand. I tried to tell him . . .' He gestured helplessly at his throat. 'Ask your officer if you don't believe me.'

Farooq glared at Knox, trying to intimidate him into buckling and retracting, but Knox held his gaze. 'Wait here,' said Farooq finally, pushing to his feet. 'I'll be back in one minute.'

III

Fear was like ulcers in Gaille's gut as she watched Khaled and his men go about their work. She'd seen murder in Khaled's eyes earlier. She had no doubt that he'd have killed them all without a qualm had Stafford's phone not rung. She knew for sure that her life depended on his say-so.

Nasser and Abdullah tore a cotton sheet into strips, wrapped them around their faces, leaving thin slits for their eyes and nostrils, anonymous yet terrifying. Faisal unwrapped a new DVD, slid it into Lily's camera. Khaled finished writing his note, came across. 'Kneel,' he said. They all knelt compliantly on the dustsheet. He thrust his note at Gaille. 'Read,' he told her.

She glanced at his Arabic scrawl, looked up in alarm. 'I don't understand.'

Khaled aimed his Walther at the bridge of her nose. 'Read.'

'Don't do it,' said Stafford.

Khaled whipped Stafford across the cheek with his Walther so hard that he cried out and fell onto his side. He put a hand to his face; it came back bloodied. He looked at it in disbelief, welling up with tears of shock. Khaled aimed down at him, but it was Gaille he looked at. 'You'll read,' he told her.

'Yes,' she agreed, feeling faint with terror. He retreated behind Faisal, arms folded, for all the world like the producer of some cheap flick, while Nasser and Abdullah, faces concealed behind their makeshift masks, stood behind them, their weapons held aslant across their chests.

Stafford pushed himself back up onto his knees, blood still trickling from his cheek. Khaled tapped Faisal's shoulder. The camera's operating light came on. He nodded at Gaille to read. It was her chance to communicate with the outside world. She might never get another. She adjusted her posture, tucking her legs beneath her, sitting up straight, throwing back her shoulders. Then she transferred the note to her left hand and raised her right hand for emphasis. 'We are prisoners of the Assiut Islamic Brotherhood,' she began. 'Our captors are treating us well. They promise to continue to treat us well unless efforts are made to find us. They assure us we will be released unharmed when our brothers, falsely imprisoned for the murder of the two girls, are released without charge. If they are not released without charge within fourteen days, the Assiut Islamic Brotherhood will not be responsible for what then happens. God is great.'

The recording light went out. Khaled reviewed the footage, nodded in satisfaction. Faisal popped out the DVD, passed it to him. He took it by its edges, careful not to leave fingerprints, then put it away in its case. Gaille's heart began to race wildly with fear. Because she understood Khaled's plan well enough to realize that if he still intended on killing them all, now would be the time.

IV

'Well?' asked Yasmine, greeting Naguib at the door. 'How was your day?'

Naguib knew what his wife was really asking. She was asking him whether he'd found his killer yet, whether their daughter was safe. He said: 'Not bad.'

Yasmine dropped a kiss on Husniyah's crown. 'Run along, beloved,' she said. 'Your father and I have something to discuss.'

Husniyah took her doll next door, though something in her eye made Naguib suspect she'd have her ear against the wall. 'Well?' asked Yasmine.

'There's no connection between the girl I found and those two in Assiut,' said Naguib. 'I'm sure of it.'

'How can you be?'

'I don't even think this girl was murdered. I think it was an accident. I think she was just a poor girl out hunting for ancient artefacts in a storm. I think perhaps something fell on her and knocked her unconscious and then she drowned. Or maybe she was climbing when she fell.'

'And then she just picked herself up and walked out into the desert and buried herself in a tarpaulin beneath the sand?'

'No,' admitted Naguib.

'Then what?'

He shook his head. 'I don't know yet. Something's clearly up. But that doesn't mean it's linked to Assiut. That doesn't make it murder.'

'But you're going to find out, yes? I have to be sure.'

'Gamal's right, my beloved. We have more pressing cases.'

'She was a young girl,' insisted Yasmine. 'I'm glad there's no murderer. I'm glad Husniyah is safe. Truly I am. But she was just a young girl, and she was from your district, and she was under your care. You owe it to her to find out.'

Naguib sighed. 'I'll speak to the *ghaffirs* in the morning,' he promised. 'Maybe they'll know something.'

V

'Well?' demanded Knox, when Farooq returned. 'What did your man say? He told you the IV stand fell over, didn't he?'

'Let's say it did fall over,' acknowledged Farooq grudgingly. 'So what? It could have been an accident.'

'Sure!'

'Very well. You pulled it over because of this mysterious intruder, this man no one else saw, this man who wants to kill you, yet who you've never seen before and can't identify.'

Knox hesitated. 'I think it might have been someone called Peterson.'

'The Reverend Ernest Peterson?' frowned Farooq. 'The man who saved your life?'

301

'I beg your pardon.'

'You heard me. He found you after your crash and risked his own life to pull you from your Jeep before the smoke got to you. Then he drove you to hospital. This is the man who tried to kill you?'

Knox went a little numb. 'I didn't know,' he said. He shook his head in confusion, baffled by this latest turn.

'You took a taxi from the hospital. Where did you go?'

'Around.'

'Around?'

'May I have something to drink, please?' asked Knox. 'A glass of water. Anything.'

'When you tell me where you went.'

'The Latin Cemeteries.'

'You went directly there?'

'You said I could have a glass of water.'

Farooq pushed himself to his feet, opened the door, shouted down the corridor. 'You went directly there from the hospital?' he asked, sitting back down.

'Yes.'

'That's strange. Because my colleagues had a call earlier. From a woman who had an intruder in her apartment.'

'So?'

'This intruder assaulted her, put her in fear for her life. And do you know the funny thing? He answered your exact description. And do you know

302

who lives right above her? Your friend Augustin Pascal. Yes. The very same man you telephoned earlier.'

'Is this really why you brought me in? To talk about Pascal?'

Farooq tapped a cigarette from a soft-pack, clamped the filter between his lips to pull it all the way out. 'Want one?' he offered.

'No thanks.'

Farooq lit his cigarette, smoke drifting from his nostrils. 'You're quite right,' he smiled. 'I didn't bring you in to discuss Mister Pascal. I brought you in to charge you with the murder of Omar Tawfiq.'

THIRTY

I

Night had fallen while they'd been in the Royal Tomb. The rocks in the wadi gleamed like bones as Gaille picked her way across them, then up the hillside. Faisal led the way, cutting a ghostly figure with the dustsheets draped over his shoulders. He walked confidently along the cliff-face path, finding places for his feet that Gaille could barely see in the gloom until he turned and picked them out for her with his torch. She took the first step, her ankles weak with fear. Then the next. Faisal smiled at her when she finally reached the end, seeking a smile in return, some kind of forgiveness, or at least of understanding; but she remembered how she'd shared her chocolate with him earlier, and gave him such a scathing look instead that he dropped his eyes in shame.

He pulled back the sackcloth curtain, nodded her through the black gash in the rock, a tree-trunk split by lightning. With his torch pointing down, the reflected light revealed a wide, low chamber, rows of voluptuous fat pillars carved from the limestone either side, the gaps between stacked high with rubble. Everyone gathered inside. Khaled led them along the passage to a shaft. A rope ladder was moored to an iron peg hammered into the ground. 'Down,' he ordered Gaille.

'What are you going to do with us?'

'Just get down.'

She dangled her legs over the drop, turned onto her front, grabbed the rope, elbows scraping on the rough stone as she probed with her foot like a tongue at a loose tooth until she found a rung. Faisal shone his torch down for her, so that she could see the plain limestone wall as she descended, the rubble floor covered with litter. In the fluttering light, she glimpsed a candle glued by its own congealed wax to a stone and a half-used book of matches, so she grabbed them both. Stafford arrived down next, then Lily. The ladder slithered up the wall like a fugitive snake, trapping them there. A mutter of conversation above, then the fade of footsteps and silence.

'Hey!' shouted Stafford. 'Anyone there?' Nothing but echo. 'You think they've gone?' he asked.

Gaille struck a match, lit the candle from it, took it to the walls, too sheer and high to climb, even if they'd had some tool with which to gouge holds in them.

'What are they going to do with us?' asked Lily. 'Did they say what they were going to do?'

'No.'

'They must have said something.'

'I don't think they know yet,' said Gaille. 'I think they're making this up as they go along.'

'How do you mean?'

She took a deep breath. The candle fluttered, giving the feeling of a vigil, as though someone had died. 'This is a mess, that's all. They stumbled upon this place by accident. They should have reported it, but they chose to loot it instead. That's a very serious crime. They'll go to gaol for years if they're caught.'

'Then why take the chance?'

'Because they're *poor*. A conscript earns maybe three hundred US dollars a year. Imagine trying to live on that. Imagine trying to marry or bring up a family. Then imagine coming across an artefact worth a thousand dollars. A single artefact. What would you do?'

'You sound almost sorry for them,' said Stafford.

'They'll let us go, won't they?' asked Lily. 'I mean they have to.'

Gaille didn't answer at once, but her silence was eloquent. 'The police will come for us,' she said.

'But they'll be looking in Assiut!'

'They'll be looking everywhere,' Gaille assured her. 'One thing the Egyptians have is manpower. We just need to keep our nerve.' The candle guttered, already burning low. They couldn't afford to waste any more. She cupped her hand around the flame to blow it out, and darkness enveloped them once more.

II

'Murder?' protested Knox. 'What do you mean, murder?'

'I mean exactly what I say,' said Farooq. 'I mean I believe you deliberately killed Omar Tawfiq and tried to make it look like an accident.'

'You must be crazy.'

'Answer me this, Mr Knox. How long have you owned your Jeep?'

'What?'

'Just answer my question, please.'

'I don't know. Ten years.'

'And tell me this. Did it have a passenger-side seat belt?'

'Oh Christ!' muttered Knox. He rocked forward on his chair, looked up at Farooq. 'Is that how he died?'

'And there *was* a driver's-side seat belt. You

308

knew that, not least because you were wearing it when you were found. So you'd agree, wouldn't you, that if the driver deliberately crashed into a ditch, there'd be every chance he himself would escape with light injuries while his passenger would be very severely injured, maybe even killed?'

Knox shook his head. 'You'd have to be mad to do such a thing.'

'Not mad. Only very highly motivated.'

'What motive could I possibly have had to do *that*?'

'That's for you to tell me, isn't it?'

'This is crazy,' protested Knox. 'Omar was my friend. I didn't murder him, I swear I didn't.'

'I thought you'd lost your memory,' said Farooq. 'How can you be so sure?'

'Because I'd never do something like that. Ask anyone.'

'We have been asking.'

'Well, then,' said Knox. But he felt a twinge. Who knew for sure what they were capable of under stress? More to the point, who knew what others would say about them?

'I hear you're quite the celebrity in archaeological circles,' said Farooq. 'I hear you can't get enough of the media spotlight.'

'I found myself in it once. That doesn't mean I enjoyed it.'

'It goes to your head, though, doesn't it?' grinned

Farooq. 'It brings you alive. And then it goes away again and leaves you feeling empty.'

'Speak for yourself.'

'You know what I think happened?' said Farooq. 'I think you found something yesterday. I think you found it on Peterson's site. I think that's why you went back after dark. I further think that you and Mister Tawfiq argued about what to do next. His colleagues say he was the most scrupulous of men. He'd have insisted on going through the proper channels, reporting it to his secretary general in Cairo. But you couldn't bear that, could you? Everyone tells me you have history with the secretary general, that you can't stand each other. The thought of him getting all that glory, all that *attention*, when it should rightfully have been yours . . . . It wasn't to be borne, was it? So you decided to silence Omar.'

'That's rubbish.'

Farooq nodded to himself. 'You know what I had to do this morning, Mister Knox? Visit Mister Tawfiq's family; inform them of his death. The very worst part of my job, as I'm sure you'll appreciate. You know much about his family?'

Knox shook his head. 'He never talked about them.'

'Can't say I'm surprised. A respected academic like him.'

'What are you getting at?'

'His father is a very powerful man, Mister Knox,' grunted Farooq. 'His brothers are all very powerful men.'

Knox felt sick. 'You don't mean . . . ?'

'I'm afraid I do. And they're not happy, believe me. They want explanations. I had to tell them you were driving. I had to tell them your Jeep had no passenger-side seat belt.'

'Oh, Christ.'

'They hold you responsible for his death, Mister Knox. And they're dangerous men, I assure you. Not the kind of men to let the death of a son and brother pass without taking certain steps.'

'They're coming after me?'

'You asked why I had you brought in,' said Farooq. 'I wanted to talk to you, yes. But I was also concerned for your safety. This is my city, Mister Knox. I won't have people murdered here. Not even foreigners. Not even killers. But I'll tell you this: I wouldn't be in your shoes, not for anything.'

'I didn't do it,' said Knox weakly.

'You'd do well to get your memory back as soon as possible,' advised Farooq, pushing himself to his feet. 'We'll meet again tomorrow morning. I'd use tonight wisely, if I were you.'

III

Khaled drove the Discovery cautiously along the wadi, only opening up at all once he was out in the open desert. The moon was low on the horizon, making the sand gleam like tarnished pewter. Chill night air blew in through the broken driver's-side window, turning his fingers to ice. He kept his headlights on; the risk of meeting anyone way out here was far less than of hitting one of the rocks that lay hidden like unexploded mines in the sand. He felt strangely calm, the situation out of his control. But luck was with him; he reached the desert track without incident, headed south towards Assiut, began to encounter other people. A farmer on his donkey. A pick-up truck. Then the traffic grew thick, cloaking him in anonymity. He crossed the bridge into Assiut. Nasser was waiting on the west bank, astride his motorbike; his route down had been far quicker, even with a Nile crossing to take into account. He waved at Khaled, fell in behind. They drove west, looking for suitable sites, found a derelict factory with an enclosed courtyard. Perfect. He scattered the belongings he'd taken earlier among the front and back seats, then doused the whole lot with fuel from the Discovery's own spare can. It went up with such a fierce blaze that it seared his skin. He climbed on the back of Nasser's bike and they drove back into town.

The Discovery would be found soon enough, but he couldn't deliver the DVD just yet. Enough time needed to pass for terrorists to snatch hostages, take them to a safe house, make the recording. Three hours, say. Then back to Amarna. They found a bench overlooking the Nile where he brooded on their situation.

A young couple walked by in the darkness. He could hear their doting voices but not make out what they were saying, and it reminded him how he'd heard Stafford's voice from inside the tomb. He went cold suddenly. What if it worked both ways? The police were sure to visit Amarna during their investigation. What if the hostages were to yell for help while they were nearby? He'd intended to keep them alive to mitigate their punishment should they be caught, but now he realized this was a risk they couldn't afford. He pulled out his mobile, called Abdullah. 'Everything okay?' he asked.

'Yes, sir,' said Abdullah. 'You want us to close the place up now?'

'I need you to do something first. I need you to silence them.'

'What?'

'You heard me.'

A moment's hesitation, then: 'But I thought we were going to—'

'We need them silenced,' snapped Khaled. 'That's an order. Am I clear?'

'Yes, sir.'

'Good. Then take care of it before I get back.'

IV

A second football match had taken the place of the first on the recreation room TV, and now was reaching its climax. Knox's two cell-mates were fans, taking it in turns to stand by the door and squint through the viewing window, wincing and cheering, chatting animatedly with the policemen outside.

Omar was dead. Finally, it was sinking in. He and Knox hadn't been old friends, but they'd grown close quickly, in that way you do. Kindred spirits. Such a gentle, thoughtful and diffident young man; it was hard to credit that he came from a family of Egyptian gangsters, though maybe that was why he'd turned out the way he had, why he'd turned to archaeology. An effort to distance himself from his own roots. Although, thinking about it, maybe it had had something to do with his recent promotion too.

The worst of it was, Farooq was right: Omar's death was his fault. He'd been driving his Jeep for years with a broken seat belt, aware that such an accident was possible, yet he'd done nothing about it. Such things somehow seemed to matter less in Egypt. Until they had consequences, at least.

A great cheer went up. Someone had scored.

He buried his head in his hands as he grieved for his friend, striving to regain his lost memory. He owed it to Omar to remember precisely what had happened, how badly to blame he'd been. But the minutes passed, slow as pouring treacle, and still nothing came.

V

Faisal followed Abdullah along the tomb corridor with a heavy tread, his AK-47 held out in front of him, as though to fend off demons. He was a quiet man by nature; he wanted only to complete his three years' conscription and go home. He believed in hard work, in Allah, in doing right by others, in marrying a good woman and having many, many children. His uncle had assured him that the army would be the making of him. Who on earth could have dreamed it would make him into this? But Khaled had given his orders, and you didn't disobey Khaled. Not more than once.

They reached the lip of the shaft, stopped. 'Who's up there?' called out the girl Gaille. 'What's going on?' Her voice was plaintive, it tugged at his heart, reminded him of how she'd given him chocolate just that same morning, how they'd laughed and joked together. How in hell had it all gone so wrong so quickly?

'I'll shine down the torch,' murmured Abdullah. 'You do it.'

'Why should I do it?'

'Are you going to let us go?' asked the girl. 'Please. We're begging you.'

'What do you think I mean?' scowled Abdullah. 'I'll shine down the torch. You do . . . you know.'

'How about I shine down the torch and you do it?' retorted Faisal. He peered over the edge, as though that would somehow resolve the issue. Gaille lit a match from a book they must have left down there, the sudden bright flare illuminating her face in the darkness, staring pleadingly up at them.

'I wish we had one of the captain's grenades,' muttered Abdullah. 'So much easier.'

'For us, you mean?'

Down below, the second woman started sobbing piteously. Faisal struggled to block her cries and wails from his head.

'We'll do it together,' said Abdullah finally. 'Then we'll check with the torch. Agreed?'

'I don't like this,' said Faisal.

'You think I do?' scowled Abdullah. 'But it's this or explain to Khaled.'

Faisal breathed deep. He'd slaughtered livestock on his farm ever since he could remember. That was all this was. Livestock ready for slaughter. 'Okay,' he said. He readied his gun; the shrieking started down below.

'On the count of three,' said Abdullah.

'On the count of three,' agreed Faisal.

'One . . .' said Abdullah. 'Two . . .'

THIRTY-ONE

I

Augustin arrived home weary and apprehensive. Farooq had treated him with such contempt since he'd decked him with his right hand that the spirit had gone completely out of him. He'd asked to visit Knox at the police station. Farooq had laughed in his face. He was normally an ebullient man, Augustin, but not tonight. He couldn't remember ever feeling this low.

A madwoman leaned over the banisters to bark at him about his rapist house guests. He lacked the energy even to yell back.

He half filled a tumbler with ice, opened a new bottle of single malt, took both glass and bottle through to his bedroom, set them down on his bedside table. Then he opened his wardrobe and lifted his stack of T-shirts. The folder had moved.

No question. No surprise, either. Knox hadn't said anything on the phone earlier; of course he hadn't, he was a man; men discuss such things, thank Christ. But Augustin had heard that slight hesitation in his voice. At the time, he'd put it down to his predicament. Only later had he realized that Knox would have needed a clean shirt, that of course he'd have seen the folder. It was the way fate worked. It gave you the punishments you deserved.

He drew out the photographs; spread them on his duvet. His favourite was the first, not least because Gaille had given it to him herself. It showed the three of them out in the desert late one afternoon, arms around each other's shoulders, grinning happily, against a backdrop of red-gold dunes, lengthening shadows, low slivers of mauve and orange cloud in a blue-wash sky. A grizzled Bedouin had taken it; they'd happened across him trudging the sands between nowhere and nowhere with the gloomiest-looking camel he'd ever seen. Augustin, Gaille, Knox. Something had happened to him that day. When Gaille had given him the photograph, he'd found it impossible to put away. He'd added to it, photos of her and Knox; others just of her.

His tumbler had somehow emptied. He refilled it.

Why have one woman when you could have twenty? In his heart, he'd always scorned fidelity.

Every man would behave like he did if only they could. Monogamy was for losers. Maybe he was just getting old, but evenings with Knox and Gaille had made him aware of the shabbiness of this life. He'd found it increasingly hard to pick up women. He'd lost his nerve, or perhaps his hunger. He'd developed a different hankering. He couldn't say what for, just that it was there, that it kept growing more severe, that it wouldn't be sated by his usual conquests. One morning, a couple of months back, he'd woken up effervescent with purpose, had leapt out of bed and had torn down a great strip of wallpaper, satisfying as a gigantic scab. He'd called in the builders that same day, had had his apartment gutted and redecorated.

The nesting instinct! Good grief! How had it come to this?

And yet it didn't feel like love. That was what Knox wouldn't understand. He was fond of Gaille, sure, but he didn't covet her or plot ways to win her. It didn't stab him in the heart when she looked at Knox in that way she had. Because it wasn't Gaille who'd got beneath his skin. It was the two of them together, the thing that had happened between them without them even knowing.

One of the unexpected hazards of archaeology was how you were constantly reproached by the lives of others. Ancient Alexandrians had had a life expectancy of some thirty-five years, less time on earth than he'd already spent. Yet so many of them had achieved so much. And he'd achieved so little.

His life was shit. He'd started buying whisky by the crate.

He lay back on his bed, his hands clasped beneath his head. He stared up at his freshly white-washed ceiling, aware it was going to be a long night.

II

'I can't do this,' muttered Faisal, taking a step back from the edge of the sump. 'I can't. I won't.'

'Fine,' scowled Abdullah. 'Then I'll do it. But I won't have you pointing the finger at me later if it all goes to shit.'

'No,' said Faisal. 'Neither of us are doing it. It's wrong. It's just wrong. You know it is.'

'And you're going to tell Captain Khaled that, are you?' snorted Abdullah.

Faisal grimaced. Abdullah had a point. He'd suffered only one of that man's proper beatings, but it had put him in hospital for a week. He didn't fancy a repeat. 'What were his orders, exactly?' he asked.

'Like I told you. To silence them.'

'To *silence* them!' snorted Faisal. 'And why did he use that particular word, do you think? So that if all this is found out, he can blame us for misinterpreting his orders. We'll be hung while he'll be let off with a slap on his wrist.'

'You think he'd do that?'

'Of course he would,' said Faisal. 'Do you honestly believe everything we've found here has been worthless, like he's been telling us? Bullshit. He's just keeping it all for himself. It's only ever him, him, him.'

Abdullah grunted. It was a suspicion they all shared. 'Then what do you suggest?'

'We do precisely as he told you. We *silence* them.'

'I don't understand.'

'These two planks. We put one either side of the shaft. Then we stretch out the sheets and blankets between them, pin them down with rocks. That'll muffle any sound, especially once we've sealed the mouth up.'

'I don't know.' Abdullah gave a shudder. 'If he finds out . . .'

'How's he going to do that? I'm not going to tell him. Are you?'

'Even so.'

'So you'd rather kill them, would you?'

Abdullah glanced down, considered the options then grimaced. 'Very well,' he nodded. 'Let's do it.'

III

Knox ached from head to toe as he struggled to sleep. Bone-weary, they called it, and they knew what they were talking about. His cell was cold, his bench hard, his companions noisy sleepers, taking it in shifts to snore. The television was still on in the recreation room, volume cranked up high. It didn't seem to bother Egyptians at all – they were born with mute buttons in their heads – but it was an aspect of life here that Knox had never quite got used to.

It was the small hours before he finally drifted off, if not to sleep exactly, then to a state of inertia near enough to it. He wasn't sure how long he'd been dozing that way when he heard a familiar voice. Gaille's voice. At first he thought he was dreaming; it made him smile. But then he realized it wasn't a dream. He realized it because of her choice of words, the strain in her tone. A jolt ran through him. He sat up, hurried to the cell door. Through the viewing window, he could just make out on the television screen the nightmare iconography of modern terrorism, Gaille and two others on the floor, two masked paramilitaries standing behind them, weapons across their chests.

'Gaille!' he muttered, disbelieving. He pounded his fist against the door. 'Gaille!'

'Quiet, damn you,' grunted one of his cell-mates.

'Gaille!' he yelled. 'Gaille!'

'I said be quiet!'

'Gaille!'

A door banged, footsteps approached, a bleary-eyed policeman peered in. He glowered at Knox, kicked the door. Knox barely even noticed, squinting past him at the TV screen. It was Gaille for sure. He called out her name again, feeling utterly helpless, bewildered. The policeman unlocked and opened the cell door, tapped his cane menacingly against his thigh. But Knox simply barged past him, out into the recreation room, staring numbly upwards, listening to her words.

The policeman grabbed his shoulder. 'Back in your cell,' he warned. 'Or I'll have to—'

'She's my friend,' snarled Knox. 'Let me watch.'

The policeman took a step back; Knox focused once more on the TV. The footage finished. The scene changed. A soberly dressed man and a woman in a news studio. No one had heard of the Assiut Islamic Brotherhood, but the authorities were confident of resolving this crisis peacefully. An inset screen appeared playing the hostage footage. Knox stared transfixed as Gaille adjusted her position, raised her right hand for emphasis. His skin prickled, though he wasn't sure why.

A door clanged behind him. He glanced around. Two more policemen were approaching, faces scrunched and mean. 'My friend,' he explained, gesturing at the screen. 'She's been taken hostage. Please. I need to—'

The first blow caught him on his thigh. He hadn't seen it coming at all, hadn't had time to brace himself. Pain spiked up his hip; he slumped onto one knee. The second blow glanced off his shoulder blade onto the back of his scalp, stars and amoebae dancing in front of his eyes as his face rushed at the floor. A sudden shudder of memory, driving the Jeep, Omar beside him, laughing together at some joke. The sharp tang of diesel. Then his hair was grabbed and someone muttered in his ear, though there was such a ringing in his ears he couldn't make out the words. His head was dropped again, his cheek banged cold stone. They dragged him by his legs across the rough floor back to his cell.

IV

Naguib went yawning into the kitchen, mouth dry, eyes gluey, eager for his first glass of morning *chai*. His wife didn't even look around, she was so riveted by her TV.

'What is it?' he asked.

'Some Westerners were kidnapped in Assiut last night. Television people. They say they were filming in Amarna yesterday. Did you see them?'

'No.'

'Apparently this woman is the one who helped find Alexander's tomb. Remember that press conference with the secretary general and that other man?'

'The one you thought so handsome?'

Yasmine blushed. 'I only said he looked nice.'

'What have they been saying?'

'Just that their car was found burned out in Assiut, that some poor half-blind man was paid to take this DVD into the television station. They've been playing it non-stop. Apparently the kidnappers are demanding the release of those people arrested for the rape and murder of those two girls.'

Naguib frowned. 'Terrorists want rapists and murderers released?'

'They say they're not guilty.'

'Even so.'

'That poor young woman!' said Yasmine. 'How is she holding herself together?'

Naguib put a hand on his wife's shoulder. The video was playing in a loop, screen-in-screen, so he could see the hostages' terrible anxiety, the freely bleeding cut on the man's cheek, the uplighting making strange shadows from their features, while the commentators took turns to deplore the ignominy this brought upon their nation, debating the steps their government would take. He too found it difficult to look away, despite his need to get to the office, clear his paperwork, buy himself some time to go see the local *ghaffirs*. But unlike his wife, it wasn't fellow feeling that kept him riveted. It was something else. His policeman's instincts were quivering deep inside. He just couldn't work out why.

THIRTY-TWO

I

Knox's mouth was sore and sticky. He wiped it with the back of his hand. It came back smeared red. He sat up on the hard bench, suffered a dizzying rush of blood to his head; had to give himself a few seconds to adjust. But that was nothing compared to the visual memory that came next.

Gaille, kneeling, terrified, hostage of terrorists.

He leaned forward, fearful he was going to be sick, but somehow held it in. He stood, walked woozily to the door, peered through the glass. The television was still tuned to the news, though someone had finally turned down the volume. There she was, reading out her statement, the words already imprinted on his mind. *The Assiut Islamic Brotherhood. Treating us well. Unless*

329

efforts are made to find us. Released unharmed when the men are released. If not released within fourteen days ...

That look on her face. Her shaking hands. She was fighting dread, terrified of something imminent, not fourteen days away. He wasn't a parent, Knox, but he felt then how a parent must feel, that desperation to help, that powerlessness. A savage sensation. Unbearable, except that he had no option but to bear it.

'Your friend is one of the hostages?'

Knox blinked and looked around. The man in the rumpled white suit was talking to him. 'I beg your pardon?'

'Your friend is one of the hostages?'

'Yes.'

'Which one?'

'The girl.'

'The red-headed girl or the dark-headed girl?'

'The dark-headed girl.' A sudden flicker of memory. *Talking to two men, one in a dog collar, the other portly like this.*

'She looks nice.'

'She is nice.'

'Your girlfriend, is she?'

Knox shook his head. 'I just work with her.'

'Sure,' smiled the man. 'That's how I react when my colleagues get into trouble. I go crazy and pick fights with policemen.'

'She's a friend too.'

He nodded. 'Anyway. I wanted to say how sorry I am that countrymen of mine could do this to her. If there's anything I can do . . .'

'Thank you.' He looked back at the screen. Something about the footage was whispering to him.

'I'm not a good man. I wouldn't be here if I was. But I can't understand how men who claim to be of Allah could think that Allah would approve of that.'

'Please,' said Knox, begging for silence.

He focused back on the screen. The footage started over. Gaille kneeling on the floor, then adopting the lotus position, raising her right hand for extra emphasis. He'd seen that posture some-where else recently. But where? He dug fingernails into his palm in an effort to force his mind to focus. Then he had it. That mosaic. The figure in the centre of the seven-pointed star.

Yes. His skin prickled.

Gaille was sending him a message.

II

The phone was ringing. It wouldn't bloody stop. Augustin did his best to ignore it until finally it went away again. But the damage had been done.

He was awake. His mouth was dry and glued; a demolition crew was at work inside his skull. Morning, then. He turned onto his side, protected his eyes from the slanted sunlight, checked his bedside clock with a groan. Hangovers weren't the fun they'd once been. He pushed himself up, unnameable things sloshing and lurching inside. Not for the first time, he resolved to change his habits. But perhaps for the first, a little flutter of panic accompanied the thought, the teenager on the lilo who suddenly realizes how far out he's drifted.

He staggered to the loo, relieved himself in an unending dark-yellow stream. Ants had congregated around the porcelain bowl, a trail of them leading across the floor up the wall and out through the half-open window. Christ! Maybe he had diabetes. That was one of the signs, wasn't it? Sweetness in your urine? Maybe that was why he felt so tired all the time. Or maybe the little bastards had just developed a taste for the hard stuff. They certainly seemed to be veering all over the place. The phone rang again, allowing him to put the unwelcome thought from his mind. 'Yes?' he asked.

'Have you seen?' demanded Mansoor.

'Seen what?'

'Gaille. On the news.' Augustin's chest tightened as he turned on his TV. He knew it would be bad, but he still wasn't prepared. He sat numbly in his armchair until he heard Mansoor shouting his name. 'Augustin? Are you still there?'

'Yes.'

'I've been trying to get hold of Knox. He's not at his hotel. He's not answering his mobile.'

'I know where he is.'

'Someone needs to tell him. It should be a friend.'

'Leave it to me.'

'Thanks. And let me know when you've spoken to him. Let me know what I can do.' The phone clicked dead. Augustin replaced it in its cradle, stunned and nauseous, yet now at least with a purpose. He splashed water on his face and body, threw on some fresh clothes, hurried downstairs to his bike.

III

'We're going to die down here,' sobbed Lily. 'We are, aren't we?'

'People will find us,' said Gaille.

'No one will find us.'

'Yes, they will.'

'How can you say that?'

Gaille hesitated. She hadn't mentioned Knox yet, the message she'd tried to send him. It was such a long shot, it seemed unfair to place the burden of expectation on his shoulders. Yet Lily was on the verge of breakdown; she needed hope. 'I have a friend,' she said.

'Oh, you have a friend!' scoffed Lily. 'We're going to be saved because you have a friend!'

'Yes,' said Gaille.

Something in her calmness seemed to soothe Lily, but she wasn't about to let herself be comforted so easily, not while she sensed she could get more. 'And just how is this friend of yours going to help?' she asked. 'Is he psychic or some-thing?'

'I told him where we were.'

'You *what*?' asked Stafford from the darkness.

'When we were being filmed, I let him know we were in Amarna, not Assiut.'

'How?'

'It's complex.'

Stafford gave a grunt, almost of amusement. 'And you've somewhere else you need to be, have you?'

'There's a portrait of Akhenaten we're both familiar with,' sighed Gaille. 'The way he's sitting is very distinctive.'

'So that's why you shifted position when you were reading out the message?'

'Yes.'

'I don't remember Akhenaten ever being portrayed that way.'

'No?' replied Gaille.

A brief silence fell. Gaille could imagine Stafford's stony expression. 'You really think your friend will deduce our whereabouts from that?' he said. 'From the way you were sitting?'

'Yes. I do.'

Lily touched her arm. 'What's his name, this friend of yours?'

Gaille breathed in deep. It felt strange saying it out loud. Like committing to something. 'Daniel Knox,' she said.

'And people will listen to him, will they? I mean, it's not much use him realizing where we are unless he can convince the authorities? So they know who he is, do they?'

'Oh, yes,' asserted Gaille, glad to be able to say something with absolute conviction. 'They know who he is, all right.'

THIRTY-THREE

I

The metal door of the interview room squealed on its hinges as Farooq backed in, carrying a tray with two cups of coffee, a pad of paper and a tape recorder that he set down on the table. 'I hear you've been making quite a nuisance of yourself,' he said.

'My friend's been taken hostage,' said Knox. 'She's sending me a message.'

'Yes, yes,' said Farooq. 'This famous message of yours. My colleagues have been discussing it all morning.'

'You have to tell the investigating team. It could be important.'

'Tell them what, exactly? That you think she's trying to send you a message, but you don't know what it is? What use is that?'

'Let me out of here. I'll find out what it is.'

'Sure. I'll let all our killers out, shall I? They can help you look.'

'Please. I'm begging you. At least notify the people running the kidnap investigation—'

'Mister Knox. Calm down. One of my colleagues has already contacted Assiut, I assure you. They'll call back if they want to know more. They haven't yet. I doubt they will. But if they do, I'll let you know. You have my word. Now, can we please concentrate on the matter in hand?'

'The matter in hand?'

Farooq rolled his eyes. 'Last night I warned you I intended to charge you with the murder of Omar Tawfiq. Or have you forgotten?'

'No.'

'Well, then. Has your memory returned yet? Are you prepared to tell us what truly happened? Why you drove into that ditch?'

'I didn't drive into it.'

'Yes, you did. And I want to know why.' He leaned forwards a fraction, a look in his eye almost like greed. 'There's something on Peterson's site, isn't there?'

Knox hesitated. Under other circumstances, he'd have resisted Farooq's clumsy efforts to make him incriminate himself. But Gaille was in danger, and she needed his help. And the key to her message lay in the mosaic on Peterson's site. 'Yes,' he said. 'There is.'

'I knew it!' exulted Farooq, clenching a fist. 'I knew it! What is it?'

'An underground network. Chambers, corridors, catacombs.'

'And that's why you drove Omar into the ditch, isn't it?'

'I didn't drive Omar into the ditch.'

'Sure!' scoffed Farooq. He grabbed his pen. 'Right, then. Tell me how to find this thing. Believe me, it'll go easier with you if you cooperate.'

'I'll do better than that,' said Knox, with as much assurance as he could muster. 'Take me out there and I'll show you.'

II

Augustin got little joy at the police station. No visits allowed for Knox; even after an offer of *baksheesh*. In interview, apparently. Come back in an hour. He went out onto the station steps, fretful, feeling the need to do something – anything – that might help. A clear blue sky, the sun still too low to offer much warmth. He rubbed his cheeks, massaged his temples, his mind leaden and fuzzy. Sometimes, in the middle of conversations, he'd start slurring slightly for no reason whatsoever.

He'd stop speaking at once, limit himself to grunts and nods. People thought him rude.

Perhaps Kostas would know something. Knox had been arrested at his apartment, after all. He got onto his bike, sped through the morning traffic, parked down a narrow alley, hurried up the front steps. The elderly Greek grimaced at the sight of him, the smell of whisky on his breath.

'Last night's,' grunted Augustin, as he went inside.

'If you say so.'

'You've heard about Knox?'

Kostas nodded. 'They arrested him here, you know,' he said, his hands trembling, his eyes watery. 'It was awful. Is it true what they said about Omar?'

'That he's dead, yes. That Knox was responsible, no. Listen, I don't have much time. I need to know what you and Knox talked about.'

'All kinds of things. The Therapeutae. The Carpocratians.'

'The Carpocratians?' A bell rang distantly in Augustin's mind. 'What about them?'

'Among other things, that they used to identify each other by tattooing the lobes of their right ears.'

'Ah!'

'Quite. That was Knox's reaction too. He asked me why biblical archaeologists might be hunting them down. That's when those policemen arrived. I think I've found the answer, though.'

'And?'

'They were quite the aesthetes, the Carpocratians. They didn't just admire the philosophy of people like Plato, Aristotle and Pythagoras, they decorated their temples with their portraits and busts.'

'So?' frowned Augustin. 'Why would a biblical archaeologist be interested in a bust of Plato or Pythagoras?'

'Oh, no,' chuckled Kostas. 'You misunderstand me. Not a bust. A painting. And not of Plato or Pythagoras.'

'Then who?'

'According to our ancient sources, the Carpocratians possessed the only portrait ever made of Our Lord and Saviour Jesus Christ.'

III

'Tell us about him,' said Lily.

'About who?' asked Gaille.

'This friend of yours. Daniel Knox, wasn't it? The one who's going to save us.'

'Oh, him,' said Gaille.

'Yes,' agreed Lily dryly. 'Him.'

Gaille swept her hair back from her brow, held it there in a bunch. 'He's just this guy I work with,

341

that's all. But he has a knack of making things happen, you know.'

'A knack,' said Stafford. 'Oh, good.'

'I can't explain it better. But if anyone can find us, he will.'

'Are you two . . . ?' asked Lily.

'No.' She sensed how thin that sounded, so she added: 'It's complex. We have history.'

'Please, Gaille.'

She sighed. 'My father meant a great deal to me when I was young. He meant *everything*. All I ever wanted was to please him. I became an Egyptologist because that's what he was, because it meant I could go away on excavation with him. That's when I first came on excavation at Amarna, even though I was still at school at the time. Then he started a new dig in Mallawi, just across the river from here. I was to be his assistant. But he postponed at the last minute, so that it didn't get underway until after my school term had started, and I couldn't go with him. Then I found out that he'd taken this man Daniel Knox in my place.' She took a deep breath. 'The thing is, my father was . . . that's to say, he preferred men to women.'

'Ah.'

'So I got the wrong idea about all this. I thought he'd put me off because he'd fallen for Knox; or, rather, because Knox had *wormed* his way into his affection, you know. But it wasn't like that at all. Apart from anything else, Knox isn't like that. My father tried over and over to explain, but I'd already turned my back on him by then; I wouldn't listen. It felt too good being angry, you know? It felt *righteous*. But time passed. I grew up. I got over myself. I began to realize how badly I missed my father. I was just about ready to swallow my pride and mend fences when I got the letter. An accident. A climbing accident.'

'Oh, Gaille,' said Lily. 'I'm so sorry.'

'It shouldn't have meant anything. He'd already been out of my life for years, after all. But it wasn't like that. It knocked me all over the place. I did all the usual stupid things. I slept with everybody. I slept with nobody. I drank. I took drugs. It took me ages to pull myself together. And my anger was one of the things that helped me get through it. Not anger at my father. At Knox. Being my father's assistant had always been *my* job, you see. It should have been *me* out there with my father on that climbing trip. *I'd* have saved him. So it followed logically that Knox had killed him. He gave me a focus of blame, you know, so that I wouldn't have to blame myself. Christ, I used to hate him.' She shook her head ruefully, struggling to believe how violent her passion had been. 'I mean, I *really* used to hate him.'

'You obviously don't hate him any more,' observed Lily. 'What happened?'

The question took Gaille by surprise. She had to consider it for a moment. When she realized the answer, it made her laugh out loud. 'I met him,' she said.

THIRTY-FOUR

I

Farooq kept his hand firmly on Knox's shoulder as he steered him through the station, more to show the world who was boss than from any fear he might run. They climbed into the back of the police car together, Hosni taking the wheel. Knox stared out through the window as they left Alexandria behind, drove west then south on the low causeway across Lake Mariut. He'd hoped the drive would jog his memory, but nothing came. His uneasiness grew. Farooq wasn't a man to mess with. Beside him, as if sensing this, Farooq folded his arms and looked out of the other window, distancing himself from Knox, preparing to blame him if the trip proved a fiasco.

They turned down a lane, crossed an irrigation channel. Two uniformed security men were playing

backgammon. A shudder of *déjà vu*, gone almost
before he was aware of it. The guard took their
names and business, called in, waved them through.
They bumped their way along a track and over a
small ridge, coasted down the other side to the
offices, parking next to a white pick-up.

Farooq grabbed Knox's collar as if he was a
mischievous dog as he pulled him out of the back.
'Well?' he asked.

Several young excavators appeared on the
brow of a ridge, sniggering at the way Farooq
was manhandling Knox. But then a man in a
dog collar strode over the ridge and all humour
instantly fled their faces, as though amusement
were frivolous, and frivolity a sin. Peterson. It
had to be. But though Knox thought he had the
broad look of his balcony assailant, he couldn't
be sure.

He strode over, looking Knox up and down with
disdain but no obvious anxiety. 'Detective
Inspector,' he said. 'You again.'

'Yes,' agreed Farooq. 'Me again.'

'What brings you back?'

Farooq threw Knox a glance. 'You remember
Mister Daniel Knox?'

'I saved his life. You think I'm likely to forget?'

'He says you've found something here. An
underground antiquity.'

'That's ridiculous. I'd know if we had.'

'Yes,' said Farooq. 'You would.'

'This is the man who killed Omar Tawfiq,' glared Peterson. 'He'd say anything to shift the blame.'

'His claims should be easy enough to prove or disprove. Unless you have a problem with that?'

'Only that it's a waste of everyone's time, Detective Inspector.'

'Good.' He turned to Knox. 'Well, then?'

Knox had hoped just being here would trigger memories, but his mind remained frustratingly blank. He looked around, hoping for inspiration. Power-station towers. A cluster of industrial buildings. Two men laying pipe with a mechanical digger. The crescent of archaeologists, holding their rock-hammers and mattocks like weapons. They reminded him of a solid truth: there was an underground antiquity around here. These people had been getting in and out without being seen. Maybe they'd restricted themselves to after dark but . . . His eyes darted to the office, its canvas extension. Could that be hiding something? But his photographs had clearly shown the shaft out in the open, so unless they'd moved the office since yesterday . . . and they hadn't, he could tell from the potholed track and this parking area, not to mention the converging footpaths in the . . .

The footpaths. Yes!

Walking back and forth day after day, they'd surely have worn a faint path by now. He looked around. Paths led away in all directions.

'Well?' asked Farooq, arms folded, his patience running thin.

A shudder of memory. After dark, running, his heart racing, slapping against a wire-mesh fence. There was such a fence away to his left, marking the power station's grounds, and a thin footpath wending towards it. It was this or nothing. He nodded along it. 'That way,' he said.

II

Augustin walked down the front steps of Kostas's building in something of a daze. *A portrait of Jesus Christ*. So Peterson's sermonizing wasn't a metaphor. He was after the real thing. He straddled his bike, rocked it off its stand, intending to head back to the police station, but then he finally remembered why the Carpocratians had been familiar. He parked once more and strode angrily back inside. 'The Secret Gospel of Mark!' he cried, when Kostas answered his front door. 'Why didn't you tell me about the Secret Gospel of Mark?'

'Because there's no such thing,' replied Kostas.

'What are you talking about? How can I have heard of it if it doesn't exist?'

'You've heard of unicorns, haven't you?'

'That's not the same.'

'It's *exactly* the same,' said Kostas. 'The Secret Gospel is a fantasy, an invention of greed and malice. It never existed. It can't possibly have anything to do with this.'

'You don't know that. Not for sure.'

'I've dedicated my life to the truth,' said Kostas angrily. 'Forgeries are a cancer. Talking about them at all, even to dismiss them, gives them a legitimacy they don't deserve.'

'Even so,' said Augustin. 'You should have told me. Our friend's in trouble. I need to know everything.'

Kostas's scowl persisted for a few seconds, but then he sighed and relented. 'Very well, then,' he said, leading Augustin back through to his library. 'How much do you know?'

'Not much,' shrugged Augustin. 'Some American woman was over here a couple of years ago, researching a book on the evangelists. Maria, I think her name was.'

'Oh, yes,' nodded Kostas. 'I remember her. Didn't you and she . . . ?'

'We went out a couple of times,' he nodded. 'She told me that Mark had actually written two gospels. One for the uneducated masses, the other only for his inner circle. This second one was called the Secret Gospel of Mark, and it contained arcane and controversial teachings, and it had something to do with the Carpocratians. But that's all I've got.'

Kostas sighed. 'First of all, there never was such a second gospel.'

'So you say.'

'Yes. So I say. The reason you've heard of it is because back in the nineteen fifties, a young American academic called Morton Smith was doing research in the Monastery of Mar Saba. He claimed to have found a letter copied out into the blank endpapers of a seventeenth-century volume of the letters of Saint Ignatius. That's not so unusual. It was a common enough practice, what with the scarcity and value of paper. It was just that this letter was previously unknown, had purportedly been written by Clement of Alexandria, and had explosive subject-matter, all of which turned it into such a major find that it made Morton Smith's name and career. What's more, by a remarkable coincidence, it happened to validate a pet theory of his, for which there was precious little other evidence.'

'How convenient.'

'He wrote two books about it,' nodded Kostas. 'One for the general public, the other for experts.'

'Like the Gospel of Mark itself.'

'Exactly,' agreed Kostas. 'One of his little hoax jokes, no doubt.'

'Hoax jokes?'

Kostas grimaced. 'To academic historians, there's all the difference in the world between a forgery and a hoax. Hoaxes are designed to show so-called experts up as gullible fools, and the perpetrator usually exposes them himself once he's had his fun. But a forgery is designed to deceive *forever*, and to make money for its perpetrator too. The first is mischievous and intensely irritating, but at least it keeps people on their toes. The second is unforgivable. Which presents any potential hoaxer with quite a problem. What if his hoax is exposed by someone else before he can expose it himself, and he's consequently denounced as a forger? He'll be ruined, perhaps even prosecuted. So hoaxers often take precautions against this. For example, they might tell a trusted third party what they're about to do, with instructions to reveal the truth on a specified day. Or they might incorporate telltale clues into their work. An anachronism of some kind, say, like the Roman soldier wearing a wristwatch in the movie. Not that obvious, naturally. But you get the idea.'

Augustin nodded. 'And what you're implying is, if someone wants to pull off a forgery, but is worried about being caught, there's a lot to be said for putting in one or two of these clues so that they can laugh it off as a failed hoax if they're rumbled?'

'Exactly. And that's precisely what Morton Smith did. He used a metaphor about salt, for example, that only makes sense with modern salt, not the rock crystal of Clement's time. And Morton is, after all, about the world's most famous brand of salt.'

'That's pretty tenuous.'

'Yes, but then he didn't want to be discovered, remember. He only wanted an alibi in case he was.'

'And was he?'

Kostas shrugged. 'Most academics immediately dismissed the letter as a forgery, but they were too kind or too timid to point the finger at Morton Smith. They claimed that it was most likely a seventeenth- or eighteenth-century forgery, though why anyone back then would have wanted to forge such a thing and just put it away in the shelves. . . . Anyway, even that won't hold any more. Everything about the letter has been analysed with modern techniques. Handwriting, vocabulary, phraseology. Nothing stands up. There's only one possible conclusion. It's a modern forgery, and it was perpetrated by Morton Smith.'

Hard experience had taught Augustin that every time an academic controversy seemed settled, some new piece of evidence would come along to kick it all off again. But he kept his expression impassive; he needed Kostas to carry on talking. 'Very well,' he said. 'This letter is a contemptible scam. Now what exactly does it say?'

THIRTY-FIVE

I

Knox had rarely felt so isolated as he did walking along the footpath. The collective ill will from Farooq, Peterson and all the young archaeologists was palpable. But he strove to look confident all the same, scanning the rocky ground as he went, hoping to see something, anything. But he reached the fence without success. 'It's here,' said Knox. 'It's somewhere here.'

Farooq glared daggers at him. '*Somewhere* here?'

He nodded south. 'That way a little.'

'I've had enough of this.'

'It's the truth. I've got photographs.'

'Photographs?' Farooq seized upon this. 'Why didn't you say?'

'They've disappeared,' admitted Knox.

'Of course they have!' scoffed Farooq. 'Of course they damned-well have!'

'Augustin saw them.'

'And I'm supposed to believe him, am I?'

'I swear it. My friend Gaille emailed them to me.'

'The one who just got taken hostage, you mean? How very convenient!'

'But they'll still be on her computer,' pointed out Knox. 'And that didn't get taken hostage. Call Hermopolis. Get them to check.'

'I've got a better idea,' sneered Farooq. 'I'll put you on the train down there so you can bring them back yourself.'

'You have to listen to me. She's got—'

The punch caught him high on his cheek. Saliva sprayed from his mouth as he staggered back against the fence. 'I have to listen, do I?' yelled Farooq, grabbing Knox by his hair, dragging him furiously back to his car, twisting and tugging viciously to make sure it hurt.

'Will that be it, officer?' called out Peterson from behind. 'Or should I expect you again tomorrow? I can have tea ready, if you let me know what time.'

Farooq's cheeks blazed but he didn't look around. He bundled Knox into the car with unnecessary force. 'Are you *trying* to make a fool of me?' he hissed, as Hosni pulled away. 'Is that what this is about?'

'I'm telling you the truth. There's something here.'

'There's nothing here!' shouted Farooq. 'Nothing! You hear me?'

They bumped their way out of the site, the car seething with silent rage, back onto the rural lanes to the causeway across Lake Mariut. Knox sank deep into despondency. His future looked unutterably bleak. He'd made an implacable enemy of Farooq. In half an hour or so, he'd be locked back up in his cell, powerless to help Gaille. And who could say when next he'd be let out?

A loud thump on the road ahead, the squeal of locked tyres. Horns blared, traffic slowed. 'What now?' snarled Farooq, as Hosni put on the brakes.

'Some idiot lorry driver.'

The other side of the central reservation, oncoming traffic slowed to rubberneck. A black-and-gold motorbike stopped by the low dividing wall, engine humming like a bumblebee, two men astride in black leathers and crash helmets. The pillion passenger tapped the driver on his shoulder, pointed out Knox sitting prisoner in the back of the police car. He unzipped his jacket and reached inside.

A sudden memory of the night before, Farooq warning him about Omar's family, how they blamed him for his death, their intent and capability. A perfect place for an ambush, this. He

reacted without even thinking, throwing open the
door while the car was still moving, leaping out,
hitting the tarmac hard, crashing against the low
wall of the central reservation, staggering dizzily
to his feet.

Across the other side, the motorbike cut back
into the stream of traffic, sped harmlessly away.
A false alarm. Hosni screeched to a halt down the
road. Farooq jumped out, gun drawn, face dark
with fury. Knox held up his hands, but Farooq
raised his gun all the same, aimed, braced to fire.
Knox turned and fled across the central reservation, dancing between oncoming traffic, using it
as a shield, then down the side of the causeway
between two startled fishermen who grabbed their
rods and ran. A ramp of sharp wet rocks sloped
down into the lake, refracting beneath the surface
to make it look impossibly shallow. A shot cracked
out behind. He took a deep breath and dived into
the dark lake waters.

II

Kostas plucked a large volume from his shelves,
licked his thumb and forefinger, checked the index,
then turned to pages of photographs of the original letter in handwritten Greek. 'This is a forgery,
remember,' he warned Augustin. 'A despicable

forgery designed to enrich and aggrandize one man at the expense of the truth.'

'Just tell me.'

'Very well.' He put on his reading glasses, squinted at the photograph, muttering each sentence to himself until he'd made a suitable translation that he then spoke out loud for Augustin's benefit.

'To Theodore.

Commendations on silencing these Carpocratians. They are those mentioned in prophecy, who fall from the narrow path of the commandments into chasms of lust. They boast of knowing the secrets of Satan, yet do not realize that they are casting themselves away. They claim they are free, but in truth are slaves of their desires. They must be opposed utterly. Even should they say something true, do not agree with them. For not everything true is the truth, nor should human truth be preferred to the truth of faith.'

Kostas looked up. 'Clement goes on to acknowledge the existence of "secret" writings. Then he says:

'So Mark wrote a second Gospel for those being perfected. He did not reveal the secrets

or the sacred teaching of the Lord, but merely added new stories to those already written, and brought in certain sayings to lead hearers into the innermost sanctuary of truth.'

Augustin smiled. 'The innermost sanctuary of truth!

'Apparently the Carpocratians tricked some hapless presbyter into giving them a copy of this supposed Secret Gospel. Clement then cites some of the more perverse sections – an absurd thing for him to do when you think about it – which is where this whole thing turns so controversial. But you need some context, first. Are you familiar with the *lacuna* in chapter ten of the Gospel of Mark, between verses thirty-four and -five?'

'Do I look like a Bible scholar?'

'Well, the text reads: "And he came unto Bethany. And then they left Bethany." You see the problem?'

'Nothing happens.'

'There's also an unexplained switch from "he" to "they". Scholars have long wondered whether some overzealous Church editor didn't cut out some problematic episode; no doubt why Morton Smith seized upon it. Listen. This is his version.

'They arrived in Bethany. A woman whose brother had died was there. She prostrated

herself before Jesus and said, "Son of David, have mercy on me." But his disciples—'

'What did you say?' interrupted Augustin. 'Did you just say "Son of David, have mercy on me"?'

Kostas frowned, perplexed by his sudden vehemence. 'Yes. Why?'

Augustin shook his head. That same subscript had been on one of Gaille's photographs. 'I'm sorry,' he said. 'Please go on.'

Kostas nodded and picked it up again.

'But his disciples chastised her. And Jesus, angered, went with her to the tomb where the young man was buried. He reached out and raised him by his hand. But the young man, looking upon him, loved him and begged to go with him. And they went to the house of the young man, who was rich. And after six days Jesus instructed the youth, and he came to him that night wearing only a linen cloth over his naked body. And they stayed together, and Jesus taught him the mystery of the Kingdom of God. And then he went to the far side of the Jordan.'

'Good God,' muttered Augustin. Linen cloths, naked bodies, overnight stays; standard fare for a

Greek mystery initiation, a worst nightmare come true for a homophobic Christian fundamentalist.

'You can see why it generated such controversy,' said Kostas. 'But, like I say, it's nothing but a malicious forgery. It can't possibly have anything to do with this ancient site of yours.'

'Maybe not,' admitted Augustin. *But what if Peterson didn't realize that?*

THIRTY-SIX

I

Farooq ran between cars and leapt up onto the causeway wall in time to glimpse Knox's dark slim shadow beneath the surface, before he lost him in the sun's reflection and the opaque churned water, so that he could only trace his progress through the diminishing trail of released bubbles. He aimed down, waiting tensely for Knox to resurface.

'What the hell was that about?' asked Hosni, stepping up onto the wall beside him.

'What did it look like?'

'Something spooked him,' said Hosni.

'Nothing spooked him,' snapped Farooq. 'He did a runner, that's all.'

'It was those two bikers. They put the fear of God in him.' He glanced curiously at Farooq. 'You didn't spin him one of your gangster yarns, did you?'

'Be quiet.'

'You did!' guffawed Hosni. 'You told him that Omar was connected! No wonder the poor guy fled!'

Farooq turned furiously on his colleague. 'I'll only say this once. One word of that bullshit gets around, I'll have your balls, understand?'

'Yes, sir,' said Hosni soberly.

'Good.' Traffic had stopped both sides of the causeway. Farooq felt eyes upon him, mutters, sniggers. His cheeks blazed. *He'd never hear the end of this!* He felt an exquisite need to take it out on someone, anyone. His finger itched on the trigger, but Knox was still underwater: the man had the lungs of a whale.

'Look!' cried Hosni, pointing out across the lake. 'There he is!'

II

Captain Khaled Osman had made sure to telephone the kidnap investigation team in Assiut bright and early that morning. He'd spoken to a senior officer, told him that he'd seen the coverage on the TV, and that Stafford and his crew had been filming in Amarna just the day before. The man had sounded deeply uninterested, the focus of his investigation clearly in Assiut. But he'd promised to send up a couple of cars to look around, take statements. Now here they were. 'A terrible thing,' he said, greeting each of them in turn, shaking his head sadly. 'Truly terrible. Tell us what we can do to help. Whatever's in our power, just ask.'

'That's very good of you.'

'Not at all. Things like this make me feel sick.'

'We'll need to see where they went. Speak to everyone who met them.'

'Of course,' said Khaled. 'You can use this as your interview room. And I'll take you round Amarna myself. We'll follow the exact same route they took.' He cast a look up at the heavens. An overcast sky, a chill wind. One of Amarna's rare but brutal storms was brewing. He beckoned Nasser across. 'I'm going out with these officers,' he said. 'Let no one in until they've finished. No one. Understand. We can't have souvenir hunters contaminating the site. Isn't that right, officers?'

'Sure,' nodded one.

Khaled climbed in the back of the first car, pointed out which direction to head. 'Making any progress?'

The driver shook his head. 'Not much. They seem to be lying low.' He gave a dry laugh. 'They can't have realized what a hornet's nest they'd stir up.'

'That bad?' asked Khaled, as a first few patters of rain stuttered on the roof and bonnet.

'I've never seen anything like it. Assiut's just a sea of uniforms. We're going door to door right now. We've already taken a few hotheads into custody. They're giving us some names. You know how it is. Trust me. We'll have these hostages back safe and sound within a week.'

Khaled nodded earnestly. 'I'm glad to hear it,' he said.

III

Knox was still heaving for air when he heard the gunshot and saw the plume of water spout away to his left. His chest was throbbing from where he'd scraped rock during his dive. His eyes burned from the sharp polluted water, so that he could hardly see as he looked around.

Lake Mariut's northern bank was just a couple of hundred metres away, fringed by clumps of reeds that offered cover. He couldn't see the southern bank at all, but he knew from memory that the lake was a good two kilometres across.

Another shot cracked, another spout of water. He couldn't wait any longer. He kicked back underwater. The lake was shallow, just a metre deep in places. Its floor was littered with masonry, relics of the dilapidated piers that had been built out onto it over the millennia. He found a chunk of

stone, held it against his chest, using it as a weight
to hold himself down while he took on more air.

Farooq would surely expect him to come ashore
on the northern bank. But the terrain was so bare
and open he'd struggle to avoid recapture even for
an hour. And avoiding recapture wasn't enough.
He needed to find that mosaic, establish his inno-
cence, help Gaille. And the way to do that was by
heading south, not north.

He oriented himself using the sunlight, clasped
the stone against his belly, then headed southwest,
propelling himself with smooth, even kicks,
pausing every thirty seconds or so to take on more
air.

THIRTY-SEVEN

I

Augustin was climbing back astride his motorbike when his mobile rang. 'Doctor Augustin Pascal?' asked a man.

'Speaking,' said Augustin. 'Who's this?'

'My name is Mohammed. I shared a cell with a friend of yours last night. A Mister Daniel Knox.'

'He asked you to call me?'

'Yes. He wanted me to pass a message to you about your friend the woman Gaille, the one who's been taken hostage.'

'What message?'

'After he saw her, he was very upset. I asked how I could help. Then this morning, before he went off to Borg el-Arab with Detective Inspector Farooq, he gave me this number.'

'What was the message?' asked Augustin.

'I would have called earlier, but they only just let me out. It's gone crazy around here. All the police are heading off to—'

'Tell me this bloody message!' shouted Augustin.

'Okay, okay.' He took a deep breath, as though trying to remember word-for-word what he'd been told to say. 'Apparently the way your friend Gaille was sitting in the video was exactly the same as in the mosaic. Exactly the same. Mister Daniel said you'd know what that meant.'

Augustin's skin tingled. *Of course!* How had he failed to spot it himself? 'Where's Knox now?' he asked. 'I need to speak to him.'

'That's what I was trying to tell you,' said the man. 'He went off to Borg with Farooq, hoping to find this mosaic. But word is they didn't find anything; and now he's done a runner.'

'He's done *what*?'

'I wouldn't be in his shoes. Not for anything. That Farooq is one mean bastard. He doesn't like anyone getting the better of him.'

'No,' agreed Augustin ruefully. 'And thanks.' He ended the call, sat there a few moments, wondering what to do, how best to help. His first thought was to go look for Knox, but that was a tall order on his own and with the police out hunting. Anyway, if he knew Knox, he'd want him to go for the mosaic, because that was the way to help Gaille. The only question was how.

II

Knox hauled himself exhausted and dripping onto the craggy southern shore of Lake Mariut. He kept low as he hurried across the exposed rocky fringe, up a slight rise and into the shadow of one of the ubiquitous Bedouin pigeon houses that stood like huge, tar-covered bells.

He felt drained from his long swim, but he didn't have time to recuperate. By panicking and running, he'd certainly quashed any lingering doubts Farooq might have had over his guilt. He'd humiliated him too. The word would already be out: a killer was on the loose. Egyptian police didn't carry their guns as fashion accessories. They'd shoot on sight. And if he handed himself in, they'd simply go to work on him with their canes, and he was quite sore enough already.

He kicked off his shoes, stripped off his shirt and trousers, laid them against the shimmering hot surface of the birdhouse. Water vapour instantly began smouldering from the cotton. When they'd dried sufficiently on one side, he turned them over.

A sixth sense made him look around. A grizzled Bedouin farmer was standing a hundred metres or so away, leaning on his staff, watching him curiously. Knox shrugged his shoulders, not unduly alarmed. No self-respecting Bedouin would willingly talk to the police. But he needed to get moving.

His clothes were already dry enough to pull back on. The twin chimneys of the power station were a two-fingered salute in the western skyline. Peterson's dig lay beyond them. He nodded to the shepherd as he began to jog.

III

It was Lily who heard the noise first. 'What was that?' she asked.

'What was what?' asked Stafford.

'I don't know. It sounded like . . . *tapping*.'

They listened together. Now Gaille heard it too. Every four seconds or so. A gentle tap coming from somewhere high above. 'Hello!' called out Lily. 'Anyone up there?' She fell silent, the echoes died away. There it was again, its rhythm unchanged.

'Something's dripping,' said Lily.

'Yes,' said Stafford.

'Listen,' swallowed Gaille. 'I don't want to alarm you guys or anything, but if that is dripping, then maybe it's started raining.'

'But this is desert,' said Lily.

'It still rains here,' said Gaille. 'In fact, I was here during a storm once, years ago. You wouldn't believe how fierce they can get. And there's a rift in the plateau directly above us, remember? If there's some way for the water to get in . . .'

'It'll all end up draining down here,' muttered Stafford bleakly, finishing the thought for her.

'But it's only drips,' said Lily.

'So far,' agreed Gaille. But right then a second drip joined the first, at a slightly different tempo. And then, a minute after that, they heard the first trickle.

THIRTY-EIGHT

I

'Have you still got that remote-controlled aircraft?' asked Augustin, walking unannounced into Mansoor's SCA office.

'I'm in a meeting,' protested Mansoor, gesturing to the three men in sombre dark suits around his table. 'Can't this wait?'

'There!' said Augustin, spotting the outsize box leaning against the wall. He opened it up, looked inside. A GWS Slowstick. Perfect. As easy to operate as they came. He checked through the components, fuel, remote controls, batteries and other attachments. Everything he'd need.

'It's not mine,' protested Mansoor. 'It belongs to the Germans. It's valuable equipment. I can't possibly let you just take it.'

Augustin hefted it to his shoulder, nodded at the suits. 'Nice to meet you all,' he said.

'You'll return it?' asked Mansoor plaintively. 'Rudi will kill me if anything happens to it.'

'You'll have it back this evening,' promised Augustin. 'You have my word.'

'That's what you said about my GPS.'

But the door banged closed behind Augustin. He was on his way.

II

Knox made good progress until he reached the power station, whose perimeter fence stretched away in both directions. Peterson's site lay on the other side; he had neither the time nor the inclination for a detour. The wire was flopping limply with age, making it hard to climb. He went to one of the cement pillars, where it was sturdier, checked to make sure he wasn't being watched, then hauled himself up. The mesh left red welts across his fingers. He vaulted over, dropped inelegantly down the other side, stumbling onto his hands and knees.

He waited a few moments in case the alarm went up, then stood and walked briskly with his head bowed across a half-empty car park outside some kind of administrative block. A side door opened as he approached and a dumpy woman came out, frowning suspiciously. He angled away from her, putting a line of parked cars between them. She put her head back inside, called out. Knox raised his pace. An overweight security guard ambled out. The woman pointed to Knox. The guard called out for him to stop. Knox broke into a run instead, aiming for the far fence. The footing was treacherous. A stone turned and sent him tumbling, wrenching his knee. He glanced around. The guard was closing in on him, a second one following, yelling for backup. Knox pushed himself up, hobbled over to the fence, climbed it, pain spiking up his leg as he landed.

The first guard reached the fence behind him, breathing too hard to remonstrate beyond wagging a finger. Knox limped away, fearful that the commotion would attract Peterson and his crowd. His knee throbbed badly, but he didn't dare slow. If the police heard about this, the place would be swarming within minutes. He didn't have a moment to waste.

III

The remote-controlled aircraft was too bulky and cumbersome for Augustin's bike, so he waved down a taxi, put the box across its rear seat, and hired the driver to follow him out to Borg el-Arab.

He'd operated many such planes before. It was a great way to photograph ancient sites, not to mention a lot of fun too. They were easy enough beasts to fly. Launching them, however, was another matter, as was taking photographs while they were up.

He parked his bike in a thin copse a kilometre or so from Peterson's site, waved the taxi in beside him. The driver was in his early twenties, with wispy facial hair and a jovial demeanour. 'What's your name?' Augustin asked him as he paid him off.

'Hani.'

'Well, Hani. You want to earn another ten?'

'Of course. How?'

Augustin got the box out of the back, opened it up. Hani's eyes and mouth made three perfect circles of excitement when he saw the plane inside. 'Can I have a go?'

'Sure. Once I'm done.'

They cut across country, keeping a wall between them and Peterson's site, until they reached a suitable patch of clear hard ground. As good a spot as any. Augustin knelt, opened the box, began assembly.

'What's this for, then?'

'I'm doing a survey for the Supreme Council of Antiquities.'

'Sure you are!'

Augustin grinned. 'Have you ever seen an aerial photograph of a field? You wouldn't believe how much detail it reveals.' He snapped the red foam wings onto the praying-mantis frame, tightened the screws. 'Ditches, walls, roads, settlements. Things you can walk over every day without even noticing, suddenly they spring out at you.' The technique had been discovered by accident almost exactly a hundred years before. The British Army had been experimenting with aerial reconnaissance on Salisbury Plain when their balloon had drifted over Stonehenge, its photographs revealing for the first time the lattice of ancient footpaths that criss-crossed the site.

'Huh,' said Hani.

'Huh, indeed,' agreed Augustin. 'I couldn't have put it better myself.' He fixed the camera obliquely to the undercarriage so that he could photograph the site without flying directly over it, then tested the remote controls to make sure everything responded as it should. 'Okay,' he said, satisfied. 'Let's do it.'

IV

Knox crept up behind Peterson's cabin office. A heated conversation was taking place inside, but the windows were closed, so that he could only make out the occasional word. Cairo. Police. Coward.

The white pick-up was still parked in front, joined by a blue Toyota 4x4, the spitting image of the vehicle in which his balcony assailant had fled. It hadn't been there earlier. Was it possible someone had moved it after the security guard had alerted them that he and Farooq were on their way in? More to the point, was it possible Augustin's laptop was still inside?

He crouched and hurried over. The glare of the sun and the dusty glass made it hard to see. He tried the door. Unlocked. He checked front and back. Nothing. He shut the door quietly, circled around, glimpsed something half-hidden beneath a dustsheet through the rear window. He lifted the hatchback quietly. Not a laptop, as he'd hoped, just a small box of pencils, pens, notepads and other such supplies. Voices grew louder suddenly from the direction of the cabin, two men thrashing it out while they walked towards him. He ducked down, tried to press the hatchback closed, but it wouldn't lock, it needed to be closed with force.

'This is madness, Reverend,' said one of the men. 'We need to leave, not chase off across Egypt on some fool errand.'

'You worry too much, Brother Griffin.'

Knox couldn't risk slamming the hatchback closed: he'd be noticed instantly. He made to get away instead, using the Toyota as cover. But the hatchback began to rise on its hydraulic arms, forcing him to hurry back, grab it, hold it down. The two men were coming his way. He was bound to be spotted in a moment. He raised the hatchback just far enough to slip inside, then pulled it down after him, holding it there by pinching the interior catch.

'How many times do I have to tell you?' said Griffin. 'Pascal has clout with these people. He won't leave this alone, believe me. He'll get the SCA to launch an investigation. Maybe not today or tomorrow, but it'll happen, count on it. And when it does, they'll find the shaft, they'll find the steps. They'll find everything. They'll ask us to explain. And what will we tell them then?'

'Careful, Brother Griffin. You're becoming hysterical.'

'These students are in *my* care,' retorted Griffin. 'They're *my* responsibility. I take that seriously.'

'You take saving your own skin seriously.'

'Think what you like. I'm getting them home. Don't you know what the Egyptian criminal justice system is like?'

'Are you suggesting God's work is criminal?'

'I'm suggesting that God helps those who help themselves, not those vain enough to think that He'll intervene whenever they get themselves into trouble. Humility, Reverend. Aren't you always lecturing us about humility?'

A moment's pause. The salvo had hit home. 'What precisely are you recommending?'

'Haven't you been listening? We get the first flight out, screw the cost. Back to the States, if possible, but anywhere in Europe failing that. And when the story breaks, which it will, we'll deny everything. We'll say we were acting with the full knowledge and blessing of the SCA. It'll be our word against theirs, and no one back home will believe an Egyptian over us, which is all that matters.'

'Very well,' said Peterson. 'You take care of your students. Leave God's work to me.'

'Suits me fine.'

The driver door opened. Peterson climbed in, the vehicle lurching slightly beneath his weight, enough to jolt the hatchback free from Knox's grasp. He tried to grab it back but it was too late, it was already rising up on its hydraulic arms. Peterson gave a weary sigh. 'Close that for me, would you please, Brother Griffin?'

'Of course,' said Griffin. And he walked around towards the rear of the Toyota, where Knox was lying in plain view, glowing golden in the slanted afternoon sunshine.

THIRTY-NINE

I

'What are we going to do?' wailed Lily, as the trickle of water turned into a stream.

'Let's not panic, for one thing,' replied Gaille. She struck one of their dwindling stock of matches, lit the candle stub, stood up.

High above her, the dustsheets and blankets stretched out between the planks were sagging visibly beneath the gathering weight of water. A drip filtered through the fabric even as she watched, splashed at her feet. There was no way to know how hard a storm this was. Hope for the best, they always advised, but plan for the worst. The foot of the sump was rubble and compacted sand. At first the water would soak away into it. But eventually it would be saturated and then the shaft would start to fill. 'We need to dig,' she said.

'What?'

She stamped the floor with her foot. 'We dig down on one side, build up a ramp on the other. That'll give the water somewhere to drain off to, and it'll provide us with a ledge to stand on as well.'

There was silence as they contemplated this, how small a response to how remorseless a threat. But it was better than nothing.

'Let's do it,' said Stafford.

II

Knox braced himself for imminent discovery as Griffin arrived around the back of the Toyota, but instead of looking down, he was staring up into the sky. It took Knox a moment to hear what had snagged his attention, an engine like a chain saw, buzzing loudly for a moment before dying away again. Griffin's frown turned to a scowl. He slammed the hatchback down without looking, marched back to the driver's window. 'You hear that?' he demanded.

'Hear what, Brother Griffin?'

'That!' He jabbed a finger at the sky. 'It's a damned remote-controlled aircraft. That Frenchman Pascal is taking pictures of our site.'

'Are you sure?'

'How many remote-controlled aircraft have you seen here since we started?'

'None,' acknowledged Peterson.

'And you think it's just coincidence there's one today, do you?'

A few beats of silence. 'Will he find it?'

'Damn right,' said Griffin. 'Have you forgotten how *we* found this place?'

'Then you'd better stop him,' said Peterson.

'How do you mean?'

'I mean exactly what I say. Take our security men. Get that camera from him before he can do anything with it.'

'We can't do that!'

'You have no choice, Brother Griffin. Unless you don't mind your precious students paying for your cowardice.'

'Fine,' scowled Griffin. 'But then we're out of here.'

'And a great loss that will be,' said Peterson. He put the Toyota into gear, lumbering away over the rutted ground, taking Knox with him wherever it was he was headed.

III

The manhunt for Knox was not going well. 'This is ridiculous,' said Hosni. 'He's got away. Accept it.'

'He hasn't got away,' retorted Farooq, sweeping his arm across Mariut's northern shore, barren and open except for a few thin clumps of reeds that they'd already searched three times. 'How could he possibly have got away without us seeing him?'

'He must have drowned then,' muttered Hosni. 'Give him a day or two, he'll bob up for sure.'

Farooq grunted. He had little faith that Knox would do the honourable thing. 'He's here somewhere,' he said, opening his car door, sitting down and turning on the heaters to blast hot air at his wet feet. 'I know he is.'

'Come on, boss. The guys have had enough. Let's call it a day.'

'He's a killer. An escaped killer.'

'You don't honestly believe that, do you?'

'If you hadn't put on the brakes, he wouldn't have got away.'

'You wanted me to crash into the car in front? Is that what you're saying?' Hosni took a deep breath, spread his hands. 'Look, boss. Maybe he is still here, but isn't it just possible he managed to slip away? Why don't I send some of the guys to check out the places he might have gone?'

'Such as?'

'Pascal's apartment, for one. And to that man Kostas, where we picked him up yesterday. Or his hotel. Or Peterson's site.'

'Not Peterson,' glowered Farooq. 'I'm not having that man gloating about Knox getting away from me again. I'm not having it, you hear?'

'Fine. I'll just have a car monitor the lane. That's all. He won't even know they're there. The others can go back to Alex.' He turned and walked away without waiting for agreement.

Farooq bridled but said nothing, aware how bad this whole fiasco was making him look. Hosni was right. He needed to recapture Knox quickly. It was the only way to regain face. Where else might he have gone? He recalled his outburst on Peterson's site, his claim that the hostage woman Gaille had a set of photographs on her computer. An uneasy sensation passed through him. If he went for those, it meant he'd been sincere in his story. But he pushed that anxiety to one side, called the station instead, had them put him through to Mallawi, where he spoke to his counterpart, a man called Gamal. 'Just wanted to give you guys a heads-up,' he said. 'Someone we're interested in may be headed your way.'

'Interested in, why?'

'Murder,' said Farooq.

Gamal sucked in breath. 'Details?'

'His name's Daniel Knox. An archaeologist. Bastard killed the head of the SCA up here, a man named Omar Tawfiq.'

'What makes you think he's coming our way?'

Farooq hesitated. Underplay it, they'd do nothing. He needed Gamal convinced it was a live situation. 'We intercepted a phone call. He's heading your way all right. He's after a computer. It belongs to another archaeologist. Gaille whatever her name is. The one who's been taken hostage.'

'Hell,' muttered Gamal. 'Just what we need. You wouldn't believe how much shit that's already stirred up. How will we identify him?'

'He's maybe thirty. Tall. Dark hair. Athletic. English. He was in a car crash; you'll see it on his face.' He took a breath. 'And be warned: he's a slippery bastard, this one. Dangerous, too. He as good as told me how he'd killed Tawfiq. Boasted about it. He'll probably be armed by now, and he won't mess around, believe me. If you're wise, you'll ask your questions later, if you know what I mean.'

'Thanks,' said Gamal dryly.

'Just doing my job,' Farooq told him.

IV

'Well,' said Tarek. 'You asked to see us. Here we are.'

Naguib nodded at the men assembled in the room, contemplating him with a variety of expressions, from indifference through suspicion to undisguised hostility. He couldn't exactly blame them. These were Amarna's *ghaffirs*, informal guards and guides traditionally left to their own devices, as long as they kept a lid on things, their jobs passed down from father to son, giving them status and income. But things had begun to change, central and regional government trying to phase them out, imposing outsiders like himself on their communities. It was no wonder they'd reacted coolly to his efforts to win them over.

'My name is Inspector Naguib Hussein,' he said. 'I am new to this area. I have met some of you before, but—'

'We know who you are.'

'I was out in the desert yesterday. I found the body of a young girl.'

'My son Mahmoud found her,' grunted Tarek. 'He reported it to you, as we've been instructed.'

'Yes,' agreed Naguib. 'And I'm very grateful, believe me. But I'm having little success finding out who she was, what happened to her.'

Tarek shook his head. 'She wasn't from around here. That's all we can tell you.'

'You're certain?'

'We know our own people.'

'Any idea where she might have come from?'

'We're not as isolated as we once were, as you

yourself know. People come and then they go again.'

'But you see them. You're aware of them.'

'We weren't aware of this one.'

Naguib leaned forward. 'We found a figurine on her. An Amarna artefact.'

An exchange of glances, surprise and curiosity. 'What's that to do with us?'

'I've heard that no one is as skilled at finding artefacts as you *ghaffirs*. I've heard that you find the sites that even the archaeologists can't find.'

'Then you've heard true enough,' nodded Tarek. 'Though naturally we always tell them straight away.'

'Naturally,' agreed Naguib, once the laughter had died down. He took the figurine from his pocket, passed it across. 'Perhaps you might have some idea where this came from?'

Tarek examined it, shook his head, passed it to his neighbour. 'Most artefacts like this are in the wadis. We're not allowed in the wadis any more.'

Naguib frowned. 'Why not?'

'Ask your friend Captain Khaled,' scowled Tarek. 'And if he tells you, I'd be grateful if you let us know. He's taken away a source of good revenue.' There were murmurs of assent from around the room.

'When did this happen?' asked Naguib.

Tarek shrugged, leaned across to confer with the man next to him. 'Six months ago,' he said.

'You're sure?'

'Yes,' said Tarek, nodding at the wall of rain outside. 'It was the day after the last great storm.'

V

It was a while since Augustin had flown a remote-controlled aircraft. But once it was up, his hands took over and he began enjoying himself. He sent the plane on several passes of Peterson's site, Hani snapping photographs at his command with the camera's remote. But then he nudged his arm, pointed to a white pick-up driving along the lane on the other side of the wall, three burly security guards on the flatbed gazing up into the sky like wise men following a star. 'I thought this was an official SCA survey,' he murmured.

'You'd better get out of here,' said Augustin.

'What about you?'

'I'll be fine.'

'I can't just leave you.'

'This isn't your fight.'

Hani shrugged but nodded, set down the remote control, slipped away.

Augustin steered the plane away along the line of the lane, teasing the pick-up after it, before putting it into a circle for long enough for Hani to reach his taxi and get away. Then he aimed

it back his way, walking briskly as he worked
the controls, his eyes fixed on it. He heard the
pick-up's engine. A cry went up. He'd been
spotted. No time for finesse now. He sent the
plane into a dive, crunching into the hard ground
fifty metres ahead. Its fuselage crumpled, its red
foam wings sprang loose. He threw down the
remote and sprinted for it. A glance around,
the three men on foot closing fast. He grabbed the
camera, tried to wrench it free, only succeeding
in buckling the catches. He picked the whole
thing up, trying to undo the clasps on the run.
He legs tangled in the fuselage, he went sprawling,
finally wrested the camera free. The first of his
pursuers was just a few paces behind, putting in
a frantic burst to catch him, diving and slapping
one of his ankles against the other, sending
Augustin sprawling. But he sprang straight back
up to his feet again, the copse just twenty metres
ahead. He reached his bike, straddled her, started
her up, glanced back. His pursuers had fallen far
behind, had come to a halt, were heaving for air.
He revved the engine victoriously, gave them a
cheerful wave as he sped out of the trees onto
the lane.

The pick-up struck him side-on. He slithered
along its bonnet, struck its slanted windscreen,
catching a glimpse of Griffin the other side of the
glass, every bit as shocked by the collision as

Augustin himself. And then he was in the air, his world spinning crazily, wondering with more curiosity than fear if it would be the last thing he ever saw.

FORTY

I

The digging wasn't easy. The sand and rubble had compacted like concrete over the centuries. Gaille's fingernails were soon ripped and bleeding from scrabbling it up. But fear kept her at it. Worms of water had started slithering down the walls, gathering in puddles at the foot.

'Could you light a match, please?' asked Lily, breathing heavily.

'We've only got a couple left.'

'But I think I've found something.'

'What?' asked Stafford.

'I don't know. Why do you think I need a match?'

The flare hurt Gaille's eyes, they'd been in the dark so long. And that sulphurous smell! She lit the candle, took it across. Lily was right. There was indeed something at the bottom of the wall. A line of hieroglyphs.

'What do they say?' asked Lily.

Gaille shook her head. The faded glyphs were hard enough to see in the poor light, let alone decipher. But the implications of their being here at all were enough to excite her. She'd assumed, from the crudely-cut walls of the entrance and burial chambers, that this tomb was simply another of the half-finished efforts that pocked these cliffs, abandoned because of the poor-quality limestone or because the Amarna era had come to an end before the prospective occupant had died. She'd further assumed that, because the layout of this place was so similar to that of the nearby Royal Tomb, this shaft was a sump designed to protect the burial chamber. But now that she thought further, she realized her assumptions were flawed. The sump in the Royal Tomb made perfect sense because its mouth was on the wadi floor, putting it in danger from flash floods. But the mouth of *this* tomb wasn't on the wadi floor. It was far nearer the top than the bottom. Flooding wouldn't have been a significant issue, at least until the rift had formed above it, so a sump served little purpose. And, anyway, how deep did they need it? They were a good six metres down already, and still not at the bottom. So maybe it wasn't a sump after all. Maybe it was something else.

'Well?' asked Lily.

Gaille passed Lily the candle to hold while she scraped away more sand. 'I don't suppose either of you have ever visited the tomb of Seti the First, have you?' she asked.

II

Augustin lay dazed in the lane for a few moments before he looked up and around to find himself surrounded by Griffin and his security guards. They looked down anxiously at him, expecting him to be grievously hurt or even dead, but he surprised them by trying to get to his feet. No chance. They picked him up and heaved him unceremoniously onto the back of the pick-up. His head, chest and thigh all throbbed violently. He felt such an urge to vomit that he turned onto his side and braced himself. But the sensation passed. He fell onto his back again, looked up at the security guard standing above him. 'If you've damaged my bike, you little fuck . . .' he warned.

The man smiled and looked away.

They turned off the lane, jolted over the earthen bridge. Throbs became stabs. They pulled up outside a low brick building. Griffin got out, unlocked and opened the steel door. Augustin bellowed as he was dragged from the back of the pick-up into the building. Several of Peterson's young crew gathered nearby, glaring sourly, as though glad to see he'd got what had been coming to him; but an angular fair-headed woman was with them too, surely the same one he'd glimpsed driving away from the site with Griffin the previous afternoon. And she looked anxious, appalled.

He was thrown down onto the floor between a rack of empty shelves and a worktable. The door was slammed shut, the key turned, leaving him in almost complete darkness. He lay there a moment, almost weeping because it hurt so much. He slid a hand inside his shirt onto his tender ribcage. No fracture that he could detect, just bruising. A fond childhood memory, leaping recklessly off a waterfall only to find the pool beneath shallower than it had looked. His mother, once she'd overcome her shock, boasting about his tungsten bones. He stifled a cry as he pushed himself up onto his feet. It pleased him to feel this much pain, yet be able to master it. It made him feel more like a man than he had for weeks. He hobbled to the door. Steel, to judge by its coldness. Neither handle nor bolts on the inside.

It was several minutes before he heard footsteps outside, the key scraping in the lock. The door pushed open, late afternoon sunshine flooding in so brightly he could only see silhouettes for a moment, three of them. An internal light was turned on, a yellow bulb dangling from the ceiling. Two people came in. The third stayed outside, closing the door behind them.

Augustin blinked as his vision adjusted. Griffin and the fair-headed young woman, carrying a tray of medical supplies.

'Here he is, then,' muttered Griffin, folding his arms.

'I want my wallet,' said Augustin. 'My phone.' Even speaking softly, the words made his ribs throb.

'Sure,' snorted Griffin. He turned to the woman. 'Well? I thought you wanted to check him over.'

She set her tray down on the ground. Ungainly, all bones and joints, with slightly beaked features. Aware of it too, uncomfortable with being looked at. Pale freckled skin, fragrant and moist with generous slathers of suntan lotion. A plain silver cross dangling from a chain around her slender long throat. She stood back up, tilting her head slightly, so that wisps of her hair fell like a bead curtain over her face.

'Who the fuck are you?' demanded Augustin.

'I'm here to examine you,' she said. 'It'll only take a moment.'

'Examine me?'

'Make sure nothing's broken, nothing's ruptured.' She frowned, perhaps made a little uncertain by his French accent. 'You know what ruptured means?' she asked.

'Yes,' said Augustin sardonically. 'I know what ruptured means. And if something is ruptured?'

She threw a defiant glance at Griffin. 'Then I'm taking you to hospital.'

Well, well, well, thought Augustin. He put a hand against his side, winced and sucked in breath. 'I think something's ruptured for sure,' he said.

A laugh like a hiccup escaped the woman; she put her hand to her mouth as though she'd done something rude. Rather to Augustin's surprise, he found himself warming to her. 'So you're a doctor then, are you?' he asked.

She shook her head. 'Not exactly. No.'

'I've been in a serious accident,' he protested. 'I could be grievously injured. I need to see a—'

A knock on the door. A young man with short-cropped blond hair poked in his head.

'What now?' asked Griffin irritably.

'The airline people,' said the young man. 'They want to speak to you.'

'I'm busy.'

'The credit card's in your name. They want to speak to you.'

Griffin gave an exasperated sigh, a boss trapped by his own importance. 'Examine him and then leave,' he told the woman curtly. 'And don't let him get you talking.'

'No,' she agreed.

'Ramiz will be outside. Any trouble at all, give him a shout. He'll know what to do.'

'Yes.'

The door closed behind him. The key turned in the lock. Augustin smiled at the woman. 'Well,' he said, rubbing his hands. 'Let's get this examination started, shall we?'

III

For the first fifteen minutes of the drive, Knox feared that Peterson would discover him at any moment in the back of the Toyota. But as they clocked up the miles, he simply grew bored, having to remind himself that he was just a few feet away from a man who'd almost certainly tried to kill him twice already.

As best he could judge, they were on a busy, good road. The angle of sunlight suggested they were heading south. Towards Cairo, presumably, though Knox had no idea why. After two hours or so, Peterson applied the brakes sharply enough to push Knox forward into the back of the rear seats. The indicator stuttered; they turned off, pulled to a stop. Peterson got out, unscrewed the petrol cap right by Knox's head. Fuel gushed in. Knox kept absolutely still lest movement give him away. The cap was screwed back on. Knox heard footsteps over the concourse. He allowed himself to breathe once more. He sat up in time to see Peterson go inside the office to pay. He climbed over the rear seats, intending to let himself out, but then he glimpsed some sheets of paper lying loose on the passenger seat, the top one a print-out from Gaille's Internet Digging Diary, that photograph of her standing outside her room with two archaeologists from Fatima's team. He froze a moment, then slid it aside to look at the one beneath it. Another print-out, this one with directions to Fatima's Hermopolis compound. So that was it. Peterson was spooked by the thought of his photos still on Gaille's laptop.

A door banged closed. He glanced up to see Peterson coming back out. He had no time to resume his previous position. He ducked down behind the driver's seat as Peterson climbed back in.

FORTY-ONE

I

'Airline people, huh,' said Augustin. 'You off somewhere?'

The young woman smiled warily. 'I'm here to check you're okay. Not to talk.'

'But what if I'm not okay? I think I'm seriously injured. I need a proper doctor.'

'You're showing remarkable resilience for a man at death's door. Besides, I know what I'm doing. I really do. And it's me or no one, I'm afraid. It was hard enough persuading Mister Griffin to . . .' She broke off, annoyed with herself for letting herself be drawn even that far, not wanting to compound it.

Augustin let it go. Push too hard now, he'd turn her against him. There was a footstool against the wall, so that people could reach the top shelves.

She fetched it, stood on it to examine his scalp, parting his hair carefully to clean the mess beneath. Her blouse was close to his face; he glimpsed flashes of her pale freckled skin between the buttons, the sturdy white cup of a sensible bra. She applied a disinfectant. He did his best not to wince. She got off her stool, stood face-to-face with him, lifted his eyelids in turn, looked deep into his eyes. Her own irises were of speckled blue, her pupils dilating in response to his. 'Take off your shirt, please,' she said.

'What's your name?' he asked.

'Please. You heard Mister Griffin.'

'Just your name. That's all I ask.'

She gave him a reluctant smile. 'Claire.'

'Claire! I love that name.' He unbuttoned his shirt gingerly. 'You know it means light in French?'

'Yes.'

'It suits you. My grandmother was Claire. A wonderful woman. Truly wonderful. She had the kindest hands.'

'Is that right?'

'Of course.' He grimaced in pain as he tugged his shirt from his waistband, discarded it. He looked self-consciously down at his stomach, wishing he'd taken more exercise recently. 'So you're an archaeologist then, are you, Claire?'

'I'm not talking to you.'

'I guess you must be if you're working here.'

She gave a sigh. 'I'm project administrator, actually. I speak and write some Arabic, you see.'

'You speak Arabic? How come?'

'My father was in oil. I grew up in the Gulf. You know how easy it is to pick up languages when you're a kid. That's why the reverend asked me along, I think. That plus my medical experience. It always comes in useful in places like these.'

'Places like these?'

Her cheeks flushed, she ducked her eyes. 'Oh, you know.'

'No,' frowned Augustin. 'I'm not sure I do. Unless you mean places too primitive to have doctors of their own?'

'I didn't mean that at all,' she protested. 'Like I said, I grew up in the Middle East. I love it here. It's just, it can be awkward enough for people to go to a doctor back home, especially youngsters. But in a foreign country, you know, when they can't even speak the language . . .' She tried a smile. 'We Americans, you know. Not the best travellers.'

'So what medical experience do you have, exactly? If I'm to let you check me over.'

She placed her palms on his chest, palpating his ribcage gently, listening intently, checking his expression for signs of pain. 'I was a medical student for five years.'

'Five years? And then you just gave it up?'

'My father fell ill.' She tipped her head to the

side, not quite sure why she was confiding so much to this stranger. 'He was out of work at the time. He didn't have . . . the *right* kind of insurance. My mother had already passed. He needed looking after.'

'So you stepped in?'

She nodded, her thoughts elsewhere. 'Have you ever looked after someone like that. Someone who's dying?' she asked.

He shook his head. 'I've never looked after anyone except myself.'

'Peterson and his church were great, you know. They did so much for us. They run this wonderful volunteer visitor programme. Honestly, we'd never have managed without them. And a hospice, too; where my father . . . you know. Plus an orphanage, and shelters for homeless people, lots of things like that. They're *good* people. They really are. The reverend's a good man.'

'And that's why you're here? To thank them?'

'I suppose.'

'How come I saw you leaving the site yesterday?'

She scratched her nose, pretending not to have heard, or not to understand. But Augustin let the question hang there, and the silence finally got to her. She looked up at him rather sheepishly. 'How do you mean?'

'I came here with the police to do interviews. Griffin was driving away from the site when we arrived. You were with him. Why did he hide you?'

404

She swallowed unhappily. 'No one hid me.'

'Yes, they did.'

She looked up. Their eyes met for a moment. Augustin felt his heart thump. Claire looked away, equally confused. 'You're fine,' she said, packing her medical supplies onto her tray. 'Bruises and soreness. That's all.'

'You know what happened that night, don't you?' said Augustin. 'You know what happened with Omar and Knox.'

'I don't know what you're talking about.'

'Yes, you do,' he insisted. 'Tell me.'

But she fled for the door instead, pounding on it to be let out.

II

'Seti the First?' asked Lily.

'An early Nineteenth Dynasty pharaoh,' answered Gaille, digging up more sand with her fingers. 'He came to power about fifty years after Akhenaten. He's buried in the Valley of the Kings.'

'What about him?' asked Stafford.

'His tomb appeared relatively simple at first. An entrance shaft leading to a burial chamber with a sump directly in front of it.'

'Just like this, you mean?'

'And the Royal Tomb, yes. But the thing is, it

turned out that the sump wasn't actually a sump at all. It was a shaft that led down to the *real* tomb chamber. It was just made to look like a sump in an effort to fool potential tomb robbers. Not that it worked, of course.'

'You think that's what this is?' asked Lily. 'A burial shaft?'

'It has to be a possibility,' nodded Gaille. 'I can't believe I didn't think of it before.'

'How deep would it be?'

'The shaft in Seti's tomb was a hundred metres. But that's exceptional. Shaft tombs are usually just a few metres deep. And these hieroglyphs must mean we're near to something.'

'What use will that be?' muttered Stafford. 'It won't lead us out.'

'Probably not,' agreed Gaille. 'But it'll give the water somewhere to drain off to. Unless you've got a better idea?'

'No,' admitted Stafford. 'I don't.'

III

There was no answer to Claire's summons. She pounded the door again. Still nothing. Augustin walked slowly over to her, as unthreateningly as he could. She backed against the wall even so, holding the tray up almost as a shield across her chest so that her medical supplies spilled to the floor all around her feet. 'Let me go,' she squirmed, refusing to meet his eyes.

'Just hear me out.'

'Please.'

'One minute. That's all I'm asking.'

She turned away, discomfited by his closeness, the gentle press of his body wherever it touched hers. 'Okay,' she said. 'One minute.'

'Thank you. I don't care what happened with Knox and Omar. At least, I do, I care tremendously. But that's tomorrow's issue. Right now I need your help because a very good friend of mine is in immediate grave danger, and without your help she may well die.'

Claire frowned in surprise. This wasn't what she'd been expecting at all. 'A friend? Who?'

'A young woman called Gaille Bonnard. She's an archaeologist down in—'

'The hostage?'

'You know about her?'

Claire pulled a face. 'She was all over the TV this morning.'

'You've seen the coverage then?' said Augustin eagerly. 'So you must have noticed her position.'

'What are you talking about?'

'The night before she was abducted, my friend Knox sent her his photographs of whatever it is you've found here.'

'We've found nothing.'

'She enhanced them and sent them back. Look at her posture in the footage! It's exactly the same as—'

'The mosaic!' blurted out Claire.

'You *have* seen it,' cried Augustin.

'No!' But her denial was absurd and she must have realized it. She pushed Augustin away from her, scrabbled on the floor for her medical supplies.

'Claire,' he pleaded. 'Listen. Gaille's sending us a message, something to do with that mosaic. We can't work out what it is because we've lost our photos. We need to find the originals. Her life may depend on it.'

'I can't help you.'

'Yes, you can. You're a doctor; you trained to be a doctor. Saving lives is your whole purpose. You've got to help her. She may die if you don't.'

'Stop it.'

'You hate what's going on here. I can tell that. You wouldn't have insisted on seeing me otherwise. I'm fine. Forget me. But Gaille isn't. Those other two hostages aren't. They need your help. How can you say no?'

'These people are my friends,' she said, pounding on the door.

'No, they're not, Claire. They're using you because you speak Arabic and have some medical knowledge and because they trust you to be loyal after what they did for your father. That's all. They call themselves Christian, but can you imagine Christ behaving like this? Can you imagine Christ running people down or locking them up? Can you imagine Christ withholding information that could save the lives of two young women and—'

'Let me go!' she begged, as Ramiz finally opened the door. 'Let me go.'

'Please, Claire. Please.'

But she tore herself away from him and out, the door banging closed behind her. He sat down gingerly on the footstool, head in his hands, aware he'd just blown his best chance; and maybe Gaille's too.

FORTY-TWO

I

The windscreen of Naguib's Lada had misted up from the storm. He couldn't see a thing. He opened the windows a slit, put on the heaters, sat there brooding on his meeting with Tarek and the *ghaffirs*, the implications of what he'd learned. This was getting way over his head. He needed to put it to his boss.

'Can't this wait till morning?' sighed Gamal. 'I'm in the middle of something.'

'It may be important.'

'Well? What?'

'I think there's something going on in Amarna.'

'Not this again!' said Gamal. 'The universe doesn't revolve around you, you realize?'

'That girl we found, she had an Amarna artefact on her. I think she found something here,

411

perhaps an undiscovered site. You know Captain Khaled, the senior tourist policeman here? He's banned the local *ghaffirs* from—'

'Whoa! Whoa! Whoa! Stop right there. Are you about to suggest what I think you're about to suggest?'

'I'm just saying, I think he knows something. I think we ought to look into it.'

'Into the tourist police?' demanded Gamal. 'Are you crazy? Haven't you learned your lesson from Minya?'

'That was different. That was the army.'

'Listen to me. You've only still got a job thanks to your friends. Go down this road again, they won't step in a second time, believe me. No one will.'

'But I only—'

'Don't you ever listen? I don't want to hear another word! Understand? Not another damned word!'

'Yes, sir,' sighed Naguib. 'I understand.'

II

Claire found Griffin shifting papers from the filing cabinets into cardboard boxes for Michael and Nathan to carry out to the pick-up. 'Well?' he asked sourly. 'How's our guest?'

'He needs a proper doctor.'

Griffin nodded. 'We're booked on tonight's flight to Frankfurt out of Cairo. I'll have Ramiz let him out the moment we're in the air.'

'Where is everyone?'

'Back at the hotel, packing. We need to get there too.' He checked his watch. 'I can give you five minutes to get your stuff together.'

'It's all at the hotel.'

'Good.' He packed the last box, slammed the drawer closed. 'Then let's get moving.' They went out to the pick-up, bumped their way out. Claire glanced anxiously back at the magazine.

'What is it?' asked Griffin, sensing her disquiet.

'He said something to me. About those hostages down in Assiut.'

'He's playing tricks with your mind. I warned you not to talk to him.'

Claire looked around. Mickey and Nathan were jolting around in the back, laughing like children. She thought that about them often, how like children they were. It wasn't their fault that bad things were going on here. They'd taken it for granted they could trust Peterson, because he was a man of God. She couldn't blame them for that: she'd done the same herself. And they were her comrades, her friends, whatever that Frenchman said. Her first loyalty had to be to them. 'Yes,' she agreed, putting Augustin forcibly from her mind. 'You did.'

413

III

The weather turned with astonishing rapidity. One moment, sunshine was falling hot through the window onto Knox's cheek. The next, the sky was covered by thick black clouds and the temperature was plummeting. Rain played a few opening riffs on the Toyota's roof, then started drumming hard. Their headlights sprang on; their wipers started flick-flacking. They slowed with the traffic around them, picking their way through the fat puddles that formed quickly on the road.

Peterson indicated, then turned off the Nile road along a winding, narrow lane. They lurched from pothole to pothole, sending up huge splashes of spray. The deluge grew more violent, the clouds so black it might have been midnight. After twenty minutes or so they slowed to a crawl, briefly sped up again, then pulled off the lane over a shale verge and onto cloying wet sand. Peterson ratcheted the handbrake, turned off his lights, wipers and ignition, snapped free his seat belt. He opened his door, paused for a deep breath, then hurried out.

Knox sat up, cramps and pins and needles in both legs. A flicker of lightning revealed Peterson splashing his way back along the road, forearm over his head as a makeshift umbrella. Knox gave him a few moments, then opened the door and launched himself out after him into the full fury of the storm.

IV

Claire watched mesmerized the news on the hotel lobby TV, her packed bags by her feet.

'Hurry up,' said Griffin. 'We're on the clock.'

'Look,' she said.

He stared puzzled up at the screen. 'Look at what?'

She hesitated a moment. There were too many people milling around. Then she said quietly: 'Our . . . *guest* told me this woman was a friend of his. He said Knox had sent her photographs of what we'd found.'

'Are you crazy?' hissed Griffin. 'You can't talk about that here.'

'Just look, will you. Don't you see it?'

Griffin turned back to the screen. 'See what?'

'Her posture. The mosaic.'

Colour drained from his complexion. 'Oh, hell,' he muttered. He shook his head. 'No. It's coincidence, that's all. It has to be.'

'That's what I was telling myself,' agreed Claire. 'But it's not coincidence. It's just not. She's trying to send a message.'

'We need to get out, Claire,' pleaded Griffin.

'We need to get to Cairo, catch our plane. I'll explain everything once we're—'

'I'm not coming,' said Claire.

'How do you mean?'

'I'm going back to the site. I'm going to let Pascal out. I'm going to show him the mosaic.'

'I'm sorry, Claire. I can't let you do that.'

She turned to face him, arms folded. 'And how exactly do you plan to stop me?' His eyes flickered to the pick-up, his students piling their luggage onto the back as if wondering if he could enlist them to help abduct her. 'I'll make a scene,' she warned. 'I swear I will. I can speak Arabic, remember? I'll tell everyone what you've been up to.'

'What *we've* been up to,' he reminded her.

'Yes,' she agreed. 'What we've been up to.'

Moisture glowed on his upper lip. He wiped it away with a finger. 'You wouldn't dare.'

'Try me.'

His expression changed, he tried to wheedle instead. 'At least let me get the guys out first.'

'Give me the magazine key and all his stuff. I'll give you time to catch your plane.'

'The Egyptians will want someone to blame for this, Claire. They'll have no one but you.'

'I'm aware of that.'

'Then come with us. I swear, the moment we're in the air, I'll get Pascal released, I'll make sure he knows everything he needs to know.'

'It might be too late by then.'

A horn tooted outside. Griffin couldn't hold Claire's gaze, he looked away in shame and confusion. 'It's not just me I've got to think of,' he said. 'They're just kids. They need to be looked after.'

'I know,' nodded Claire. She held out her hand for the key and Augustin's belongings. 'You'd best get going,' she said.

FORTY-THREE

I

Knox tailed Peterson to a high wall with a neat row of well-spaced date palms standing like sentries in front. Fatima's Hermopolis compound, as he'd expected. He kept a good distance behind, but even so Peterson may have sensed something because he suddenly whirled and glared into the darkness. Knox froze, trusting the deluge to hide him. Peterson turned forwards again, reached the main gate, oil lamps fluttering weakly either side, a sign inviting visitors to ring the bell. But Peterson had no intention of doing that. He hurried past, reached the end of the wall, turned down the side, splashing over the waterlogged sand, looking for another way in. The back gate was evidently locked from the inside and wouldn't open. He completed a full circuit, paused in the shelter of a date palm.

After a few moments' reflection, he wedged his boot between the wall and the tree-trunk, lifted himself up, looked over the top to make sure there was no one there, that he could drop down safely on the other side. He hooked a leg over the top, straddled it, lowered himself down before letting go and landing with a splash and a grunt and a clatter. But then only silence.

Knox considered ringing the front bell, raising the alarm. Peterson would have one hell of a time explaining himself. But it wouldn't be a picnic for Knox either; and he couldn't risk getting banged back up in gaol. So he wedged his foot like Peterson had done, grabbed hold of the top, hauled himself over. Peterson had had a minute's head start, but Knox had local knowledge. He took a short cut between the lecture hall and kitchens, reached the courtyard with the sleeping quarters. All the lights were off, but he spotted Peterson beneath an awning when he turned on a pocket torch to consult his print-outs, work out which was Gaille's bedroom. Something clattered inside the kitchens. There was a muffled curse. A cry of exasperation went up. 'Stay where you are,' yelled a man, as doors flew open all around the courtyard. 'Put your hands on your head.' An ambush. Peterson turned and fled, all the policemen chasing after him, shouting orders, waving torches, leaving Gaille's French windows tantalizingly open.

Knox hurried forwards in out of the rain, shoes squelching on the terracotta tiles. Her laptop was open on her desk. He yanked out its leads, packed it into its case, slung it over his shoulder, was making for the French windows when he heard footsteps, saw the beam of a flashlight. He dropped to the floor, rolled beneath the desk. Two policemen came in, stomping their feet. 'Tonight it rains,' grumbled the first. 'Nothing but sun for six damned months, and tonight it rains like the world's on fire.'

'I'd better call our friend in Alexandria,' grunted his companion. 'He'll want news.'

'Not *this* news,' muttered the other. 'I think he'll . . .' He trailed off. Knox noticed the glazed slug's trail of mud he'd laid on the floor, leading directly to him. He sprang out from beneath the desk, startling the policemen, barging between them, out through the French windows into the courtyard. Other policemen were returning bedraggled and empty-handed from their chase. Knox ran the other way, towards the rear of the compound. The back gate was bolted top and bottom. The top bolt slid easily but the bottom one was stiff. He had to jiggle it before it would open. Footsteps splashed behind him. Torch-beams picked him out. He hauled the door towards him but it clogged on the bloated earth. He squeezed through but it snapped closed again, snagging the laptop so that he had to twist it sideways to pull it free. But then he was out in the desert, laptop slapping his backside as he ran.

The rain continued to hammer. He glanced back. Torches flashing, people shouting. A low fence ahead, he hurdled it in one stride, but his feet slid from beneath him on landing. Lightning illuminated an SCA sign as he picked himself up, trousers sticking wetly to his legs. He headed towards it, looking for anything familiar; conditions had been very different on his last visit. He heard gates open. An engine roared, headlights sprang on full-beam, casting his shadow out ahead, making the fat raindrops glint like jewels. He foolishly glanced around, ruining his night vision, then clattered headlong into a protective railing, tumbled over it, clinging on to avoid falling into a pit, hauled himself to safety. A ladder was tied to the wall. He climbed down into darkness, fumbling in vain for some way out.

A vehicle pulled up above. Doors slammed, people shouted. A torch shone down, briefly illuminating a corridor to his left. He hurried down it, blindly feeling the walls, the ancient windows and niches in them informing him he was in the animal catacombs. He twisted and turned, looking upwards for a glimpse of the sky, a ventilation shaft through which he could escape. Torchlight ahead. He turned back. Light that way too.

He felt the walls, found a window, climbed through it into a cell, half-filled with debris and sand. An eerie place, made all the more so by the fluttering approach of a torch. A mummified baboon stared glassily from a niche in the far wall. Baboons had been revered around here as the personification of Thoth, Egyptian god of writing, associated by the Greeks with Hermes, which was how Hermopolis had got its name. Hundreds of thousands of baboons had been buried in these catacombs, which stretched for miles.

Heavy wheezing outside, the rasp of a lighter, the orange pulse of a cigarette. Knox pressed himself against the wall. A man's backside appeared in the mouth of the cell as he sat down to enjoy a smoke.

II

Augustin had just about given up hope of being released that night when he heard footsteps approaching and then a tentative knock on the magazine door. 'Mister Pascal? Are you in there?'

'Claire?' He pushed himself aching to his feet. 'Is that you?'

'Yes.'

'I thought you'd left.'

'I came back.' A pause, an intake of breath.

'Listen, you are telling me the truth, aren't you? I mean, that your friend's a hostage; that finding the mosaic might help her?'

'Yes.'

'Only I'm likely to get in a lot of trouble for—'

'I'm telling you the truth, Claire. I swear it. And my name's Augustin.'

A key turned in the lock. The door opened. Claire was standing there in the moonlight, her hands clasped in front, looking very scared and very young, for all her height. 'I'm in a foreign country,' she said. 'I've broken the law. At least, the law's been broken, and I'm going to be the only person the authorities have available to punish. I don't have any family back home to make a fuss. I don't have any friends here. Mister Griffin as good as told me that he'll disown me once he gets everyone back to America. It's not that he wants to, you understand, it's just that he'll have no choice. So I'm scared. I'm really scared. I'm not good at being on my own. I'm not good under pressure. If I tell you where this thing is, I'll need someone to help me through what happens next. Someone who'll fight for me the way you've been fighting for your friend.'

'I'll fight for you,' said Augustin.

She dropped her eyes. 'You'd say anything to get out of here. I can't blame you for that, but it's true.'

He made his way slowly across to her, not wanting to spook her. He put one hand on her shoulder, lifted her chin with his other, until she finally met his gaze. 'I'm not a good man, Claire,' he told her, looking deep into her eyes. 'I'm the first to admit it. I have all kinds of vices. But I have one virtue. I stand by my friends, whatever it takes. Help me now, you'll be my friend for life. I swear this to you. And you can believe it.'

Her expression clouded for a moment. But then a smile spread radiantly across her face. She handed him his wallet and phone. 'Then come with me,' she said. 'I'll show you what you're looking for.'

III

The sump was filling quickly, water snaking down the walls, soaking into the floor, puddles growing into pools, mirroring the acid anxiety eating away inside Gaille. 'Light a match,' grunted Stafford. 'I got something.'

It sputtered when she struck it; the moisture had got everywhere. She nursed it carefully into life, held it down low. Stafford paddled away water so that they could all see. A carved brick at the foot of the wall. A *talatat*. They all looked at it a moment, then at each other, wondering what it signified. The burning match scorched Gaille's fingers, she yelped and let it go, the darkness returned.

'Dig it out,' suggested Lily. 'Maybe there's something behind.'

They went at it in shifts, their progress thwarted by a large stone buried in the rubble immediately in front of it. But they kept going, and soon were able to jiggle it back and forth like a loose tooth, feel its outline. There was another brick to its left, a third below. Perhaps a whole wall. It was Gaille who at last gouged out enough of the sodden ancient mortar to lever out the brick. They'd all hoped the water would start draining away at once, but it stayed obstinately where it was.

She reached into the hole where the *talatat* had been, encountered solid wall behind. But when she scratched at it, it came away beneath her fingernails like plaster.

They took it in turns to dig, but the water level was rising all the time. It wasn't long before they had to take deep breaths and duck their heads underwater even to get at it at all. 'It's no good,' wailed Lily. 'We're getting nowhere.'

'We have to keep going,' insisted Gaille. 'We just have to.' And the alternative was clear in the strained cracking of her voice.

FORTY-FOUR

I

Smoke from the policeman's cigarette put a tickle in Knox's throat; he had to fight his urge to cough. More footsteps approached outside. 'Get up, you lazy so-and-so. We're to do a full search.'

'Yes, and I'm searching this bit.'

'That's what you want me to tell Gamal?'

'Very well,' he sighed. He pinched out his half-smoked cigarette, replaced it in his pack, lumbered away.

Knox waited for silence before he emerged from hiding. He was barely out when he saw the flashlight return. 'I told you it was the other way,' said one, turning the corner. A moment of complete stillness as they stared at each other. Then one yelled for backup while his colleague grabbed for his gun.

Knox fled into the dark, guessing at every junction, left, right, right, the sounds of chase all around, managing to avoid it until he reached a dead end, the passage ahead choked with sand. Torches coming up fast behind. No going back. He clambered the mound, a few inches of headroom between the top and the ceiling, enough to wriggle through, the laptop dragging like an anchor. A strobe of light ahead, followed by a crash of thunder. A ventilation shaft.

The sand grew waterlogged as he squeezed towards it, then up and out into the storm once more, straddling a safety rope, splashing across the sand, his breath coming fast. A flutter of distant lightning illuminated the landscape; he looked for cover, saw only a white-painted bench in a ring of date palms. He ran towards it, glancing around as the first policeman emerged from the shaft, waving his torch the wrong way, chasing off after shadows.

Knox's spirits lifted, he was going to get away. But then a branch snapped in front of him, he looked ahead, saw a man standing there, flung up his hands. Too late. A fist smacked his cheek, dazzling stars from his eyes, sending him staggering onto his backside. Peterson, fists bunched, teeth bared, mucus trailing from his left nostril, mania in his eyes. 'You!' he muttered in disbelief. 'How did you get here? Satan brought you, didn't he?'

'You're mad,' said Knox, scrambling away, fearful not just of Peterson but also that the commotion would attract the police.

'Sodomite!' spat Peterson. 'Abominator! Agent of Satan!'

'You're fucking crazy.'

'The day of reckoning is at hand,' he cried. 'Don't you understand? The rapture is finally upon us. The world is about to look upon the face of Christ! Upon His grace. His infinite mercy. Mankind will fall to its knees in worship. To its knees! That's what has your Master so scared, isn't it? That's why he sent you to stop me. You filthy creature of Satan. The great battle is starting, the Lord is set to triumph, there's nothing you can do. It's written! It's written!' He crawled astride Knox. Knox kicked up at his groin, but to little effect. He scrambled away, but Peterson jumped on his back, his knee on Knox's nape, grabbing the laptop strap, hauling it against his throat, choking him. 'Your Master has no power any more. You hear? The Reign of the Beast is at an end. The victory of the Lord is at hand. Can't you see it? The Lord is with me, and He's mightier than armies.' He gave another heave; the strap bit like a garrotte into Knox's windpipe. 'At the time that I visit them they shall be cast down, says the Lord,' exulted Peterson. 'I will fight them with my outstretched hand and my strong arm, even in anger and fury and great wrath.'

Knox had both hands on the strap, but Peterson was too strong. Knox couldn't breathe, his lungs were straining for air. He pushed himself to his feet, Peterson clinging to his back, staggered over to the bench, climbed up onto the seat then hurled himself backwards so that Peterson hit the ground hard, car keys and other belongings spilling from his pockets, jogging his grip for just long enough for Knox to twist free, scramble away, heaving in high-pitched whines of air, both hands nursing his raw throat.

'I am the Alpha and the Omega, says the Lord,' cried Peterson, getting back on to his feet. 'I am the One who comes from all eternity. My name is Vengeance. I am the Destroyer.'

A shout across the sands, a torch-beam picked out Peterson. He turned to see four policemen splashing through the rain. Knox crouched, hurried for the thin cover of the trees, dropped flat. Behind him, Peterson seemed torn, eyes flickering between the policemen, Knox, the laptop, his scattered car keys and wallet. But finally he decided on what was most important. He unzipped the laptop from its case, opened it up, picked up a whitewashed limestone brick and crunched it down on the keyboard. Letter keys and shards of broken plastic sprang off in all directions.

'Stop!' yelled a policeman.

'And they shall go forth,' shouted Peterson. 'And

they shall look upon the carcasses of men that have transgressed against me.' He brought the stone down again, smashing through the casing into its wired heart. 'Their worm shall not die, neither shall their fire be quenched. They shall be an abhorring unto all flesh.'

Lightning showed his frenzied eyes, serpents of long silver hair slithering over his face, spittle on his chain, enough to persuade the first policeman to wait for his comrades. 'The time of the Lord is upon us! You hear? Get down on your knees, you filthy heathens. You are not worthy.' He brought the brick down again.

A second and third policemen arrived. They jumped Peterson together. He stood up from the mud with them clinging to his arms, strong as Samson. He staggered a short distance, trying to shake them off. But then the fourth policeman arrived, and he clubbed Peterson on his temple with the butt of his gun until Peterson collapsed to his knees and then slumped face-first into the mud.

The policemen stood around his prostrate form, hands on their knees, breathing hard. One gave Peterson a vengeful kick in the ribs; but another rolled him onto his side to clear his mouth away from the water, while a third cuffed his wrists behind his back.

'There were two of them,' panted one. 'They

were fighting.' He gestured vaguely towards where Knox was lying with his cheek pressed into the waterlogged sand.

Torch-beams flared half-heartedly his way, then disappeared again. 'I vote we take this one to Gamal,' grunted one.

'It's about time the others did something,' agreed another. They lifted Peterson up by his arms and dragged him back towards the compound.

II

Claire led Augustin across the broken ground. Two construction workers in hard hats were standing beside a yellow mechanical digger. 'They've been laying a pipeline next door,' explained Claire. 'I asked them if they wouldn't mind earning a little overtime.'

Augustin laughed appreciatively. 'You're quite something, Claire.'

She ducked her head to hide how pleased she was, walked on a few metres, stamped the loose earth beneath her feet. 'Here,' she told them. 'Dig here.'

'You're sure about this?' asked Augustin.

'I'm sure.'

'And that this is the right place?'

'Yes.'

He pulled out his mobile, held it up for her to see. 'I need to make a phone call. A friend of mine at the SCA. We can trust him.'

She hesitated, but then nodded. 'Yes.'

He dialled Mansoor's number. 'It's me,' he said. 'I'm at Peterson's site. You need to come out here.'

'But I'm in the middle of—'

'Now,' said Augustin. 'And bring some security with you, if you can. We need to put this place under guard.'

III

'Found your killer yet?'

Farooq scowled at his smirking colleague. 'You shut up,' he warned. 'You just shut up.'

His face was burning as he wrote out his report. Hatred for Knox dripped like acid in his heart. He'd had people out looking all across Alexandria, but the man had simply vanished from sight. He didn't know how it was possible. A humiliation that would take years to live down. His phone began to ring. Maybe it was news. 'This is Farooq,' he said, snatching it up.

'Gamal here. From Mallawi, remember? We spoke earlier.'

Farooq sat up in his chair. 'You have news for me?'

'Maybe. We think your man was here.'

'You think? How do you mean, you *think*?'

'He got away.'

'I don't believe this! How could he get away?'

'We'll get him, I promise you. It's just a matter of time. And he wouldn't have got away at all if you'd warned us there'd be two of them.'

'Two of them? How do you mean?'

'He had an accomplice. He gave us the slip, but we've got him now.'

Farooq scowled darkly. Augustin! 'A Frenchman, yes?'

'Can't say. He's not talking. Won't be for a while yet, either. Resisting arrest, if you know what I mean. But a foreigner, certainly. Maybe early fifties, tall and strong. Long hair with streaks of grey. And he's wearing a collar, a white collar. You know, like those Christian preachers do.'

'A dog collar?'

'Yes. Exactly. Does that make sense?'

'Yes.' Not Augustin after all. Peterson.

'What's going on, then?' asked Gamal.

'I don't know,' said Farooq grimly, getting to his feet. 'But I promise you this. I'm going to find out.'

FORTY-FIVE

I

Augustin watched raptly as the scoop of the mechanical digger munched great mouthfuls out of the earth. He turned to say something to Claire but she'd moved off a little way, hands clasped in front, fingers twining, nervous of her ordeals ahead. He walked across, wanting to reassure her, but not knowing quite how. 'Do you know what Peterson was after?' he asked gently.

She shook her head. 'He never really included me in that side of things.'

'Did he ever mention the Carpocratians?'

'Once or twice,' she nodded. 'Why? Who were they?'

'A Gnostic sect. Founded in Alexandria. Based here and in Cephallonia. They were reputed to own an artefact that your reverend craved. A portrait of Jesus Christ, the only one credibly attested before the relic boom of the Middle Ages.'

Claire gave a grunt. 'I suppose it had to be something like that.' She turned to him. 'Did he find it, then? Is that what sparked all this off?'

'No. He found something else.'

'What?'

'There's a text called the Secret Gospel of Mark. At least, there isn't, but some people fear there might be.' He gave her a precis of what Kostas had told him: how the letter had been repudiated as a forgery, but how Peterson had found something on the walls of this place that had made him worry that maybe the secret gospel had existed after all. A mural depicting Jesus and another man emerging from a cave, while a kneeling figure implored: 'Son of David, have mercy on me'.

'So?' asked Claire.

'The Secret Gospel described precisely such an incident. This mural is proof that this incident really happened, and therefore is strong evidence that the Secret Gospel is authentic after all.'

'But why couldn't the mural simply be depicting a similar incident?' she frowned. 'Like with Bartimaeus, for instance?'

'Bartimaeus?'

'You must have heard of him. The blind man

who pleaded with Jesus to heal him. He used those exact words. It's in the Gospel of Mark, I'm sure. And in Matthew too.'

It was Augustin's turn to frown. He'd been certain of his reasoning. But then he saw the answer, and it made him laugh. 'I'm not the only one who didn't know that story. Your reverend didn't know it either.'

'Of course he did,' protested Claire. 'He's a preacher.'

'Yes,' agreed Augustin. 'But an Old Testament one. Fire and brimstone, not love and forgiveness. Have you ever seen his website? On and on about the word of Christ, but all the references are actually to Deuteronomy, Leviticus and Numbers, never to the New Testament, never to Christ himself.'

'You can't be serious.'

'Tell me, then. You must have heard him. preaching. Can you ever remember him citing Christ?'

The digger's scoop scraped something solid at that moment, saving her from having to answer. The driver stopped and reversed away, allowing Augustin to scramble down into the pit. He cleared the hatch with his foot, lifted it up to reveal the steps beneath. His heart swelled with unfamiliar sensations as he nodded up at Claire. 'Thank you,' he said.

II

Knox retrieved Peterson's car keys from the wet sand, his wallet and mobile too. There had to be a good chance the police had found the Toyota, were waiting in ambush, but he had little choice other than to chance it, and luck was with him. He turned on the ignition, peered through the misted windscreen into the dark night, unable to see a thing, yet not wanting to risk his lights. A distant shudder of lightning gave him a snapshot of the open sands, enough to drive blind across them until a second shudder gave him another glimpse. When he'd put some distance between himself and the compound, he turned on his lights, reached the line of trees that marked the border between desert and cultivated land, trundled on to a field of sugar cane, pushed on inside, hiding himself behind a wall of stalks, facing outwards should he need to run for it. Then he switched off his lights again, turned on his heaters instead.

Now what?

Gaille was in Assiut, some seventy kilometres south. No chance of getting there on the main roads, not with the police out hunting. And not even a 4x4 would make it across the desert in this weather. Not that it mattered anyway. By destroying the laptop and his photos, Peterson had denied him any chance of deciphering Gaille's message.

It was only then that he remembered the remote-controlled aircraft flying over Borg. He grabbed Peterson's mobile, punched in Augustin's number. It kicked into voicemail. He composed and sent a text message instead, asking his friend to call back the very moment he got it. Then he settled down to wait.

III

Farooq arrived at Peterson's Borg el-Arab site to find the security guards gone, the office deserted. But away to his right he could see a mechanical digger with its lights on, a car parked next to it, two navvies chatting with a burly security guard. He drove over. There was a great mound of earth and fill next to a huge pit in the ground, stone steps leading down into an underground chamber, a generator muttering away at the foot.

'How about that, boss,' said Hosni cheerfully. 'There was something here after all.'

Farooq gave him a look fit to cook a kebab as he got out and strode across. 'What's going on?' he demanded.

'Restricted area,' said the guard. 'SCA jurisdiction.'

'Murder investigation,' snapped back Farooq. 'My jurisdiction.' He pushed his way past the guard, hurried down the steps, anger seething in his heart. The sound of voices led him along a passage to a chamber where Pascal was photographing a mosaic while Mansoor and a young fair-headed woman looked on. 'What the hell is this?' he cried.

'What does it look like?' retorted Augustin.

'How dare you come down here without me? This is a crime scene. I'm in charge! Me! I make the decisions. No one does anything without my—'

'Haven't you caused enough fucking trouble?'

'Who do you think you're talking to?'

'You've made a fugitive of my best friend,' snarled Augustin. 'Sort that out or I'll talk to you any fucking way I choose.'

'Where's Peterson?' demanded Farooq. 'Where's Griffin?' The woman took a step back into the shadows. Farooq whirled on her. 'And who's *she*?'

'A colleague,' said Augustin. 'From the SCA.'

'Is that right?' asked Farooq, turning on Mansoor. 'She's one of yours?'

'I . . . ah . . . that is . . .'

'She's one of them, isn't she?' exulted Farooq. He turned to Hosni. 'Arrest her. Take her to the station. I don't care what you have to do to her, just make her talk.'

'Don't you dare!' shouted Augustin, stepping in front of her. 'Leave her alone.'

But Farooq drew his gun and levelled it with such intent at Augustin that he moved reluctantly aside. 'Obstructing the police,' he gloated, as Hosni led Claire away. 'Be careful or I'll have you too.'

IV

'You look worried,' said Yasmine, greeting Naguib at the door.

'I'm fine,' he assured her, taking off his soaking jacket, picking up Husniyah, carrying her through to the kitchen. 'That smells good,' he said, nodding at the pot.

She draped his jacket against the stove, the better to dry. 'Tell me about your day,' she prompted. He didn't reply, just stood there staring blankly at the wall. She touched his arm. 'What is it?' she asked.

He gave a loud sigh. 'An Englishman called Daniel Knox,' he said. 'The guys across the river are out looking for him. I've been listening in on the radio.'

'So?'

'Wasn't he the other person at that press conference? The one at which they announced finding Alexander's tomb, I mean. With the secretary general and the hostage girl?'

'Yes,' she nodded. 'Daniel Knox. I think you're right.'

'They're saying he's a killer.'

'He didn't look like a killer.'

'No,' agreed Naguib.

'He looked nice.'

'So you kept saying,' scowled Naguib. 'But the question is, what's he doing down here?'

'What are you getting at?'

'A killer on the run runs *away* from trouble. This one's running into it. Why? Because of the hostage woman, I'm sure of it. He knows something, and it's leading him here.'

'Have something to eat. Worry about it tomorrow.'

'Something's going on in Amarna, my love. I'm not sure what, yet, but it's got to do with those tourist police.'

'Oh, no,' she said. 'Not this again.' She glanced at Husniyah. 'We've only just got settled here. If you lose your job . . .'

'Tell me not to pursue it, I won't pursue it.'

'You know I won't do that. But what about your colleagues? Won't they back you up?'

He shook his head. 'I asked Gamal. He told me to drop it. But I can't.'

Yasmine was silent a moment. Then she took a breath. 'Do what you have to do. Husniyah and I will stick by you always, you know that.'

His eyes glittered as he pushed himself to his feet. 'Thank you,' he said.

'Just don't do anything crazy. That's all I ask.'

He nodded as he pulled on his jacket. 'I'll be back before you know it.'

FORTY-SIX

I

Streams were still pouring down the walls, the rate not slackening at all. If anything, it was getting worse, leaving Lily marooned with Stafford on the small island they'd created, thigh-deep in water that would soon be up to her waist and then her throat unless something changed and went their way. She gave a full-body shudder of dread and cold, teeth chattering wildly. It took all her strength not to let the hysteria take hold. She was so young, and felt the desperate unfairness of her predicament, but also reproach for herself. It was one thing to have one's life ahead, all those infinite possibilities, another to look back and see how little she'd made of what she'd had so far.

Gaille surfaced, heaving for air after her latest

shift attacking the *talatat* wall. 'Any luck?' asked Lily.

'We need to keep working.'

'It's getting us nowhere,' snapped Stafford. 'Haven't you realized yet?'

'Then what do you suggest?'

'We conserve our strength,' said Stafford. 'That's what I'm going to do. Maybe we can swim out of here.'

'Swim out!' mocked Lily.

'If this rain keeps coming down like this.'

'We'll drown before then,' cried Lily. 'We'll all drown.' Her indignation was too much for mere words. She slapped at the sound of his voice. To her surprise, she struck his bare chest. He'd taken off his shirt. 'What are you doing?' she asked.

'Nothing.'

She reached a hand across, felt something bob in the water. A water bottle, its cap screwed on. He grabbed it back from her; she heard the sound of wet cloth, felt out the knotted sleeve of his shirt, bulging with Popeye muscles. 'You're making yourself a life-jacket,' she said.

'We'll all be able to use it.'

'He's making himself a life-jacket,' Lily told Gaille. 'He's using all the water bottles.'

'It's a good idea,' said Gaille.

'They're *our* water bottles. Not *his*.'

'This is for all of us,' said Stafford unconvincingly. 'I just didn't want to get your hopes up before I knew it would work. Anyway, isn't it your turn to dig out this bloody wall of yours?'

It was. Lily paddled across the shaft, took several deep breaths, dragged herself down to the *talatat* hole, ears and sinuses aching from the pressure as she scratched furiously at it, a crust of plaster beneath her nails, progress pitifully slow, especially as the rising water was making the task harder and harder and soon it would be impossible even to—

Her world crashed in suddenly, the water a ferment; something striking her shoulder, spinning her around. She kicked instinctively upwards, half aware already of what must have happened, the planks and sheets and blankets and the rocks pinning them over the shaft mouth had all been brought crashing down by the accumulated weight of water. She surfaced, spluttered, flapped around in the darkness.

'Gaille!' she cried. 'Charlie!' No reply. She reached out, touched something warm, a torso, a man's shirtless torso: Stafford. She felt his neck, his head, a great indentation in the cranium, soft hot pulp smashed like a dropped fruit. She shrieked and pushed him away. 'Gaille!' she cried, searching the darkness with outstretched fingers, the flotsam of sheets and blankets and a wooden plank. She touched a forearm, felt the shirt, knew it was Gaille, dragged her up the mound and lifted her head from the water, allowing her to cough out liquid from her airways, but giving little other sign of life. All the same, Lily hugged her against herself, weeping copiously with grief, terror and loneliness in the dark.

II

'I'm getting you a lawyer,' Augustin yelled out to Claire, hobbling up the steps after her. 'Not a word until he arrives. Understand?' She nodded as she was bundled into the back of the police car, her complexion alarmingly pale. 'I'll be right behind you,' he promised. 'I won't let you out of my sight.' But as the door slammed closed and they began pulling away, he remembered too late that he'd crashed his bike.

Mansoor came to join him. 'Don't worry. It'll sort itself out.'

'What's that supposed to mean?' snarled Augustin. 'You know what it's like here once people get caught up in the system.'

'What are you so worked up about her for? She's one of them, isn't she?'

'No, she's not. She's one of us. She made her choice and she chose us.'

'Yes, but—'

'You have to drive me back to Alexandria. I need to get her out.'

'I can't,' grunted Mansoor. 'This place comes first. You must see that.'

'Bullshit. We already have security. Get on the phone, arrange more if you want. Everything else can wait till morning. It's already waited two thousand years, after all.'

'I'm sorry, my friend.'

'I gave her my word,' protested Augustin. 'I promised I'd stay with her.'

'Yes, but—'

'Please, Mansoor. I've done a lot for Egypt, haven't I?'

'Of course.'

'And for you too.' Mansoor's son was studying medicine at a prestigious university in Paris, thanks in large part to strings pulled by Augustin.

'Yes.'

'And I've never asked you for anything in return before.'

'What are you talking about? You're always asking for things. How about my GPS, that remote-controlled aircraft? Where is that, by the way?'

Augustin waved his quibble aside. 'I'm serious, Mansoor. Claire's not at fault. She's really not. She's behaved well in difficult circumstances. She's risked her whole future to put things right. You saw

Farooq. He wants a scapegoat. Someone to interrogate, to bully, to take his anger out on. If he can't
find Peterson or Knox, he'll make do with her.'

Mansoor sighed. 'What can I do?'

'Tell him that Claire was a whistleblower, the
one who originally contacted the SCA with
concerns about Peterson and this dig. Tell him she
was the reason Omar and Knox came out here in
the first place.'

'He'll never believe me.'

'He doesn't have to. Just as long as he can't
prove anything.'

Mansoor grimaced unhappily. 'You really think
it'll work?'

'There's only one way to find out.'

'You'll owe me big for this.'

'Yes,' acknowledged Augustin. 'I will.'

III

Knox was blasting warm air into his shoes when
the mobile finally rang. 'It's me,' said Augustin.
'Sorry I missed your call. Troubles of my own.
Where are you?'

'Hermopolis. Long story. Listen, was that you
flying that plane over Peterson's site?'

'You saw that? Yes. And we've found the site,
too; we've found everything, the mosaic too.'

'You fucking beauty.'

'I haven't had a chance to study it yet, but I can send you a photo. This number, yes?'

'Please.'

'Any news of Gaille?'

'Not yet.'

'You'll find her,' said Augustin. 'I know you will.' He paused, searching for the right thing to say. 'I don't believe in much, but I believe in you two.'

'Thanks, mate,' said Knox, unexpectedly touched.

The photograph came through shortly after, but the mobile's screen was too small for him to make it all out, so he turned on the Toyota's interior light, fetched a pen and notepad from the box of supplies in the back, sketched out the figure inside the seven-pointed star, then added the clusters of Greek letters. But hard though he stared at it, it made no sense. He punched the dashboard in frustration. He'd imagined that everything would fall into place if only he could find the mosaic. He'd been wrong.

The notepad was too small to make it easy on his eyes. He went back to the box for some sticky-tape and a cheap pair of scissors, then drew the figure and each of the seven clusters of letters on separate sheets and stuck them to the Toyota's windscreen in the rough pattern of the seven-pointed star. Such heptagrams had been favoured symbols of the alchemists, who'd believed it had taken seven stages to convert the leaden soul into the golden sun. He dredged up what little else he knew about them. They'd been a talisman against evil, a symbol of God, of the divine form. *The divine form.* Wasn't that what Augustin had called hermaphrodites? When everything came from one thing, that one thing must by definition be both male and female. Atum masturbating into his hand. The Androgyni. Adam Kadmon. His thoughts drifted uselessly to a halt.

He began switching the clusters of letters around on the windscreen, looking for patterns, anagrams. But then he heard an engine rumbling nearby and hurriedly switched off his interior light. A truck prowled into view, turning this way and that, using its beams like twin searchlights to illuminate great swathes of the sugar cane. They swept past where he was hiding, throwing thin bars of yellow light over the pages, settling for a moment on two of the clusters, *Θε* and *ΔI*, before moving on once more. If he hadn't had divine forms on his mind, no way would he have spotted it, but *ΘεΔI* transliterated into English as *thedi*; and *theoeides* was Greek for the divine form. A third possible link to a single concept all within one diagram. Could it really be coincidence?

The headlights vanished as the truck drove on.

He gave them twenty seconds or so before his impatience grew too much for him and he turned his interior light back on. His spirits dipped as he saw that the two clusters $\Theta\varepsilon$ and ΔI weren't adjacent, but then he realized they were connected by the unbroken line that made up the seven-pointed star. He jotted down the cluster at which the central figure was pointing, then followed the line all the way around.

$$K\varepsilon N \ XA\Gamma \ HN \ \Theta\varepsilon \ \Delta I \ TP \ \Sigma K$$

He stared down at these letters, trying to impel his mind to the solution, until suddenly the answer burst like sunlight in his mind. But he had no time to celebrate. The truck's headlights sprang on at that moment, full beam and directly at him, dazzling him through his windscreen.

FORTY-SEVEN

I

Knox switched on his own lights, stamped down his foot, surged out of the sugar cane, the Toyota throwing up great sprays of water; startled faces in the truck, the driver wrenching his steering wheel, his passenger calling in back-up. He sped alongside the field until he spotted a track, swung down it, driving by feel, stalks drumming against his flanks.

Headlights in front, a car speeding past on a road, he spilled too fast out onto it, charging into the tilled field opposite before swinging around, accelerating away. He rounded a tight bend, saw two police cars blocking the lane ahead, slammed on his brakes, muddy tyres struggling for grip on the saturated surface. He put it into reverse, but another police car was coming up fast behind. He steered off the road, down a short embankment into a quagmire field, changed to four-wheel, gained traction, the pursuing police car bogging down behind. He reached an abandoned railway spur, turned left, jolting along the sleepers, checking his mirrors, hoping he'd got away. But then a pair of headlights appeared in his rear-view, shuddering over the tracks, and then a second pair. He looked left and right, but the track was bracketed by water-logged ditches that even the Toyota would struggle to get out of.

A freight train clanked slowly into view ahead, a monster with dozens of carriages. He tried to beat it to the junction but it got there first: there was no way past it, wouldn't be for another couple of minutes at the rate it was going. The police were catching up fast, their sirens sounding, lights flashing. There was nothing for it. Knox stuffed his pockets with the phone, wallet, scissors, pen, anything of potential use, jumped out, ran to the train, grabbed hold of a ladder, climbed up onto the roof. The train had appeared from his left and therefore was heading south, maybe even as far as Assiut, where the search was on for Gaille. But Knox had no interest in Assiut any more. He'd figured out the mosaic, why Gaille had tried to bring his attention to it; and the solution beckoned him not south but east.

He found a ladder on the other side of the roof,

climbed down, jumped from the moving train, winding himself on landing. The Nile was a good couple of kilometres away. He tore through a thicket, out into a field, his feet splashing up gouts of water as he ran, the secret of the mosaic ablaze in his mind.

ΚΕΝΧΑΓΗΝ ΘΕΔΙ ΤΡΣΚ

Akhenaten, Theoeides, Threskia.

Akhenaten, Divine of Form, Servant of God.

II

Reception on Naguib's police radio drifted in and out. He smacked it in exasperation with the heel of his hand. The crackle of static gave way to a burst of speech. 'He's getting out. He's getting out.'

'Seen him.'

'He's going for the train. Stop him.'

'He's boarded! He's boarded!'

'Follow him.'

'Stop the train. Stop that damned train.' A burst of static. 'What the hell do you mean, you don't know how? Follow it, idiot. Get ahead of it. Wave to the driver. I don't know.'

Naguib released his Lada's handbrake, coasted down a slight incline to park in the shelter of trees as close to the Nile's edge as was prudent in this dreadful weather. If his bearings were correct, this was all happening a kilometre or so upstream. He turned his headlights on full, the camber aiming them down so that they painted brilliant yellow ellipses on the Nile's foaming surface, the reflected light illuminating a million raindrops from beneath.

He felt, for an exquisite moment, that delicious moment of stillness when you don't have the answer quite yet, but you know for sure it's coming. And then it arrived.

Light coming from beneath.

Yes!

How blind he'd been! How blind they'd all been!

III

The local fishermen had hauled their rowing boats high up the Nile bank in anticipation of the storm, turned them turtle. It took Knox a couple of minutes to find one with a pair of sturdy long slats for oars. He righted it, dragged it down to the water, glanced back. No sign of chase. With luck the police still believed him on the train.

He pushed out into the fast-running current, jumped aboard, began to row, his mind whirring with the implications of the mosaic. Was it truly possible they referred to Akhenaten? Or was his imagination running away with him? He'd never given much credence to Amarna-Exodus theories. For all their superficial plausibility, there was precious little physical evidence to support them. He was an archaeologist; he liked physical evidence. But the mosaic changed everything.

Akhenaten, Theoeides, Threskia.

It wasn't just *theoeides* that linked to Akhenaten. *Threskia* did too. The Greeks hadn't had a word for religion. *Threskia* was as close as they'd got. It had denoted anything done in the service of the gods, and the people who did it too, which was why it was sometimes translated as 'servants of the gods'. Scholars still debated fiercely the etymology of the word 'Essene', but it quite possibly meant something very similar, as the word 'Therapeutae' almost certainly did. And then there was the name Akhenaten, the one the heretic pharaoh had chosen for himself. For it literally meant 'One who is useful to the Aten'; or, more simply, 'Servant of God'.

The current was fierce, storm-water swelling the Nile as it raced downstream towards the Delta and the Mediterranean. And maybe that was significant too. After all, why should a mosaic of Akhenaten be found on an ancient site outside Alexandria? If the story of the Exodus were even faintly true, and if the Atenists had indeed become the Jews, he could see an explanation.

Plague had ravaged Egypt during the Amarna

era. Perhaps it had started during the reign of Akhenaten's father, for he'd famously commissioned hundreds of statues of Sekhmet, goddess of disease. And it had certainly persisted throughout Akhenaten's reign, as made clear by independent Hittite texts as well as the human remains recently found in Amarna's cemeteries, which showed stark evidence of malnutrition, shortness of stature, anaemia, low life-expectancy; all the classic indicators of epidemic. That fitted neatly with the Exodus account. After all, God had warned Pharaoh to let his people go by inflicting a series of plagues on Egypt. Historians and scientists had long sought to explain these plagues with natural phenomena. One theory argued that they'd actually all been triggered by a volcanic eruption, specifically the eruption of Thera in Santorini sometime during the mid-second millennium BC. It had been a blast of extraordinary magnitude, six times more powerful than Krakatau, the equivalent of thousands of nuclear warheads flinging one hundred cubic kilometres of rock into the atmosphere, debris crashing to earth for hundreds of miles around, just like the hail of fire described in the Bible. And, in the ensuing days and weeks, a great cloud of ash and smoke would have blacked out the sun, turning the world to darkness, just as described in a second plague.

The rain was still bucketing down, slopping

around in the foot of his boat. Knox rested his oars for a while to bale it out with his cupped hands.

Volcanic ash was strongly acidic. Excessive contact not only caused sickness and boils, it could kill cattle too. Its high iron-oxide content would turn rivers red, suffocating fish. But other species would thrive, particularly egg-layers whose predators had died out. All their eggs would hatch for once, triggering mass infestations of lice, flies, locusts and frogs. So a volcanic eruption could legitimately explain all the biblical plagues except the slaughter of the first-born, and Knox had even heard ingenious explanations for that.

But it didn't stop there. From a distance, an eruption looked like a pillar of fire by night, a pillar of smoke by day – just like the one followed by the Jews as they'd fled. And if they'd truly started from Amarna, their obvious route would have been north along the Nile, taking them in the direction of Thera. In fact, by Knox's reckoning, a line drawn between Amarna and Thera would pass almost directly through the Therapeutae settlement.

A glow ahead. In the deluge it was hard to make out. But then he realized it was a pair of headlights, pointing directly out over the Nile. Maybe they were out looking for him. He stopped rowing at once, lay down in the boat, let the current drift him through the beams, hoping he was far enough out to remain unseen. The darkness swallowed him again. He picked up the oars once more, rowed towards the bank, his mind back on ancient riddles.

The Chosen People. That's what the Jews considered themselves. If any one episode proved the truth of their special covenant it was surely the moment when God parted the Red Sea to help them escape, then brought the waters back to destroy Pharaoh and his army. But actually, according to the Bible, God hadn't parted the Red Sea at all. That was a mistranslation. He'd parted something called the 'Sea of Reeds' instead.

Scholars debated vigorously where this sea was, many placing it in the ancient marshlands of the eastern Nile Delta. But it would certainly have been an appropriate name for Lake Mariut too, surrounded as it had been by reeds, and directly abutting the Mediterranean in places. Tsunamis were well documented along that stretch of coast, triggered by underwater earthquakes or volcanic eruptions. The first sign of a tsunami was the sea being sucked away in a massive ebb tide, creating acres of new dry land. It could stay that way for hours too, plenty of time to enable an escape, before a huge tidal wave swept in, destroying everything in its path.

The Nile's eastern bank came into view ahead.

Knox stopped paddling and let momentum drift him in.

The Therapeutae had sung antiphonal chants celebrating the Exodus and the parting of the Sea of Reeds. And so he asked himself a startling question: was it possible that they'd chosen that particular site not out of fear of pogroms, or a wish to be left alone? That, in fact, the Therapeutae weren't some small offshoot of the Essenes, but that their Borg el-Arab site actually commemorated the great miracle of Exodus itself?

The boat's keel scraped earth. He jumped out, hauled it up the bank out of the river's reach and stowed the oars. He was about to head on up the slope when he heard a distinctive noise behind him. A handgun had just been cocked. He stopped dead, slowly raised his hands and turned around.

FORTY-EIGHT

I

It was a sultry evening, not made any more comfortable by the malfunctioning air conditioning inside Cairo Airport's Terminal 2. Griffin was sweating profusely by the time he and his students reached check-in, his anxiety levels off the chart, certain it had to be showing on his face. But the woman behind the desk was fighting a yawn as she beckoned him forward. She took the fan of passports he offered, printed out their boarding cards, checked in their luggage, then muttered something that he didn't quite catch, thanks to a buzzing in his ears that he sometimes suffered under stress. 'I'm sorry?' he said. He leaned in close as she repeated it. But her English was heavily accented and he couldn't make it out.

She sighed, exasperated, scribbled a figure on a

piece of paper, turned it to show him. His heart was pounding; he could feel the dank pools of sweat beneath his armpits. He fished out his wallet, pulled out a thick wad of twenty-dollar bills, begging her with his eyes to take however much she wanted, just as long as she let them through. She glanced over her shoulder, saw her supervisor standing there, turned back to him with downcast eyes, plucked a single note from his sheaf, made a calculation on her screen, then gave him his change in Egyptian pounds. His heart-rate relaxed a little, only to pick up again as they queued for passport control. But they got through that safely too, leaving him feeling drained and nauseous with relief. He found a restroom, leaned against a sink, studying himself in the mirror, the greyness of his complexion, how old he looked, the wild trembling of his hands.

He felt a twinge of guilt as he thought of Claire, but he shut her from his mind. One thing at a time. Boarding would start in forty-five minutes. With luck, in two hours or so, they'd be out of Egyptian jurisdiction altogether. Then he could worry about Claire.

He ran cold water into his cupped hands, brought them up to meet his face, almost as if he was at prayer. He dried himself off with a paper towel that he screwed up and threw at an overflowing bin, so that it fell onto the floor. Conscience pricked him: he picked it up and put it in his pocket. Then he practised a smile in the mirror and concentrated on holding it in place as he went back out to rejoin his students.

II

In the darkness, it took Knox a moment to see the policeman sheltering beneath the trees, his handgun pointed slightly to one side, prepared to use it, but not yet. He was short and slight but he carried himself with calm self-assurance, so that Knox didn't even consider running. 'You're Daniel Knox,' he said.

'Yes,' agreed Knox.

'I am going to ask you some questions. Lie if you wish, that is up to you. But you'd be wise to tell the truth.'

'What questions?'

'To start with, what are you doing here?'

'Looking for a friend.'

'Who?'

'Her name's Gaille Bonnard. She was taken hostage a couple of—'

'I know who she is. But she was abducted down in Assiut. So what are you doing here?'

'I don't think it happened in Assiut,' said Knox. 'I think it happened here.'

'My name is Naguib Hussein,' said the policeman. 'My wife and I, we saw you on television one time.

It was you, wasn't it? With this woman Gaille and the secretary general, announcing the discovery of Alexander's tomb?'

'Yes.'

'My wife said how nice you looked. It twists me inside when my wife says that about a man. I think that's why she says it. But their names stay with me too. So when I hear on my radio that it is Daniel Knox my colleagues are searching for, I think, ah, he is worried for his friend the woman, he has come to see if he can help.'

Knox jerked his head in the direction of the far bank. 'Have you told them that?'

'It would do little good, I assure you. My boss does not think much of me. And he's already told me once today to stop pestering him with my crazy ideas about strange goings-on in Amarna.'

'Strange goings-on?' asked Knox.

'I thought that might interest you,' smiled Naguib. He lowered his handgun, gestured along the bank. 'My car is that way,' he said. 'Perhaps we should get out of the rain and tell each other what we know.'

III

As long as she could remember, Lily had struggled with thoughts of killing herself. Mostly they were just blinks, gone as quickly as they'd arrived, locked safely back in their box. But sometimes the thoughts wouldn't leave. They'd stay with her for hours, days, even weeks. They'd build and build until she'd think she'd never get through to the other side. Whenever it got too much, she'd hurry to some place of sanctuary, lock out the world, let the tears come. *I wish I were dead*, she'd yell. *I wish I were fucking dead*. And she'd mean it too. At least, her wish for oblivion felt sincere. But she'd never done much about it, other than edge near the platform as trains hurtled past, or stare hungrily up at the top-floor balconies of high-rises.

The water was coming down as relentlessly as ever. Lily was kneeling throat-deep on the mound, her arms around Gaille, supporting her head on her shoulder, allowing the rest of her to float. The chill had long-since penetrated right into her bones, so that every so often she'd break into violent shudders.

Strange childhood memories. Standing in the shadows outside a party, trying to summon the courage to knock. Her neck burning at half-heard remarks. A stray dog she'd once seen, trapped in a garden by two callous young boys so they could throw stones at it, how she'd ducked her head and hurried past, scared of what they'd say if she tried to intervene. How those whimpers and yelps had haunted her for days, a stain upon

her soul. Her whole life dictated by her birthmark, a birthmark that didn't even exist any more.

'I'm not like that,' she yelled out at the darkness. 'I'm not fucking like that, okay? That's not
how I was made.'

It was one thing to think about death in the
abstract. There was something noble, romantic,
even vindicating in the prospect. But the real thing
wasn't like that. All it provoked was terror. Another
set of shivers wracked through her. She clenched
her eyes in an effort not to cry, tightened her grip
around Gaille. She'd never believed in God, she'd
always felt too bitter with the world. But others
did, people she respected, and maybe they knew
what they were talking about. Beneath the water,
her hands clasped tight. *Just let me live*, she begged
silently. *I want to live. I want to live. Please God,
I want to live.*

IV

Claire was hustled through the corridors of the
police station to a small interview room with greasy
yellow walls and an ugly acrid smell. Farooq made
her sit on a hard wooden chair he placed deliberately out in open space, so that she didn't even
have a table to hide behind. Then he prowled round
and round her, jabbing his cigarette at her, thrusting

his face into hers, spraying her with spittle that she didn't dare wipe away. He had a gift for languages, it turned out. He used it to abuse her in Arabic, French and English. He called her a whore, a thief, a slut, a bitch. He demanded she tell him where Peterson and the others were.

Claire hated conflict. She always had. It made her feel unwell, provoked an overwhelming longing to placate. But she remembered what Augustin had told her. 'I want to speak to a lawyer,' she told them.

Farooq threw up his hands. 'You think a lawyer can help you? Don't you realize how much trouble you're in? You're going to gaol, woman. You're going in for years.'

'I want to speak to a lawyer.'

'Tell me where Peterson is.'

'I want to speak to a lawyer.'

'The others. I want their names. I want the name of the hotel you've been staying at.'

'I want to speak to a lawyer.'

'I'm going for a coffee,' spat Farooq. 'You need to get wise fast, you stupid bitch. It's your only chance.' He stormed out, slamming the steel door so hard it made her jump.

Hosni had been leaning against the wall this whole time, arms folded, neither condoning nor intervening. But now he cocked an amused eyebrow at her, pulled up a chair that he set obliquely to hers, instantly reducing the sense of confrontation. 'I hate all this,' he sighed. 'It's not right, bullying nice people. But he's my boss. There's nothing I can do.'

'I want to speak to a lawyer.'

'Listen, you need to understand something. Farooq's been made a fool of today. He's lost face with the guys. He needs a victory, however small. Something to show them, you know. I'm not defending him. I'm just telling you how it is. Give him something, anything, and this can be over for you, just like that.'

She hesitated. Augustin had promised he'd be right behind her, but she'd kept glancing out of the back of the police car, and there'd been no sign of him. She remembered how short a time she'd known him, how little she knew about him, that she had no reason whatever to trust him, other than her instincts and her heart. 'I want to speak to a lawyer.'

'I'm sorry. That's not possible. You must see that. This isn't America. This is Egypt. We do things the Egyptian way. And the Egyptian way is to cooperate. That way everyone benefits. Where are your colleagues?'

'I want to speak to a lawyer.'

'Please don't keep saying that. It's discourteous. You don't strike me as a discourteous person. You're not, are you?'

'No.'

'I didn't think so. You look nice. Out of your depth, sure. But nice. I promise you, if you trust me, I can help you sort this out.'

She glanced around at the steel door, not just locking her in, but locking help out too. 'I . . . I don't know.'

'Please. I'm on your side, I really am. I want to help you. Just give me some names. That's all I ask. We didn't write them down earlier. Give me some names and I'll get Farooq off your back, I promise.'

'I can't.'

'You have to. Someone has got to pay for what's been going on. You must see that. If we can't find anyone else, it's going to be you.'

Tears of self-pity pricked the corner of her eyes. She wiped them away with the back of her hand, wondering what time it was, whether Griffin and the others would have boarded their plane yet, be safely on their way. 'I can't,' she said again.

'I hate to see women being bullied. I really hate it. It's against our culture. Please just tell me the names of your colleagues. That's all.'

'I can't. I'm sorry.'

'I understand,' he nodded seriously. 'They're your colleagues, your friends. It wouldn't feel right. I appreciate that. I *admire* it. But look at it this way: they've left you here alone to face the consequences of their actions. They've betrayed you. You owe them nothing. Please. Just one name. That's all. I can convince Farooq you're on our side if you give me just one name.'

'Just one name?' she asked wretchedly. 'That's all you want?'

'Yes,' pressed Hosni gently. 'Just one name.'

V

In the dryness of Naguib's Lada, Knox marshalled his thoughts. So much had been going on, it was difficult to know where to start. He told Naguib about Peterson and the underground site. He showed him the mosaic photo on his mobile's screen, how it matched Gaille's posture in the video. Then he explained how the Greek letters pointed towards Akhenaten and Amarna.

Naguib nodded, as though it meshed with his own thinking. 'We found the body of a young girl out in the desert two days ago,' he said. 'Her skull had been bashed in; she'd been wrapped in tarpaulin. She was a Copt, which is a very sensitive issue round here right now, so my boss told me to drop it. He's not a man to stir things up unnecessarily. But I have a daughter. If there's a killer on the loose . . .' He shook his head.

'Good for you,' said Knox.

'The investigation didn't go as I'd expected. I'd assumed rape or robbery, something like that. But it turned out she'd drowned. And when we found an Amarna figurine on her, a different scenario began to take shape in my mind. A desperate, poor young girl who's heard of valuable artefacts being flushed out of the wadis by storms like these. She makes her way out to the Royal Wadi, she comes across a figurine, tucks it away in her pouch. Perhaps a rock crashes down on her. Or perhaps she glimpses a gash in the cliff-face and tries to climb up to it, but slips and falls instead. Either way, she lies unconscious face-down in the rain-water until she drowns.'

'Then someone comes across her,' suggested Knox. 'They too see the gash in the cliff. A newly discovered tomb just begging to be plundered. So they wrap the girl in a tarpaulin and take her out into the desert to bury.'

'That's what I began suspecting,' agreed Naguib. 'And so I got to wondering, what if your friend Gaille and her companions spotted something while they were filming in Amarna? What if *that's* why they disappeared? I spoke to some local *ghaffirs* earlier. They no longer have access to the Royal Wadi. They were banned by the senior tourist policeman here, a certain Captain Khaled Osman, the day after the last great storm.'

'Jesus!' muttered Knox. 'Have you told anyone?'

'I tried to earlier. My boss wouldn't hear me out. You don't build a career in the Egyptian police by taking on the sister services. Anyway, I had no evidence to offer, only suspicions. But then, just before I saw you, I realized something. You remember that hostage video?'

'You think I'm likely to forget?'

'Did you notice the lighting?'

'How do you mean?'

'Think back. You could see the underside of the hostages' chins, yes? All the shadows were being cast upwards. That's because the light was coming from beneath. Everyone's been working on the assumption that they're being held in some house or apartment in or around Assiut. But private houses and apartments don't have floor-lighting like that. In Egypt, you only find such floor-lighting in one kind of place.'

'Historic sites,' said Knox.

'Exactly,' said Naguib. 'That video wasn't filmed in Assiut. It was filmed in Amarna.'

FORTY-NINE

I

'Mister Griffin?'

Griffin looked up, startled, to see two uniformed airport security men in front of him, regarding him with polite but knowing smiles. His insides lurched, he felt sick. 'Yes?' he asked.

'Would you come with us, please?'

'Where to?'

The taller of the two nodded to a glass-fronted office the far side of the departures lounge. 'Our interview room.'

'But my flight's about to board.'

The smiles tightened. 'Please. Come with us.'

Griffin's shoulders sagged. A part of him had known this would happen. He wasn't the kind of man life gave breaks to. He turned to Mickey.

'You're in charge,' he said, handing him his credit card. 'Get everyone safely out. Okay?'

'What about you?'

'I'll be fine. Just get everyone home. I can rely on you, can't I?'

'Yes.'

'Good man,' said Griffin, patting him on the shoulder. With a heavy heart, he followed the two security men across the carpeted departure lounge floor.

II

'So what do we do now?' asked Naguib.

'Can't you take it to your boss?'

'He won't listen. Not to me. You know how people get. As if you're a burden specially designed to test them. And what do we have, in all honesty? Lighting. A mosaic.'

'But we're right,' protested Knox.

'Yes,' agreed Naguib. 'But that's not enough. You have to understand how Egypt works. There's so much inter-service jealousy and rivalry. If the tourist police so much as hear that we're accusing them of being behind this . . .' He shook his head. 'They'll fight back hard. It'll be a matter of honour. They'll demand evidence, scoff at it, counterattack, accuse us of all kinds of evils.

My boss is my boss precisely because he knows how to avoid this kind of confrontation. Believe me, he won't even hear me out, not unless I can give him irrefutable proof.'

'Irrefutable proof? How the hell are we supposed to get that?'

'We could always find the hostages ourselves,' muttered Naguib, half joking. But then he shook his head, discounting the thought. 'Amarna's just too big. And the moment Khaled realizes we're out looking, he's sure to cover his tracks.'

'Yes,' nodded Knox, as the glimmer of an idea came to him. 'He is.'

III

Griffin felt the tremors in his hands like soil feels an impending earthquake. He clasped them together in an effort to still them. 'Can we make this quick, please?' he asked. 'Only my flight leaves in—'

'Forget your flight.'

'But I—'

'I said forget about it.' One of them pulled up a chair, sat down, leaned forwards. 'I'm afraid we have some irregularities to deal with before we can let you leave.'

'Irregularities?'

'Yes. Irregularities.'

'What kind of irregularities?'

'The kind we need to deal with.'

Griffin nodded. All his adult life, he'd felt deficient. Living a lie, they called it. The lie that you were adequate. He looked out through the office window onto the departures lounge, his students milling around the gate, conferring heatedly, glancing anxiously his way, delaying their boarding to the last moment. They looked so young, suddenly. They looked like children. All of them had been aware of the clandestine nature of their excavation. But they hadn't cared. They were God-fearing, they were American, they were immune from consequence. But now that their immunity was being stripped from them, they realized just how vulnerable they were. Horror stories about foreign gaols, judicial procedures in which they wouldn't understand a word, their whole futures at the mercy of people they despised as heathens . . . No wonder they were scared.

He looked back at the security men. Whatever they knew, they evidently knew it only of him, or they'd have stopped everyone flying. His students were his responsibility, his job was to buy them time, whatever the personal cost. And, realizing this, a serene calmness descended upon him. 'I don't know what you mean,' he said.

'Yes, you do.'

'I assure you.'

They shared a glance. 'May we see your passport, please?'

He fished it from his pocket, along with his boarding pass. They took their time inspecting it, flipping slowly through the pages. Griffin looked around again. The lounge was empty, the gate closing. His students were aboard. A warm wave of relief, the chill of loneliness. Apple pie and ice cream.

'You come often to Egypt.' A statement, not a question.

'I'm an archaeologist.'

The two security men glanced at each other. 'You are aware of the penalties for smuggling antiquities out of the country?'

Griffin frowned. He was guilty of a lot of things, but not that. 'What are you talking about?'

'Come on,' coaxed the man. 'We know everything.'

'Everything?' And, just like that, he got the feeling that this was nothing, that they were fishing.

'We can help you,' said one of them. 'It's just a matter of the right paperwork. We'll even take care of it for you. Pay us the amount owing, you won't have to do another thing.'

The relief was so intense that Griffin couldn't help but sag in his chair. A shakedown, that was all. After all that anxiety, just a fucking shakedown. 'And how much would that be, exactly?'

'One hundred dollars,' said one.

'One hundred dollars *each*,' said the other.

'And then I can catch my flight?'

'Of course.'

He didn't even begrudge them their money. It felt strangely as though they were messengers from some greater power, as if this was some kind of penance. And that meant he still had time to turn things around. Get his students home, make sure Claire was okay, then do something with his life of which he could be proud. He counted out ten twenty-dollar bills, added an extra one. 'For your friend in check-in,' he said. Then he walked out through the door and across to the departure gate, a great weight off his shoulders, a little strut back in his stride.

IV

Naguib found Captain Khaled Osman sitting out the storm in his quarters, listening to his men gossiping as they shared a *shisha* of honey-flavoured tobacco.

'You again,' scowled Khaled. 'What is it this time?'

Naguib closed the door behind him to shut out the storm, brushed down his sleeves, flicking droplets of water onto the floor. 'A vicious night,' he remarked.

'What do you want?' said Khaled, pushing himself to his feet.

'I tried to phone,' said Naguib, gesturing vaguely out of the window. 'I couldn't get a signal. You know how mobiles can be.'

Khaled's jaw stiffened. He put his arms on his hips. 'What do you want?'

'Nothing. Nothing particular, at least. I just wanted to give you guys a heads-up, that's all. We had a report earlier.'

'A report?'

Naguib raised an eyebrow, apparently as amused by what he was about to tell them as no doubt they would be to hear it. 'One of the locals has been hearing voices.'

'Voices?'

'Men's voices,' nodded Naguib. 'Women's voices. Foreigners' voices.'

'Where?'

'I couldn't make sense of it exactly. I don't know this place as well as you. And he wasn't the most coherent of witnesses. But somewhere in Amarna.'

'What do you expect us to do about it?'

'Nothing,' said Naguib. 'It's just, with every-thing that's been going on, I'm going to have to look into it.'

Khaled stared incredulously at him. 'You want to go out *in this*?'

Naguib laughed heartily. 'You think I'm crazy?

No, no, no. But if it's okay with you guys, I'll bring him back here first thing tomorrow; he can show me the place. You're welcome to come along with us, if you like. It's a long-shot, I know, but with these hostages and everything . . .'

'Quite,' nodded Khaled stiffly. 'In the morning. No problem.'

'Thanks,' said Naguib. 'Till tomorrow, then.'

FIFTY

I

Captain Khaled Osman clenched his fists as he stood at the window watching Naguib drive away. When his tail-lights had vanished into the storm, he turned to Faisal and Abdullah. 'Voices,' he said icily. 'Someone has been hearing voices. Men's voices. Women's voices. *Foreigners'* voices. Explain this to me, please.'

'It must be some mistake, sir,' whined Abdullah, backing away. 'A coincidence. Tourists. Journalists.'

'You're telling me you've allowed tourists and journalists into the site?'

Abdullah dropped his gaze. 'No, sir. But maybe they sneaked in while . . .' He trailed off, aware his boss wasn't buying it.

Khaled folded his arms, glaring back and forth

between him and Faisal. 'You didn't do as I asked, did you?'

'We did, sir,' said Abdullah. 'I swear we did.'

'You killed them?'

Abdullah's complexion paled a notch. 'Kill them, sir?' he swallowed. 'You never told us to kill them.'

'*What*?'

'You told us to silence them, sir,' volunteered Faisal. 'That's exactly what we did.'

Khaled's face was stone. 'Silence them? And how precisely did you do that?'

'We spaced those planks out over the shaft,' nodded Faisal. 'We covered them with sheets and blankets. No one could possibly have heard them.'

'And yet someone has,' pointed out Khaled. 'And tomorrow morning the police are going out looking for them. They're going to hear their voices again.' He thrust his face into Faisal's. 'We're all going to hang because you disobeyed my direct order. How does *that* feel? Does that make you feel *proud*?'

'They won't come back till morning,' pointed out Nasser.

'Yes,' agreed Khaled. It was the first sensible thing anyone had said. He checked his watch. They still had time. 'Get pickaxes and rope,' he ordered. 'And anything else we need to open the place up and close it again.' He touched his Walther instinctively. Much though he cherished it, it wasn't the best tool for the job in hand. He opened up his locker, clipped two of his army souvenir grenades to his belt. 'Come on then,' he scowled, opening the door into the maelstrom. 'We've work to do.'

They ran through the deluge, clambered into the cab, then set off for the Royal Wadi, unaware of the passenger hitching a ride on their roof.

II

The water had now reached Lily's chin. She had to tilt back her head to breathe. Her left arm was aching from holding up Gaille, still breathing faintly but not yet conscious. She transferred her to her right. She'd climbed as high as she could go on the mound, but it was being eaten away bit by bit beneath her feet. She gave a sob of fear and loneliness.

The time was fast coming when she'd have to choose. She could perhaps ride the rising tide, supporting herself on the few meagre holds in the limestone wall, but no way could she do so while still holding Gaille. She was already too close to exhaustion. And the longer she held on, the more of her own precious reserves of strength she'd burn up. Letting her go was the only sensible strategy. No one would see. No one would ever know. And even if they did, they'd agree she'd had no choice.

Right, she told herself. *On the count of ten.*

She took a deep breath, counted the numbers out loud. But she trailed to a halt at seven, aware she couldn't do it. She just couldn't.

Not yet, at least.

Not yet.

III

Naguib watched Khaled and his men drive off towards the Royal Wadi in their truck, exhilarated that the first part of Knox's plan had gone so sweetly. He got out his mobile, called his boss.

'You again!' sighed Gamal. 'What this time?'

'Nothing,' said Naguib. 'At least, I've been listening in on all the chatter. You aren't looking for some fugitive Westerner, are you?'

'Of course we bloody are. You know we are.'

'Only I think he might be here. A tall Westerner, maybe thirty, thirty-five. His face pretty badly banged up.'

'That's him! That's him! Where is he?'

'He was in a truck with some other people.'

'Who?'

'I didn't see. I just saw them drive off towards the Royal Wadi.'

'Keep on them, you hear me,' yelled Gamal. 'We'll get there as soon as we can.'

'Thanks.' Naguib disconnected, nodded to Tarek, sitting in his passenger seat, an AK-49 across his lap.

'All set?' asked Tarek.

'All set,' agreed Naguib.

Tarek grinned and lowered his window, gave the sign to his son Mahmoud at the wheel of the truck behind, a dozen *ghaffirs* in the back, all armed to the teeth, champing at this chance to get their own back on Khaled.

It was time to roll.

FIFTY-ONE

I

Claire's cell-door banged open and Augustin burst in, closely followed by a short, slim man in a beautifully cut charcoal-grey suit. 'Have you told them anything?' asked Augustin.

'No.' It had been close, though. She'd been on the verge of opening up to Hosni when Farooq had returned, bringing confrontation back with him. Hosni had rolled his eyes in despair, had even allowed himself a complicit smile at Claire, both aware of just how close he'd got.

'Good girl,' exulted Augustin, planting a kiss on her forehead. But then he took a step back, as though worried about overstepping his bounds. 'I only mean, it's important you take proper legal advice first.'

'Of course,' she agreed.

'Great. Then come with me.'

'I can go?'

Augustin nodded at his companion. 'This is Mister Nafeez Zidan, Alexandria's finest lawyer. I've had to use him once or twice myself. You know how it is. He's made the arrangements. You're free to leave, as long as you agree to come back tomorrow afternoon. That's okay, yes?'

'You'll come with me?'

'Of course. And Nafeez too.'

'Then it's fine,' she said. She turned to Nafeez. 'Thank you so much.'

'The pleasure is mine,' said Nafeez.

She clung to Augustin's arm as he led her out towards the lobby. Suddenly, she couldn't get away fast enough. 'We had to agree to certain conditions to gain your release, I'm afraid,' he told her. 'The important thing was to get you out tonight.'

'What conditions?'

'For one thing, your passport has been confiscated and won't be returned until the investigators are satisfied.' He opened the front door for her, then led her down the front steps and opened the back door of Mansoor's car which was waiting at the foot. 'I've also had to assure them you won't try to leave the country before then.'

'I won't,' she promised, climbing inside. 'But how long will it all take?'

'It won't be quick,' admitted Augustin, sliding

in beside her. 'Things in Egypt rarely are.' He took her hand in both his, gave it a reassuring press. 'But you mustn't worry. It's going to work out fine. Mansoor and I have worked out a story that—'

'Ay, ay, ay, ay, ay!' protested Nafeez from the front, covering his ears. 'I can't hear this. I'm a lawyer.'

'Forgive me, my friend,' laughed Augustin. He turned back to Claire. 'Just trust me. It's going to be fine. It's who you know in Egypt that counts. Usually I hate that about this place. Tonight I welcome it. Because I know a lot of people, Claire. A lot of connected, powerful people. I'll call them all if I have to.'

'Thank you,' she said.

'I've made some other commitments on your behalf. I've undertaken to be personally responsible for making sure you show up for all interviews and court appearances, should it come to that, which it won't. But I'm afraid that means you're going to have to stay as my guest for the time being.'

'Won't I get in your way?'

'Of course not. It'll be my pleasure.'

She glanced down at her hand, still pressed between both his. He realized what must be going through her mind, blushed furiously, let go of her hand, shifted away along the back seat. 'No!' he protested. 'It won't be like that at all, I promise you. You'll have your own bedroom. At least, it'll be my bedroom, but I won't be in there with you, I'll be on the couch in the living room, I'll just grab a blanket and a pillow, I've slept there before, it's fine, it's comfortable, much more comfortable than the bed actually, I don't know why I don't sleep on it all the time, anyway you'll be completely safe, that's the point, I give you my word.'

He broke off his schoolboy blathering, drew a deep breath, looked directly into her eyes to see if she'd bought it, evidently came to the conclusion that he still needed to give it one last push. 'Honestly, Claire,' he insisted, 'I'd never dream of taking advantage of you like that, not after everything you've just risked for me.'

There was a heartbeat of silence.

A second heartbeat.

'Oh,' she said.

II

Lying exposed to the full savagery of the thunderstorm on the roof of the truck, Knox looked back down the road and realized a major weakness in his impromptu plan. Even with the truck's headlights on full beam, visibility was dire. But Naguib and Tarek wouldn't be able to use their lights without giving themselves away. And driving without lights in these conditions would be almost impossible.

A vicious squall buffeted the truck. It lurched so sharply sideways that water sloshed from the top and Knox had to cling desperately on. Their tyres regained grip, but they slowed down after that to a more prudent pace. He looked behind again. Still no sign of anyone. They reached the end of the road and parked by the generator building. An appropriate place for all this to end. Geometry might be a Greek word, but it had been an Egyptian science, developed in response to the annual Nile inundation which flooded the surrounding land, meaning that owners of valuable property needed reliable ways to determine what land belonged to whom when the waters receded, while the authorities had needed fair methods to work out taxes too.

That these skills had been used by Egypt's architects was proved by the orientation and proportions of the Great Pyramids. Yet talk of 'sacred geometry' made Egyptologists uncomfortable; it smacked too much of New-Age thinking. And while the Egyptians had clearly had both the knowledge and the ability to incorporate it into their city planning and architecture, the archaeological record showed that they hadn't often had the inclination.

At first glance, the city of Amarna seemed designed to fit its landscape. But a British architect had recently mapped the key sites, with remarkable results. Amarna, it seemed, hadn't been haphazardly laid out at all. The entire city was in fact a vast rectilinear open-air temple that straddled the Nile and faced the rising sun. What was more, if you drew straight lines from each of the boundary stele through the main palaces and temples, they all converged on a particular point, like the rays converging on the sun in so much of Amarna's art. And that focal point was right here at Akhenaten's Royal Tomb. It was as though he'd seen himself as the sun, shining eternally upon his people and his city.

The truck's doors opened. Khaled and his men hurried out, hunched beneath waterproofs, their torch-beams feeble things quickly lost in the massive darkness. Knox's mobile couldn't find a signal, overwhelmed by the storm and the high walls of the wadi. He was on his own, for the time being at least. Water slopped over the edge as he lowered himself down. His shoes squelched as he walked, so he kicked them off and tossed them into the night. Then he followed Khaled and his men along the wadi floor, wading barefoot through the storm-water as it cascaded like rapids across the scree.

III

Abdullah glowered at Khaled's back as they laboured up the hillside and then across the plateau, his feet soaked and sore and cold inside his ill-fitting boots. What madness this was! No way would they be able to make it down that sorry excuse for a path in such a torrent. But Khaled had anticipated this. There was a protruding spike of rock on the hilltop above the tomb mouth. He tied a slipknot in one end of a coil of rope, slung it around this spike, then tossed the rest over the edge. 'Down you go, then,' he told Abdullah.

'Me?' protested Abdullah. 'Why me?'

'We wouldn't be in this damned mess if you'd followed my orders.'

'You should have been clearer,' muttered Abdullah.

'On the phone? On the phone?'

Abdullah grudgingly took hold of the rope. He gave it a couple of tugs to test it. It promptly rode up the spike and came free. 'Look!' he said.

'Stop whining, will you?' said Khaled, looping it back around, pulling the knot tighter. 'Just climb.'

'Don't worry,' murmured Faisal. 'I'll keep an eye on it.'

Abdullah nodded gratefully. Faisal was the only one he trusted. He fed the rope through his belt, fastened his torch-strap around his wrist, traded his AK-47 for Nasser's pickaxe, which he slung over his shoulder. Then he lowered himself backwards over the edge, like he'd seen on TV, but his boot slipped on the slick rock, he crashed into the cliff-side, hanging on desperately while Khaled and Nasser laughed themselves sick. He was still muttering curses when he reached the relative sanctuary of the tomb mouth.

The cement had formed a crust, but hadn't yet dried underneath. It came away easily when he attacked it with the point of the pickaxe, fragmented grey mush washing down the cliff-face. He made a hole large enough to reach his arm inside and set his torch down at an angle to light his work, then hacked out more cement. Lightning lit up the wadi all around. He braced himself for the crack of thunder, but just before it started he could have sworn he heard a different noise, that of automatic gunfire. He anchored one hand inside the tomb, leaned out and looked up to find out what the hell was going on. But there was no one up top to answer his question.

IV

It was pure luck that Khaled saw the man. He just happened to be glancing back when a lightning bolt illuminated the entire plateau, revealing him crouched some thirty paces away, mobile phone in his hand.

The knowledge of how he'd been tricked was both instantaneous and complete. Instead of fear, Khaled felt only a great and visceral rage. He snatched Nasser's AK-47, turned back towards the man. Darkness had fallen once more, he couldn't see a thing, but he sprayed the horizon all the same, hoping providence was with him.

'What is it, sir?' asked Nasser.

'Company.'

Lightning shuddered again, revealing the man crawling on his belly like the snake he was. 'There!' he yelled, firing another burst. 'Get him.'

FIFTY-TWO

I

Knox fled across the hilltop as gunfire skittered around him, the night illuminated by muzzle flash and a distant strobe of lightning. It went dark again and he flung himself sideways, tumbling down a rift in the hilltop into a shallow lake created by the deluge. He tried to duck beneath its surface as the three men ran up, but the water wasn't deep enough.

'Did we get him?'

'He went down.'

'Then where the hell is he?'

'He must be here somewhere.' Torches probed the darkness, flurried across the water's surface, heavy raindrops glittering golden in their light. 'Who is he, anyway?'

'He must have been in our truck.'

'You think that policeman knows? You think this was a trick?'

'Of course it was a trick!'

'Son of a dog. We're done for.'

'We're not done for! We're not done for! This one's here on his own, isn't he? We just need to silence him. That's all. Once he's gone, no one will be able to find this place. They won't be able to prove a thing.'

'But we—'

A sharp crack; someone had just been slapped. 'Follow my orders, damn you. He's here somewhere. He must be.' One of the men shone his torch around, the beam flashing again over where Knox was half-hidden in the water. But this time the beam stopped, came back, fixed on him. 'There!' he cried.

Knox pushed himself to his feet, splashed up the side of the rift, then fled headlong. But now he was penned between the rift lake and the cliff's edge. Gunfire ripped the night behind him. He threw himself down by the spike of rock, grabbed for the rope looped around it, slithered over the edge, slick wet fibres slipping through his grasp as he fell, wind buffeting him, spraying mist into his face. He finally gained some grip on the rope, his palms scorching as he juddered to a halt, glanced down to see Abdullah standing on a thin ledge below. He shouted something that Knox

502

didn't catch, swung at his ankles with a pickaxe. Knox danced away across the rock face, but his sideways movement pulled the slipknot loose from the spike of rock and suddenly he was in freefall, plunging down the sheer cliff-face towards the rocks beneath.

II

Naguib was driving almost blind, his sidelights rather than headlights on, only the faint glow of the whitewashed kerbstones to show him the road, steep embankments studded with rocks either side, eyes constantly playing tricks on him, blurs all over the place, his tyres banging the sides, wrenching round the wheel.

They had to have fallen way behind by now. Too far behind. He muttered a prayer and switched his Lada's headlights on full, stamped his foot down on the accelerator. It proved his undoing. A sudden squall lifted up the light car and threw it sideways, aquaplaning them over the kerbstones and then crunching into a boulder, the sickening noise of crumpled metal, seat belts snapping tight against their chests. He and Tarek glanced at each other. No time to waste in recrimination or regret. They jumped out, ran over to the truck that had pulled up alongside, helping hands hauling them up into the back; drenched, bedraggled, feeling rather ridiculous as they found places to sit, and the truck pulled away again.

'Nice driving,' muttered someone, earning himself a laugh. But then another buffet of wind almost sent the truck over the edge, and the laughter promptly died.

III

Knox hurtled down the cliff-face past Abdullah towards the wadi floor. But he was still gripping the rope tightly in both hands, and its other end was looped through Abdullah's belt, so that the momentum of Knox's fall transferred instantly to him. Knox slammed against the cliff, grabbed rock, let go of the rope. But Abdullah wasn't so fortunate. His knees buckled, his right foot slipped from the wet narrow ledge, his hand was ripped free from its hold inside the tomb. He tumbled shrieking past Knox, clawing the sky, and slapped the rocks beneath with a sickening thump. Then only silence.

A cascade of stones clattered by. Knox looked up to see Khaled on the cliff edge, pointing down his torch and aiming his pistol, squeezing off four rounds that pinged and whined off the rocks. Knox scrambled up to the ledge where Abdullah had been, gaining the protection of a slight overhang. There was a gaping hole in the rock, he saw, big enough for him to squeeze through. He tumbled through to the other side. A torch was lying on the ground. He picked it up and shone it around a chamber, ankle deep in water. He splashed over to a passage leading off and then down. 'Gaille!' he shouted. 'Gaille!'

A cry ahead. A woman's cry: high-pitched, short, terrified. Not Gaille, though. Lily, the other hostage. And panic rather than relief in her voice. He raised his pace, running headlong, almost didn't see the shaft in time, stopped teetering on its waterfall brim, regained his balance, shone down his torch, picked out Lily fifteen or twenty feet below, clinging to the wall, surrounded by a flotsam of crushed water bottles and wooden planks, keeping Gaille's head above the water with the crook of her elbow, but crying out in pain and exertion.

'Hold on!' cried Knox.

'I can't. I can't.'

He looked around for some way to get down to her and then back up again. Any way. He saw an iron peg hammered into the floor, but there was nothing to tie to it. And Abdullah had taken the rope down with him on his plunge.

'Help!' cried Lily. 'Help!' A spout of rainwater fell on her open mouth, catching in her throat, making her choke and splutter, flailing around in the water, letting go of Gaille, who promptly slipped beneath the surface.

'Gaille!' yelled Knox. 'Gaille!'

Lily splashed over to the wall, clawed onto it with both hands. 'I'm sorry,' she wept. 'I'm sorry.'

Knox had no time to think. No time at all. He gripped his torch tight, yelled out in fear, and leapt feet-first into the shaft.

IV

Khaled stared down into the darkness as Nasser and Faisal ran up to join him at the cliff's edge.

'What happened?' asked Faisal. 'Where's Abdullah?'

'He fell,' said Khaled. He turned to his two men. Faisal looked white-faced. Abdullah had been his friend. Nasser, by contrast, looked relatively composed, considering their situation, at least. 'He took the rope down with him,' he told Nasser. 'We need it. Go fetch it.'

'But I—'

'Do you want to get out of this or not?'

'Of course.'

'Then do as you're told,' spat Khaled. 'Fetch me that rope.'

'Yes, sir.'

V

Knox burst through the surface of the water, plunged on through, drawing his feet up as he went, striking the floor of the shaft hard, banging and scraping his feet, ankles and backside, his head slapping the wall, rough surfaces scouring his calf and arm, wind punched from his lungs, sucking in water. He kicked instinctively for the surface, coughed and spluttered it out, breathed gratefully in, oriented himself, pointed around his torch. 'Gaille?' he asked.

Lily shook her head wretchedly, all her energy needed to cling to the wall.

Knox swam around, feeling out for her. It wasn't easy with the rainwater cascading down. He kicked beneath the surface. The shaft wasn't large, yet he couldn't find her. Another breath, another dive, his hands outstretched, fingers brushing something soft. He grabbed at it but it eluded him. He went after it and then he had it, a shirt, an arm, his hand closed around a wrist, kicking for the surface, lungs burning for air, pulling Gaille after him, an arm around her as she reflexively coughed out water, gasped air.

He found a handhold on the wall on which to anchor himself, carrying Gaille slumped unconscious upon his shoulder. He shone his torch around this drowning prison, Lily fighting hysteria beside him, and the question formed unanswerable in his mind: *Now what?*

FIFTY-THREE

I

Nasser was wheezing hard by the time he brought the rope back up to Khaled and Faisal at the top of the cliff.

'Abdullah?' asked Faisal.

'No,' said Nasser.

Faisal looked sickened. 'It's over,' he said. 'We're finished.'

'What are you talking about?'

'What do you think I'm talking about? Abdullah's dead. How are we going to explain this?'

'We say we got worried after that policeman visited with his story about mysterious foreigner voices,' scowled Khaled. 'We say we decided to go out searching for them ourselves. Abdullah slipped and fell. A tragedy, but not our fault.

It's that policeman's fault for feeding us false information.'

'No one will believe that.'

'You listen to me, you snivelling little coward,' shouted Khaled. 'We see this through. We see this through together. You understand?'

'Yes.'

'Yes, what?'

'Yes, sir.'

'That's better.' Khaled glared back and forth between Faisal and Nasser, then looped the rope around the rock once more, thinking about how to make best use of his limited resources. No way could he trust Faisal up here alone; he'd run like the coward he was the first chance he got. 'Nasser, you stay here. Guard our backs. Faisal, you come down with me.'

'But I—'

Khaled pressed the muzzle of his Walther against Faisal's cheek. 'You do exactly as you're damned well ordered,' he yelled. 'Am I clear?'

'Yes, sir.'

II

'Others are coming,' gasped Lily, clinging to the wall. 'Please tell me others are coming.'

'Yes,' Knox assured her. 'Others are coming.'

'Then where are they?'

'They'll be here as quick as they can,' he promised. 'There's one hell of a storm going on.'

'You're Knox, aren't you? Daniel Knox?' She nodded at Gaille. 'She said you'd come for us. She said you'd save us.' But then she looked around, realized he was in no position to save anyone, had to fight back the tears.

'It's okay,' he assured her. 'It's going to be okay. You've done really well.' He shone his torch around again, to change the atmosphere as much as anything, picking out the wooden planks and empty water bottles floating in the water, the sheer walls, the rim a good fifteen feet above their heads. He felt his pockets. He still had the scissors from the car. But even if he could gouge holds in the limestone, the shaft would have been far too high for him to climb out on his own, let alone with Gaille and Lily to worry about.

He adjusted Gaille in his arms. Her head lolled back, revealing an ugly gash in her scalp leaking watery blood. 'What happened?' he asked.

'Those planks were across the top,' sobbed Lily. 'They must have come crashing down. I was underwater, trying to dig through the wall.'

'Dig through the wall?'

Lily nodded vigorously, her hope rekindling. 'We found some *talatat* down there. We got one out, hoping we could give the water somewhere

511

to drain off to. But then everything came crashing down. Stafford was . . . he was . . .'

Knox nodded. He needed to check this out. 'Can you hold Gaille a minute?' he asked.

'I can't,' wailed Lily. 'I'm sorry. I can't. I just can't.'

'Please. Just for a little while. You've got to try.'

She looked unhappy, but nodded all the same. He passed Gaille over, took out the scissors, gouged a deep groove in the wet limestone wall, slotted one end of a wooden plank in it, then lowered the other end like a drawbridge against the wall opposite until it had jammed at an angle. He swam across the shaft, hauled himself up onto the higher end, jumped up and down on it until it had wedged so tight that it was bowing in the middle. Lily was beginning to cry out with the strain. He took Gaille back from her, pulled her up onto the plank, laid her out on her back, then helped Lily up too, gave her his torch to hold. 'I need to go and check out that *talatat* wall,' he told her. 'I won't be long.'

He packed his lungs with air, dived for the foot of the shaft, felt blindly along the rocky debris until he found the hole where the brick had been. He attacked the softened plaster with the scissors, hacking it free. His lungs began to protest. He kicked for the surface, filled his lungs once more, returned back down, aware how little time he had should Khaled and his men come in after him.

III

Khaled descended the rope first. He'd planned to wait on the ledge for Faisal, but curiosity got the better of him. He shone his torch inside the entrance chamber to check for an ambush, then advanced warily along the passage, perversely excited by the situation.

Noises ahead. He froze, crouched, aimed his Walther. But it was only water splashing into the shaft. With luck, it would have saved him a job. He continued his advance, catching another noise now, almost in harmony with the first, a woman sobbing. He tiptoed to the rim of the shaft, peered down.

Gaille was stretched out on a wooden plank just a little above the rising water level, her head in Lily's lap. No sign of Stafford, nor of their mysterious pursuer. But then the water boiled and he appeared, gasping for air.

Khaled put his Walther quietly away. Handguns weren't designed for jobs like this. Besides, he'd always been curious about what a grenade could do in a live situation. He plucked one from his belt, pulled the pin with his teeth, then lobbed it into the shaft.

FIFTY-FOUR

I

Movement caught Knox's eye. He looked up to see Khaled toss the grenade down the centre of the shaft, froze for a moment as he watched its lethal arc. Lily saw it too, screamed and closed her eyes, bracing her body against mutilation and death. Her shriek shocked Knox into action. He dived towards the grenade, arms outstretched, some futile notion in his mind of trying to throw it back up, impossible though he knew it to be.

It slapped the heel of his right palm, heavier than he'd anticipated, like a ball of lead, throwing up a splash as it bounced from his hand. He reached after it, fumbling it with his fingertips, finally grabbing it, but already deep underwater, no time to think, only to kick deeper and thrust it into the *talatat* hole, then turn and kick for the surface, hope the limestone would protect him from—

The explosion ripped through the water, his world spinning crazily, bell-towers clanging in his head, arms flapping uselessly, mind scrambled, swallowing water, unsure which way was up. His head struck rock, scraped along it. He stabilized himself, kicked upwards, broached the surface, coughing and hacking for air, splashing around with Lily, the plank dislodged by the blast. And then something suddenly gave way. The water all gushed out, leaving him, Lily, Gaille and the planks stranded bewildered on the shaft floor.

He looked up. Khaled was staring down in dismay, fumbling for his handgun, muzzle flashing, bullets ricocheting wildly. Lily recovered first, throwing herself through the gaping hole that the grenade had ripped in the wall into a new chamber, half filled with water. Knox scooped up Gaille and tumbled after, bumping into something bulky and soft: Stafford's body, floating face down. He glanced at Lily, her torch making eerie patterns in the rippling water. She shook her head and turned away, not able to talk about it.

A narrow dark arched passage led off the chamber. Lily said something he couldn't catch, his ears still ringing from the blast. But her meaning was clear enough. He nodded for her to lead the way, then adjusted Gaille in his arms and set off after her.

II

Khaled reloaded his Walther as he stared down at the hole in the side of the shaft. *What the hell had they found down there?* Footsteps behind. Faisal was hurrying up, drawn by the blast, the shots. 'Look!' said Khaled, pointing down. 'I told you we just had to keep digging.'

Faisal stared incredulously at him. 'You're worried about that now?'

'We need to get down there. We need to finish this. Go get the rope.'

'Rope? What rope?'

'The one we climbed down on, idiot. Get Nasser to throw it down to you.'

'But we need it to get back out.'

'We'll use the path. The rain has to stop sometime, doesn't it?'

'But—'

He smacked Faisal across the cheek with the barrel of his Walther. 'That wasn't a request. It was an order. Now carry it out.' He watched Faisal stalk away, fretted for him to return with the rope, then anchored the slipknot around the iron peg, tossed the rest down into the shaft. He was about to go first when he realized what a perfect spot it would make for an ambush, so he took Faisal's AK-47 from him. 'You go,' he said. 'I'll cover you.'

'Unarmed?' snorted Faisal.

'Here,' scowled Khaled, giving him his Walther. 'Take this, then.'

'Why can't we just—'

'Don't you want to see what's down there?'

'Yes, but—'

'We're going to be rich,' insisted Khaled. 'The three of us will have more money than you've ever dreamed of. Just do as you're told.'

Faisal looked sullen as a mule, but he tucked the Walther into his waistband, grabbed hold of the rope, tugged it to make sure it was secure, then lowered himself over the edge, climbed without incident down to the foot.

Khaled allowed himself a little smile. *The three of us indeed!* First Abdullah, then Faisal. What a tragic night for his unit it looked like being.

III

Gaille's head lolled against Knox's shoulder as he picked his way carefully over treacherous submerged rubble, Lily out in front, her torch playing shadow-theatre on the walls. The corridor sloped gently upwards so that soon the water was only calf-deep, making progress easier, but forcing Knox to concentrate harder on his footing. Maybe that was why Lily noticed the murals first. 'What are they?' she asked, illuminating the gypsum-covered wall with her torch.

He went closer to examine them. Faded paintings of stunted trees. Row upon row of them, column after column; the motif endlessly repeated, like ancient wallpaper. And the same on the right-hand wall, too.

'Well?' asked Lily.

Knox shook his head. He'd never seen anything like it before. At least, trees and other vegetation were common enough in Ancient Egyptian art, but only as part of greater scenes, typically filled with people, livestock, water, birds. Never just one tree endlessly repeated like this. *Or was it just one tree?* Those to his right looked distinctly different from those to his left. The Egyptians had been meticulous about such things. But this was scarcely the moment for detailed investigation. They continued on, emerged from the water altogether, were able to see that the passage wasn't sloped but rather was cut with long, shallow steps that had been turned into a gentle ramp by the thick covering of sand, rubble and dirt.

Something glinted on the floor where Lily had stepped. He swept it with his foot to reveal a metallic strip running down the centre of the passage. 'Over here,' he said. 'Let's have some light.'

Lily shone down her torch. 'Jesus!' she muttered. 'Is that . . . *gold*?'

'Looks like it.'

'What *is* this place?'

A memory sprang then to Knox's mind: Kostas describing the link between Harpocrates and Akhenaten, the Luxor Temple on which were depicted wise men coming from the east to celebrate his birth, and the gifts they brought with them. These trees on the walls, not trees at all, but shrubs. Specifically, frankincense and myrrh. And suddenly it all started to make a kind of sense to him, this Exodus quest he'd so unwittingly started out on.

'What is it?' asked Lily, reading it on his face. 'Do you know where we are, or something?'

'I think I do,' said Knox slowly. 'I think we're in the Cave of Treasures.'

FIFTY-FIVE

I

The storm was finally raining itself out as the truck arrived at the end of the Royal Wadi road and parked next to Khaled's truck. Naguib jumped down. The place was still awash with water; all around them was the sound of it trickling and splashing down the hillsides.

Tarek tapped his arm, pointed up at the cliff-top. 'See that?'

Naguib squinted. The cloud-cover was just beginning to disperse, and one or two stars were peeking through, enough to show the silhouette of the wadi cliffs. He shook his head. 'See what?'

'A man. He ducked down. He's hoping we haven't seen him.'

'Can you get us up there?'

Tarek nodded. He led them close to the base of

the cliff to avoid making easy targets of themselves, then east along the wadi. It was Mahmoud
who made the grisly discovery of one of Khaled's
men lying spread-eagled on the wet rocks. Naguib
knelt down. A single glance was all it took to know
it was too late for this one. They climbed the side
of the wadi, the light growing stronger all the time.
'Spread out,' murmured Tarek as they reached the
top.

'And if we meet anyone?' muttered a voice.

'Order them to surrender,' said Naguib.

'And if they won't?'

'You've got a gun, haven't you?' said Tarek.

II

'The Cave of Treasures?' asked Lily.

'A famous place in Jewish legend,' Knox told
her. 'A cave in a desert beside a great river. Adam
and Eve were sent there after being expelled from
the Garden of Eden. But that was only the start
of it. There's a whole literature on it, not least
because many of the Hebrew patriarchs were
supposedly buried inside. Adam and Eve themselves. Abel, after being murdered by Cain. Noah.
Abraham. Jacob. Joseph. Some even say Moses.'

'Pretty big damned cave.'

Knox nodded. 'Jewish archaeologists have been

hunting it for centuries. Quite something to find the tombs of all those Bible legends.'

'So what would it be doing in Egypt? Shouldn't it be in Israel?'

Noise behind them. Someone had started wading through water. The passage ahead showed no sign of ending, though it curved sinuously this way and that, limiting their horizons. 'You've got to understand,' he told her, 'that the Bible isn't historical. It's a collection of folk-tales designed to convince the Jews that they'd brought their Babylonian exile and the destruction of the Temple upon themselves. That's why so many of the stories follow the same basic moral path.'

'Man makes covenant with God,' murmured Lily. 'Man breaks covenant. God punishes man.'

'Exactly,' said Knox. He set Gaille down a moment, giving his arms a rest, flexing his fingers. 'One explanation is that the person or people who put the Bible together actively looked for stories that fitted this pattern. But there's another possibility. Take Adam and Eve. The first man and woman, right? Yet even the Bible tacitly admits there were other humans around.' He picked Gaille up again, continued walking. 'Cain was branded for killing Abel, for example, so that others would know not to harm him. Which others? He married and had a son called Henoch who founded a city, which you can't exactly do if you're alone in the world. So maybe Adam and Eve weren't the first humans in a *biological* sense, only in a *spiritual* sense. That's to say, maybe they were the first to understand the true nature of God.'

'Akhenaten and Nefertiti?' said Lily sceptically.

'Think about it,' said Knox. 'Here you are, living in Amarna. It's your paradise, your Eden, your Promised Land. You're certain nothing can go wrong, because this is the home on earth of the One True God, and you're under His protection. But something *does* go wrong. You're expelled, forced to flee in the night, then to leave Egypt altogether. How is this possible? Surely the only explanation is that you made your God angry for some reason, that you failed him in some manner. You vow never to let that happen again. You renew your covenant. And in return God gives you a new Amarna, a new Eden, a new Promised Land. But not in Egypt this time. In Canaan.

'Decades pass. Centuries. The people of the Exodus splinter into different settlements, different tribes, each with their own identity, though still with that common bond of flight from Egypt. They pass their stories down from father to son, time after time after time, so that they gradually blur with narrative invention and blend with local folklore until, hundreds of years later, they're not only unrecognizable from what really happened, but from the folk-histories of their neighbours too, even though they're describing the same events.

'Then the Babylonians arrive. They defeat the Israelites in battle, destroy their temple, take them into exile. They become introspective, wondering once more how such a calamity could have overtaken God's chosen people. They look to their heritage for answers, gathering all these different traditions together and weaving them together with their favourite Mesopotamian and Canaanite myths to create a single narrative about Adam and Eve, Abraham and Moses, all those journeys back and forth between Egypt to Canaan, all those Edens and Promised Lands and New Jerusalems. But in fact these stories aren't about numerous patriarchs and ages and places at all. They're about one patriarch, one age, one place. They're about Akhenaten and Amarna.'

'It can't be,' muttered Lily weakly.

'Did you know that Akhenaten solicited gifts of exotic animals from his brother kings? He kept them here. The whole Amarna plain would have flooded during the annual inundation of the Nile. All those animals would have had to be loaded onto rafts. Remind you of any Bible story at all?'

'It *can't* be.'

'When Adam and Eve were in the Cave of Treasures, God gave them the very first possessions ever owned by man: gold, frankincense and myrrh. We even know how much gold they got. Seventy rods of it. Which is really odd, because a rod's not a unit of weight, but of *length*. About five metres, as it happens. Much the same as each of these steps.'

'So seventy rods would make three hundred and fifty metres,' murmured Lily.

'Yes.'

Ahead, the passage opened up into a chamber, the golden thread coming to an end at the base of the wall opposite. 'So how far do you reckon we've come?' she asked.

'About three hundred and forty-nine, I'd guess.'

III

Khaled joined Faisal at the foot of the shaft, peered through into the new chamber and passageway. A man's body was floating face down in the water. He lifted his head by a hank of blooded hair to check. Stafford, the TV presenter. One down, three to go. He dropped him again, held his flashlight and the AK-47 at the ready as he waded through the chamber then along the passage. 'Well?' he snapped at Faisal, who was holding back. 'Are you coming or not?'

'Let's just get out of here,' pleaded Faisal. 'We've still got time.'

'And then what?'

'What do you think? We vanish.'

Khaled hesitated. A new life somewhere no one knew him. Port Said. Aswan. Or over the border into Sudan or Libya. It was easy enough buying a new identity if you had contacts and *baksheesh*. But a new identity was only the start. And the prospect of starting over in a new land with nothing to his name made his heart sink to his boots.

Leave now and he'd be poor forever. He wasn't designed for poverty. He was designed for good things. And they were so close. At the very least, he had to see what lay at the end of this passage. 'We're finishing this,' he said. 'Trust me. No one will ever find out.' He smiled encouragingly, then turned his back on Faisal and walked on, knowing that the man was weak, that he'd buckle and follow.

And, sure enough, he did.

FIFTY-SIX

I

Knox laid Gaille down, brushed hair from her brow and cheek. The cut in her scalp was clotting, her complexion was perceptibly healthier, her breathing stronger. He stood up, took the torch from Lily, shone it around the new chamber, took it to the left-hand wall. It was coated with gypsum, and there were markings visible beneath the thick coats of dust. He took off his wet shirt, wiped it down, bringing a night-time scene to vivid life: people huddled in their beds as robbers roamed their houses, while outside lions prowled, snakes slithered, crocodiles lurked.

He went to the wall opposite, cleaned that too. A daytime scene. Akhenaten and Nefertiti handing out gold necklaces from a palace balcony while farmers went about their work, cattle grazed in the fields, ducks flew over the reeds and fish leapt in the lakes, all sporting in the beams of sunlight.

'It's *The Hymn of the Aten*,' he murmured. 'Akhenaten's poem to his sun god.' He illuminated the left-hand wall. 'That's the world by night,' he said. 'Lions coming forth from their dens, snakes preparing to strike.' He pointed right. 'And this is day. "Cattle and sheep welcome in the dawn, birds take wing as you appear. Boats sail upon the waters, all paths open through you."'

'What good is that?' said Lily, her voice cracking a little. 'We need to get out of here.'

The sunbeams converged towards the upper left-hand corner of the wall, Knox noticed. Yet they didn't meet. They hit the junction with the neighbouring wall before reaching their focal point, then promptly vanished. He turned the torch upon this wall, noticed something that had eluded him before. It wasn't a single flat surface, as he'd first thought. There was a recessed V-shaped section in its centre, set perhaps half an inch behind the rest, and it was actually at the base of this V that the golden thread stopped.

He placed his hand upon it, colder, smoother and altogether more metallic than he'd expected. He stepped back, illuminating the whole wall and the golden thread in the floor, and it reminded him of something. 'It's like a wadi,' he said, pointing out the valley-shaped V to her. 'You know, the one the sun rises over to make the sign of the Aten.'

'Then where's the sun?'

'Exactly,' nodded Knox. He went back to the wall, rapped his knuckles against it, listened carefully to the echo. He rapped again. Yes. No question about it. It was hollow.

II

Naguib, Tarek and the *ghaffirs* advanced cautiously across the hilltop, taking turns to scurry from cover to cover, keeping low to avoid showing their silhouettes.

'Stay back!' cried a panicky voice from the darkness. 'Don't come any closer!'

Gunfire rattled to Naguib's left, muzzle fire leaving orange blurs dancing on his retinas. 'Stop!' he cried. He turned to Tarek. 'He has information. We need him alive.'

Tarek shouted out the order. Silence fell.

'Listen,' called out Naguib. 'I am Inspector Naguib Hussein. You saw me earlier. We know what's going on. We know everything. You're surrounded. Lay down your weapon. Put your hands over your head and then stand up.'

'Go away. Leave me alone.'

There was laughter at this, the idea was so

ridiculous. 'You don't have to die,' called out Naguib. 'You can surrender. A trial. A lawyer. I'll tell the court you helped us in the end. Who knows how it will turn out? But otherwise . . . you don't stand a chance.'

'He'll kill me.'

'Who'll kill you?'

'Captain Khaled, of course. He's mad. He made us do it. We didn't want to. It was all his idea.'

'Then help us stop him. The courts will have mercy on you. But right now put down your gun and surrender. You hear?'

'You won't shoot?'

'You have my word.'

Something clattered on the rocks. The figure of a man rose in the darkness ahead, arms above his head. Within a moment, he was swarmed and pinned to the ground, Naguib kneeling beside him, asking about the others, where to find them.

III

Knox put his shoulder to the wall, tried to slide it to one side, lift it, press it down. Nothing worked. Down the passage, splashing noises were replaced by the scuff and patter of footsteps. By Knox's best estimation, they had a minute at the most. And there was nowhere to hide, no way to spring an ambush. It was getting through this wall or nothing.

'Look!' said Lily. She steered the torch in his hand at the base of the wall. It was difficult to make out, dark against a black background, but there was an ankh-shaped hole there, the approximate size of a man's hand. He went a little numb. The ankh was the great Egyptian symbol of life. It had evolved from a hieroglyph for magical protection, though there was still furious debate over what that glyph had originally symbolized. A ceremonial knot, said some. Or perhaps a sandal. Others claimed that it had represented the sun rising over the horizon, or even the fusion of male and female genitalia, a kind of hermaphroditism all of its own. But looking at it right now, Knox couldn't help noticing how much it looked like a keyhole.

'Hurry,' said Lily. 'They're getting closer.'

Ancient Egyptians had invented mechanical locks at least five hundred years before Akhenaten. They'd typically been simple, wooden, cylinder-and-tumbler devices, fastened to posts outside doors. But there was no reason they couldn't have fashioned more sophisticated examples. He knelt, pressed his cheek to the limestone floor, angled the torch. It was hard to see inside, but he glimpsed jagged teeth and an internal cylinder, components large as a child's toy.

Memories of a desert drive with his late friend Rick, veteran of the Australian special forces. Killing time discussing methods of picking locks, the tools you needed. He opened up his scissors, twisted and turned the two blades until he'd wrenched them apart. Far too large and clumsy for a modern lock, but not for this. He pressed one blade against the cylinder, gently jiggled the tumblers with the other, listening intently as they clicked into place.

'Quickly,' begged Lily. 'They're getting closer.'

'Please,' he said. 'I need silence.'

The final tumbler slotted into place. He tried to twist the cylinder clockwise. It wouldn't shift. He went counter-clockwise instead. It gave reluctantly, protesting at being disturbed after so long. Thirty degrees, sixty, ninety. And then it stopped altogether, no matter how hard he strained.

'Come on!' wailed Lily.

He lay on his back, slammed the wall with both bare soles. Nothing. He kicked again, a third time, a fourth. Something clicked inside. A releasing latch perhaps. The floor began to tremble, shaking dust into the air. The tortured groan of metal on rock as counterweights went to work. The wall began rising with painful slowness, like the curtain of a theatre. Its metallic surface began to glow in the torchlight, a yellowish tint to it, brighter and brighter, too golden to be silver, too silver to be gold. Electrum, then, a naturally occurring alloy of the two, so highly prized by the Egyptians for its sunshine dazzle that they'd coated the capstones of pyramids with it. And then the disk of the Aten itself appeared, climbing slowly up the wall. The sun was rising over Amarna.

FIFTY-SEVEN

I

Knox shone the torch beneath the still-rising electrum curtain, illuminating the artefacts spilled across the floor behind, dulled by thick coats of sand and dust, yet still glowing brightly enough to give an idea of their material. Ivory, faïence, alabaster, leopard skin, shells, semiprecious stones. And gold. Everywhere, the lustre of gold.

The curtain was now high enough for Lily to squeeze beneath. 'Come on, then,' she said, reaching back for the torch. Knox grabbed Gaille's arms, dragged her after him beneath the curtain into the crowded chamber, a narrow aisle wending between high stacks of artefacts. He picked her up, his mind swimming, trying to take everything in. Bronze candlesticks, an ebony staff, a model sailboat, a copper snake, a wooden headrest, an

537

ankh of green jade. Two life-sized black-and-gold
sentries on eternal guard, lapis lazuli eyes staring
belligerently in challenge. Lily hurried by, taking
the fading torchlight with her. The artefacts grew
more regal. An embossed gold chariot rested upon
its yoke-pole next to a double throne. A golden
statue in a niche. An ornate couch with a single
wooden oar fallen against it. Bowls of rubies and
emeralds. He bumped against Lily; she stepped to
one side and pointed the torch so that he could
see for himself what had made her stop. A flight
of electrum-covered steps on which stood two
massive gold sarcophagi. He looked at them in
quiet awe, aware the world would never be quite
the same again. Akhenaten and Nefertiti. Adam
and Eve.

But there was no time to dwell upon the
discovery. Torchlight behind; a burst of automatic
gunfire. Knox dived in search of cover, trying to
heave Gaille over a gold couch, but he slipped and
Gaille fell from his arms. He reached back for her
just as Khaled arrived, torch clamped beneath his
armpit, firing from his hip, forcing Knox to retreat
into the darkness, abandoning Gaille to his mercy.

Khaled approached slowly, the Aladdin's cave
of treasures blooming and fading as he turned this
way and that, Knox searching desperately among
the ornaments, gemstones and furniture for something he could wield. It went dark again as Khaled

turned away. Eighteenth Dynasty grave-goods were ritual in nature, Knox knew, designed to equip the pharaoh for the trials of the afterlife. Howard Carter and Lord Carnarvon had found a composite bow in Tutankhamun's tomb. They'd found a dagger of hardened gold. What he'd give for that!

He reached out blindly, trying not to make any noise. His hand lighted on a statuette of some kind. He took hold of it, but it was made of worm-eaten wood, too light for his purpose. He set it back down, continued his exploration. His finger-tips brushed something colder and heavier. His spirits soared as he realized what it was: a mace, the kind that pharaohs had used to smite their enemies. His lips tightened almost into a smile. That was more like it.

II

Once Nasser had started to talk, he wouldn't stop. He wanted to tell Naguib everything, blaming it all on Khaled.

'The path?' cried Naguib. 'Where's this damned path?'

Nasser pointed it out to him. Naguib hurried off, shining his torch over the edge; his heart leapt into his throat at the fall that awaited any misstep. But he held his nerve and his footing too, made it at last along the precarious slick limestone to the ledge and the mouth and inside, then ran headlong down the passage to the rim of the shaft. Automatic gunfire echoed from below, sounding a great distance away.

A rope was slung around a metal peg in the floor. He grabbed it, lowered himself over the edge. Another burst of gunfire. At least it wasn't over yet; he still had time. A hole in the wall, chest-deep water, wading through it as fast as he could, his gun held out ahead, yelling exhortation to keep himself going even though he half expected at every moment to encounter a blaze of gunfire from ahead; sick with fear, wondering how Yasmine and Husniyah would take the news if anything should happen, yet not letting it slow him either, for he'd given Knox his word, and this was his nature, and he'd rather have his loved ones grieve for him than be ashamed.

III

Khaled advanced slowly into the treasure chamber, artefacts glowing as his torch ran over them, before dying back down to a reddish smoulder. He couldn't believe his eyes. More gold than he'd ever dreamed of; and he'd dreamed a lot. He'd be the wealthiest man in Egypt with all this, the wealthiest in all the world. Houses, yachts, planes, women, power: everything he'd ever coveted, that he'd always believed his due. But how to make it his? How to get out of here and make it his?

'Guard my back,' he ordered Faisal. 'No one comes through. Understand?'

'But we can still—'

He thrust his face into Faisal's, jammed the muzzle of the AK-47 into his belly. 'That was an order,' he yelled. 'Are you going to obey it?'

'Yes, sir.'

He turned face front again, searching the golden nooks and crannies with his torch. The woman Gaille was lying on the floor. At first he assumed her dead, but there was little sign of blood or trauma. He stooped, checked her throat, found a flutter of pulse. Still alive. Maybe he could use her. He stood up, aimed down at her face. 'Come out,' he shouted, his voice ringing around the chamber. 'I'll shoot her if you don't. I mean it. Come out.'

Nothing happened. Not so dumb. He considered executing his threat, but decided against it. Killing her would only show the others for sure what fate awaited them, encourage them to fight all the harder. He advanced further, jagging his torch sharply this way and that, hoping to catch them by surprise. An intake of breath to his left, he turned towards it, his torch lighting up Lily cowering behind her forearms in the narrow gap between a throne and a painted wooden chest. She gave a soft whimper when she realized he'd seen her, began to shriek and carried on shrieking. He slammed the butt of his AK-47 into her forehead, if only to shut her up. Her temple smacked against the chest, she slumped unconscious at his feet. With two women now captive, the dynamic had changed. He could shoot one simply to show he was in earnest, then threaten the other to force the man to reveal himself. He aimed down at Gaille once more. 'You've got five seconds,' he said. 'Four. Three. Tw—'

A blur in the reflection of one of the golden sarcophagi; the man launching himself from the stacked treasures, swinging a mace in both hands. Khaled ducked, but not quickly enough. It caught his shoulder, leaving his left arm dangling numbly, his torch clattering to the floor. He swung the AK-47 around, catching the man across his cheek, the mace spilling from his grasp. He grabbed for it but Khaled clubbed the AK-47 on the back of his head and he went down hard.

Noise way back down the passage. A man yelling out and splashing through water. He recognized his voice too. That damned policeman Naguib! And he'd be here in a minute, no doubt bringing others with him. Hatred twisted Khaled's heart like a towel being wrung dry. He'd only wanted to make a half-decent life for himself. What had he done to these damned people, that they insisted on ruining it?

The man groaned and turned onto his side. Khaled's left arm was still too numb to use, but he didn't need it to fire the AK-47. He aimed down, was about to pull the trigger when he had a better idea. He turned the gun on Gaille instead, wanting the man to watch these two women die, to know that all his efforts had been in vain. He felt a gloating sensation in his belly as his finger tightened on the trigger. The loudness of the shot in the confined space took him by surprise. The way it echoed, the orange glow of muzzle flash reflected in all this fabulous gold. The AK-47 dropped from his grasp, clattered to the ground. He was surprised to find himself falling then lying on his side, saliva leaking from his mouth, the salty taste of it. The second shot punctured high on his ribcage, kicking him onto his back. He looked up to see Faisal standing above him, *Faisal* of all people, pointing his own beloved Walther down at his chest, a look of perfect calmness on his face.

He tried to ask the question, but for some reason his mouth wasn't working any more. He had to ask it with his eyes instead.

'She gave me chocolate,' answered Faisal. 'What did you ever give me?' Then he raised the muzzle to Khaled's face and pulled the trigger a third and final time.

EPILOGUE

It was the worst part of Knox's day, arriving at the hospital without knowing whether Gaille's night had gone well or badly. His heart began to pound as he pushed through the double doors into reception, his mouth drying unpleasantly. But a nurse leaning against the counter saw him and nodded genially. 'She's awake,' he said.

'Awake?'

'Just after you left last night.'

'What?' he protested. 'Why didn't someone call me?'

The nurse gave a 'not-my-business' kind of shrug. Knox had to hide his exasperation. There were times when Egypt drove him crazy. But then relief took over; he was too glad to be indignant. He took the steps three at a time as he hurried up to the second floor, bumped into a doctor coming out of her room.

'How is she?'

'She's fine,' he smiled. 'She's going to be just fine. She's been asking for you.'

He went inside, half expecting to find her sitting up in bed, smiling brightly, bruises healed, bandages removed. It wasn't like that, of course. Her black-ringed eyes slid to the side to see who'd just entered, she managed a smile. He showed her the flowers and fruit he'd bought, made space for them on the windowsill. Then he kissed her forehead and sat down. 'You look terrific,' he told her.

'They told me what you did,' she slurred. 'I can't believe it.'

'Nor should you,' he agreed. 'I paid them a fortune.'

A little laugh; a wince of pain. 'Thanks,' she said.

'It was nothing,' he assured her, covering her hand with his. 'Now close your eyes and get some rest.'

'Tell me first.'

'Tell you what?'

'Everything.'

He nodded, sat back, composed his thoughts. So much had been happening, it was hard to know where to start. 'Lily sends her love,' he said. She'd flown back home with Stafford's body, but there was no need to go into that just yet. 'And we've been on TV a fair bit.' A contender for understatement of the year, that. It had been pandemonium since that night, everyone wanting to take credit for the discovery of Akhenaten's tomb, while simultaneously distancing themselves from the mayhem that had surrounded it. Knox had been happy to let them fight between themselves. All he'd cared about was getting Gaille to the nearest decent hospital. The fear had been eating at him ever since, that he'd got to her too late; a fear so intense it had forced him to acknowledge to himself how much deeper his feelings for her ran than ordinary friendship.

But once he'd seen her – and Lily too – safely into the hands of competent and motivated doctors, he'd done his best to answer the questions the police and the SCA had thrown at him. He'd told them about the Therapeutae and the Carpocratians, their Borg el-Arab site, the figure in the mosaic and the Greek letters that spelled out Akhenaten's name. He'd told them his theories about the Exodus and, when the tiredness had got too much for him, he'd foolishly shared his wilder ideas about Amarna and the Garden of Eden.

He'd woken, the following morning, to a media firestorm. The tomb of Akhenaten and Nefertiti was by itself quite enough to draw all the world's major networks; but someone had leaked his theories too, and that had taken the story to another level. Reputable journalists were excitably reporting as fact that Akhenaten and Nefertiti had been Adam and Eve, for how else could details of their last resting place have been described so precisely in the Book of the Cave of Treasures. And they were claiming that the riddle of the Exodus was conclusively solved too: that the Jews had been Amarna's monotheists forced to flee Egypt by Akhenaten's reactionary successors.

But the backlash had started at once, historians mocking the putative link between Amarna and Eden, claiming that the Book of the Cave of Treasures had been written two millennia after Akhenaten, making any connection purely coincidental. And religious scholars had weighed in too, ridiculing the notion that Adam, Abraham, Joseph and the other patriarchs had all been Akhenaten, pointing out the Creation and Flood accounts predated Amarna, insisting that Genesis wasn't a concertina simply to be squeezed that way.

But it was Yusuf Abbas, secretary general of the Supreme Council for Antiquities, who'd had the most sobering effect. First, he'd dismissed Knox as a glory-hunting sensationalist, not a serious archaeologist. Then he'd observed that the Amarna tombs had been inhabited by pioneering Christian monks in the early centuries AD, making them a far more plausible conduit for any knowledge of Akhenaten held by the Gnostics of Borg el-Arab.

And once you took their mosaic out of the equation, everything else was mere speculation. Even Knox had to acknowledge it was a plausible explanation. And, just like that, what had briefly seemed clear was opaque once more, fertile territory for academics to squabble over for the next hundred years.

As for the Reverend Ernest Peterson, one night in custody had done for him. According to Naguib, he'd not so much confessed to his crimes as boasted about them, bragging of his sacred mission to find the face of Christ and bring the world to the light. He'd admitted responsibility for Omar's death, and told how he'd tried to kill Knox again and again. How he'd gladly do it all over. A Soldier of the Lord, he called himself. A Soldier of the Lord who was about to spend the rest of his life in an Egyptian gaol. Knox wasn't a vindictive man, but there were times he had to laugh.

Augustin had visited the afternoon before. He hadn't stayed long; he'd needed to get his new girlfriend Claire back to Alexandria. Knox had taken to her at once. Tall and gentle and shy, yet with an inner strength, a million miles from the glamour of Augustin's usual conquests. Yet in all the years he'd known him, he'd never seen his French friend so obviously smitten, so proud of another person.

Gaille's eyes had closed. He watched her for a while, thinking she'd fallen asleep. But then she suddenly opened them again and reached out a hand. 'Don't leave me,' she said.

'No.'

She closed her eyes again. She looked at peace. She looked beautiful. He checked his watch. He had a full day on. The police wanted to talk to him again. Yusuf Abbas had summoned him to the SCA's Cairo HQ to explain himself. And rival newspaper groups from around the world had been calling non-stop, bidding eye-watering amounts for his exclusive.

Let them bid.

He pulled a paperback from his pocket and settled down to read.